CYCLADIC GIRLS

PATRICK GARNER

AEGIS PRESS

First published 2019 by Aegis Press
Northborough, Massachusetts

10 9 8 7 6 5 4 3
Copyright © Patrick Garner 2022
Revised October 2022

Garner, Patrick
Cycladic Girls / by Patrick Garner.
ISBN 978-0578-589-268

Front and rear cover artwork by Patrick Garner.
Front cover photograph © Getty Images.
Typeset in Baskerville.

AUTHOR'S NOTES

Cycladic Girls is Book II of *The Naxos Quartet*, which chronicles the appearance of the ancient Greek gods in our world. All four books are stand-alone novels, but the reader is encouraged to begin the series with *The Winnowing* (Book I), followed by *Cycladic Girls* (Book II), *Homo Divinitas* (Book III), and *All That Lasts* (Book IV).

———————

Cycladic refers to the Cyclades (derived from the word "circle" in Greek), which are islands in the Aegean that appear to form a circle around the ancient Greeks's sacred island of Delos. Well-known nearby islands include Naxos, Mykonos and Santorini.

Unattributed poems are by the author.

A glossary of deities appearing in this volume is included at the end of the book.

The characters in this story are not based on living persons. Only the gods and goddesses are real.

Comments and feedback are welcome. You are invited to leave a review with Amazon and/or contact the author at patrickgarner@me.com

PROLOGUE

To those who insist, "Where have you ever seen the gods,
and how can you be so assured
of their existence, that you worship them in this way?"
my answer is, For one thing, they are perfectly visible to the eye.
—Marcus Aurelius, *Roman Emperor*

S hortly after the goddesses held their convocation at my Pennsylvania estate, I became aware that the nymph, Timessa, had fallen out with Artemis. Although she was well-known as one of the Goddess's favorites and was, chronologically, millennia old, she began to argue repeatedly that self-discovery was imperative. At one point Artemis remarked to me that no other nymph had rebelled.

I suspected Timessa encountered something at Vassar during her studies, some idea that appeared revelatory. Or perhaps it was simply the shock she endured the morning that Laine's plot disintegrated into chaos — the morning that Aisa fell backward into the toxic "gifts" that had been set aside to mail to selected scientists. After all, Timessa was the only one, other than me, who witnessed the event. She had warned the three Fates to avoid the poison, to no avail.

Within a day, the Fates were dead, something no one in the tribe had imagined possible. I suspect Timessa held herself somewhat responsible for the debacle. She had encouraged Aisa's pirouettes, and when the child lost her balance, decades of Laine's planning were destroyed.

A fair characterization too is that many in the tribe feared the disaster would lead to a collapse of the old cycles, that human time-driven birth and death would implode. But that has not occurred.

For weeks after that unimaginable day, Timessa slept restlessly, if at all. She duly returned in the fall to her studies at Vassar, rooming as before with her oldest friend, Filly, who, like Timessa was a semi-divine nymph. Both returned to our estate after a semester, Timessa claiming to have lost interest in her molecular biology. She told me later that exploring genetics, protein and organic chemistry, and the other courses Laine had encouraged her to pursue, seemed frivolous, even traitorous.

Artemis later related, "Although I had protected her for millennia, on her return she was changed. Her obedience turned to recalcitrance, her equanimity to angst. So I granted her pleas and released her to the wild. Now we shall see."

Rather than being bereft at her new status, Timessa reveled in it. As a girl with many of the attributes of a goddess, she appeared to the ordinary human as if an angel, her face aglow, her skin flawless. And her direct knowledge of almost every western culture since before Homer made her formidable, when she chose to engage.

Artemis granted her financial security and she left honorably. Danaë and I hosted a low-key party for her on the eve of her departure. No one spoke of her plans, although she seemed sanguine, unaffected at being cut free.

Because Artemis had far less confidence that Timessa could navigate successfully, I admit to keeping tabs on her, a self-assignment I found surprisingly effortless. I could follow her closely enough. My goal was her safety — to track her without interfering with her day-to-day choices. Consequently, my narrative here is that of an observer, howsoever partisan.

Although I knew Timessa well, I could not have anticipated her trials. Or her successes. Like Artemis, only rarely did I have to intervene — and even then, I did so surreptitiously.

My name is Jackson Night. A half-decade before, Laine — or as she was known formally, Lachesis, one of the three Fates — extended my life-span by an unimaginable factor. She transformed me so that I might linger millennia as her plaything. As a master geneticist, she simply rearranged my DNA. With this came abilities beyond those of mortals.

What Laine could not do was prognosticate, as she never anticipated her own demise, an event that occurred within months of my metamorphosis. My first memoir, *The Winnowing*, reconstructs those tumultuous months, and the whirlwind year that swept me into a world of Greek divinities.

I am aware that my dispassionate references to nymphs, goddesses, a-mortals and fanciful events associates this work with fantasy. To assume so would be an error. The divine live and walk, however veiled, among us today.

And Timessa? She had avoided human suffering for millennia, and now, without warning, was plunged into a maelstrom of change. Gods and humans are more alike than not. She sought out her darknesses, and reveled in the light that bathed her, more and more frequently, in its lumi-nescence.

This is her story. You may judge, but I see it as one of struggle and triumph.

CHAPTER 1

Tribes once bent to grey-eyed Athene. All of this now gone:
dark eddies, Ionian girls once fawns
twisted and down
as if origami goddesses found
on a sidewalk in the rain.

The angel before her said, "Now, you are of the few, blessed among the many."

Although the afternoon was warm, Timessa shivered, asking, "What's your name?"

"No-name."

Timessa was certain angels did not exist. They were from the mythology of ancient desert tribes. She had lived with gods and goddesses for millennia, and had never encountered one. Yet two days before she moved in with Josef, she had a dream in the early dawn. From a slight elevation she saw herself and the angel in a field of uncut grass. A butterfly darted through the flowering asters scattered through the field.

She was in a summer dress sitting sideways on a blanket on a gentle slope. The angel, a golden-haired young woman, sat beside her. That this being was celestial, that it co-existed with goddesses, was impossible. Regardless, she was apparently as real as the goddess Artemis.

The dream-angel's wings glistened as if they had been coated in shellac. Her lower gown was folded primly under her legs. Timessa looked around and thought, *Uh-huh.* She saw a bottle of wine off to the side with glasses. The sky and field behind them stretched to infinity.

With an imperceptible touch, the angel ran her fingers along Timessa's shoulders/ She shifted on the blanket, and said in a whisper, "Now I'll tell you the meaning of life. Isn't that what all seek?"

Smiling, she began to speak, but she spoke too quickly. The words blurred and Timessa could catch only scattered phrases. She concentrated, yet the words whirled past her. In frustration Timessa cried, "I can't understand!"

The experience was similar to my own a half decade earlier, when I had dreamt of a massive hawk, one that had come to dictate truth from Hawk to Man. The hawk's words, like the angel's, were inscrutable.

Now, in Timessa's dream, the angel paused, her eyes flashed angrily, and she lifted her hand as if in warning … then she waved it in an idiosyncratic circle as if Timessa's request were inconsequential. Smiling, she brushed Timessa's cheeks. With a curious serenity, the angel resumed speaking. Yet now, waspishly, she spoke even faster.

Timessa had an overwhelming sense that she was incapable of understanding, that the message was in fact perfect in its delivery; it was she who was imperfect. She understood she was failing. She tried to concentrate on each word, but instead, almost dreamily, noticed the angel's lips and became lost watching the angel speak. Yes, her angel was petulant. With a sigh, the angel made a soft whistling sound as an extraordinary finale to what Timessa was certain were immortal words.

Then there was silence. Timessa looked into the angel's eyes.

The angel said, "Now you know what no other knows."

Timessa nodded solemnly. She wanted to admit to this being that she could not remember a word, but the angel leaned forward, her eyes fixed on Timessa's. The angel put a hand on Timessa's neck, drawing her close and kissed her. After a long moment, during which Timessa almost lost consciousness, the angel pushed away. Timessa had had the sensation of slipping into death, of being suffocated by an overwhelming force. Did the angel not know Timessa was almost immortal, a nymph and favorite of the goddess Artemis?

Released, Timessa gasped. The angel was still inches from her face. Timessa marveled at the angel's fiery eyes, filled with — what — love? For the first time, she noticed the angel's halo, a glowing saucer behind her hair.

Timessa was swept with euphoria. Yet she knew the visitation was over. Without a word the angel kissed her hair, stood, and shook her wings. Bending her knees slightly and bounding off her feet, she took flight. As she flew farther away, she became gradually transparent until invisible.

Timessa lay down on the blanket in the endless grass and stared upward. She was dizzy, wonderstruck. She was also unexpectedly aware that she was without clothes. Certainly she had been dressed when the dream began. Now she was not. She saw her clothes lying on the edge of the blanket. Good; she could dress later. She felt oddly consecrated. *Wait,* she thought as she felt herself returning to normalcy. *Don't let it go. Make this last.*

But the singularity dissipated. So she savored the sun on her skin and allowed herself to drift. Then she sat abruptly, sensing someone watching. Yet the field was empty. She lay down again slowly, pulled the blanket over her hips, covered her breasts with her hands, and told herself to reclaim the angel. *Reclaim it!* She wanted to memorize it all.

You are of the few, blessed among the many. That phrase. She had been singled out. Why? She could think of no reason. Perhaps Artemis had set it up.

And the kiss. The angel's face had been wholesome. Until the kiss, Timessa had felt secure, protected. But she sensed there was no virtue in that kiss. There was eroticism only, and beyond that, dark death. What seemed chaste was not.

Why did she taste annihilation in the angel's kiss? Her fingers had circled Timessa's breasts; the angel had not allowed her to breathe. How close had she come to death?

And she remembered the burning eyes: such knowledge, such detachment. And the name, No-name. Then too she thought of the angel's hackneyed phrase, *I'll tell you the meaning of life.* B-reel dialogue. She rarely dreamed — was it a portent of something momentous?

Tired, she dreamed that she turned on her stomach, closed her eyes and fell into a thoughtless sleep. Sleep inside sleep. Then the hotel alarm clock startled her awake. Two days later she signed an agreement to rent a room at Josef's house in Cambridge, Massachusetts.

❧

Although strange events had occurred over the four months she had rented from him, Timessa found Josef generally agreeable. She would admit to personal ambiguity, but he influenced none of that. Further, she was subject to an new eroticism that, like a rumbling electrical charge, constantly played throughout her lithe frame. But those were issues she would have experienced regardless of Josef. Even the remarkable incidents that occurred she attributed to her naiveté.

One of those events revealed Josef's physical anomaly, but I leave her discovery of his peculiarity to a later description.

Timessa remembered her interview with him a day after she had answered an ad for a housemate. On a winter day, he met her on his front porch, and rather than inviting her inside, asked her to sit in one of the chairs outside. They both ignored the cold.

Josef was tall, she thought, almost six feet, with a soft creamy look, his eyes relaxed and green. Yet he had an odd manner of looking at her sideways while he spoke, then punctuating the end of his sentences by shifting his gaze directly to her eyes. In other circumstances, she thought, such mannerisms would have been rude. It was a stare, she reasoned, like a flashlight pointed into a vast darkness that suddenly redirects as a fierce beam. The effect, although obnoxious, also was mildly hypnotic. In a psychic sense, she felt probed as they talked.

So it was with a careful eye that she looked at him, guessing his age to be twenty-eight. Beyond inquiring about her unusual name, he asked few questions, and she found herself saying far more than she intended. She wanted to impress him and went on about her invented childhood and her concocted academics. Her contrivances included describing poems she had published in minor journals — which she had not — recognitions in video and film, and even that she had been captain of her high school hockey team. She said nothing of her years at Vassar or of nymphs and Artemis.

How stupid, she thought to herself as she spoke, yet she went on, his eyes never leaving hers. After a quarter hour, finally dreaming up a story of how she'd wrecked a family car when she was seventeen, she made him laugh, although his laughter struck her as odd, almost feminine. And as he went silent again, she wondered what made the laughter so incongruous.

"If you had to characterize your current state of mind, what would you say?" he asked at the end.

Startled, Timessa asked, "What?"

"Your state of mind."

She paused. "Okay. I get it. In transition, I guess …"

Abruptly, he stood and invited her inside to look around. She liked the interior immediately, the immense windows, the kitchen, the square rooms. The available bedroom was pleasant, furnished with a window overlooking a back garden. His bedroom was remarkable for its endless quantity of angels, statues, pictures of angels, small tabletop sculptures and figurines of angels. She saw a red pinstriped bathrobe on his closet door — silk, she guessed.

What she remembered later about the house was Josef's remarkable collection of celestial beings. One gilded angel with a softly painted face, about a foot and a half tall, stood off to the side in an illuminated glass display case. He had said, "Looks like you."

She guessed forty-five or fifty figures might be scattered over several table tops. She thought uneasily about her dream — would she find the face of the angel in the field here among his figurines?

When she asked him about the array, he said, "Angels of mercy. God knows I've needed them …" His comment was factual, not conversational. As he spoke, he closed the bedroom door. Wanting to ease any misunderstanding, she quickly remarked about the bathroom across the hall with its triangular stained-glass windows, one green window atop a red. He remained silent.

Back on the porch, they discussed costs. She had no sense of money. Whatever amount he quoted was acceptable. Near the interview's end, she asked, "Why are you renting a room?"

He replied without elaboration, "The house is too big for one."

Then to his final inquiry, Timessa assured him that she didn't smoke. They shook hands. Within a week she was living on Summer Street, surprised that she had so readily agreed to share the space. Still, there was a sense of inevitability to her having done so, a tiny harmony she could measure arising from life itself having shifted ever so slightly, of loose pieces aligning.

Josef appeared to accept the stories she created. Within hours of Artemis setting her free, she had begun to craft a tale of frailty and miscalculation. She posed as a young woman fleeing a marriage that had lasted only months before she had slipped away one afternoon while The Husband was at work. The Husband was a clumsy lover. He criticized her poetry, her posture, the way she slept on her side, her movies, her first name, and her cinema books.

Acquiring The Husband, she told Josef, had been a mistake. All The Husband wanted was to talk about food. Or bands. Or Etta, the wife of a friend. Or television shows, which she admitted she never watched.

The made-up marriage would have happened impulsively, suddenly one winter weekend. She would not have wanted a prolonged courtship, would have dreaded such a thing even as a child. When Rick, The Husband proposed, on a second date, she accepted on the condition that the event occur within a week. An event of this immensity, she would have rationalized, should not be overthought, and the proposition would have to be taken as a stroke of fate, of predestination.

She elaborated to Josef that in the second month of their marriage, Rick told her he was going to video their lovemaking, which she refused. He said it was for a friend of his who had girl problems, and the friend would learn how to treat a woman from watching how he treated her. A week later, having uneasily dismissed the incident, she found a camera, hidden in a bedroom closet, a tiny green light pulsing on its front.

War, she would have thought. *Okay*. Without reacting visibly, she would have left the bedroom, found a hammer in the basement and returned to the bedroom. Without hesitation she would have smashed the eye. There would never have been a word between her and The Husband regarding what she had found, or how she had reacted, but she was amused the broken camera remained dangling from a cavity. A day later, tearless, packing her cinema books, photographs and clothes, she would have left as impulsively as she came.

Josef, she thought, was different from her fabricated Husband. In as much as the Summer Street house was a self-contained domain, Josef was its creator. More mysteriously, within a week of moving in she became convinced that something about Josef that was as authentic as The Husband was a fraud.

Timessa concluded that Josef was at his essence psychotropic, that the very carbon dioxide he exhaled was hallucinogenic. She knew it made no sense. Then she thought: he's a shaman. That was it. Josef had a whiff of a conjuror. Unlike Artemis who simply and solely was a goddess, Josef seemed a half-mad, half-savvy, half-adept being who could slip in and out of any role.

So, she thought, he was like her, a chameleon. Confirming her suspicions, one night as he sat in a dark room, she saw his eyes, bright and alive, orbs of inquiry, blazing.

As remarkable, she thought, Josef showed little interest in her as a woman, a disorienting trait because Timessa relied on that premise when she dealt with men. His interest seemed brotherly. His curiosity was remote, never salacious, and at best vaguely voyeuristic. Although she had fabricated the story of her husband and the hidden camera, she checked her own room and was relieved to find nothing.

At first Timessa found Josef's disinterest vexing, even cloying. But she fell quickly into a sisterly role, one she began to think of as appropriate to the home's family atmosphere. She had created no brothers in her background, and allowed Josef, as he wished, to slip into that role.

But one of his traits irritated her. He spent his waking hours at home in the bathrobe she had seen on her first visit, wearing it much like a smoking jacket, pulled tight at the waist and covering his chest, a crisp V of material just below his neck. That, and sock-less loafers, were his inflexible dress. When she tried to kid him about it, he grew short.

One night over drinks Josef spoke briefly of his family. His grandfather, an industrialist, had left him money.

As he spoke, the ground may as well have parted for her. As Josef knelt, his robe opened slightly and she glanced quickly, inadvertently, into the loose garment that had been meant to bind the swelling and the coy tumescence: a woman's breasts. The robe no longer hid his secrets. She saw shadowed aureolas, a girl's nipples, breasts loose and unintentionally unbound in the opened silk. Stupidly she thought to herself, *No bra.*

She felt her heart pound. No more than a split second passed. She looked up as quickly into his eyes, saw his panic as he cried loudly, standing, gripping his robe to his throat, "Fuck you. Just go fuck off —!"

Another night, as if Josef's world had not been ripped open earlier, he invited her to a "sitting," where he would look into her past. When he appeared, he was unremarkable except for restless fingers that danced tip-to-tip upon themselves, seemingly disconnected from his consciousness.

They sat across from each other at a small table, his fingers fluttering. She was now far more confident, aware she had intel on the man. Or was he not a man? She glanced at his chest: it now was as flat as a punctured tire. Josef must have bound himself more tightly than before.

He wanted this meeting because the night before he too had dreamed. In his dream he sat in a classroom before a thin girl who lectured about Timessa's past. In the dream she had said, *My name is Kore. Listen carefully.* He had duly remembered the details, although, as in many dreams, they seemed nonsensical.

After a moment of silence, he turned to Timessa and said, "Here is what I see. When you were twenty, you studied avant-garde poetry , cine dance, metrical films, the history of independent cinema —

"Experimenting as all of us do, you smoked Marlboros. Then, within a day, you quit."

He continued. "And you liked martinis. You would say to friends, 'It's not a martini if it's not stirred and cold as hell.'"

She laughed. He clearly was inventing all of this. Little did he know of inventions. "Where did you come up with all of this? Marlboros, martinis?"

"Dreamed it all last night." Josef caught her eyes and said, "Your irises are violet."

"Yes," she said. "A divine trait, I'm told." She was certain, regardless of his intelligence, that he would not catch her dissembling.

"Then, a week before you moved here," he said carefully, "and several days after you left The Husband, something occurred. You returned from a friend's dinner party —"

She smiled. She had not attended anyone's dinner party.

"— to the apartment you briefly shared with a girlfriend, rifled through your forwarded mail and found a letter from a girl you had known in high school, whom you had forgotten and could not even picture."

"Oh?" Timessa said, surprised. "What was her name?"

"Kore Serowik. You thought, when you saw the letter, who the hell is that? The postmark was smeared but you could make out, Rue d'Alsace, Charleville. The stamp was French, the letter itself undated." Josef paused. "Should I go on?"

What? she thought. Impossible. She had invented a Kore Serowik months before, an imagined girlfriend from an invented past. Invented, then rejected as ludicrous. Invented her without these details and without emotions. Timessa had played out dozens of potential backgrounds for herself, dismissing most. Kore was just one of many.

She nodded.

He smiled, picked up an envelope on a table between them, and pulled out the folded papers. "I'll read the letter. I apologize for its length."

"*Dear Timessa,*" he read, "*The hot winds of this industrial slum in France blow south, onto me, through my bones. Here I am, sitting through it all without you.*"

Timessa stopped him. "What the hell are you doing?"

He smiled. "Reading from Kore's letter."

This invention exceeded mere amusement. He was going places she had never imagined, taking her small inventions and creating the same theatre she had witnessed time and again with Artemis. But with Artemis she had been safe. Now she didn't know and couldn't anticipate Josef's intent.

He continued, "*I just want to say, Timessa, you're special. You're someone who can see …*"

Timessa smirked. Josef had gone to great effort with this odd contrivance. And why?

"*Remember the last time we saw each other? You smiled. Like some seraphim.*"

He shook the letter at her, as if to emphasize its importance. What she was hearing seemed impossible. Impossible that he now held a letter from a concocted girlfriend. She'd never told anyone. Kore had existed as her invention for five minutes at best. Even the girl's last name, Serowik, was one she'd twisted from *serow*, an obscure goat-antelope that Artemis once had hunted in Japan. And *Kore* was ancient Greek for maiden.

He smiled, "I'm almost through —" She shrugged. He continued,

"That last time … You made me cry. That too came back, all of it returning with ridiculous force. I've felt stupid for so many years —"

Josef stopped, dropping the letter from his hands, dramatically allowing the pages to scatter at his feet. In the silence he shrugged. "Convincing stuff."

She said, "Where did that come from?"

"Hand-delivered to me this afternoon."

"By whom?"

"A girl in her twenties. Said she was your friend. That you'd left it behind."

"That's preposterous. No one knows I'm here."

He smiled. "Then I must have conjured it … for your entertainment."

"As if you're a sorcerer?"

"Sorcerers deal in mysteries. Not me. I prefer pure dialectics."

" 'Dialectics' ? That's Greek, Josef. The Greeks used the term: a dialogue to discover truth."

"Is that what we're doing, Timessa? Exploring truth, plumbing the soul?"

No, she thought. *That's not what we're doing.* Angels, sorcerers, souls — all fictions. Yet the letter existed. He'd held it in his hand. She picked it up. "What did this girl in her twenties look like?"

"About your size. Mousy hair. Eminently forgettable."

"You should have invited her in. Perhaps I'd have had something to say."

"The moment the letter was in my hands, she turned and fled."

"Fled?"

"Ran. The whole incident lasted seconds."

She knew too little of men, yet she was aware he concealed as much as he disclosed. Tiring of the small deceptions, she said, "Enough. You mentioned martinis. Do you make them?"

"That's possible," he smiled. As he went to the kitchen, she collected the letter from the floor, rereading parts of it. She imagined her imaginary friend: a tall, dirty blonde who dyed her hair and cried at the slightest provocation. Kore. She thought: *Yes, I devised Kore. An invention become real.*

A stupid letter, an epiphany. Could she now create things simply by imagining them? To imagine something, then see it manifest? She thought suddenly, *Perhaps nothing is true, no barrier between the material and the imagined. What if whatever I think exists somewhere, in some form?*

Josef stood before her, offering a pink martini. She took the conical glass, feeling childlike and simple. Ignoring him, she suddenly felt euphoric. *Think of a Kore and a Kore appears.* It was all amusing.

The senseless realization made her laugh. She was free, free from running with Artemis and a hundred nymphs. Surely the girl's delivery of the letter proved something. *Think of a Kore and a Kore appears.* Was she acquiring new power?

Timessa felt weak, dizzy and then, through the silliness and joy, suddenly gloriously sleepy.

She stood and drank the entirety of the martini as Josef watched. "What was the address on the letter?"

He picked up the envelope: "I told you. Rue d'Alsace, Charleville. France."

"Ingenious. Hand-delivered by some girl."

"Said you'd left it behind."

"I never received a letter to leave behind. The French address? Concocted."

Stooping, he picked up the envelope. "Yes, Rue d'Alsace, Charleville. There's a stamp that reads, Liberté."

Nymphs were fearless. If her invented character had hands and legs and had become real, the once-imaginary girl could have become anything — a university professor, a hacker, a fashionista, a chef. She could be sweet or menacing. Timessa shrugged. *Whatever,* she thought. When at risk, nymphs became ninjas, cool-headed warriors.

If Kore's letter was meant to be threatening, it wasn't. Instead, it amused her. Although Artemis had protected her throughout her life, the goddess's protection was a nicety. Timessa could fend for herself. What was intriguing was that a backstory she believed she had invented had now become physical; she thought of the mousy-haired girl fleeing Josef, the letter in loopy script.

With a small smile, she said, "All well and good, but I'm off to bed."

When she woke late the next morning as the sun colored the room in golds, she lay motionless, replaying the sequence of her life's events. She knew intuitively that she had needed to escape the tribe, to recreate herself away from Artemis, to create a life as foreign to the old as possible. That desire made sense.

All nymphs should learn to live and love independently, however briefly, she thought.

She turned on her side, the sheets falling off her shoulders, her hair tangled, reddish-yellow in the early sun, and as she yawned, she caught her image in the mirror and stared into her dark eyes. Quickly, she was bored, lost in self-mockery and in the ridiculous complexity of her situation.

New answers led to new questions. She wanted to avoid them. Revelation to ruination would not do. Chaos theory. Thermodynamic laws. She knew it all too well. Damn Vassar.

Time to cut my hair, she thought, *or become an archaeologist.*

Yes, yes. *Yet nothing to uncover,* she whispered to herself. *Nothing to excavate or love. I've lived it all. Seen too much. Let the dust cover up all the lies I've concocted in the last month, and the inevitable chaos that must occur as long as I play a human game.*

As she slowly dressed, she thought, *And now I go forth to excavate my invention, my Kore Serowik.*

In her dream the angel of the grasses had held Timessa's arms and said, "You are of the few, blessed among the many," and in the same breath whispered, "Now I'll tell you the meaning of life."

But the meaning of life had eluded her. It had eluded her in the dream, throughout her endless life, and was elusive even now.

Perhaps Artemis was prescient when she had freed her so readily. Did she expect Timessa to return in tears?

CHAPTER 2

You clearly see the the future
and the steppingstones along the route.
—Pindar, *to Delphic Apollo, the* Ninth Pythian Ode

I n her bedroom with early sun a blur behind an overcast sky, Timessa watched rainlight shifting on the curtains as clouds accelerated randomly. She sat up in bed breathing heavily, impatient and angry with herself. Any thought was preferable to those she had. She was thoroughly tired of the dreams that ran in nightly loops. Artemis had protected her from nightmares, but no more.

Now there was nothing Timessa could do. *Dreams are made in cinematic time,* she thought. *And I know what that's worth. Nothing. Nothing I can do. Reinvent myself — so what? It'll do no good. Who in the human world controls their dreams?*

These conversations with herself were a waste. She wrote in a notebook, *Dreams are as lasting as fireworks. Yet their thunder reverberates.*

On a slow afternoon she took Josef aside, lowering her voice and said as if complimenting him, "Kore's letter? A one-off."

On another afternoon she said portentously, "Dreams are but illumi-
nations of a journey's twists —"

"You accuse me of empty lectures," he laughed. "while talking foolishly. How can I take you seriously?"

"That's how I talk."

"It's dishonest. You hide behind it."

She shrugged, admitting to herself that phrases such as these were to
shield her before she had had a day or days or sometimes weeks to
process her sleep-made memories. It was just dream talk, smoky images
to marvel and laugh at when her mood was appropriate.

Once, she theorized that her dreams were like unexpected replies to
personal ad queries, except her replies seemed like the product of an
automaton, a robotic device that worked in shadows and darknesses,
weaving strange events, having the audacity, the malevolence to reply.
These unrequited reveries always played out like old windup toys,
mechanical and clunky. And yet Timessa knew that her bold talk and
pseudo research were just that — theories, talk, tiring explorations, all
laid out with caveats and excuses. In reality, she couldn't guess the
meaning of a single dream.

They were one of two extremes. The usual dreams were classic, soft
sequences, acts from short plays that crawled in slow motion through
diffused light, dream-voices muffled, dreams with voices as rare as first
editions. In these dreams, someone's hand would almost grab her hair,
and always, she woke in fear.

But *these* dreams never bothered her. These were drab, and she knew as
much. What she could not reconcile were the stranger ones, those with
detailed sequences, dreams that were cinematic, maddeningly encyclopedic,
each with rich conversations left echoing in her memory, dream voices
without filter that were as crisp as professional recordings, dreams with a
camera panning over silver buckets of ice set in checkerboard patterns on
polished countertops, dreams that might startle her awake with a whispered
phrase, *Go mercilessly against the forces that oppose us* — or that might wake her, a
harsh phrase uttered by someone inches away — *Now you see it clearly, right?* —
at which moment she would wake, lying sideways with her hair matted to her
forehead, her belly wet, her chest soaked, replaying the senseless sequences.

Each morning as she lay awake, she was certain she could analyze the patterns, break down the meanings and the words, the utterances from the faces she had just kissed or touched, that she could prevail and control it all if given time. But for Timessa, as for all beings, there never seemed sufficient time.

Aware of these divinations, she sat upright and quickly wrote out each nightmare's metronymic dialogue — tick tock, tick tock, the images escaping from her fingers now like trout, slipping in and out of the nets in her mind, time passing, the left strap of her nightgown down her arm, her hair tangled.

"Dreams can be deconstructed or reconstructed — it's fucking obvious," she would say out loud.

Yet she hardly believed herself, for talking of her dreams reminded her, as so much reminded her now, of the totemic *Obrero en heulga, asesinado*, a 1930s Manuel Bravo photograph of a fallen worker, royal and asleep in death, blood dried in a long streak across his cheek like a warrior's makeup, sunlight hard on his open, pinstriped shirt. For instance, she would say some fatuous phrase, *Conjuring the narrative*, and immediately see herself lying dead on a street, blood like a star melted onto her open shirt, across her breasts.

She had first seen the Bravo photo in a book published with an exhibition of his work. In her first year at Vassar she had sojourned to New York City with Filly. They spent afternoons at MoMA or the park, evenings at galleries off West Broadway, late nights in the remaining bookstores in the Village. But seeing the *Obrero* had transformed her. Of the thirty-two images in the show, this photograph spoke most clearly of fear and death and mortality, and of the radiance of flesh.

The print cost $4,200, an enormous sum at that time. When she returned to school she contacted Artemis, and the $4,200 appeared in her account. Timessa forwarded a check to the Witkin Gallery, desperate that the silver Bravo image be hers.

But now as she awoke at Josef's, dazed, she felt herself a recreation of the *Obrero*, on her back, her arms out and hands open perfectly in death. Still half asleep, she looked down at her chest for splattered blood, then shuddered awake.

For three succeeding evenings as she slept, she entered a dark and dreamless bliss, emerging each morning as if from a deep pool into sunlight streaming through her room. The Bravo print, framed simply, hung now across from her, away from direct light.

Then the reversion came. On the fourth night, a new dream, slippery and dangerous, spilled like cabernet into her sleep, coloring what had been days of clarity and uninterrupted purity. Incongruous in its juxtaposition of imagery, the dream was tremulous, jarring, sexual.

The same day, Timessa received a short email, a poem from a sender whose address was kore@slomo.com. The email read,

> *... Golden rivers gone turbid,*
> *streams boiling like thrashing snakes*
> *through a hazy floodplain ,*
> *a plundered land where men and women*
> *walk no more as separate beings*
> *but instead intertwine in single flesh ...*

She startled when she saw it. The sense that this new email was intended as something ingenious left her giddy, although the phrase she used in her notebook was *vertiginous*, which seemed far weightier. Since leaving Artemis she had been adrift, expectant, wide-eyed ... awaiting a thunderous event. Was Kore what she awaited? There was a deliciousness to it all.

Later, wondering what she knew (versus what was sheer conceit), she thought of Josef's breasts. Was she making something of nothing? It didn't seem possible. And because Josef would not discuss the incident, she wondered what, as the weeks passed, she really had seen. Was the entire event simply a hallucination, a byproduct of the wine intermingled with her silly dreams?

What was he, and who was she to judge him anyway, as she found herself doing when he went silent, voiceless, when they now passed each other in the house? She would look at his chest with sidelong glances, and say to herself, *It's not that whatever he is is good or bad, it's not that I'm judging ... I just want to know.* But as matters stood between them, she could not satisfy even that.

Disheartened, or alternately aroused (for she admitted she was, in some indeterminate fashion), she would imagine finding him in bed, asleep on his back. She would sit beside him, slowly pulling down his robe, peeling it off his shoulders as he slept, her eyes unable to avoid his ribs, the soft light from a table lamp casting deep shadows on his beautiful, forbidden breasts, which she would see again.

And in these fictions, Josef would, at times, waken, open his eyes and look into her own, watching as her eyes moved from his face to his chest; he would be expressionless as she stared down at him in the intense quiet of the night. In this recurring fantasy, breathing rapidly, Timessa would feel her heart pounding against her own soft breasts.

She would imagine, *Oh, he's beautiful.* Then, *Why do I care? I don't!*

And she would imagine Josef reaching over and touching her, smiling and sighing, rolling his eyes at the preposterousness of it all. They would laugh, cautiously. And as a song sometimes plays itself repeatedly in our heads, Timessa would hear in the space between them the sound of a dove, balancing on a wire in the distant street, moaning softly to itself, or to its distant sisters, as the sun rose flush and pink:

OH-oh, OH-oh, OH-oh

Or she would hear a wind that seemingly had entered the bedroom on its own, that would twist like an endless sheet around the bedposts until, in exhaustion, it sighed and collapsed in a shapeless *whoosh* onto the floor.

CHAPTER 3

In spring, the forsythia are the first to bud
followed by the merry willows, the basswood,
then the row of maple trees
dancing in a southern breeze.

On the morning that Timessa replied to Kore's email, feeling utterly
foolish, Summer Street was hit by a spring storm that broke tree
branches and coated the street in ice. Their electricity never failed,
although Josef had warned her about New England storms.

By late afternoon, temperatures rose to 50 degrees F, and she went
out, bought a latte, pastries, and shopped for groceries. Maintenance, she
normally would have called it. But throughout, she could not shake a
feeling. Was it that dreaded dull familiarity at some incident, that simple
illusion that this all had happened before?

Nothing happens twice, she thought, or repeatedly, or in recurring
patterns. Not really. Fractal theory, she knew, is no more real than finding
spirals in every natural shape — an aimless, mathematical pursuit. Why
not apply the geometry of geomorphology to memory, or suggest the

slippery curves of rivers as a panacea for our snaking remembrances, none of which we can recount a week after they occur?

This smothering by the imaginary, come-to-life Kore was like a river's slow sinuosity. In fact, how could an imaginary friend appear — from a time that never occurred — and reverberate today? Uncertain whether she should even answer the email (doing so might only enhance the absurdity), she rewrote the reply several times, then finally kept it brief.

Dear Kore,

Please do not contact me again as you are my invention, not my friend.

I cannot help, whatever you need, regardless of what you may imagine.

Timessa

Barely a day later, Kore replied,

Dearest Timessa,

Relationships are fascinating, yes? I spent hours last night, thinking about your reply.

Time is too short not to live fully as ourselves. I find doing so — living as myself — a struggle and am not interested in pretending otherwise.

I thought I might temporarily hold the upper hand, but no, at this moment, you remain the wizard.

Still, what I know you do not yet. So much is about to occur. You have far to go. I will hold the light for you to see.

Remember, I am your enduring friend — and so much more.

Fondly, Kore

Turning from her computer, Timessa looked at the Bravo photograph, then out a window into the night. The streetlight seemed unusually dim, the trees around it shifting gently, ice from yesterday's storm gone from the stiff branches.

She halfway expected to see this Kore standing by the light, facing her window, waving or gesturing or calling her name. *Oh, Kore Serowik,* she murmured to herself, *I accept you as my progeny. A figment prodigy, a thing without molecules and atoms. Yet my force has given thee propulsion.*

She heard Josef in the kitchen, noisily pulling glasses from the dishwasher, opening and closing cabinets. Wearily, she opened her door. His back was to her as he put dishes away, the red robe wound tightly around his waist.

"Is that robe," she said, "the only thing you own?"

He turned slowly toward her, a clean plate in his hand. To her surprise he smiled, and said, "I own other robes as well."

"Why don't you wear them?"

"I do," he said. "I never wear the same robe more than a week. Then, it's off to the cleaner."

"What a liar!" she said. "You always wear the same damn robe. The same red robe —" She liked the sound of *same red robe*. It had a certain power, a lyricism.

Twirling the plate at the level of his head until stopping it with a flourish, Josef said quietly, "What, you don't know? All my robes are red, identical, you idiot." He smiled widely, adopting an angelic look, perhaps copying one of the statues in his room.

Vaguely hurt by his words, Timessa suddenly understood. He owned a quiver of identical robes. Or was he teasing? And when had she qualified to be called an idiot?

Warily, she leaned against the door, careful not to return his smile. " 'All my robes,' huh? How many red robes do you own, Josef?"

"Enough." He turned, returning to his work.

A long moment passed before she walked up to the sink, stood beside him and, to irritate him, clicked the fluorescent light under the cabinets on and off, once, twice. As she was about to click it again, his hand covered hers. She froze, then slowly withdrew her hand, looking away.

Josef shrugged. "You look like the angel in a da Vinci painting, *Virgin of the Rocks*. Probably my favorite seraphim. Same curling hair, glazed, half-open eyes. She wears a robe like mine."

"So give me a robe to wear," she said. "Your robe."

Placing his right hand, fingers wide, across his chest, he shook his head. "You're rather dangerous, Timessa-thing." For a moment they exchanged looks. Then in control, he smiled again. "Tell me more about the … about your old best friend. Surely there's some secret we can share."

She played along. "Yes, Kore. I saw her last when we were seventeen or eighteen. I don't remember. It would have been the end of high school. She was not terribly attractive —"

"Unlike yourself."

"Maybe she had a crush on me. We weren't really even friends. Not what I'd call friends. She was a prodigy, or maybe a curiosity —"

"Prodigies are rarely admirable. Misfits, usually."

"Don't make fun of me." She reached into one of the open cabinets, grabbed a coffee cup, then set it down. "I'm not apprehensive. She claims she lives in Europe. Yet that was probably her, handing you the letter." She shrugged charmingly.

In a mock German accent, he said, "An unattractive girl …" He went on, "I want to meet her. At least for longer than a few seconds."

She pushed his shoulder gently. "Never."

"Who knows. She and I might hit it off."

Timessa cocked her head. "You said I looked like an angel. A da Vinci. That's the nicest thing you've said."

"The Virgin, she's about your age, although angels are always ageless. Kneeling or sitting sideways. Her hand is out, pointing with a single finger at the Savior. Sweet baby Jesus, dimpled and fleshy, sits beside her. Rocks or a grotto in the background, copper-colored light, yet all of it surrounded by an ominous background —"

"And what's the similarity? I mean, between me and …"

"I don't know. No, I'm not being honest. I do know. Same beautiful eyes, lips. I thought so the first time I saw you. Not that I'm implying anything, but for angels in paintings, she's one of the best."

Timessa unexpectedly teared. Josef looked away, and she saw his embarrassment. She wanted to tell him how she felt, her gratitude that he would listen, that he was here. That Kore presaged some new thing, perhaps even what she awaited.

Instead, surprising herself, she walked away.

CHAPTER 4

*The lilacs swollen in the surge
of spring with blooms,* Trifolium repens.
*Corollas and calyxes are pollinated
and ovaries emerge.*

K ore's secret:
Hair shorter than Timessa's, lighter, parted down the middle and consciously unwashed — she woke on her stomach and rolled swiftly onto her back, stretching, her arms out over her head, her legs tensed in a stretch for seconds until she relaxed in a sigh. With a breath and an exhalation, she rolled onto her side and sat on the edge of the bed. The room was empty except for an old writing desk with a laptop. Light drifted in through a single window as if the light were heavy smoke. The window itself seemed suspended, a painting on the wall. The only thing pleasing about the old house was the beach location.

She evaluated her contact over the week. What Timessa could not yet know was that she, Kore, had camouflaged herself, inserting herself in Timessa's memory as if she were Timessa's invention. But she was not. Instead, she had come like subtle ganglia, a network of thoughts, synapses connecting invisible roots which masqueraded as real experiences — not one memory different in sensation than a real one. Except that she, Kore, was the creator, not Timessa. And for that one night, she had appeared to Josef as well. How easily humans believed dreams.

The technique was audacious, duplicitous. Yet the approach was effective. Timessa felt no threat. In fact, because she found Kore's emergence amusing, she even anticipated the next contact.

Kore found herself wound tight with a fidgety electricity. She smiled with an angry appraisal of the past night, and with an enraged sense of hollowness, and an awareness of the hours in the partial day that remained before the repetitive emptiness of night.

Another secret Timessa could not know was that, if she had not been destined, Kore would want her. In their brief contact, Kore had felt a powerful attraction. She was drawn to naivety, and few beings were as sexually naive as nymphs. Yet nymphs knew desire; their inquisitiveness made them covetable. Timessa's beauty left Kore distracted and irritable.

Pushing her hair to the side, Kore thought, *I look like an Armani model, shirt open, rootless, romantic, carefully disheveled, supple.* This observation would have been accurate except that the typical glazed eyes required of these models, the urbane and worldly gaze of dissipation — was absent. Instead, her eyes were savage.

She stood, walked to the desk across from her bed, and touched the laptop's keyboard, waiting restlessly for the screen to light, for the previous night's writing to appear as thin hieroglyphics backlit on the glass. After a moment of disgust — the usual armored anticipation she consciously affected — Kore began to read, forming the words with her lips, falling into the rhythm, the phrasing of the short poem:

> *Bootlegged apple juice, absurd as her brief love.*
> *Men, women dreamt her demonic light,*
> *Woke describing it as a molten gold,*
> *Her astounding flesh aglow — a mercury,*
> *or bioelectrical alchemy, a sexed virus black*
> *As Black Death, a small bird burrowing into bones*
> *as sleepers slept in reverie —*

She stopped, highlighted Black Death, replaced it quickly with plague. She reread *astounding flesh aglow*, wanting to strike it as well, but stopped. The phrase sang in its impurity: the neighborhood girl's sumptuous soft flesh had been ridiculous. *Keep it*, she thought, *the words are appropriate, like knives.* She pushed her hair away from her eyes again, read,

... a sexed virus black
As the plague, a small bird burrowing into bones
as sleepers slept in reverie —

Yes, she thought.

She saved and exited the file. Some truth was there, maybe, caught between the lines, some scratches in the surface of the past evening's shadow play. She did not even know the girl's name, the anonymity important to them both, yet now infuriating. The girl had come to her room bearing an apple in cupped hands, silent, a small smile in the corners of her wide lips as she closed Kore's door, offering the fruit.

Kore recognized her as a girl who lived nearby; they had passed at times in the street, the girl's face always on fire as if she were a divinity. Many women's faces burned like hers until they fell off some fragile continental shelf, tumbling forever down a narrowing shaft, faces finally blank and worn.

But that had not yet occurred to this one. More distressing to Kore — or perhaps more disquieting — the girl resembled Timessa. They had the same cheekbones and small breasts, for which Kore had a weakness. Now the girl stood before her, burning in her yellow robe, capricious and bearing a token.

"From this I can make bootlegged apple juice," the girl said after a moment. "It's always sweet."

Her voice was lovely, with a desolate, pleading impetuosity. "With this single apple I can make an orchard's worth of forbidden juice —"

"Like wine from water?" Kore said, looking into her eyes, standing slowly from the desk. "Are you offering me miracles?"

The girl nodded, "Yes, that's it —"

The girl's smile was charming, childishly winsome. Kore stepped closer, touched the girl's shoulders lightly and the girl closed her eyes.

"Why?" Kore asked. "Why me?"

"Because ... you attract me."

"Is that it? Why do you think I feel anything for you?" The girl closed her eyes again, offering herself. Kore pushed the bathrobe off her right shoulder and kissed her neck. She found soft, immaculate flesh, pulsing with a curious fire. After Kore unknotted the narrow sash and the bathrobe dropped to the floor, the girl spoke again, for the last time, with her hand up, as if in some imperious warning.

"No. No further. Not until you take the apple from my hand."

Kore understood, taking it, biting it, chewing the pulp while the girl watched her carefully, her eyes half closed. Then Kore threw the apple aside, the fruit bouncing noisily into a corner. Her temper flared. "I'm not used to taking orders. If you stay you do what I say. Or you leave."

The girl half opened her lips and turned her head slightly. She raised her wrist, showing a silver bracelet with silver coins, and undid the clasp, letting it fall to her feet. Kore placed her hands on the girl's waist. The girl drew forward. Preposterous analogies, Kore thought, even as they touched — the riddled apple, nipples taunt, bracelets clattering with silver coins, everything but tiaras bursting into flame. But what was most unsettling was that, as she explored the girl, she imagined she was touching the unsullied nymph.

She whispered, "Are you simply some undone Eve?" but the girl shook her head, putting a finger on Kore's lips, leading her to the bed.

Soundlessly, the girl floated onto the unmade sheets and waited, eyes fluttering and wide. Kore took off her clothes. As the girl pulled her down, their faces inches apart, she thought abruptly, *She could be Death. In her beautiful face, there, beneath the flesh, her bones the bones of Death's archangel …*

And then as she moved her legs between the girl's, she thought, *A succubus, come to count my teeth … Possibly a demon-thing, Incubi in the guise of girl, here to take me on this afternoon …*

Finally, now on her back, surrendered under the girl, she cried out loudly — and in the heat they were consumed. And again, feeling guilt, she thought of Timessa, of ravishing the nymph as thoroughly as she had this girl.

After the apple-bearer left, she returned to her desk. A poem flowed from her in minutes without revision:

Bootlegged apple juice, absurd as silent love …

When she'd finished she fell exhausted onto the damp sheets, into the lingering perfume of the girl. When she woke hours later, she thought, *Okay, okay, okay, the sun is up and you are obligated now to rise, as all sad heralds of the sun arise* —

And Timessa will be neither your lover nor your naive prey. She is yours to proclaim. You are her augur, nothing more.

꫶

Now Kore was in disguise. Once she had been a revered goddess — Eos, the goddess of dawn, trumpeting the daily arrival of her brother Helios, the sun. But the duty she believed to be eternal ended, as Helios himself was taken more and more for granted. Cut free, she drifted off into machinations far less glorious.

For millennia, since her duties as his herald ended, she had relentlessly lived on and off, repetitiously appearing, dying, being reborn, at times bursting from the darkness, sometimes lingering in an unremembered purgatory for a century or more. She knew that in a painful, wearied breath, she had last expired in 1891 at the age of thirty-seven, lost in a fever, rotting from the legs down, in hell and in oblivion in seaside Marseilles.

Yet she would remind herself that vagrant time travelers do not look back, for the future itself quickly begins to resemble the distant past — a cycle of disappointment, achievement, and eventually, disdain. And always, half-filled, tremulous elation begins in the life that turns in time to silent, repetitious sorrow. She recognized the dichotomy.

Once she began to fend for herself, life had passed like a camera's flash. Although she was musically gifted, she played violin for the joy alone, much like a gypsy whose touch plumbs depths that often are better unexplored. Kore reveled in her native talent, playing songs flawlessly from memory, sometimes singing simultaneously in a voice that perfectly matched the notes. Wherever she landed she was considered a phenomena, and yet had no pride whatsoever in her work. Her attitude was careless and dangerously passionate, and her performances fraught with risk.

Once while playing an obscure concerto at the Sanders Theater in Cambridge, she began dancing while she played, a frantic, frightening dance that mesmerized the select audience who followed her rare appearances. Then she stopped, halfway through a line, letting the last violin note drag on endlessly while she shuffled her feet in tiny steps. After a long silence, she stopped, sighed, looked out across the audience. There was wild applause. That concert was the first where she began to quote poetry. And dance. On this earliest occasion, she laid her violin down, stood on the small stool by her side and said, "I now recite a poem I wrote last night ..."

Sometimes, during the rare moments of reflection she allowed herself, she felt violated by some tidal river, the plumes of rack and sea salt driven up into the gullet of the uplands of her thighs in a violent wedge of sharks and phosphorescent cells, oceanic matter that then washed headlong, driven by an angry moon, back into the depthless brink that fell away — and so she was, tossed asunder, brilliant in her brief spectacles before always being forced to flee to some dark land.

In the 1870s her flight had been to Ethiopia and Egypt. Now it was New England, where she read for pocket change from her scathing books of poetry in small cafes in Somerville and Jamaica Plain, a word hawker with a violin slung over her neck appearing as a glowering muse on every Poet's Night.

Kore was intolerant of sentimentality of any kind at any time. She held a single, millennial-old credence that was as eternal and as resilient as her charred soul. Her tenet — a complex propaganda — was that life was hypocrisy, that life without suffering was hallucinatory, bounded, made of lapping rings of sensuous derangement.

A poet's obligation was to destroy hypocrisy by word and deed and furious intelligence. And oh, sweet goddess, here she was in coastal Massachusetts, two towns away from Cambridge, living as an itinerant off the literati of Harvard and the satellite universities that were connected to it as if by glowing ganglia. These children, these students and their wizened keepers seemed to thrive on her insults, her taunts and coarse behavior, readily buying her dinner, booze, books and drugs.

In this privileged locale, she was well-placed to nourish Timessa, who had wandered into Boston solely on a whim. Kore had been chosen for this, to be the forerunner. She would hold the light.

An April interview in *The Boston Globe* opened further venues, and within a year Kore was invited to be a guest lecturer in contemporary literature classes at Harvard and Tufts. Her inflammatory persona — here she could again be Dawn — was reinforced by her willful ignorance of contemporary literature, although she could speak at length, and on an apparently intimate level, about the visionary poets of 19th century France. To anyone listening, Kore seemed on a first-name basis with Hugo, Gautier, the mawkish Leconte de Lisle, Verlaine, Rimbaud, and the opium-drenched visionary, Baudelaire.

She mixed colors, sounds, exotic rhythms, and a meteoric passion with a profound literary knowledge, leaving the huge classes stunned, and at times, in applause. "Dreams," she would cry at the end, "dreams are like cultivating fog! Why do we pander to the past?"

Girls would weep, and young men feel restless, inadequate, incapable of understanding her allusions. The men would remark later over drinks on Commonwealth Avenue about her fervor and insolence, secretly admiring her unkempt looks and arrogance. She was, they would say, unlike any woman they had met. And their girlfriends would giggle that she was like a resplendent nightmare — no one to take home, but someone certainly to inspire. To each other, privately, they would wonder how she loved, and what sort of lovers she took — that is, if she ever paused a moment from her work to look into the eyes of a man or woman.

The young women knew from hearing her poems, as their boyfriends could not, that Kore was consumed with love, wrestling with its sad minutia, its canyons and its nameless trails. They watched her eyes carefully as she looked out across the classes, hoping she would linger alone on theirs, that they could somehow sit later in a state of impossibly safe ecstasy over coffee with her on an endless night under immaculate stars, shivering as her hand brushed their arm, as she gestured widely while reading melancholic poems about innocence and love, wanting more than anything in their lives to take care of this ferocious girl-child.

But Kore had no interest in these girls. She was an immanentist, a being who always was and would be. And she knew that Timessa's potential was to eventually channel the energy that sustained the universe — that Timessa was Gaia's child, however momentarily unaware.

Consequently, Kore lingered in the Boston area solely because

Timessa lived near, for Kore knew that Timessa, not herself, was the blessed. This she knew as intimately as she knew the violin, or the works of her spiritual double, the mad Rimbaud.

Yes, she knew, Timessa was the one. Timessa was the luminous one, the high priestess, although Timessa herself was still blind.

Kore's secret mission, unfolding imperfectly, was clear. She was the herald, the messenger; she knew the terminus and would hand Timessa the light, a burning cosmic light. Gaia had told her to go forth and illuminate the way, to herald Timessa as she did the sun in the earliest years of the world.

She would be Timessa's Charon, her boatman over the Styx who, like one interpreting natural signs such as the flight of birds or the marrow of cracked bones, would point her toward inevitable revelations.

CHAPTER 5

From darkness to light
things shown, things said and done:
the lilacs rise toward the sun
the rivers again at flood height.

Days after Josef told her she looked like the angel in a da Vinci painting, Timessa received an email from Kore, which read,

Dear Timessa,

I fear that if given the choice you'd make me vanish without a moment of remorse. With a small exhalation, you'd blow me out.

You should know I am your protector, although I'm aware that like all innocents, you remain blissfully unaware. Or do you?!

I struggle to properly describe our small dynamic, but I have learned in my lifetimes that what seems revealed often vanishes. So it was with the horsemen and the apocalypse. Odysseus and the Sirens. Prometheus and the eagles. But that was long ago.

I dreamed a simple scene last night: dark smoke rose in the distance. Then I woke. I woke.

Ignore all of that. Here, the words are all for you.

Oh Timessa, do you know yet what they mean?
Fondly, Kore

In her room, alone at noon, Timessa looked outside at the barren trees. She read the email repeatedly. Her room smelled faintly of olives. Or of smoke. She cracked a window.

Resplendent in a red robe, Josef moved easily from room to room, straightening a vase, shifting a plant, casting his eyes across the order of his territories. Occasionally he would stop and tighten his robe. Fresh coffee brewed. Coffee cake heated in the oven. Timessa had gone by herself to a cinema.

"A matinee?" he had said.

"Foreign — you read the reviews, I'm sure, "she said. "A takeoff on *Last Tango in Paris*."

Josef found it ironic. When he met her, she noted that she loved film, had received some award for a script. Then she said that hated film, hated cinema. Now she had gone to a matinee.

"The perfect escape," she had said. Seemingly hesitant, she'd noted having received another email from Kore, then smiled.

There'd be a Bertolucci symposium at the Brattle Theatre, he recalled.

"I'm so enamored of Italian cinema!" she had laughed. "All the jump shots, cultural stuff, weird POV, the directorial courage — not like American crap," she concluded. "Art, Italian art. I was a fool to give it up —" She seemed besotted, enraptured. Josef carefully smiled.

She was due back shortly. Walking down the hallway, he stopped at her bedroom, impulsively opening the door. He observed, as in the past when he'd been in her room, she was neither meticulous nor careless. Her bed was made, clothes hung, with the exception of a couple blouses thrown across a chair. A black bra lay on the dresser. He opened the top drawer, then closed it rather than see intimates. Turning clockwise around the room with his hands on his waist, he wasn't sure what he wanted or why he'd wandered in. Curiosity, perhaps.

The famous Bravo photo hung over her bed. He didn't understand how someone could enjoy such a ghastly piece. Possibly he would loan her an angel figurine, something to offset the severity of the piece. He bent over and fluffed up her pillow. Then he smiled at a thought.

Retracing his steps to the kitchen, he opened a cabinet and took down chocolates. He chose one wrapped in gold foil, held it up between his thumb and index finger as if it were a jewel, and returned to her room. He placed the candy in the middle of her pillow, squaring it with the edges, carefully centering the glittery piece.

Looking around a last time, he saw a 3x5 postcard leaning against a bedside lamp. His interest quickened as he looked closer and confirmed his first impression. Da Vinci's *Virgin of the Rocks*. Picking up the card, he turned it over: a piece from Boston's Museum of Fine Art. She had remembered.

Hearing the timer, he left her room, not bothering to shut the door. Back in the kitchen the cake smelled ready and coffee was made. He poured a cup, sliced a wide piece of cake and sat at the table, tapping his fork thoughtfully. *How long had it been?* he wondered. Three months? Timessa had been a roommate for some time. And like all roommates, they revealed, inadvertently or not, secrets and confidences as weeks turned to months.

He had stopped trying to impress her. She was far too intelligent. Books he loaned her had probably gone unread. Two months out of the last four she had spent reading and rereading Artaud's *The Theater and Its Double*. Now she was talking about ideas for a screenplay. Next month she might be thumbing through *How to Find an Agent*. She was pretty enough to act, but seemed embarrassed when he'd suggested it. Too cerebral, he thought.

She once had accused him of treating her like a sister, and a younger one at that. And indeed, she had been correct. But he hadn't rented her a room seeking more.

He had been a fool to let her see him as she had. That he'd never intended. But now she knew. Or guessed. And he doubted that the knowledge had disgusted her — that had been his fear. That was always his fear. But with Timessa he had come to believe that on the contrary, his bisexuality, as it was that in the truest sense, physical as well as by inclination, was intriguing.

Yet he knew he put a gloss on it, remembering a girl he'd dated in his teens and the beating he took from her brother, who had responded to her screams. Josef would never forget the look of contempt as the boy hit him repeatedly. That was more than a decade ago. He'd learned to be careful, his slips increasingly rare.

And Timessa? Was she looking for love? No, he thought, she's looking for salvation, for the visionary from anywhere who reveals some purpose for all of … this. And aren't we all seeking the same thing? So, although he had never said so, he thought of her as an unrealized angel, a being in waiting, one of his seraphim.

Josef had acquired his first angel while finishing school in London. A friend invited him to visit his family on long weekends. Arrayed along a window sill in the dining room was a row of carved angels, standing like large toy soldiers, each performing a separate task. One held a prayer book, one preached the good word, one held a sword overhead, another a candle against the darkness of the world.

Josef was completely taken by them, and was gratified that the father allowed him to handle each. The carvings were German, and he estimated them to be 150 to 200 years old. Each was painted in bold colors with gilt trim, accented in antler bone. On the last day of Josef's last visit, the father said, "One of these is yours. Pick the one that moves you most," and Josef picked the one with a red robe, a long silver sword and wings.

That began what became an obsession, and the start of his collection. He now had sixty-seven angels, each catalogued and listed by height, material, date of acquisition, origin, age, seller, creator (if known), cost, and probable value. He had selected most of them for amusement or for their singular character. Two were large plastic pieces from Brazil, gaudily hand-painted and electrified so their faces glowed when illuminated. Several were valuable.

One bronze he bought a year before supposedly dated to the 18th century; he now believed it had been misattributed. His research at the Fogg Museum in Cambridge, and later in Florence at the Museo Nazionale del Bargello, led him to believe the work had been sculpted by Donatello himself, probably circa 1440. An elderly gentleman and fellow collector had offered him the piece, and said he'd bought it in Europe at the end of World War II. Josef had paid well over $20,000, careful to suppress his excitement during negotiations. After a year of research, he was certain about the attribution.

His sole acknowledgment of the value of the piece was to isolate it from the other figurines. A friend of his was a cabinetmaker, and Josef had make an aged cherry case for the Donatello. It came with glass doors, antique pulls and dovetailing. The bronze angel stood on a marble base inside the case. It was in a gown, held a scroll and had an ellipsoidal halo of beaten gold behind its long hair. The angel was female, although Josef had never attributed meaning to the gender of divine beings.

Most angels were men, many were asexual and a few were clearly female. The gender of this angel was immaterial to him: it was clearly imbued with a unique energy that left Josef dizzy when he handled it. The detail was exquisite, the casting technique lost wax and the patina delicate. Today, to his shock, it reminded him of Timessa, her face a perfect match for the angel's.

Timessa viewed his angels on occasion, always acting like she was in a museum. One morning she went into his bedroom as he was arranging them and said, "What is it about you and these damn angels?" He smiled because she smiled. She asked about the Donatello, touching the case, not knowing its attribution, and Josef had simply said, "It's my favorite."

She had knelt before it a long moment, then said, "I think it looks like me." Her voice was toneless, and her comment no more than an observation.

Her apparent disinterest gave Josef confidence, and he did not discuss its age or value. In fact, the first time she formally viewed the collection, he emphasized the Brazilian pieces, the Christmas angels from a knick-knack shop and showed her the piece that had started it all. She indulged him, asking few questions, saying, "How nice" or, "Colorful." Referring at the end to the Donatello, she remarked, "This is an old piece that isn't depressing."

"It came with the case," he lied. "I almost didn't buy it because it takes up so much space."

She looked at him a moment, then beamed. "But out of them all, this is the only one that seems alive. That's why you got it, right?"

When he said nothing, she smiled. "I mean it could be by some old master or something. Have you had it checked?"

"Oh, that's not why I have them. If I started worrying about their value, I'd stop having fun."

She stretched slowly, looking bored, then said, "Do these have anything to do with you?"

"What do you mean?" he asked.

Now her eyes were almost dancing, and she looked at him inquisitively. "All these angels. Have you ever thought about it?"

"Don't try to complicate things. It's just a hobby."

"That's like saying, 'My grandfather was just a mechanic.' "

"Timessa, when you clear your own head, we'll sit down and look into mine. When they threw me out of Groton, I returned to Boston and spent a month in analysis. Then my mother sent me back to England after reading the doctor's reports. I think she wanted me out of the country, out of sight."

"Did it do any good?"

"What? Analysis?

"You know what I mean. Did the doc recommend angels as a cure?"

"Psychoanalysis is based on the belief that individuals often are unaware of many of the factors that determine behavior. These 'unconscious' factors may create unhappiness, sometimes in the form of recognizable symptoms and other times as troubling personality traits, difficulties or disturbances in self-esteem …"

"That's good. What crap."

"I memorized it long ago."

"Sounds like a month of analysis wasn't enough."

"And I missed half the sessions. At the end the doctor suggested I consider a career in the circus. When he said that, I said, 'What?'

"He stood, saying quietly, 'Josef, I can't help you. And I'll deny I said this, but you're fucked up.' "

"Oh my god …" Timessa held her hands together as if praying. Josef liked her intensity. "What did you do?"

"I wanted to kill him. Instead, I walked out."

Timessa had tears in her eyes. "Oh!"

"I saw him last month at a theater opening. He was simply an old man. I turned away the moment I realized who he was."

"Would he have recognized you?"

"Probably not."

That exchange had happened in early summer, and she had not brought up his angels again. In fact she had become more and more distracted by the letter and emails she received from Kore. Josef now was the de facto recipient of almost all her entreaties: what should she do? Once he said, "In the same way that professional analysis becomes an intimate partnership, your relationship to this woman is becoming that. Are you aware?"

"No, impossible."

Sooner or later, he thought, Kore would go too far, and she would reveal her identity. Who she was, where she was.

Having no choice, he, like Timessa, waited.

CHAPTER 6

Nothing is analogous, all is inside out
the sudden mutation
according to plan, or no plan (a random
thing, an anōmalia*).*

K ore had not slept for two days. Between noon on a Tuesday, when
she woke with sudden inspiration, and the following Thursday,
driven by her unwavering belief in the mission (her "Timessa mission"),
she had written a movie script. She knew Timessa was considering
writing one. Beating her to it would be a great opportunity for Kore to
express some ideas, to foretell events. Maybe Timessa then would take
her more seriously. As it was, she had awoken Tuesday with all of it —
the characters and plot and motivations — inexplicably complete.

In its beginning, Kore's movie was dedicated to Timessa. The tone of
the story was purely contemporary, with modern characters who had
familiar sensibilities. Yet it harkened back to ancient Sparta. Kore well
remembered the regime: a warrior-society that discouraged love, a city-
state with dual kings, a people who treated their young women as
breeding chattel. The script emphasized betrayal, sex and death.

Now Kore was finished. She typed, "The End," centering the text four or five lines below the last line of dialogue. Yet she felt stupid. She deleted the phrase, allowing the script to terminate on the final spoken word. She checked her printer for paper.

Then, everything seemed hallucinatory. The computer's screen glowed. The printer drummed out sheet after sheet; she stood for a moment, feeling dizzy, and sat quickly.

As her heart quieted, she read the printed version. The dialogue was clean, the voices real. All in all, she thought, her story seemed half-true. She liked the title, *Not Her Man*. And she'd had no need to cast the parts in her mind; that had happened before she had begun. Laetia, Timessa's surrogate, would be played by Madonna, the celebrity Madonna circa 1985, when she was young. Amy, the tough street girl, would be played by a high school punk, perhaps recruited from a local school.

The Boy would be played by the current jock dream-boy. She didn't care who, as long as the boy was genuinely cruel. He'd be just another self-absorbed young man, knifed at the end, deserving his fate.

But then there was the Old Man. That was another matter. The Old Man would be played by Marlon Brando, but the Brando of the early 1970s, when he was still muscled, cynical, threatening and sad. In *Tango* he had been sadder than even Jack Kerouac in the years before his death. What had Kerouac died from? Leaping cats, litter boxes, nightmares and alcohol. Then smiling to herself, she thought she might cast Kerouac instead. The Old Man was weak, a blowhard, yet he had a certain strength. Brando had become an embarrassment.

Kerouac was a good choice, she thought, and rhapsodic enough, sensitive enough that he wouldn't dominate Timessa's doppelgänger, the dangerous Laetia. For Laetia was a goddess with a long knife, one who would gut her man like a fish. Gut her boy-man with a silver, shining blade.

Pleased with her creation, Kore sent the script to Timessa from the Harvard Square post office. As she left the building she looked up into the overcast sky. In a half-trance she crossed the street to a cafe and ordered an Americano. A dozen people sat at tables. One man stood and walked over to her table, chess board in hand. "You play?" he asked.

Play, she thought, aware of the dozens of meanings. He danced before her eyes, his entire body expanding and contracting as if he were taking huge breaths. She knew her problem was exhaustion. She should be in bed. Alone. Before she could answer, a waitress brought her drink. Rolling the hot cup between her hands, she looked at the man and said, "Sure. I play."

❧

Eighteen hours later Timessa opened the large envelope. The script was unbound. A yellow note stuck to the front page read, "You are Laetia. Madonna is Amy. The Boy is whatever boy next door you thought about when you were fourteen. And the Old Man is Kerouac — Jack, probably not a name you know. There's violence and sex. But all justified —"

Timessa slammed the manuscript down. She looked down the hall and yelled, "Josef!"

"What?"

"You won't believe. She's beginning to drive me crazy."

He appeared, looking preoccupied.

"Look —" She held up the mailing.

"Kore," he said flatly. "What now?"

"A movie script."

He picked it up and paged through. He stopped at every other page or so, skimming, smiling or shaking his head. Finally he placed the script back in her hands and said, "I've been thinking. We either call the cops, or we can turn this thing inside out. Why not? Let's invert it. From mystery to immense amusement."

"I don't get it." She tried to read his silence. "We'll pretend she's entertainment?"

"What if she's a saint? Like us all. There's a god in each of us."

"There's not."

"Perhaps we celebrate each time she knocks," he said. "Otherwise, she's got us."

"You mean, 'Hooray! More from Kore'? "

"Exactly. In this case, a script."

Cautiously, she said, "Okay. But a martini first."

She had been wondering what came next. Each missive, in whatever form, felt vaguely mission-critical, a component that, when fit with the other pieces, would reveal something, perhaps Timessa's purpose, her trajectory. She had invented Kore, yet her invention was no longer under her control. Or so it seemed.

In some respects, she waited on Kore's next move. Each week promised a new disclosure. And now she held a small unveiling.

Josef returned after a few minutes with a drink. They sat together and she laid the manuscript between them. Without saying more, they began to read.

"NOT HER MAN"
by Kore Serowik
For Timessa

The writing was concise, the characters nuanced and the dialogue laconic. Timessa guessed that, if produced, the screenplay might run twenty or thirty minutes.

A young woman, Laetia, clearly was intended to represent her. The theme was sacrifice. In the movie the girl sacrifices herself to a character called Johnboy, who marries her but does not love her. Instead, he loves an older man.

The young woman's hair is sheared on her marriage day, which she allows. She also has a friend, Amy, who, in the end, betrays her.

Josef observed, "Amy seems to mirror Kore. Not a sympathetic character."

"Yes," she said quietly. "It's an interesting technique. I mean, to write yourself in as an unlikeable character."

Johnboy cannot get his new wife pregnant and keeps her confined to the house. At one point the script depicts her being forced to have sex with him while she is restrained by the older man. She eventually fights them off, and that scene is a turning point. No longer the naive wife willing to sacrifice everything, she sees through Johnboy's scheme to use her to produce his child.

After the attempted rape, his hostility is so continuous that Laetia flees. He confronts her in a park as she is visiting with Amy, who turns out to be Johnboy's ally and helps corral Laetia. When he grabs Laetia's neck, demanding she return, she knifes him.

"Redemption?" Josef asked.

"None of this has anything to do with me."

Josef said, "Perhaps she's framed it like a prophesy. She's saying it *will* happen."

"No," Timessa said, "too subtle, if so. But something like it might occur. Something with the same flavor." She paused. "I'm impressed. She's really quite good at this."

"I'd like to read it again," he said. "On some starless night."

She laughed. "That would give it too much emphasis. No, I'm throwing it out."

&

Minutes later, Josef said, "I like the way she ends it."

"You liked it, huh?"

"That's not what I said." Josef got up and walked into the kitchen. "I'm making an omelet. Want one?"

"Sure. A single egg." She flipped mindlessly through the pages. "Why do you think she wrote it?"

"For you. It reeks of you, even if half of it is indirect."

"I don't agree."

"The most significant thing is her relationship to Johnboy, right? At first she allows herself — hell, she wants to be — subsumed," he said. "She allows it and all the while she knows about this Old Man and The Boy. Then she kills the boy at the end. So she wins, I suppose —"

She could hear him cracking eggs, then beating them. "Add milk," she directed. "And whatever that seasoning is you use —"

"Out of milk … What about the part where her hair's cut?"

"Symbolism," she said. "But of what?"

"Don't you know the story?" he asked.

"There's a story?"

"2,500 years ago. Sparta. A girl's hair was sheared as a matter of custom when she married."

Timessa realized his allusion but couldn't admit that she knew. "Now you're being obscure."

"I could be wrong, but the script made references to Greece. The tradition was cropped hair, a simple ceremony, followed by a harsh marriage bed."

"I see. I'd never heard that." Of course she had. She remembered that Hasidic Jews have a similar tradition. Regardless, she pretended to be puzzled.

He worked quickly making eggs. That Kore had posed this as a movie was ingenious. Timessa herself wanted to write one. Kore had done so, her screenplay complete with directorial cues and camera directions.

"Nothing Kore does," Josef said loudly, "is without meaning. Maybe we should have her arrested."

"Did you see the postmark?" she asked.

He picked up the envelope. "Local."

"Not just local," she said. "Harvard Square. Mailed yesterday."

"We're on a need-to-know."

"Yes." Timessa stretched out on the couch, her feet on the armrest. Suddenly everything seemed amusing. "I've got it. Call me Laetia from now on. Laetia Timessa. LT. Can't you see the initials stamped onto my handbag?"

"Imaginative."

"I think she's onto something. I've always liked Timessa. But now I like Laetia. I could take it on as a pseudonym."

He said nothing for a moment. Omelets were ready and he put them on plates. "You want toast with this?"

"Sure ... there's something you've never told me —"

"What?" He had tried to keep the conversation light and had succeeded all too well. She'd been amused for much of the reading. But not now.

"You've said almost nothing about your mother." She paused. "Is she still alive?"

"She died while I was in London, a month before I finished school. She had a lot of money, which she'd inherited when her father died."

In an amused voice she cried, "Did you inherit it all?"

"Yes. That's how I can afford silk robes and tacky angels." He set plates on the table, neatly arranging cloth napkins and silverware. "Orange juice?"

She said, "You look sad."

"Let's talk Kore," he said. "That'll cheer me up."

"One thing I disliked about her back in high school was that name. 'Kore Serowik.' That's horrible. She's done better with Amy. So let's talk Amy. Laetia and Amy."

"I'm used to you getting wide-eyed every time she sends you something."

She held up a piece of omelet that she'd speared. "It all fits, really. Poems, dreams, amateur theatrics …" She spoke while chewing. "But this is different. She's waved a wand, I think. You know how much I like movies."

"This month."

"It's perfect." Timessa speared another piece of omelet and circled the fork overhead. "Can't you see the pixie dust? It's magical!"

"It's not that simple," he argued. "It's confusing. Too many voices, everyone in conflict with everyone else. No protagonist to love."

"No, you're wrong."

"Now *I'm* wrong?"

Timessa squinted. "And I like the ending."

"Here's how I'd redo it," Josef said. "She tells them to leave and the Old Man refuses. He stands and they wrestle. She cuts him but he gets her around the neck and begins to squeeze 'til she's out of breath. Then just before she faints, she knees him, hard. They break apart, and the Old Man scrambles up and grabs Amy, or Kore, by the hand and they run like hell. Laetia lays on the ground watching —"

"No," Timessa said. "I'd make her an Amazon. Think of how she grabs The Boy near the end. She kills him without a blink. So then she traps the other two and they know they could go down in a moment. She's powerful. But instead of killing them, she walks."

"Laetia, the Amazon. Or the angel. Which will it be?" He said it with irony, but he liked Timessa's reaction. If she could take this latest delivery with a sense of power, why not play along?

And, he thought, the script was hermetic. There was eroticism, combined with a sense of prurience. And Laetia was a woman in transition, clearly unformed and metamorphic. Timessa once had described herself to him as "in transition."

He finished eating. "Too bad there wasn't a return address. You could write a critique. 'Loved the twists and turns. Oppressed woman finds revenge. Catharsis and delicious ending, all in the best bloody traditions of the silver screen …' "

Timessa gave him an odd look. "I'll email her."

"I'm not sure I'd acknowledge. One way or another."

She pouted. "Then I have to wait for the next surprise?"

"Or perhaps," he said, "she'll knock on the door."

"No," Timessa said, shaking her head. "Not yet. That comes later."

He looked at her carefully. She sat with her fingers pressed against her cheeks. Her hair had come undone. He tried to catch her eye, but she looked through him, seeing something far away. Then she said, "I'll meet her, you know. I'm certain. Not sure if that's good or bad."

CHAPTER 7

Timessa knew something was happening. Multiple stories, fantastical characters, multifarious incidents. She'd created a childhood, schools, imaginary friends, passions and experiences. She had balanced them all so far, but was aware of the snowballing complexity. Each had seemed ingenious at the time. But she had not anticipated Kore.

A day after she and Josef read the script, she received a brief text. It read like an an order:

Meet me at the cafe at the
corner of Prescott and Broadway.
10:00 a.m. tomorrow. —*A*

Artemis. Her goddess. Timessa broke into tears. Why? Within minutes she received a second text, this from Kore. It was as brief.

You have not written to say
you love my script.

Timessa responded to Artemis, affirming the meeting. Of course she would; she had no choice. Kore could wait.

That night she dreamed she was locked in a room with the three sisters, the Fates, and they were eating toxic acorns. She could barely distinguish them as their gowns were the same brown as the walls and furniture, as the acorns. At some point Laine offered Timessa an acorn and she recoiled in horror, waking in a sweat.

In the morning she dressed and undressed and dressed again, trying a half dozen outfits before settling on a conservative black skirt and beige blouse. She brushed her hair far longer than usual and put on makeup, then wiped it off. She tried to imagine meeting Artemis but was unable. She would simply go, regardless of the outcome. They had had no contact since Artemis released her to "find" herself. Yet her financial accounts remained funded and her tether to the tribe remained, however unacknowledged.

Timessa had no idea that I observed her regularly, or that I communicated my observances to Artemis. Of course I was partly responsible for her exposure to Laine and for her last months with the Fates before they self-destroyed. I had failed to protect her at the end, to anticipate what might occur. I would not repeat my error.

Timessa appeared at the cafe at 9:50, and sat with a coffee, waiting restlessly. At precisely ten o'clock, Artemis appeared, accompanied by Filly, Timessa's oldest friend. Both nodded to Timessa as if they were casual friends. Timessa stood, but the goddess and the other nymph sat immediately, motioning Timessa to do so as well. Artemis's outfit was similar to Timessa's, except her blouse was accentuated with a leather belt hitched below her breasts. Filly wore jeans and a hoodie, her face impassive. Timessa understood the dynamic immediately. Still, it was good to see them, whatever the circumstances.

Timessa spoke first, whispering. "Goddess —"

"Timessa."

A waitress appeared and Artemis ordered coffee for the table. Then she turned to Timessa. "Jackson tells me that things have become a mess."

Timessa nodded, trying to engage Artemis's eyes but the goddess was expressionless. "Things are okay."

"Remember the father of the Fates?"

"Phanes."

"Yes. His wife was Nyx, who appeared at the trial."

"I remember. I haven't forgotten anything."

"And what was his sex?"

"Lachesis called him double-sexed."

"Yes, he could go either way."

Timessa flushed. To the goddess her thoughts were transparent. "I have not strayed."

"When you were freed you became free."

"But I have not … done anything like that."

"Yet your thoughts are not pure."

Timessa smiled carefully. "Nor have they ever been." Filly's mouth flickered — a tiny smile.

Artemis deflected the comment with another. "You room with a herm."

"Josef. You're calling him a hermaphrodite?" She paused. "Yes, he has a girl's breasts. I've wondered about the rest. Is that why you mention Phanes?"

"Phanes and this man are not duplicates. One was immortal, the other is *not*."

"Josef," Timessa paused, "… is no threat."

"No," Artemis agreed. "The threat is Kore."

Timessa looked away, into the shadows swallowing Prescott Street. She had not intended to discuss Kore. The goddess touched her hand. "Timessa, you invented her, didn't you?"

"Yes."

"No, you did not."

"But I did!"

"You have been fooled."

Timessa looked down, then into the goddess's eyes. "I don't understand."

"Kore found you, not you her. You tell yourself she's a concoction, an ingenious creation of yours. Something you made up for what you call a backstory."

"I have to have a childhood. Everyone else does."

"Kore is real. Not a concoction."

"She can't be."

"Do imaginary friends write letters, or send emails and texts?" Timessa grimaced and shrugged. "Like a parasite, a worm, she planted herself in your mind. And did so in the guise of a fantasy of your own making. What you thought you created was her invention, not yours. She is the ingenious one."

"Is that why you've come?"

Artemis simply looked into Timessa's eyes. After a moment she said, "No nymph has ever taken a journey such as yours."

"I am grateful."

"That I allowed this to occur?"

Timessa toyed unconsciously with the upper button on her blouse.

"May I ask a question?" Artemis nodded. "I am surrounded by constant allusions to angels. From Josef, from this Kore. And in dreams as well. You have always taught that angels do not exist."

"Seraphim," Artemis said. "Creatures of Christianity, an order in their so-called celestial hierarchy."

"One who appeared before me in a dream kissed me at the end. It might have been the kiss of death."

"The belief in them pre-dates Christianity," Artemis said. "We are older than these things by a millennium."

"But are they real?"

"Not in our world. But you have crossed over into a darker place, a primitive world of conflict and violence."

"The human world?"

Artemis smiled. "As Filly often says, you are the most innocent of the tribe. Here, in this place, you are at risk of losing everything."

She felt chastened, small, and tried to breathe evenly. "So you are saying angels exist."

"For humans, yes. As you extend across both worlds, you will be subject to what manifests in their domain. Are you surprised?"

She wasn't sure. She was aware their faces glowed. In comparison to the other women at the shop, their skin was burnished, blooming. "Both Josef and Kore have implied I am one."

"An angel?" Artemis laughed. "Are you?"

"Of course not! How could I be?"

"This darker world has dark angels and angels of death. Some are messengers of whatever god humans believe exists. Some are beautiful and many androgynous, like Phanes." Artemis put her hand on Timessa's. "I am sorry I cannot anticipate what you may encounter or what you may become."

Timessa broke into tears at the same moment the waitress appeared. She waited while Timessa wiped her face, then asked, "Anything else?"

Artemis shook her head, waving her away.

"And Kore?" Timessa asked. "What is she?"

"We're not sure. A specter perhaps, but real. A thing of the material world, I think."

Filly whispered, "Like a wraith, a spirit."

Artemis went on, "Yet of the flesh. She exists here, not there. She thrives in the winds beyond the enclosure I maintain to protect us all. And you have attracted her."

"I don't understand."

"You're a nymph. Your face shines, your psyche seeks the sun. And love. You are envied by the others. They would have your purity. You've heard the phrase, 'like a fly to honey'? There will be others like her. They will claim to exalt you, while their efforts will be self-serving."

Artemis paused. "Remember our word, *Akrasia*. You are now a sparrow, as free as any bird. But birds are easily snared, baked and eaten in pies. Or become hawk-bait when they feel safest. Be vigilant."

The goddess retreated into a worrisome formality, and neither she nor Filly spoke for minutes. Timessa nervously wove her fingers together, picked up her cup and set it down. When Artemis and Filly stood, Timessa rose as well and the goddess motioned, "Sit. Leave after we do." The nymph slowly sat and watched the two stride out, turn east on Broadway and disappear into the bright sun.

They had talked for thirty minutes. She stood, leaving several bills on the table. Feeling a vague deftness at her accomplishments — at the least she had survived for a third of a year on her own — she left, following the goddess's path onto Broadway, half expecting to find them waiting on the sidewalk. Instead, looking across Broadway, she saw a large hound sitting beside a building. It was grey and muscular and she knew immediately: Orthrus, in its single-headed iteration. Even at eighty feet, the beast's eyes glowed red and inscrutable. She nodded to it, as an acknowledgement was necessary. Then she looked away. She knew what its appearance meant. Artemis had assigned it to observe. And guard, if necessary.

She scanned the roadways and sidewalks for the two. They had vanished.

The goddess's absence made Timessa unexpectedly realize that since her withdrawal from the tribe, she had slept every night without company. Doing so was a small revelation as she had always depended on someone holding her, stroking her sides until she slept. For years it had been the goddess herself, or Filly, or even for a brief time when Timessa stayed at my mansion, me, however reluctant I had been at the time. The realization that she needed none of us gave her hope, a small sense of independence — it felt an antidote to Artemis's innuendoes and warnings.

Even at Vassar Timessa had been constantly accompanied by Filly. Now, in what the goddess called "a darker place," she had endured without the security of companionship for months. She wondered, years before when she and Filly were allowed to attend the university, if Artemis had anticipated her flight, had prepared her even then for all of this.

And Artemis was clear, she thought, that Kore was not benign. Was she instead *malign*? Filly had called her a wraith.

As she slowly walked down the sidewalk paralleling Broadway, ruminating about the events of the last months, Timessa was shouldered by a girl about her age who had been walking toward her. The blow sent her sideways a foot, and she staggered a moment before looking at the girl.

"Sorry!" the girl said. Then she looked startled. "Timessa! It's you!"

Inexplicably, she knew: Kore. The girl's hair was light, parted down the middle, a strange softness in her cheekbones, her lips thin and eyes lambent. As Timessa scanned her face, the girl broke into a grin and took her arm.

CHAPTER 8

Any of these things, the best planning done
by generals, upended in a quake or eclipse of the moon.
Any of these things. The mere glance
she gives equivalent in energy
to the gesture of victims burnt on a stake, madly
blowing one final kiss from the hot debris —

Timessa's instincts were defensive. As quickly as the encounter occurred, Timessa ended it, brushing off Kore's hand and driving her fist into the girl's sternum. As a nymph she was trained in self-protection. And as Lachesis had once described her to me, she was capable of being an assassin, acting without conscience and constraint. If threatened, she could kill, and had.

In this instance and in real time, Timessa acted abruptly. Artemis's visit had been prescient. As quickly as the goddess had departed, Kore had appeared.

At the strike Kore wobbled, falling sideways into the street, crying, "Hey!" as she went down.

A heel strike to the head would kill her instantly. But Timessa paused.

They exchanged looks for a breath. Kore's lips curled into a strange smile.

Timessa turned and sprinted east down Broadway, crossing the street in front of several cars and running into the public park in front of the Cambridge library, finally stopping in the small playground beside an older woman who held two children. Timessa had dashed six-hundred feet and as quickly, swiveled, looking back. She saw no pursuer. The woman frowned and said, "Are you all right?"

Timessa nodded, continuing to scan the area. What was the likelihood of such an encounter? None, she thought. The girl fit her image of Kore perfectly. Their meeting must have been a setup. Even as Artemis and Filly left the cafe, Kore must have been approaching. The three probably had passed each other. Artemis would have known, and allowed the confrontation. Timessa was not winded by her sprint, but was incredulous.

One of the children pointed at her and said, "She's so pretty, Mommy!"

The woman said, "Hush," and dragged the children toward the swings. Timessa eyed a bench facing a circular walkway but continued east through the library grounds. Pausing seemed foolish, although Kore, if she wanted to follow, would be visible by now. The dog, Orthrus, was a master at stealth; she assumed it was nearby.

Timessa exited the grounds onto Ellery Street and turned north. Josef's house was only blocks away. She decided that sprinting the eighth of a mile was sensible, and darted toward the house, pausing twice to look for Kore.

At the house she climbed the steps and sat on one of the porch chairs. If Josef were home, he'd sense her here; he was good in that regard. She settled into the old chair and crossed her legs. Artemis, Filly, Orthrus, Kore — all had appeared within a short time of each other. Although Timessa felt herself inconsequential, her search for herself even indulgent, the advent of these beings seemed to argue otherwise.

Josef opened the front door. "That wasn't long."

She smiled. "A boring outing. But pleasant. I walked through the library grounds."

He shrugged. "Have you had coffee?"

"Yes. A cup or two. Quiet here?"

He nodded and sat across from her, aware she was fidgeting. "I'll be out this afternoon doing some research. I have an appointment at the Widener."

"Harvard?"

"One of the libraries. You can come if you promise to be good."

"There's a word for that."

He waited, smiling. She said, thinking of Artemis's word. "Yes, *Akrasia.*"

"Like crazy?"

"Pretty close. Probably its derivation. Anyway," she said, "Angelology is not my thing."

"Funny that angels always protest angel research."

"Is that true?" She opened her palms in a silly gesture. "Perhaps angels just *are.*"

They sat in silence for minutes, then she said, "I ran into Kore this morning."

"What?"

"I was leaving the cafe and she collided with me. Purposely, I'm sure."

"How did you know it was her?"

"I just knew. She even shrieked something like, 'Timessa, it's you!' "

He said nothing, studying her face. She seemed content to wait, but finally he asked, "So what happened?"

"I shoved the hell out of her and ran."

"I'll bet that was a pretty fast run."

"Yes." She smiled. "She didn't follow."

Josef stood and said, "That's not the way to greet an old friend."

"I confirmed one thing. She's corporeal, Josef — alive."

"I'm not surprised. Ghosts don't write movie scripts. Or send emails."

She stood. "I'm moving on. I've almost forgotten her."

❧

More than four months had passed since Timessa's dream of the angel, the two of them on a blanket in a field. The night after the morning she'd encountered Kore outside the cafe, she dreamed again of the angel,

Golden-haired No-name. The dream was short, lasting no longer than her confrontation.

No-name was younger, perhaps no older than twelve, a half-woman. As Timessa began to speak, the angel exhaled fire. Timessa recoiled and the dream dissolved. Oddly, the imagery did not trouble her, and she woke remembering it all. The predominant image was No-name's lips pursed in an O, her tongue belching flames, a roar of heat accompanying her bellicosity. And there were her eyes, arced slats under blue eyeshadow. Yet she appeared as a girl-child.

In the morning Timessa wandered out to the backyard. Josef had set up a lovely cedar bench between old apple trees and blackthorn shrubs. Timessa was drawn to its privacy. She decided to inventory her stories, real and fabricated. They were increasingly problematic. The surging intensity could not continue. She was certain all of it could be reversed — decelerated, she thought, mouthing the word. *Decelerated.*

Life was partially a matrix, sounds, colors and senses, and she was fully capable of brushing grays over the wide swaths of red, white over the darknesses. She sat on the bench, putting her feet on a nearby stone.

She practiced thinking nothing, but that lasted only moments. She began to see Kore's startled face, Artemis's stern expression, Filly's reticence, No-name's eyes — and hot eyes of the divine Orthrus. All watched and assessed, measuring, waiting, anticipating. Yet, she thought, I am not a pending revelation. That is not who I am at all.

She closed her eyes and sighed. Rather than finding peace, she saw No-name exhaling flames. She opened her eyes, taking in the small garden, and laughed. *What did everyone want?*

She stilled herself, swept with an odd wordlessness. She was aware of a golden light that seemed to have dropped from the sky; it bleached the green colors of the garden, washed all intensity from the arbor, blanching the reds of the climbing roses. The grass was a monochrome of pale golds. For the first time in years, she sat stupidly, aware yet stunned that she now seemed without a thought. After a moment she became aware of a small yellow butterfly hovering several feet away; she watched it dart among flowers. As she allowed herself to follow the movement of its wings, she breathed, conscious that minutes had passed without her inhaling. The butterfly stopped on a bloom, floating, pulsing, alive.

I am Timessa, she thought. *Not Laetia, not an imaginary human girl. I am a-*

mortal. I cannot get sick and I do not age. I am no one's angel. Any transitioning I do is of my own choice. I owe no one anything. I have childhood memories, but they are all from a period of four or five years in Greece, all from millennia ago. We grew fast, three times faster than villagers, and Artemis allowed me to reach adolescence by the time a human child was six. Those times were good, and I was loved.

I am not immortal. Although humans are fond of using the word for the divine, no thing is genuinely immortal. Birds and grasses and men and gods all begin and end, endlessly recreated and endlessly destroyed. Gaia sees to that. Our race, the divine gods of ancient Greece, is a-mortal; destroying us is difficult, onerous. We experience death only by violent destruction. Or extraordinary toxin. In the hierarchy of things, we are high. But in due time we, too, will go.

For a while she aimlessly scanned the garden. The grasses had returned to green, the golden hue gone. The small butterfly still wavered from flower to flower. She wondered about its lifetime. Was it weeks or months or years? *And me,* she thought, *I have invented a human adolescence, a childhood of convenience, a necessity in this place away from Artemis. Its invention has not canceled or negated my past as a nymph. Although I am in the wild and outside of the goddess's magical sphere, I remain who I am.*

Yet there was the unresolved business of Kore, what Timessa had once believed was a sheer concoction, her invention —

That had been her reality until the goddess stated otherwise.

Artemis had called Kore a worm in her mind. That Kore had fooled Timessa into believing she was a fantasy of her own making. That the invention was Kore's, not hers.

And now Timessa knew Kore was, as she had told Josef, a corporeal thing. She was real. Or a convincing facsimile. The girl had grabbed her, and she in turn had struck Kore down. Flesh on flesh. *We both qualify,* she thought to herself, *as phantasmagorical. Known, yet enigmas.*

If this enigma-thing has wormed itself into me, she reflected, it must have a purpose. All things do. Nothing exists without an aspiration. Or at least, a function. And Kore seemed, to this point, to be purposely bewildering. She thought of the old Greek phrase *anakalypteria,* the lifting of the veil at a wedding. Too, there was *anagnorisis,* the recognition. With Kore there had been *anakalypteria,* the veil pulled aside. Now Timessa awaited *anagnorisis,* the revelation. Yet there was none; the lifted veil increased the mysteries.

Josef wandered outside. She heard the backdoor open and then footsteps as he approached. She sighed, not willing to share her reflections. As she knew he would, he broke the lovely silence. "Sorry to bother you. This just came by FedEx. Unusual enough that I thought I should interrupt."

She took the envelope from him. Her name was written in red block letters in the address — no last name, just "Timessa." He turned to go and she said, "No, stay. I'm expecting nothing. Who knows what might be inside."

She quickly opened the envelope. Inside she found what appeared to be an old playing card. On the front was a vintage etching of a water-wheel being turned by a blindfolded, naked woman. At the top of the wheel, a couple was cavorting. And at the bottom of the wheel, a man in a red shirt flew off into an abyss, his arms akimbo. The card read, LA ROUE DE FORTUNE.

She knew: a Tarot card, a thing of superstition. Touching it, she felt defiled.

Josef said, "The Wheel of Fortune. It signifies destiny, future."

"It looks frightening."

"Some interpret it to mean first happiness, and then, disaster. Or first, endearment, then death. Others see it as more sanguine."

She flipped the card over, knowing what she would find. The back was signed in a crooked calligraphy, *Kore*.

CHAPTER 9

Ah, Apollo —Theodosis took you down as well.
All of you. It was coming clear as hell.
You and Hyacinth
cut down by the unholy Holy Patriarch

J ackson here:
   I mentioned at the end of the first volume of this recollection that after the Fate's deaths, I made tentative efforts to revive the male gods. The efforts came to nothing and largely were research — first steps in what I assumed would be a long undertaking. According to Laine's explanations (I'm going back to an evening seven years ago when she still pretended to be my daughter), no male god had reanimated when the Fates chose to return. Her claim was that "the male gods spiraled into unrecoverable darkness" and that the nymphs and goddesses "vanished incognito into wildlands in what is now France, Spain and Greece."

The claims struck me as nonsensical, but I was on a need-to-know basis. And certainly not in a position to challenge her.

I have mentioned that, now as the sole male among this divine tribe, I have never shaken my disquiet that none of the men reanimated. Could I expect the same? Could their failure be attributed to weaker chromosomes? I doubted it — divine genes are not identical to human.

After the Day of the Pyres when the sisters were cremated in the amphitheatre, I decided to explore the possibility of reviving the males. Perhaps lives were recoverable. Danaë found my efforts touching, or perhaps foolish. But I have persisted.

Restoring Dionysos, Apollo, Hephaistos, Ares, and even Danaë's father, Poseidon, would affirm that gender was not, as Laine avowed, the cause of their failure to reanimate. As time passed I wondered if she purposely had left them comatose. They would have been competition, which she disdained. Regardless, my explorations have continued these intervening years. Danaë is, of course, enthralled at the possibility her father might live.

I first had to determine the place of their retreat. Laine always had been elusive about the locale. She had emphasized that those who chose dormancy did so around 390 CE. I spent over two years substantiating the retreat's location. Danaë was invaluable, and even Artemis helped. Her recent suggestion to focus on her place of birth proved invaluable.

In the end I confirmed that the male gods, along with the three Fates, "retreated" to the sacred island of Delos, the epicenter of the Cycladic islands. Islands surrounding Delos include Amorgos, Anafi, Andros, Ios, Kea, Kythnos, Milos, Naxos, Santorini, and a half dozen others. Three thousand years ago, Poseidon selected Delos for Leto to give birth to Apollo and Artemis. Consequently, in ancient Greece it was the most sacred of locations, a destination as hallowed as Delphi or Eleusis.

That was then. Today, Delos is a desolate, broken isle. It prospered between 490 and 88 BCE, becoming wealthy with a booming slave trade, immense banking facilities and a vast body of worshipers serving numerous temples and as many gods. Apollo had a large temple, as did Poseidon and Dionysos. Near the end, temples were erected even to Egyptian gods such as Isis.

Overlooking the ancient city is Mount Kynthos, and at its peak were temples to Zeus and Athene. Victors in the Delian Games climbed a long roadway to its pinnacle to receive laurels.

But Delos was doomed, prospering for less than half a millennium. In 88 BCE, King Mithridates of the Black Sea raided the island, destroying part of the island and killing thousands. Disaster struck again in less than twenty years when Athenodoros leveled what was left and killed whomever remained. As a consequence, the island lay in ruins until modern times when archeological excavations began. The gods who chose to retreat in 390 CE found the site in ruins, the perfect sanctuary for their melancholy exodus.

I suspect Apollo, Dionysos, Ares, Poseidon, and the others assumed their withdrawal would be brief, akin to what we might call a restorative, and not the 1,600-year-long interment it became. Laine may have played a role in that as well, but her motivations are a mystery. Regardless of the catalyst, I was convinced the gods lay in divine suspension. I suspected Laine's protestations that they had descended into unrecoverable darkness were another lie.

Frankly, Timessa's ongoing misadventures — as I viewed them initially — were an immense distraction. She was easy to follow, and I felt a responsibility for ensuring her safety. But doing so prevented me from focusing fully on my research, which was my real passion. I became convinced that the island housed them, but Delos comprises more than 1.3 square miles.

Were they ensconced in the peak of Mount Kynthos, or hidden near the sacred palm tree planted in honor of Apollo, or in the base of the altar in the amphitheatre? For some weeks Artemis toyed with me as I hounded her with my banal questions. Near the Naxian lions? The House of Masks? Below the Sacred Lake (which was now dry and difficult to imagine as ever having been a lacustrine wonder and center of worship)? Artemis knew, but pretended otherwise.

One night in bed, Danaë whispered, "If you were Artemis and had to retreat, if you were the goddess and were in a place sacred to you, one with a temple built to glorify you, where would you go?"

"To my temple?"

"Yes, but she had no temple in Delos. Apollo, though, was persuaded to take the long sleep. His temple was the largest there and the most glorious."

I looked at her, blank. Then I knew: "The gods retreated to Apollo's temple!"

"It lies between the agora and the Sacred Lake, in the center of the habitation, the most blessed of the places on the sacred isle."

"So it's the temple ..."

"A subsurface floor below the footings, a small warren of conclaves, was hidden from all but the highest priests. It remained intact even after repeated attacks on the island. Pirates never discovered the foundation's chambers. I'm not certain, but it's a reasonable location, and would have appealed to Apollo's sense of harmony."

"So they lie in Apollo's temple."

"Perhaps. In a long sleep. Since the human year 394."

Danaë would be proven wrong — the ruins of the temple held nothing — but the temple's stones were the spark for my eventual discovery.

I'd struggled to reach this conclusion. Now I believed I knew, but the truth — or at least the apparent truth — left me underwhelmed. It seemed absurd that the male gods had willingly gone to lie together below temple ruins on a ransacked island in the Mediterranean. They had ruled the world for millennia. I was to believe, that after thousands of years of adulation they simply shrugged and followed the Fates into the darkness, saying to each other, "We're tired of attacks, of the libel and of constant mockery. Enough!"?

Perhaps I'd imagined something grander. Then again, I knew too little. In reality, now that I knew when and where, knowing felt like knowing nothing. Or far too little. For instance, how were their bodies situated? Were they in rows, lying on their backs like wounded soldiers from an ancient war? Or in hermetically sealed pods? Or were they sitting in a golden circle, propped atop thrones and watching each other through narrow, dazed eyes, incognizant as the years passed?

And were they even comatose, as Laine had said? I laughed aloud, to Danaë's surprise, saying, "What if they sit around some magnificent card table playing games and carousing through the endless hours of the days and nights, freed of responsibility, reveling in their freedom?"

She looked at me without humor, as if my lack of respect was abhorrent. "They agonized for some time before leaving us. No one entered that darkness with an easy heart."

I rolled onto my back, studying the bedroom ceiling. "There's got to be more. No being, divine or human, willingly gives away immense power, let alone their lives. None of them would have readily acknowl-edged failure or accepted such a retreat. Each was powerful enough to destroy cities. Together they could have eliminated vast regions with a single nod. They easily could have been thwarted the attacks by the new religionists on so-called pagans. I never bought Laine's explanations. And I still don't."

She lay quietly, then said, "It was what we were told."

"Did all of you simply trust the Fates?"

"It was only Lachesis, but even she went off to sleep. We watched them walk away. How could we doubt them? Beforehand, we gathered briefly. We were not asked to concur, just to listen. Hundreds of us gath-ered in a vast meadow outside Athens. The sun was low, just touching the treetops. When Lachesis, my father and Apollo finished speaking, many of us began to cry."

"And then what?"

"Those who had committed to leave, left. There were no second thoughts. I watched their backs, admiring the magnificent robes each wore. It was the last time I saw my father or any of the others. Then Lachesis and her sisters reappeared."

"It's as if you're describing bulls led to sacrifice."

"Led into the labyrinth. But not to Hades, which is permanent. Delos became a place of sleep. Or so we were told."

I turned again, facing her. "I'm not through with this. I'm convinced that in time we'll know whether they were led to sleep or slaughter."

Danaë half-smiled. I knew she had long reconciled their end. Now she simply indulged my quest, probably certain that the outcome would bring further sadness. She knew it occupied me. Whatever her doubts, she played along, allowing me to blunder where I would ... even if where I wandered was into the gods's necropolis.

Yet inexplicably, I remained optimistic. And now I believed I knew their resting place: a ruined temple in Delos that lay 153 kilometers from Athens. And I knew that I would travel there, kick a few stones, pretend to be an archaeologist, and hike Mount Kynthos to watch the sun drop into the sea. With luck, I would open a divine time capsule and excavate what remained of the glorious Greek gods. With greater luck, their lives would be recoverable.

In the morning I checked on Timessa and observed her having coffee in Josef's kitchen. She idly turned a tarot card in her left hand.

When Josef had seen it, he said, "The Wheel of Fortune." And indeed, it showed exhilaration and misery. Its assumption was that all happiness ends in ruin. The man being thrown off the wheel, the one who wore a tattered red shirt, was being tossed into an abyss, his arms flailing as the naked woman turning the wheel looked away. Was that the fate of humans? An abyss, a silent scream? No wonder religions prospered.

As Timessa sat indolent, she remembered: Lachesis had granted no favors to supplicants, and Aisa cut the delicate cord of life without a qualm. They were robotic in their machinations. As a nymph she hadn't really cared. Now, as a pseudo-human girl, she could empathize.

Timessa knew that humans were born, lived a life as short as mayflies, as the *Ephemera danica*, then perished, their memories extinguished, and all memories of them lost within generations. From her perspective, fate was barbarous and remorseless to them all. The Wheel of Fortune was not a poor representation. Yet in humans she also had seen exultation and ecstasy. And she knew that for some, the euphoria of the couple at the top of the card never diminished. Love lasted through life's short moments.

So she wondered: did the tarot card disregard love, or was love an entrapment, an enticement and hoax before a human was hurled to humiliating death? She had never known that type of love.

Josef walked into the kitchen, watching her play with the card. She turned the back of the card to him, flashing the signature: *Kore*. "You haven't destroyed it yet," he said.

"As the Fates destroy humans?"

"Have you considered that she's toying?"

"I'm no longer sure."

He poured himself coffee and sat. "You've lost your sense of humor."

"Blame me?"

He shook his head. "Wrong guy to ask. I'm a bit hungover."

"Scotch?"

"No, all-night transfusions of brandy. I admit to being a bit shaken myself. A movie script, a confrontation with the real Kore, then a gypsy's tarot card."

"Whatever it is, is directed at me."

"I suppose. Yet, if so, the card could have been La Mort."

"Death?"

"Death, destruction, sudden loss. Instead she left things ambiguous. The Wheel can turn for good or bad. Perhaps she's hedging. Or doesn't know," Josef said.

"I'm really quite sick of her. Once she was intriguing, but she's growing tiresome."

"You're hard to please."

"Now," she smiled. "I must eliminate her. Deconstruct her atoms. Fashion her into something else. I'm imagining a voodoo doll, to start. Then a small pile of ashes left outside for the rain to scatter where it will."

He stood. "Maybe we're putting too much into all this. She's somewhat ingenious, and you've fallen for it. As she hopes, I suspect. Have you responded to yesterday's FedEx?"

"Not a chance."

"Then don't. Let's discourage contact. In time she'll go away."

"Why do you say that? Even now I feel she's somewhere close."

Timessa's cell phone binged. She picked it up hesitantly, set it down, then picked it again. Making a face she tapped the message: a weather service alert. It read, *Severe storms possible at 2 p.m.*

Timessa turned her cellphone toward Josef and said, "Good news. I'd take that any day."

CHAPTER 10

Blue mascara, moon-lit brows
in a dress with yellow petticoat,
tea length, endless crinoline, tight
at her hips, blood-red bows
doubled at her waist.

Several days later Timessa returned to the same cafe on Broadway, as much to exorcise Kore as anything. Sitting in suspension for a half hour, she drank lattes and ate scones. As she was about to leave, a woman in her 40s stopped beside her and asked, "May I join you for a moment?"

Without waiting for a reply, the woman sat, handing her a business card and said, "My name is Seneca. I represent Great Insights Agency. GIA dominates the New England fashion market. Places beautiful girls for local shoots. I noticed you as I came in."

Timessa studied her a moment and knew that she was who she said she was. Sensing no deception, Timessa smiled carefully. "Why speak to me?"

"You have a unique look. I think we could keep you busy. Interested?"

"You're suggesting I model?"

"Have you ever?"

Timessa shrugged. "No. You're joking, right?"

"It pays well. There's glamour. Some drudgery. You're the right size. The market's looking for lithe girls right now. I love your nose. And your cheeks are adorable."

Blushing, Timessa looked down at the card. It read, Seneca Ibsen, Agent, Great Insights Agency, Cambridge. She looked up at the woman. "I'm a student. But I'm bored. Would modeling un-bore me?"

"A GIA model is never bored."

"What's it pay?"

"$500 a day to start, but with your face, $2,500 to $5,000 within a few months. We'll need a screen test. Some girls are more photogenic than others."

Timessa laughed. "No lingerie."

The woman said, "Lingerie pays double and triple the usual rate."

Timessa shook her head no. The money meant nothing. But she could imagine fashion itself as a steppingstone to cinema or theatre. She perhaps would be seen in an ad, and invited to audition for something big. At the least it would be an adventure, a diversion. She thought, *Artemis has a keen sense of fashion and might be amused.*

The following afternoon Timessa appeared at the agency's studio, and after headshots and full body snaps, she was signed. Seneca promised that her images would be on their website by week's end, saying with endearing enthusiasm, "You're a natural. You'll be deluged with gigs."

Her first gig occurred less than a week after signing. She and another girl modeled bridal dresses for a regional manufacturer. After the show, a local haute couture designer, a couturier to women on Nantucket and the Vineyard, approached her. Would she represent her Newbury Street shop? After negotiation with GIA, the designer secured Timessa under a three-month contract; the couturier agreed she could continue to work high-end shows.

Timessa succeeded quickly. Show runners liked how she held cigarettes. They raved over her confidence. She skipped the usual tryouts and the heartbreak of rejections. As Seneca promised, the work poured in. The agency struggled to schedule the gigs. Soon she was making $15,000 a month.

A few days later when Timessa went downstairs for morning coffee, she found the house quiet. She'd gone back to her room and dressed slowly. There was no rush this morning. She had slept well. A rain squall had swept through the city after midnight. She woke, listening to rhythmic metallic bings as the storm passed over and had gone back to sleep.

When she woke she remembered a series of dreams, all related to fashion. In one she was backstage, a dozen dressing rooms teeming with models, dispassionate girls rarely older than seventeen, each with hair gelled or sprayed or pulled back in feinted disarray, most being pinned into clothes or having makeup applied. The dresses they wore were high-necked, some open at the chest to reveal identical blue bras.

A casting director swept in and exclaimed, "Anyone shorter than five-foot-eight? Bye-bye." Girls turned and left, stumbling out.

He then cried, "Hips bigger than ninety centimeters, thirty-five and a half inches? Don't waste anyone's time!"

Odd, she thought, in one of the dressing rooms the girls were chanting in French as if in a polymorphic chorus. The words in the dream repeated monotonously,

Nous fêtons le soleil —
We celebrate the sun —

Over and over. In a later dream just before she awoke, she had become one of them, standing in a claustrophobic room. She was being fitted in a dress. Two older women were arguing whether to tighten it further.

A girl, perhaps no more than eight, stood officiously on a stool braiding Timessa's hair. The girl was in a yellow jumper and was humming as she worked. Her hands were delicate and her fingernails glossed white. As a matching touch, she wore white eyeliner.

A man in his thirties — a couturier she thought — stood before her, smiling. Then he frowned and pulled at the tight material covering her breasts. He pulled at the front and the sides.

"I expected a bigger girl. Your boobs? Too small." He spoke into the back of the room. "This one's not what I need!"

She had broken into tears, but almost immediately a woman dressed in what appeared to be a physician's lab coat pushed the man away. She cupped Timessa's breasts and said in a lilting voice, "Your breasts, my dear, have promise, regardless of Immanuel's comment."

When Timessa awakened, she was puzzled and touched herself. No one had ever criticized her chest. And she had never seen such vast dressing rooms.

Recently her dreams had become ornate, curious, almost melodious reveries. Memorable ones occurred almost every night. She attributed last night's to the week she had spent with Seneca visiting fashion shows in New York City. The agent had taken her into back dressing rooms, and Timessa had been overwhelmed at the grand whirl of it all, at the half-dressed girls waiting on long benches for a call, or at the lines of girls being dressed by fitters.

She was heartbroken seeing them all, thinking, *All beautiful children. Human beauty is so fleeting. Do they even understand?*

They would all be ground down, or dead, in such a short time. *Ephemera. Ephemera danica.*

Now in her own room, in Josef's house, she felt that, if she looked into her mirror, she would see a new woman looking out, manifest in some frightening way. Feeling brave, she did exactly that, leaning into her bedroom mirror. But there was nothing new, no one special.

Timessa scanned the clothes she had laid on her bed. The red-buttoned blouse worked well with the black check skirt. She put on a bra and the blouse. The morning sun was bright and the trees outside her window glinted from the rain. She shrugged and sat on a chair by the window, her blouse buttoned but her skirt still on the bed.

In the silence Timessa leaned back and closed her eyes. She wasn't tired, but had a slight headache. Then she stood abruptly and slipped on the checked skirt, zipping it up. Looking in the mirror, she liked the look. Her eyes followed her hip line. There was a magic there.

At that moment she shivered inexplicably, wondering suddenly if she were alone. The room felt full. She thought: *All I want this morning is normal. Want to be a normal girl.*

Yet she knew she wasn't normal and wasn't a human girl. She was reminded of something Artemis had said once at the sacred pool, something like, "We can stand up to our hips in the water. But are we really wet?" What she meant was that reality differed from appearances: what we appeared to be was never what we were.

Closing her eyes again, she stepped away, away from it all, took a breath and rose on one foot to turn delicately on her toes, elbows out, fingers cupped together. She balanced, all the disdain and confusion instantly gone. Gone, gone, stamped out. She knew she risked imitating Lachesis, who had herself imitated Gaia. She remembered Aisa imitating them all, her caricature of Lachesis's pirouette eventually bringing down the Fates forever as the child fell backward into a stew of toxic acorns. But that was years ago. Now, because of Lachesis, no one danced. Yet she would.

For good measure, because she could and none of the other nymphs dared, Timessa spun once and slowed, viewing herself in the mirror.

Pleasant, she thought.

Then she remembered something else Artemis had said, this as Timessa prepared to leave the tribe: "You will exceed every female you encounter. Not because you are special but because you are a divinity. Being divine is not better, just different. So, be careful, Timessa. Otherwise you may wander into darknesses you cannot imagine."

Seneca had said last week, "Soon, you'll eclipse all my girls."

Timessa knew Seneca sang a song of seduction and that the goddess counseled something more circumspect. Perhaps, she thought, both were wrong. Yes, perhaps I will excel, but not as either imagines.

Recognizable artwork was placed strategically throughout Josef's house. Timessa knew too little to recognize them. A six-foot long Calder mobile, its black and green discs lazily turning as if under power, hung in the dining room. Near it a massive Rauschenberg combine was mounted on a stark wall as if lifted from the MoMA. On a wall across from it was the Warhol silkscreen of Marilyn Monroe, its pop colors still, after decades, an outrage.

A friend of Josef's, a producer of the *Star Trek* movies, visiting before a lecture series at Emerson, had stopped by and said, "Not to be tacky, Josef, but the artwork in this room alone is worth —?"

Unlike Josef's friends, she knew nothing. She was a savant, yet ignorant of contemporary art. When he casually had shown her the Warhol, she had said, "Who?" Her fascination, if she had a fascination with anything he displayed, was with his angels. She remained a charming riddle.

Another week passed. One grey morning Josef wandered into the living room. Timessa was sitting on a couch that overlooked the backyard. She wore a pale yellow dress with black dots the size of pearls and she had tucked her legs under herself, a water glass in hand. One arm dangled on the couch back. On a nearby wall hung Josef's John Singer Sargent painting, *Eleanor*. It was of a girl of a similar age sitting in a high Chippendale chair, her arm at the same angle as Timessa's. In the painting the girl, Eleanor, looked away. The Calder mobile lazily turned.

"Hi, Josef."

"Timessa."

"I have a shoot this afternoon. Then I'll be back."

Something about her dress reminded him of an evening when he was fourteen, shortly before his chest transmogrified. He had been invited to a dance at a private girls's school. It was an old institution and looked out over a bay on the Gulf. He could not remember what he wore, but he remembered that the girl he danced with had been in a pale dress like Timessa's. He remembered too that the girl was slight, still very young. They had danced once or twice. He was no longer sure. But the memory of the humid evening, the lights on the masts of sloops and catamarans dancing on the water, was the first romantic magic he'd tasted — and he remembered each second of that night. A good evening, he thought. One that only someone utterly inexperienced could have treasured.

He could no longer recall the girl's name. He wasn't sure he ever saw her again, but it didn't matter. His hand on her back, their touches — that was otherworldly and even in hindsight, far more important than any later relationship he'd known. He likely had been too unsure of himself to have made contact afterward. Or maybe she moved or was transferred. Or perhaps she did not reply to a letter he sent to the school to her attention. He liked imagining that he had sent such a letter.

He was so innocent then, he thought. Like Timessa now. Although Timessa was, in her naivety, glamorous as well, certainly more urbane than he would ever be.

She turned to him. "What are you thinking?"

He apologized, saying, "Daydreaming. One of my flaws."

She could have goaded him. He'd left himself open, but instead she smiled softly. "I've been sitting here thinking of my afternoon. I'll be modeling skirts and dresses. Daring, supposedly. The designer is introducing them here before a show in Paris. She has no faith they'll be loved. She thinks that she's failed, that nothing will sell. She's run out of inspiration. I think she hopes I'll save her ass."

"Is that true?"

She looked down. "If the show sells locally, I'm supposed to own the runway in the Paris show. You know, become the girl who launched a thousand slips."

He smiled at the pun. "And that occurs when —?"

"In weeks. Just enough time for her to add a ribbon as an accent, or raise a waist line a quarter inch. Enough time for me to pack a bag before I'm sent across the seas."

He sat across from her. She seemed oblivious and finally said, "I've never liked France, Josef."

"You've been?"

"I lived outside Provence for years."

"You'd never said."

She smiled. "There's a lot I've never said."

She thought briefly of the tribe surviving in the back hills and wildlands of France and Spain, of Artemis hiding them from the scattered farmers who themselves hid from bandits, thieves and invaders. The sacred tribe had scrambled for hundreds of years after Emperor Theodosis had declared pagans criminals. Those were good years, but she was glad they'd finally left.

Stretching gracefully, she said, "Seneca picks me up in five. A limo. I'm making her a fortune and must play the part."

Josef stood and bowed, saying, "Then perhaps we'll talk when you return."

She sauntered out, fully aware that he watched her as she left. At the door to the hallway, she turned. "Oh, got a text from Kore late last night. The first since forever."

He cocked his head. "And?"

"It said, 'Beware, as now … gods serve man, not man these gods.' "

"Which means?" he asked.

"It's inscrutable. Kore's *always* inscrutable."

With a shrug she left, her right hand raised head-high, making small circles with her long fingers as she walked. He was certain she took none of this seriously. When several nights earlier he had called her his enigma, she had replied, "Ενιγμα," then smiled, saying, "Old Greek for the word. So much softer, don't you think, in the original?"

He had said nothing. How could she know something so obscure?

CHAPTER 11

Rainlight penetrates rain
as sea-salt penetrates sunken bones —
soon there will be no justifications …
Everything is moving at speed.
There is no longer need
for explanations.

The morning after Danaë affirmed that Delos was where my hunt would end, I booked tickets to Athens. Danaë agreed to come. The trip would be New York to Munich to Athens, ending with a short flight from Athens to Mykonos.

From there we'd take a catamaran to the ancient, hooked cove at Delos, appearing for all purposes as tourists, a final leg of less than a half hour over a distance of 10 kilometers. Delos, in ruination, was glamorous Mykonos's sacred sister to the southwest.

We could have willed ourselves from Pennsylvania to Delos in a matter of moments; Danaë had shown me the maneuver some time before. I tested the novelty several times, shifting a few hundred miles once. But she wanted to experience what she called a "globe-trot" for the first time. So we would journey the long way, the human way, or so I viewed the expedition.

Danaë had been to Delos repeatedly, but her last visit was before Mithridates raided the island in 88 BCE. We spoke little about the details of past trips. She seemed disinterested in reviving the past, yet I suspected she would prove invaluable as I poked around the stones. And as we both shifted shapes at will, we would quietly change appearance, if necessary, before we left Mykonos. Danaë's natural luminance and beauty would be too memorable, and we would need to be forgettable once we arrived.

She mentioned she'd seen Apollo's temple shortly after its construction in the 6th century BCE, and again off and on until about 100 BCE. Her memories, at least those she would discuss, were of a cosmopolitan, wealthy island, its residents confident and rich. Its primary currency had for some time been slaves. And banking — measured in gold and silver ingots.

In Rome's last years, it had replaced Athens as the island's benefactor, and Roman conquests through the Mediterranean after 166 BCE continued to generate hundreds — sometimes thousands — of new slaves for market every month. The island's affluence inevitably became too tempting to brigands and raiding powers.

We would leave when weather was favorable in mid-April, and stay as long as necessary. Filly agreed to watch our three boys. As the date approached, Danaë grew visibly excited. She had not left the estate since our coupling years before. On one night as we talked in bed, she said, "The poppies are everywhere in early May. Wildflowers, migrations of birds and, I hear, topless girls on the beaches."

"That's Mykonos. I suspect there'll be no topless girls roaming the ruins of Delos."

She laughed. "But we might see goats and sheep. And the slopes of Kynthos will be a carpet of blooms. There's a hallowed path to the pinnacle."

She told me that after 500 BCE, no one had been allowed to give birth there. The island was sacred to Apollo and had been purified by the Athenians. At one point mid-millennium, Athens had excavated all burials and taken the dead to Reneia, an island less than a half mile away. With a single, assertive declaration, birth and death had been banished from the god's sanctuary. She knew of no other place with such a history. Yet I couldn't help but think the ritualistic cleansing did them little good. Mithridates swept the island at will one red dawn.

And as interesting as I found the history, I still puzzled over the vanished gods, who, we now acknowledged, had apparently dispersed there. My focus was their location and whether their *essence* was somehow intact, as I cared nothing for the graveyards of Reneia, or dirty Athens, or the countless sheep she expected to see, hauled by boat from Mykonos to graze between stone walls on the ancient slopes.

I remembered, too, that the Fates did not simply reappear. Twenty-five years ago, when Laine lit the fuse for their return, they followed the ancient path of nativity, with a mother and father, merging their consciousness with new bodies.

And if I found that the gods even were recoverable, what means would be required to bring them back? And was it thoughtless to take Danaë, who conceivably could come face-to-face with the remains of her father, preserved in some form, in a state that left the once-mighty Poseidon, the sea-god, no more able to move than a fly caught in prehistoric amber?

I was in the crowd watching Timessa the afternoon she modeled the designer's skirts. My monitoring usually entailed only distance viewing, at which I'd become adept. It was a lazy technique; I could close my eyes and watch her movements from anywhere, and hear conversations. I was uncomfortable intruding into her privacy but knew no other way to protect her.

And the technique wasn't perfect. For instance, I could accurately sense action around her for a diameter of up to 50 feet. A threat twice that distance was difficult to anticipate. But my skills sufficed for enhancing her safety. I knew Artemis watched her independently. Between us, we surveilled the girl perhaps more than necessary. But my disquiet about her activities continued, so I maintained vigilance.

I should clarify that, when I say I "watched" Timessa modeling clothes, I mean that in this instance I appeared physically in Somerville, at the opening. As I did, I chose to show myself as a new fashion critic from the *Boston Globe*. It was better that she not know her every move was monitored. Artemis had appeared days before; for Timessa to then see me within a few days might have shaken her self-confidence.

None of this explains my earlier error. Or Artemis's. Neither of us had anticipated that Kore would appear near the cafe, let alone send letters and emails for weeks before. Neither of us understood what she was or what she represented. I was shocked that Artemis was uncertain, referring to Kore as an eidolon or phantom, which felt far too vague. When I cornered her one evening, she said, "I know you're watching Timessa. Good. We have to remain alert."

Danaë shrugged and turned away when I asked her opinion. I trusted no one else.

Concluding that Kore was a presence beyond the tribe's encounters, I sensed nothing when I first saw her. She was a cipher, yet, rather than being of no importance, she seemed the opposite. I say that, aware that Kore was a zero, a hovering, sinister nothing. Living beings have a cohesive molecular anatomy, a unique vibration that I can use to instantly recognize the living from the inert. Kore emanated no sentient attributes, yet she existed.

Neither Artemis nor I could explain her singularity. I could not imagine anything as alarming. But then, like the others, I was sure she foreshadowed some event, whether light or dark, like an ancient herald, warning those she enveloped that some event was imminent.

I sound portentous, but I simply reflect my concerns. The goddess and I might hover near Timessa, yet if we could not be certain what was dangerous, we could not anticipate the danger. Consequently, I suggested to Danaë one evening that we take Timessa with us to Delos. She appeared startled, saying, "What? I thought I knew you."

"You do. Why look so shocked?"

"Delos is *our* adventure. I don't want some shifty nymph along. What an awkward threesome —"

"Are you jealous?"

She looked at me cautiously. "No."

"You are."

Her eyes flashed. "Why take her?"

"I won't be able to keep track of her from thousands of miles away."

"Let Artemis."

"We've been double-teaming."

"She can find someone else to play."

"No one else can project."

She paused, her eyes becoming distant. "You're genuinely afraid for Timessa, aren't you?"

"Yes. She's a naif."

Danaë paused, then said, "She's my friend, not yours. I've known her forever."

"Sure, but I feel some responsibility for her leaving us all."

"Why?"

"A week before she announced her departure, we spoke. She told me she had no idea who she was, that the bliss of being a nymph was gone. That she wanted to escape from Artemis's care. That it was like a spider's web, oppressive. That she needed to prove herself."

"I'm not impressed."

I continued. "Perhaps it's an old story. But I stupidly said, 'Then go. Strike out. Challenge yourself.' "

"What did she say?"

"Nothing. But then a week later she asked Artemis to sever her protectorship."

"I see ..." A moment passed. "And now you watch her constantly."

"Not quite. But I do check in."

Danaë whispered, "I'm opposed. But I'll not fight you over it. You decide."

The next morning I told Danaë that I'd approach Timessa when I went to Somerville. I'd invite her to accompany us, that she could view our trip as a chance to revisit old grounds she'd seen when Delos was in its glory. She'd be under no obligation to serve anyone. She'd simply go as an explorer, whether in search of herself or the old gods.

Danaë acknowledged that Timessa had been to Delos with Artemis multiple times, that both of them knew Delos as well as anyone. She grimaced and acquiesced.

In the end I wasn't sure of my decision. At the least I would owe Danaë for her concession. Her irritation was unmistakable.

❧

At the fashion opening. T (my old nickname for Timessa) walked lazily down a narrow aisle built in a flat S-configuration, the surface a faux leopardskin. She did so repeatedly, wearing different skirts each trip. Theatrical lights followed her from beginning to end. The room was predominately women, with three men, including myself, scattered among them.

The show, modeled exclusively by Timessa, went on for some time. As she sauntered back and forth, I scanned for Kore, but saw no one who matched her description. There was palpable excitement throughout the show, with numerous gasps and occasional applause from the audience. When T modeled the final piece, she stopped and bowed and the entire audience rose and applauded. Graciously, she turned and acknowledged the designer, saying, "Not me — she's the star."

Almost immediately a small staff rolled out food and drinks. The gathering went on for some time, with Timessa mingling with the shifting groups of women as if she had been modeling for years. She posed with dozens of the designer's patrons, always professional, poised and graciously self-aware. I never left my seat, pretending to take notes and watching attentively. Near the end the designer approached me, smiling. "You're from the *Globe*, yes?"

"Indeed. And I'm impressed with what I've seen."

"In that case, I'm delighted." She put out her hand.

I stood. "Would you introduce me to your model?"

"Everyone wants to meet her. A special girl —" She gestured to T, who casually joined us. She looked at me quizzically. The designer said, "Timessa, meet the *Globe*'s new fashion reviewer."

She half-bowed, saying, "My honor." As I smiled, she paused briefly. "You look familiar."

"Everyone says that."

T gazed at me for a moment, then said, "I was certain. Perhaps a party —?"

The designer interrupted and said, "You must have questions about the show."

"My article will be, essentially, a rave. I understand you are going from Boston to Paris in another month. May I predict success?"

She laughed, saying, "Success as long as Timessa comes!" After a few minutes of small talk, they wandered off, but not before I stopped T and asked, "I have a question for you. Could you humor me when this is over?"

She looked at the designer, who nodded, and Timessa said, "Of course. Give me five."

I sat, pretending to complete my notes. In a few minutes she returned, suddenly cautious. I had not indicated my question and suspected she was not used to interviews. I invited her to sit. As she did, she said, "I'm nothing special."

"T, it's me, Jackson."

She gasped, and pushed back in her chair. "What?"

As she stared I allowed my appearance to slowly change. In seconds I was myself. "Sorry to startle you."

She scanned me in disbelief. "Yes, your eyes," she said. "That's what looked familiar. But I like you better in the original."

I walked her out of the show and to a bench in the center of a nearby park, and said, "I only have moments. You should know I've decided to bring the male gods back. I think it's possible."

She frowned. "Why tell me?"

"They're in Delos, probably below Apollo's temple."

"It was destroyed thousands of years ago."

"The perfect retreat for them, don't you think?"

"I don't think about it."

I said nothing, simply looking at her. Finally, I said, "Danaë says you've been there. That you both visited Delos a couple times."

"Many times, with Artemis. So what?"

"Take a break and join us when we go. We'll be a couple weeks. You'll be no one's nymph, just one of us. It'll be like a vacation, a chance to think about all of this —" I gestured into the street, at the people hurrying by. "It might do you good to get away."

"No, I'm going to Paris."

"That's a month from now. We'll be finished in Delos a week before."

She needed assurance that Artemis was not involved, that she wasn't being used. I spoke lightly. "You and Danaë will be my archaeologists. This will be unique."

Hesitating, she said, "Jackson, there a dozen nymphs you could ask. Or even Artemis."

Knowing I had moments to persuade her before she stood, I said, "We go way back … Remember that day Danaë almost beat you up?"

She laughed for the first time. "Over kisses. She's a fierce protector."

"I suspect she'd say, 'Properly jealous.' "

"She threatened to cut out my tongue."

"Her anger passed. Long ago. She's agreed that having you along makes sense."

"So it was your idea."

Then I knew I'd won. "I'm eager, frankly, to hear what you've learned since you've been away."

T smiled. "When do we go?"

"This weekend. We're flying Boston to Munich to Athens to Mykonos."

"It's a good time of year to go."

"Pack light. Meet us Saturday morning in the terminal. Nine o'clock, Air France."

We hugged briefly and as she pushed away from me, she broke into tears, wiped them haphazardly and smiled.

CHAPTER 12

Mystagogos, nauseous
and Nausicaa, losing mad Odysseus
said with her parting kiss,
"Forget not, I gave you life —"

I watched Timessa leave, cognizant of doves circling and the dozens more strutting expectantly around the bench, waiting on sandwich crusts. I thought briefly of the primeval crows intended to serve as the jury at the trial years before. In comparison, these birds were dull, their eyes demanding, petty. Ignoring them, I connected with Timessa, who by now was five blocks away. She walked fast and I sensed Artemis as an invisible nimbus surrounding her.

Assured that the girl was safe, I focused on finding Kore, whom I suspected to be near. She seemed to exist solely as Timessa's twin, not quite an alter ego but, at the least, a *thing* skulking, a menacing shadow. My conclusions felt portentous. Yet, whatever she was, some entity was actively sending texts, emails and even scripts. Too, she had collided with Timessa on a street, and Timessa had shoved her away.

Detecting Kore was easy. Not surprisingly, she was at a table at the same coffee shop where Timessa had met Artemis, Filly, and later, Seneca. Without bothering to change my appearance, I walked up to the counter. When a barista looked up, I said, "A double latte." He nodded and I turned, scanning the shop. Kore ignored me and I joined her at the table.

She looked up and said, "That chair's taken."

"I'll leave if someone claims it."

She looked me up and down, a smile flickering on her mouth. "Monsieur Asshole."

As she spoke I examined her: corporeal, female and darkly inscrutable. I sensed fearlessness. There was no transparency: she was simply blank. "You're Kore."

"Not a question?"

"No."

"Perhaps it's true," she smiled.

"And I am?"

"No idea." I'd seen a flicker of interest, but it vanished.

I spoke rapidly, "Let's talk about Timessa."

We locked eyes. She said, "The lovely one." It was a declaration, bereft of emotion.

"Are you stalking her?"

"My, you're direct. You're a cop?"

"I'm not. But I am direct. This conversation might last seconds. One never knows."

"But it goes on, doesn't it? If you're not a cop, maybe I should *call* the cops."

A waitress brought my latte. I looked at Kore. "A drink?"

"No."

She shook her hair. It was unkempt, light gold. She said, "I, too, shall be direct. I've been waiting for you." Her eyebrows were full, brown. Her overall look was ethereal, scrubbed. She glowed with an odd delicacy.

I wanted ominousness, an enemy. Instead I encountered ennui. I had roused caution, but now knew it meant little.

"Have you?" I asked. She said nothing, her eyes on mine. I sighed, "Who and what you are?"

Laughing, she abruptly waved her hand at the waitress. "A latte like his. But small —" She then turned to me. "Minutes ago you pondered what I am, and concluded I'm … what? Timessa's dangerous shadow? I'm flattered."

So she read thoughts. Of course. Otherwise how could she know Timessa's? Humans had no such capacity. Still, she was a blank, elusive. I whispered, "Must I ask again?"

"Probably. Good to ask again." The waitress stepped over with her drink. Kore took the latte and turned to me. "It's been pleasant, you tracking me down and all." Then she stood, saying, "You'll have to wait a moment for answers —" and strode casually, drink in hand, toward the rest rooms.

I waited five minutes, then another three. Catching the waitress's eye, I motioned to her. "The girl I was sitting with … She went to the restroom awhile ago and hasn't returned. Would you mind checking?"

She smiled, saying, "Not one of my duties," but walked into the back, quickly returning. "No one there."

Admonishing myself for not keeping a lock on her movements, I scanned for her: nothing. Widening my search, I knew Kore had vanished. The moment had passed. Timessa was home. Exasperated at myself, I returned home to Danaë.

On Friday Air France texted a confirmation of our Saturday flight. For the first time in months, I texted Timessa in turn. She responded immediately with "K."

Danaë and I packed lightly, assuring ourselves we could buy whatever we needed in Greece. From Athens we'd fly Olympic Air to Mykonos.

I booked two rooms at a hotel on Agios Ioannis beach on Mykonos. The beach was small and away from the denser developments on the island, and the hotel was famous for a movie, *Shirley Valentine*, filmed there in the late 1980s. Our rooms would look out onto the northeastern slopes of Delos. The hotel's website showed photos of an open-air bar beside the Mediterranean. I imagined drinking ouzo while Danaë sampled wines.

Early that evening we spoke about my encounters in Boston. I noted that Timessa was a sensation in the fashion scene there. Danaë seemed unsurprised, saying, "She's shilling for the fame, the attention. It's easy. She's stunning and no one's ever flattered her." She kept shifting the conversation back to Kore, knowing immediately what I'd seen and said. She, too, was puzzled.

We took an early morning flight, from Philly to Boston, landing about eight with an idle hour before Timessa arrived. We waited at a café in the main terminal, watching people pass. At one point Danaë asked, "Do you sense her nearby?"

"Timessa?"

"No, Kore."

I focused on the terminal, then the entire airport, then the city. "Nothing."

Danaë smiled. She saw Timessa before I did, and stood and waved. T saw us and briskly pulled her carry-on in our direction. T seemed unusually reticent and I asked, "Everything okay?"

"Yes, great."

I didn't press. She'd left us all months before, implying she might never return, and now she sat beside Danaë, one of her oldest friends. And I had appeared without warning a day before to invite her on a trip she never anticipated … and for the outlandish purpose of poking around ruins for old gods. It must have seemed incongruous, the three of us awaiting a flight to take her back to Greece. There would be time to ascertain her mood.

Our flight to Munich seemed interminable. I was more restless than either of the two. They chatted endlessly about events in the past. Timessa kept referring to La Porcheria, a river valley in Sicily. The tribe apparently had spent several centuries there, until the wildlands became cultivated. Their conversation shifted to memories of what is now Herzegovina. That area sheltered them until Muslims overran Christians, and the tribe was forced into southern France. I had the impression they could have talked about these lost times for days.

We landed in Germany Saturday afternoon, and after a brief layover, continued to Athens, a flight that took almost four hours. I had booked rooms at a small hotel a half block from the Archeologic Museum. After an unremarkable night, we flew early Sunday afternoon to Mykonos. The weather was glorious and the flight less than an hour. A driver took us to Agios Ioannis, where we had time to unpack and stretch before dinner.

As advertised, the place looked over the sea to Delos, a brown-grey hump rising from the waters a short distance away. As darkness descended, Delos disappeared into the daemonic sea, not a light visible on its broad flank. Its position above the horizon blocked the stars behind it. Their absence hinted of some *thing* upon the waves.

Alone in the open-air bar at the hotel, I drank ouzo until Danaë appeared. "Very civilized," she said. "That is, your choice of locations."

As if a ghost, Timessa materialized, standing beside the table. Neither Danaë nor I commented on this apparent new power. Instead, Danaë gestured for her to sit and said, "An hour ago we could see that old whale of an island. Now Delos has vanished into the night. Πλοῖον, a barnacled ship, a massive ancient thing. Imagine its memories."

I almost said, "Or its emptiness," but caught myself. Danaë knew my thoughts and frowned. Instead, I said conspiratorially, "It'll be back at dawn."

Neither commented, and neither accepted wine when the waitress asked. We sat in silence listening to the sea lap the shallow beach, small lights from the nearby hotels flickering off the waves. Finally, Danaë said, "I can't sense what lies ahead. Nothing. Tomorrow's a blank."

I smiled indulgently, taking her hand. "There's a large catamaran that leaves around nine. We'll take that, debark in the old harbor and go exploring. No pressure. We'll just kick some stones and take photos like everyone else."

Timessa said, "At the last minute, I went on the web and looked at images of the place. Everything on Delos looks dead, dead, a city of the dead."

"You knew that," Danaë whispered. "Don't act surprised."

T shrugged. I had a second ouzo, not certain I liked the heavy aperitif. It exuded a faint mist, anise-scented and exotic. As our waitress filled my glass, she said, "This variety is still made near Mount Athos. Monks invented it there. Two shots are fine; three will do you in." She smiled.

Danaë looked at me. "Then no more for you."

After a short time we went back to our rooms. I knew Timessa needed four hours of sleep. Danaë and I did fine with less, so after we were certain she was asleep, we returned to the small café and sat for an hour in darkness without speaking. I felt as if the Greece of myths and relentless tragedies was exhaling, shaking off its bloody legacy — and that we were its sudden chroniclers, its empty-headed heirs.

Danaë whispered, "Perhaps even imbeciles in our naivety."

I, like Timessa, now questioned my decision to come. What had I been thinking? Only then did Danaë slip her hand into mine.

CHAPTER 13

All then lost
the groves burnt,
the oaks axed, tossed
aside and stacked in pyres.

A s the sun rose, climbing up the raw slopes of Anatolia, now Turkey, a hundred miles to the east, I stood on the beach on Mykonos watching the flanks of Delos slowly warm. Homer had called this the "rosy-fingered dawn," the daily gift by the goddess Eos. Although I admired the pinks striking Mount Kynthos, last night's misgivings had not vanished, and I viewed the island with apprehension.

Twenty feet above me, the café was opening. The waitress who had served us the night before waved, calling, "Coffee?" I nodded, bounding up the stone stairs from the beach. Danaë appeared moments later. She smiled and sat beside me.

"We leave about nine?"

"No," I said. "We go nowhere."

She looked disappointed. "But I'm eager."

"Poor timing. I can't explain it."

"Last night's foreboding?"

I half-smiled. "It's occurred to me that once we navigate to Apollo's Temple, we might get jumped by a gang of angry, half-dead gods."

"Attacked by zombie divinities, huh?"

"Who knows? Your father might be furious you married me." Before she could speak I corrected myself. "That is, that you chose me to couple."

She loosened her cover-up, a red bikini showing beneath. The sun was already turning hot and we sat quietly, the delicate tide barely sounding against the shore. As the waitress refilled our coffee, Timessa walked down from the hotel. She moved with her new model's stride, taking slow, long steps that rocked her hips.

Danaë made a light wolf-whistle, and T waved her hand dismissively, saying, "I know I'm late. Sea breezes always do me in." As she sat she looked across to the ancient island. "I thought it might have shaken off its ill temper. Wrong again."

Danaë said, "I remember such a different place."

Timessa said. "Music, dancing, celebrations, crazy gods. Gold and silver in every trader's fingers, tetradrachms fresh from the Athenian mint and everything for sale."

"Silver coins were stamped with Athene's profile, remember?" Danaë smiled. "Her owl on the reverse."

I was impatient and, frankly, not interested in their reminiscences. I said, "Then Mithridates showed. The walls came tumbling down, the party over. The marble columns and the palm trees and the dead lying together in the sun. Must have been quite the stink. And now we've arrived to rake through the remains."

"My," T said, "you're cheery." She shook her hair. "When do we leave?"

"Not today."

"Oh. I wouldn't have gotten out of bed so soon."

As she spoke I saw movement toward the hotel. A rough-hewn man of about forty-five with an unkempt beard ambled over to us. With fierce eyes he looked at us. In a Greek-British accent he slowly said, "So you're crossing to the island of the dead. Why?"

"Just looking around. We're like all the other tourists here."

He watched me, his head oddly sideways. "Going over myself to pick up some sheep. Boat's big enough for four."

"We'll take the catamaran."

"I'm cheaper."

"Why the offer?"

He extended his hand to me. "I'm Charon. Call me Charlie."

"Jack." I looked at Danaë. "Danaë here, and Timessa."

The man barely acknowledged them. "Going in about 30 minutes, and will be back in the afternoon. You'll be pretty tired by then. My offer's my offer." He looked amused but also willing to leave at the slightest sign of disinterest.

On instinct, I said, "Fine, where's your boat?"

He shrugged. "It'll be waiting down there —" He pointed to the beach. "Wear shoes and hats. Can get hot on the island. By the way, I own this place." He thumbed backward toward the hotel. "Graze my sheep over on Delos. Done it since Socrates."

I assumed he meant his family went back into antiquity. I smiled, "You never mentioned what you'll charge"

"One obol."

"Obol?"

Danaë frowned. "The silver coinage of classic Greece."

"I like to shine 'em up like little mirrors." Grinning, he gestured toward the waitress. "She'll have one. Just ask." He turned and walked away.

As if on cue, the waitress came up and pressed an old coin into my hand and shrugged. I looked at it: a honey bee was stamped into the crude spit. The piece was thin and I was tempted to bend it. As if reading my mind she said, "Don't. You'll need it to get across."

Danaë turned to me. "I couldn't read his thoughts."

"Nor could I."

"What's your instinct?"

"Local color," I guessed. "If he owns this place, he's got to be okay."

Timessa interjected, "We'll be fine."

We exchanged looks. Danaë grimaced but looked resolved. The three of us quickly changed clothes and stuffed a few pieces of fruit in our pockets. As he had promised, Charlie had tied up his boat against a couple stones by the beach. The craft looked to be about twenty-feet long and rust-colored as if the wooden planks had oxidized.

We went down to the boat and he stood in the center, offering a hand to each woman. A single board extended from side to side and we sat. There were no life preservers. A small engine was strapped into the back and clamped against the transom. He pushed the starter, thick smoke belching as the engine caught after a few tries, the boat trembling as the engine misfired for over a minute before finally running well.

The boatman grinned manically and, standing with his feet apart, swiveled the craft out into the sea. "Onward to the island of the dead!"

The Mediterranean was dark and its waves increased as we pulled away from Mykonos. Charlie's eyes were igneous and focused southwest. He seemed to have forgotten us, his beard windblown and right hand tightly clenching the steering arm of the small engine. The boat was beginning to slap against the chop. I raised my voice, "How long?"

"A quarter hour. Most of my passengers pray it'll take forever —"

"What?"

Danaë caught my eyes and shook her head no.

We were midway between Mykonos and Delos with a steady wind raking on a slant between the two islands. Timessa shivered. I braced myself against the gunwales, asking him, "You've done this all your life?"

The boatman showed his teeth, shaking his jowls as wind caught his beard. "Once ferried riders across a river. That was long ago. Same boat, though." He scowled, raising his voice, then turned the throttle higher. "Fast as it will go —"

T looked at me. "His name is Charon."

I shrugged. She continued, "A Charon ferried the dead across the river Styx."

Shaking my head, I turned to Danaë. "Tell me what's going on."

Her face was carefully neutral. "The Styx separated the world of the living from the dead. Charon poled the dead to Hades."

I swiveled back to the boatman, aware he was inscrutable. None of us could penetrate a thought. Charlie — Charon — was not being evasive; he simply was impenetrable. He looked down at me, laughing and said,

"The sun still shines on Delos. Hades never saw a ray of sun. I far prefer this route, although my passengers are fewer than before."

We were almost there. *Delos*. He looked away and raised his hand in a greeting, and as I turned, I saw a lone man standing in the waves on shore. We were several hundred feet from the island. The man was dressed in a cloak and, unlike Charon, was clean-shaven. The boatman bawled, "Hermes!"

The man raised both hands, open-palmed, in greeting. It was the gesture Laine had used to greet Artemis. Charon bent, grabbed a coil of thick rope and tossed it overhead to the man on shore. "Pull us in, my friend!"

As we got closer I could see the man was young, probably my age, muscled where his cloak opened, moving easily. He caught the line and tied it to a post, then pulled us in. Within moments the prow sliced into the shore, grinding as it drove into the sand. For the first time I noticed that the boat's oar rungs and pins were hand-beaten, probably bronze. Wooden dowels pinned the oak and pine skeleton of the shell. I felt Charon's hand on my shoulder. He growled, "You've arrived. My payment?"

I fumbled in my pocket for the obol, shoving it into his calloused palm. He pointed toward his associate. "He will guide you today. And he will know when I return and will bring you back on time."

"We need no guide."

"Whether you do or not, he guides the honored through this forsaken place." The two women had stepped out, and as I put a foot on land, Charon abruptly turned and revved the engine. The boat backed into the black sea and made a sharp arc toward Mykonos. I noted he had not picked up any sheep.

Our uninvited guide was as impenetrable as Charon, and I instantly suspected him being complicit. Danaë surprised me when she said, "Hermes. I met you once many years ago. You were a trickster god."

The man nodded, saying, "So it was. And is somewhat today. Should I remember you?"

"I ran beside Artemis, she of the silver bow."

He bowed slightly. "Of course. You will appreciate my services."

I vaguely recalled that Hermes was the emissary of the gods, and the patron of thieves and athletes, moving freely between the worlds of the living and the dead. I cut in, "You know why we come?"

"I know as much as I need to know."

"And will we succeed?"

"Succeed? At the least we will proceed," he said.

Timessa said, "You talk in circles, cunningly."

Hermes smiled, "Chastised by a nymph! Ah, the world is upside down. Once you would have trembled at my face."

She giggled. "My apologies. I was simply observing."

He scanned her with a kind expression, putting a hand on her cheek. "Once a nymph, but perhaps a nymph no more. Metamorphoses?"

She blushed and smiled naively, shaking her head. "Compliments from a trickster. My goddess would have said, 'O beware.' "

"Follow me," he said. "I will take you directly to the temple."

Hermes reminded me a bit of Laine when she had appeared at my door — flush cheeks and blue eyes. He scanned me quickly and said, "Do not compare me to Lachesis."

I nodded in bewilderment. There seemed little he didn't know. I asked, "Why are you and Charon still in this world? I was told the entirety of the male pantheon had gone."

"The boatman could not abandon his duties. Who would ferry the dead?"

"And you?"

"I guide them, like I shall you, once he drops them off on the shore."

Danaë said quickly, "This is Delos, not Hades."

"Where everything that lived died millennia ago."

She retorted, "And all the dead went to Hades. That place is not this."

"Oh," he said. "I find the two rather interchangeable. But I'm tiring. Let's strike out for the ruins. It's a twenty-minute walk." He turned and started down a narrow path that led inland. We followed. I guessed the time about ten. The sky was cloudless, and Hermes walked swiftly, as if impatient, as if having wasted time explaining the obvious. With his back exposed, he looked immensely powerful, as if he were a charioteer. Or an ancient discus thrower.

In fifteen minutes we stood on a small rise. I looked down into a rectangular area perhaps a quarter-mile square, a vast plain of scattered stones, roofless columns and a grid of dirt roads: the old city. Hermes spread his arms and intoned, "Behold, the sacred heart of the Athenian empire, its bones left for vultures."

T pointed into its center, asking, "Was that the temple?"

He took her wrist and moved it slightly. "See the palm tree? The temple once stood beside it to the right."

Timessa broke into tears, nodding. "Heartbreaking."

I said, "Enough. Time to explore."

The path widened as we picked our way down into the interior. Before we began to mingle with the wandering tourists, I noticed Hermes pause, and imperceptibly change appearance: he now wore a golf shirt, baseball cap and khaki shorts, a water bottle strapped to his waist. We exchanged glances and he said, "Best to wear disguises."

"Sure. But the chances of anyone here recognizing you are pretty slim."

"Perhaps."

"Let's get closer to the temple," I said. "without drawing attention to ourselves." I still questioned his company. We easily could have accomplished this much without him.

We wound closer, passing the row of Naxian lions. Timessa pointed north, to a half-acre dry bowl with a single palm. "That was the sacred Palaestra lake," she said.

We passed it, stopping beside a ruin to its right. I turned to Hermes, who smiled. "Yes, Jackson, the temple you seek."

I was now Jackson. None of us spoke.

Finally, Danaë whispered, "I knew it was down. But this? Oh my god."

I wasn't sure how to proceed. I was certain that what I sought was here. And I suspected that Hermes, as much as I distrusted him, knew. I turned to Danaë and T. "Suggestions?"

They simply stared. The sun was now overhead and to my shock, I sensed nothing. What had I expected? Perhaps immediately to know which broken marble I should overturn, which cracked stone covered the stairs that descended to the catacomb. Instead, I watched as an older couple passed between us and the ruins, the man turning briefly to eye Timessa and Danaë.

Hermes said, "Must I wait for you to ask?"

"As if you knew a thing."

He gripped my arm and pulled me toward the stones. "They speak," he said. "You must listen carefully."

In the midst of hundreds of marble blocks, he pulled me down and made me sit. "What do you hear, Jackson?"

At first I heard nothing. Then I heard faint sounds that became louder: the screams and butchery of Mithridates's raid, the cries of a massacre. Hermes shook me powerfully. "No, not that. The gods came here together, on their dismal mission, hundreds of years after that. You're indulging. Focus on why you're here."

I looked around. Danaë and Timessa squatted before me, then T stood. "Let's walk around," she said. "Look for signs."

I squinted, trying not to show my disappointment. "Sure, do so. Hermes and I will stay here and talk."

He raised an eyebrow and watched them leave. "I'm surprised. You're resisting my suggestions."

"You mean, 'Listen to the stones'? Give me something real —"

"Close your eyes, Jackson."

I did, irritated at his sudden camaraderie. I heard nothing new — a dry wind, distant voices speaking a guttural German. Or perhaps the voices were colloquial Greek. Deep tones. Men speaking of the weather. I opened my eyes, expecting to see tourists nearby. Yet we were alone.

"Close your eyes again, my friend. Listen again, and again —"

I obeyed, instantly detecting a flute playing in the distance, a shell tambourine keeping an archaic beat. Then, I heard the voices again. A low male voice said, Πλοιον. *Ship or boat.* Then I heard, Ακροπολιη. *Acropolis.* Opening my eyes, I saw no one. Hermes smiled, "The receptors are not visual. Look and you shall not see. Listen, and the stones will sing."

Standing, I saw the girls some hundred feet away. I was pleased to see them holding hands. They seemed unaware of what we heard. Danaë was golden, resplendent; she was Aphrodite's mirror and she had chosen me. As I watched her move, Hermes said, "You're easily distracted. We are in pursuit of fire, not water — men, not women. Close your eyes again —"

The instant I did, I heard far louder voices, arguing, angry, the words unrecognizable. I heard, Βρομιοσ, then, ακρασια. *Dionysos,* and *crazy.* Something was thrown, the ground below us trembled momentarily.

"They're arguing. How do I find them, Hermes?"

"Close your eyes."

Τιμη. *Honor.* A single, loud voice echoed over the stones. I suddenly visualized stairs, an opening. I swiveled and saw a square slab flush with the ground. On it was carved, *A*. Hermes nudged me. "Alpha. Is it what you seek?"

The beginning or the end? Was I to raise the stone? I knelt beside it, seeing side notches, finger-holds. The stone was about a meter square, wide enough for a man's shoulders. Wide enough for a god to pass from light to dark. I turned to Hermes for confirmation. He shrugged, and I slipped my fingers into the notches, looking around. We were alone, the nearest tourist hundreds of feet away.

Before I could lift it, the stone darkened: Danaë's shadow. She said, "Jackson, are you sure?"

I looked into her eyes and released the slab. No, I wasn't. Wasn't sure of anything. Sensing more movement, I turned and saw Hermes laughing.

"He found an apparent way in, and he hesitated!" His laughter increased. I closed my eyes, hearing, Αινιγμα. *Enigma.* Yes, that.

I knelt beside the slab. The gods spoke, the stones spoke, and Danaë looked to Timessa, who said nothing.

CHAPTER 14

The light that through the dark glass drove
as if it were an infinite force
that only an equal force could move,
was in her eyes.

As I hesitated Timessa stepped up to Danaë, linking arms. She whispered to me, "Our guide is testing you. Don't be fooled. There's no entryway, no stairs into a secret place —"

Hermes continued laughing, his watering eyes flitting from face to face. Timessa said, "It's grander than that. Ask him again —"

Before I could speak, Hermes said, "The girl understands. Far more than you. You're looking for the obvious and denying the divine."

I caught Danaë's eyes and she shook her head. Timessa saw something we didn't.

Sensing my confusion, T said, "Athens once banned all deaths on Delos. The dying were banned. Bodies were buried elsewhere. Old burials were exhumed. This is the birthplace of Artemis and her brother, Apollo. Athens banished death in their honor.

"Τιμή. No *honor* is greater than life. That is why they outlive all other living things."

I retorted, "What does this have to do with anything? You've said nothing I don't already know." I paused. Had I ever been angry with her? Irritated, amused — but not angry. Like Laine in the past, Timessa was lecturing me.

Hermes smiled at my transparency. He said, "She is emerging into something new. She's no longer a nymph-girl. See her as a chrysalis, a promise."

Timessa continued, ignoring him. "Once the island allowed only life. Then it collapsed. Athens had fallen, its Roman successors were weak and it succumbed, capitulated to waves of pirates until there was nothing left. Its poles reversed. I had to stand here, now, absorbing the energy to understand. But I do. There's nothing here."

The others were silent. Timessa looked irritated.

"Well and good," I said. "Impressive. But the male gods? Hermes insists the stones speak. I sense life, not death. When I close my eyes I hear arguing —"

"Ancient voices? Just the wind," she said, kicking a piece of marble.

The breeze shifted slightly, and the scattered grasses bent sideways, their brown sheaves and pale blades flashing in the heat. A bird wheeled overhead, but I couldn't make it out. A hawk, a crow?

Hermes interrupted my thoughts. "I offer that it's impossible the gods would do the obvious …"

I smiled wanly. "You're saying that I'm chasing illusions? Or are you suggesting they're not here at all?" I picked up a broken stone and threw it toward the dry lake.

I said, "Perhaps they're over there." Picking up another stone, I threw it toward the harbor. "Or there. Old gods watching ships go by."

"You," Hermes said, "are being derisive. Yet, my friend, you're near."

"How would you know?"

"I am the guide."

I hesitated. Of course, he would know this place better than anyone. Still, I couldn't see beyond what he called the obvious. There was more. He was saying so, and continued, "Remember, Jackson, I guide the living to the land of the dead. And I guide those who want to escape. Not all are dead, and not all who are tired want to die. There are ways to rest, and places to sleep."

Timessa said excitedly, "Obfuscate as you wish. I know it suddenly! They *have* unwound here!"

Confused, I said, "I thought you said they *weren't* here —"

"Not under *this*," she said, picking up a small shard, "or here, beneath the temple."

Hermes interjected, "I brought them here. Your instinct, Jackson, that this spot was hallowed, is correct …

"We gathered here, six of us, where we now stand. It was a summer afternoon. Apollo himself spread his arms, saying, 'We come to rest in Delos. Surrounded by the sea. Always under sun by day and stars by night.' Then those who wanted release let out a mighty cry that rolled like thunder over the waves."

I shook my head, "You, Hermes, remain elusive."

"I await your understanding. You come as a discoverer, not as someone seeking entertainment. Only a child wants a map marked with an X."

Timessa spread her arms, her hair catching in the wind, the locks adrift. Almost mockingly she asked Hermes, "Did Apollo open his arms like this?"

He nodded. She spread her arms wider. "Like *this*?"

Again, he nodded, smiling. "Yes, almost exactly like that."

She said, "I encompass the entire island, don't I?"

He stepped forward, touching her cheek as he had done at the landing. "You, my dear, encompass the world. And here, on this broken atoll, your fingertips touch the shores, the mount, the hillocks, and the slopes." She grinned, slowly turning on her toes, taking it all in.

"Yes," she said, "their abode. Here. In its entirety!"

Then I understood. The gods were here, but not in some dark catacomb. She was saying they had chosen to infuse the island, fill it all, let their essence fill its entirety. They *were* Delos.

Hermes cried, "Yes!"

I understood and I knew. There was no part of Delos that wasn't quietly alive with their concealed divinity. They were not on the island; they *were* the island.

Hermes whispered, "They chose to bless this land with their lives.

And even now they sigh and argue and hiss and sing as the wind passes over the stones. They speak and the stones respond. The sands and grasses are their lips. Their murmurs are everywhere. But few can hear. And fewer understand. Until today, until you came. I was one of the last."

I took his shoulders. "How? How do I interact with stones? You're telling me the gods merged with everything?"

"They are cognizant. Each remains himself."

"To communicate do I raise my voice, and sing out, 'Apollo? Hephaistos?' "

Hermes looked at the sun angle and said hurriedly, "No time left today. Charon will be waiting. We have a quarter hour to depart."

Without delay he turned and headed back. We looked at each other, and Timessa said, "Intermission. The next act, I think, may be astonishing." She lowered her head and followed him, stopping after a few steps to turn and wave us on.

The sea on the Mykonos side of the island had calmed. As Hermes had sensed, Charon stood beside the old boat, a long pole in his hands. Our guide cried, "That pole's not long enough for where we go!"

"It's to beat off the impudent. What took so long?"

"They're a curious lot. Not content to simply gawk." Charon half-listened, swinging his pole randomly. I was glad we were separated by twenty feet. "No more of that," Hermes cried, stepping into the boat. "Now get us back. No one here has eaten for too long."

Neither man spoke on the return. Two days passed before Charon would be available again. And Hermes seemed in a foul mood when we landed by the hotel. I wondered if they might write us off.

Before we parted I saw Timessa speaking quietly to Hermes and overheard a few words. "Artemis ... Lachesis ..." I presumed she wanted him to know more. I guessed he already knew. Hermes was a mind reader, wily and well-networked. His appearance had surprised us, but our arrival had been anticipated.

We spent time the next day in Chora, the old town, wandering the narrow, stone streets. None of it was to my liking, but Timessa was taken by the high-end shops. We were all mildly surprised to find a poster of her in a dress shop — her reaction, "Oh my!" In it she slouched in a grey skirt and tight blouse looking grim, her hair disheveled. Danaë smirked, "So that's what you've become —"

That was the highlight of our day as the town was deluged with tourists. We saw no one interesting, and I tired of men constantly scanning Danaë and Timessa. Danaë was the more beautiful of the two, but T strutted as if on a catwalk. Conscious of the attention, they linked their arms in mine and we shopped without buying, letting time pass.

The next day was eventless. I spent hours making notes about Delos — its terrain and appearance, my impressions, Hermes's insinuations. We walked the beaches of Agios Ioannis in the morning, collecting pottery shards and bits of colored glass washed in by the tide. In the late afternoon, Charon appeared in the café and said gruffly, "We leave in the morning at nine."

I asked whether Hermes would come.

"If he chooses. He hasn't spoken since we returned."

"Would it help if I asked him personally?"

"He is not available," Charon said as he left.

The three of us ate together as the sun set. Our usual waitress stopped momentarily and pressed an obol into my hand, saying, "For tomorrow."

Danaë smiled. "The table's being set. We're a small spectacle. There's whispering in the shadows. As in, *What will the visiting divinities do next?*"

I looked into her eyes for a moment. "What *will* we do? Once on Delos, how will we raise the dead?"

"I think we won't," Danaë said.

Timessa nodded. "Yes, perhaps the dead aren't dead. Maybe like an unexpected breeze, they'll come to us."

That night Danaë and I made love. Later, I failed to sleep and, leaving her under the sheets, wandered down to the dark café. I slumped in my wicker chair on the patio overlooking the dark whaleback of Delos, questioning myself, reviewing Hermes's comments, considering options for our return. An hour before sunrise, I thought I saw a light on the island's slope. It blinked twice, went dark for minutes, then blinked again. But I was tired and may have confused it with reflections from a hotel on

Mykonos. No one could be on Delos. The Greeks were uncompromising about the island's sanctity.

After some time I began to muse aimlessly and the sky lightened. As the sun rose in an unusual fire, Danaë appeared, clearly upbeat. "Eos woke."

"Eos?"

"The goddess of dawn. I'm excited about today. I have a hunch."

I smiled. She was aglow and must have slept well, however briefly. I took her hand, saying, "When we arrive, stay by my side."

She looked surprised. "Of course. Why would you even say that?"

"An odd misgiving. We should be careful not to separate."

Timessa appeared before breakfast. Sitting with us she said, "Storms today. Rain in the next hour."

I scanned the darkening sky. "Perhaps. I wonder how bad."

Danaë sighed. "None of us brought rain gear."

The waitress, from several tables away and clearly listening, interrupted. "The hotel stocks slickers. Just ask Charlie before you launch."

Charlie, I thought, the friendly proprietor. No, *Charon*. As I nodded, a sideways deluge swept the hotel. The rain was hot and we moved our chairs under cover. It remained constant and an hour later Charon appeared, wearing a yellow raincoat, and carrying several similar jackets. "They all have hoods," he said. "We leave in five."

The wind was gusting. I asked stupidly, "Should we just wait until tomorrow?"

"No, we go today."

Danaë glanced at me and T shrugged, saying, "I don't care —"

And so we stood, pulling on the heavy rubber jackets. They weighed enough to be ancient, circa 1950s and, I guessed, Norwegian. We pulled the hoods up, tying them tightly with the long cords sewn into the edges. The waitress looked us up and down, saying nothing. I was aware that she was as opaque as Hermes.

Charon gestured for us to follow, and we descended to the old boat. He had the engine running, for which I was grateful. Again, he helped the women on, and grabbed the steering rudder. Lifting his head, he suddenly sang into the rain, "O Poseidon, grant us passage!"

I caught Danaë's eyes. Poseidon. Her father, lost long ago with the other male gods. She appeared grim at his outcry, even shaken, but the rain may have contributed to her pallor. She looked away, squinting into the storm.

The boatmen wheeled the craft in an arc and pointed the bow toward the island. As if Charon's prayer had been answered, the waters smoothed suddenly. There was chaos port and starboard but a flat, calm corridor before us as the boat surged ahead. I noticed Timessa grinning and Charon stood, legs wide and confident as the boat cut effortlessly through the wine-dark sea. He cried again, "Our thanks to the sea-god! Now, to Delos! To the dead!"

Though the waters had turned to glass before the bow, the rain intensified, beating on us, its noise deafening. I was aware, too, of the boat's engine. Its roar seemed harsher than during our first trip. Charon said loudly, to no one in particular, "The tourist runs will all be canceled. No catamarans. You're in luck. You'll be alone."

Yes, that made sense. And explained why he insisted we go today. Yet I still had no idea how we'd proceed. "Will Hermes meet us there?"

Charon nodded.

Within minutes I saw the old beach and a lone man standing in the tide: Hermes, dressed only in a wet robe. Once again, Charon threw him the line, and he pulled us ashore, and tied down the boat. In the rain, conversation seemed inappropriate, and Hermes did no more than nod in acknowledgment of our arrival, although Timessa made a point of hugging him briefly. He scowled.

On this second trip, Charon lingered, braced in his boat, waiting, almost expectant. Hermes turned to him and said, "You will know when to return."

The boatman cocked his head and gestured with his hands, as if to move us along. As the rain sheeted he cried, "You could not have prayed for better skies!"

With that the four of us turned toward the island's center, Hermes striking out ahead. I thought briefly of Dante and his admonition at the Gates of Hell, "All who enter here, abandon hope."

Aware of my gloom I found myself saying small prayers to Artemis. Doing so seemed to banish my premonitions. Danaë and Timessa's enthusiasm, even in the pellmell rain, was obvious. I kept walking, my eyes at Hermes's back, refusing to turn to see if Charon remained.

The rain slowed us, the trail a small stream soaking our feet. Timessa was the first to remove her shoes, throwing them into the brush and crying, "Away, away!" Danaë and I took off our shoes, but stuffed them into the large pockets of our slickers.

In fifteen minutes we had mounted the overlook and were gazing down into the ruins. The stones had turned dark, shining in the rain, the landscape desolate. Hermes gripped my arm, saying, "Even in a storm, old stones speak."

I looked into his eyes and saw an emptiness as vast as the field of broken marble scattered before us. Then he laughed. The outburst was offensive and I shook him off, turning back to the ruins, measuring with a glance the wide wet roads that led to nowhere, roads that once sang with commerce and plenty. Death had swung its scythe. Even in the storm, the sacred lake beside Apollo's temple was bone-dry. Danaë said, "Let's keep moving — I'm getting cold."

So we descended into the rubble, with Hermes taking strange, wide steps as if a child. We advanced toward the lake, a lacustrine wave of grasses, fescues, glabrous sedges shining in the rain. As we approached the old temple, Timessa began to dance, opening her yellow jacket and circling the sky with her arms. Danaë cried, "You'll get wet!"

T laughed. "Oh, but this is how we raise the dead!"

Hermes stopped in the road, frozen, shaking his head. He might have been a Zen hermit, his dark robe soaked, the wet linen tied at his waist with rope. His eyes followed Timessa's dance. He slowly grinned. Then he reached and gripped my arm again, leaning into me and saying, "She's dancing the old Dionysiakos, a dance of phalluses and lust and mysterious insights. Delos was famous for its marble cocks at every entry-way, many of them larger than your arm —"

I shook my head, and he continued. "The dance is a celebration. It calls Dionysos, the god of wine, madness and fertility. He, too, lies in all these sands."

T had thrown her slicker into the grass and her thin skirt was red, short and vaguely licentious, although in any other locale it would have appeared simply contemporary. But here, worn with her white blouse, held together by a single center button, it was clearly otherwise. To my shock Danaë linked arms with her and they circled the stones, dancing in a dance and an ecstasy utterly foreign to me.

At one point, minutes into their *dansant*, Danaë took T's hips, Timessa shoving back, the two grinding together. I found it oddly obscene. Timessa, whom I knew to be a virgin, groaned.

Hermes elbowed me, grinning at the display. At that same moment a young man materialized, standing a few paces from the pair, stroking a black, short beard. He wore nothing, his sleek muscles slick with rain. His face, as theirs, appeared ecstatic, his eyes rolling.

I could feel Hermes tense, then say, "Διονυσοσ!" *Dionysos*.

CHAPTER 15

Eros, chaos, death —
—Lachesis

The man moved, his steps an archaic dancer's. He wove between the girls, circling with them, stepping with immense confidence and apparent joy. Surely, I thought, he was one of the five lost gods, one of the defunct, diffused divinities who had been ingrained in the sands and stones.

Timessa apparently had intuited an incantation that raised him up. Not from the dead, but from the suspended, from the ranks of the numbed and lamented.

They stopped moving and T squatted with Danaë. Beside them knelt the dazzling god. His hand stroked T's cheeks; both girls had bright, almost varnished eyes. I sensed they were semi-blind, that the god was an irresistible force. From their expressions the two may as well have been ancient maenads, whose lives were solely the god's to play.

Hermes whispered, "A frenzy. Typical of him. He's testing his old powers, confirming that the enchantment still enchants the beautiful."

"It does."

"You know of Dionysos?"

"Yes, the son of Zeus and a mortal woman."

"He's a deity of madness, delirium, euphoria. The two girls cannot shake free, but he will release them soon …"

As if on cue Dionysos turned to us, and as he did, he palmed T's breast. The gesture was deliberate and his fingers circled her as if he were delicately unscrewing a lid. In response, her eyes fluttered. He grinned briefly, reluctantly letting her go and said, "Hermes, you were the last to see me so many years ago, and now the first to greet me as I wake."

His face and beard shone with rain. He appeared faintly effeminate, his gestures soft and strangely sinister. He caught my eye and said, "Jackson Night. The first of us in millennia. Lachesis's creation, am I right?"

I watched him warily, remembering the stories of his frenzied women, mere girls tearing bulls apart, eating birds alive, wrenching trees from the ground. His maenads danced endless nights in drunken raves, and there were tales of violence. He was a dangerous god, seductive and unforgiving.

I took a step toward him, and said, "Your reputation precedes you."

"Indeed," he muttered, bored at my cliché. "Now that I'm carnal once again, I have so much to do."

I pointed at the girls. "Not with them."

He grinned, a fearless expression as if I had challenged him. "Both easily mine. Shall we see?"

Hermes interjected, "Don't underestimate him, Dionysos. He wields different powers, yet ones as great as ours."

Dionysos growled, then turned. A second man suddenly appeared and tapped his shoulder. Hermes whispered, "*Ares.*"

So, I thought, god two, a divinity of chaos and destruction, whose lover and sister had been Enyo. Her name meant discord. So, Timessa's magic continued.

Dionysos stepped back and spit on the ground between them. "Ah, you now! I felt safer when you were dispersed in the sand. No longer. A pity. I thought perhaps you'd been immobilized for good. All salute the mighty Ares!"

Ares wore a grey chiton, a bronze knife hanging loosely at his side. I guessed his age to be similar to mine.

He bent, drew his knife and savagely slashed at Dionysos, who easily stepped aside. He advanced quickly, continuing to seek some vulnerability on the wine-god's part. But Dionysos danced away from each thrust, saying, "Mighty warrior, those years asleep did no good. You always fought like a girl —"

Silent before the insults, Ares stopped, sheathed his knife, put his hands in front of his belly as if cradling a ball and with a slight *whoosh*, vanished. He had not spoken, but Dionysos did again, saying, "No matter where he goes, he'll do no good."

Hermes turned to me and said, "They fight like sisters, but are dear friends."

Dionysos looked around, then pointed at me. "Did you like our little show?"

Danaë was suddenly at my side, whispering, "He taunts you. It's how he picks apart the weak —"

"I know. Stay at my side."

Dionysos watched us, finally smiling as if we were inconsequential. He caught my eye and said, "So you await the missing three." At my silence he said, "Apollo, Hephaistos and Poseidon. May be that they sleep too deeply and will disappoint us all. Perhaps they were weak and will never wake."

"Perhaps."

"Why did you want us back?"

"Lachesis told me that the male gods had descended into an unrecoverable state. In time I came to disbelieve … It's clear she lied."

We faced each other, Dionysos unwilling to move against me, yet unable to retreat. Timessa sidled up to him. "I've never seen you without your thyrsus —"

Hermes leaned close. "The thyrsus: a giant fennel stalk, phallic, crowned in ivy, used by the god in ecstatic dances."

Dionysos smiled at Timessa, putting his hands between his legs. "You want to see my thyrsus, girl?"

She giggled and danced around him, as if circling a maypole. She had read him well as the tension was broken and she danced away, back to Danaë, where they linked arms. They swayed in silly turns and

Dionysos laughed. After a few minutes Timessa retrieved her rain jacket, slipping it on as the rain increased, dancing again to a silent beat.

The god watched, unfocused, in a reverie as she moved before him. I suspected he was not fully awake, that 1,600 years of lying in suspension had left him disoriented. Yet he lived. And his wit and sense of invulnerability seemed complete. I had proven Laine wrong.

I say I, as if I had solved the mystery. I had not; I knew I had only been a small catalyst. The spark had been Timessa. She had danced in some arcane ecstasy, steps I guessed that went back to the beginning of these beings. Her fire, her ebullience had been bright enough to reanimate the gods.

I glanced to Danaë, for, I suppose, affirmation, and she nodded, blowing me a kiss. I hardly understood what had just occurred, but there was time. And in time, I suspected more would emerge.

I turned to Hermes. "We must stay until they all appear."

He shook his head. "We are done today."

"We have to leave?"

"Yes."

Over the sound of the pounding rain, I yelled, "But there are three more."

"Perhaps they are the missing, the unrecoverable. Who knows?"

"You know, don't you?"

He shrugged. "Charon waits." Then he stepped up to Dionysos. "There is room for one more on Charon's boat."

He bristled. "If I go, no one is to say my name. When we leave this island for another, I will simply be called ... the stranger."

Hermes shrugged, saying, "Sure. You were always such."

For a moment we stood together. Then all of us, including Dionysos, turned and trudged down the narrow path to the boat.

Charon throttled the engine back and glided the boat onto the hotel's narrow beach. The stonewalls winding down the slopes of Agios Ioannis shone like ebony snakes in the rain. As we stepped onto the sand, the rain lightened, turning to a thin drizzle. Dionysos looked around as if a time traveler, assessing the structures, paved road, overhead utility wires, and decorative lights hung around the patio. He scowled, turning to the girls. "Which of you fillies spends tonight with me?" Slipping his arm around Timessa, he whispered, "For hours of bliss."

She pushed him away, playing gullible, trusting but confused. "Not I, sir. Taking me like that would create a small war between yourself and Artemis. I am pledged to her, and not to any man. Or to any god —"

Danaë was now under my arm, her face in my shoulder. Dionysos was becoming annoying. I had not had to use my ability to change shape in some time, but in caution I allowed my muscles to swell, my stance to widen. From behind Dionysos I could see T, shaking her head to dissuade me from engaging.

Charon stepped between us. "No girls tonight," he said. "These two will never be yours, Dionysos."

"Wrong," he said.

"There will be time for your proclivities," Charon said, "but get on your feet first. You're hardly conscious, yet already on a prowl."

Charon held Dionysos's arms as if between metal jaws. Surprisingly, the god slumped his head, then looked up angrily. "Is there lodging for a stranger?"

Charon pointed up the stairs to the hotel. "Second floor, third door on the right. Accommodations are simple." He turned him with a single rotation. "Go on, get some rest." Dionysos stumbled off, slowly maneuvering the steps. I was glad we had not fought. But I reminded myself: he manipulated men, and I was something more.

By now the drizzle had ended. We took off the rain gear, which Charon gathered. As T buttoned her blouse, smiling at her own indecency, Danaë whispered to me, "The Agios beach calls. Do you mind if I take a short walk? It's been a crazy day …"

We kissed and she stepped into the light wake, shuffling away, turning once to wave. I watched her half-cavort, skipping through the water, causing small rainbows from the showers she kicked into the late afternoon sunlight. T stood beside me and said, "She looks happy."

Then I saw a lone woman some hundred feet ahead of her, standing, legs apart, a sentinel no less rapt at her movements than I. Another minute passed. Then Danaë looked up from collecting shells and saw her as well. She stopped, her arms opened and I heard her squeal: "Goddess!"

I was stunned. Artemis now on Mykonos? Had she known Dionysos would appear? Was she anticipating another god's emergence? I thought of Apollo, her brother, and realized I knew too little about their relationship. Perhaps he would be next. Regardless, I viewed her arrival as an augury, her presence as always propitious.

Danaë and her longtime champion joined us in minutes. Artemis was smartly dressed in a stripped skirt and black blouse and had slung her sandals over her shoulder. She wore a gold spiral necklace I'd never seen. Her eyes flashed and without prelude she asked, "Where is Dionysos?"

Charon half-bowed, saying, " Artemis … He's more tired than I have ever seen him. But then he has been without substance for quite awhile. Imagine lying for centuries as nothing more than atoms."

"Yes," she said. "A shame."

"That he's back?"

She smiled. Charon returned her smile, saying, "To your question, he's retired for the night."

Timessa giggled and said, "Charon gave him the boot. He's up there," she pointed. "in his hotel room. Sulking, and demanding to be called The Stranger."

The goddess nodded. "Strange is appropriate. He's the gentlest, yet most savage of us all." She paused. "But let's celebrate our small reunion. Wine, olives?" She looked at me. "Or is it ouzo?"

"Perhaps. And ambrosia for the goddess who stands across from the island of her birth."

She scanned me dispassionately. "Indeed. And I never understood the Delians. Apollo was celebrated with a rich temple while I was ignored."

Timessa said quietly, "We've always heard that your mother, Leto, promised the islanders glory if they built a temple to Phoebus Apollo."

"All glory to the baby boy," Artemis said dismissively. "An ancient prejudice."

"Then, too," T said, "she promised that if that temple went up, the island would be impregnable forevermore."

Laughing, Artemis said, "Our mother was taken by Zeus, and addled ever after. The islanders should never have believed a word —"

I said, "They had a good run. It lasted centuries."

Danaë interjected, "Until the pirates came."

Bantering, we mounted the steps to the patio and sat at a large table, ordering bread and wine, drinks and olives. Charon left to attend to business. No one talked about the circumstances that brought us together. Instead T inquired about friends left at the estate, and Artemis filled us in on the exploits of our sons. Danaë's eyes glowed as the goddess described their adventures. Finally, the goddess turned to me and smiled. "Jackson, you've raised the dead."

"Not at all. Not me. Timessa's dance was too much even for the divine.Ares, Dionysos. Neither could resist —"

Timessa said. "It's always about sex."

"But," I said, "we've only awakened two. Three more asleep."

Artemis looked at me without emotion.

I continued. "Years ago Lachesis told me there were five — Ares, Dionysos, Apollo, Hephaistos, and Poseidon."

"Lachesis's words."

She was probing, yet I knew she never did so without already knowing.

"Goddess, I wasn't aware you attended the Delos conclave, that you were present when Apollo and Lachesis chose to retreat."

"Jackson, there's much you don't know."

"Were there five gods? Or did Lachesis lie again?"

She said nothing. T, and even Danaë looked away. Finally the goddess whispered, "Yes, there were five. Those who haven't reanimated are Apollo, Hephaistos and Poseidon. And one of those three is lost." She took Danaë's hand. "No tears. The great sea-god lives."

Danaë sobbed, finally standing and coming over to sit beside me. As I looked over the sea, the night seemed particularly dark. It was as if the hotels surrounding us had dimmed their lights in deference. Even the air felt heavy, a salt mist that left our drinks with an odd piquancy.

We were one of three tables that night, nine people, four of whom were in disguise. The others knew nothing of our divinity. Or of the antiquity of the women. Even Artemis, the golden one, appeared as any other young woman. I was no more than a young man with three attractive girls, one or two who might have been models. But that was not unusual on Mykonos. Our waitress had mentioned one of their guests had been Mick Jagger, and in the 1950s, Brigitte Bardot. Celebrities, like us, sought the same beaches and views and anonymity.

As our meal was being served, Charon stepped out of the darkness,

the consummate emcee, his arms open to his guests. A light illuminated
his face.

"My friends," he smiled. " I have a special treat for you tonight. We
bring you entertainment!"

Lights switched on behind him, dimly illuminating a quickly assembled bandstand and three musicians. I might have called them a band,
but the three were more an ensemble from a bygone time. A young,
handsome man sat in a cushioned, armless chair and to each side stood a
girl no older than fifteen, both dressed in thin, flowing gowns tied at the
waist with ribbons. He cradled an elaborately decorated lyre and the girls
held pan pipes at their lips. I instantly thought, *These are ancient Greeks, not
of this time. What has Charon conjured?*

The lights dimmed and the young man closed his eyes and settled
into a strange, unexpected stillness. After a long moment, he looked up,
scanning his small audience, gazing from face to face, settling on Artemis.
She covered her mouth with her hand as he sang a single, three-syllable
word: *Ar-te-mis* …

Then striking crystalline notes on the lyre, while the two girls played
the pipes in an odd harmonic, he sang,

> *Lovely sister, who followed me*
> *With her silver bow in Delos,*
> *I greet you now*
> *My notes like endless singing swallows*
> *In that lovely place —*

Απολλωνος. Apollo. The glorious Phoebus Apollo sat before us.

As he sang he grew more radiant, his body afire, his lyre echoing
through the nearby hills of Mykonos. The archaic song reverberated off
the sea, resonating off the grasses, through the umbrellas that lined the
beach. Within minutes the audience had grown to dozens, men in shorts
and girls in bikinis from nearby hotels clamoring for a view. To our side I
saw Charon in tears. And Artemis appeared shocked, her caution and
self-control awry.

Danaë whispered, "He's back —!"

Without interruption one song led to another, Apollo's eyes never
leaving his sister's face. After three songs, the last ending,

Silver Artemis, Artemis, Artemis
Let us reminisce
About our mother, Leto
How she gave birth to the best
Children of all the gods,
Best in what they say and do,
Gave birth to us
On lovely, living Delos —

Artemis rose and put her arms out. He set aside his lyre and stood. Charon moved to a wall switch, and the lights on the small ensemble went out. The three musicians and Artemis vanished into the darkness. Charon turned to the crowd, saying, "Be gone, all of you! The entertainment ends. Be grateful for what you saw —!"

The place emptied and I was taken in a powerful bear hug — Apollo! His hair was golden and he was laughing. He then pulled Artemis into our embrace, released me and clasped Danaë, then Timessa in turn. His voice was filled with immense love. He said, "My deliverers! What took so long?"

CHAPTER 16

We shifted to a private area on the patio. There were seven of us. Apollo introduced the two girls as Aigle and Arlea, twins with divine parentage. They seemed innocent and reminded me of Artemis's nymphs, both equally transparent. Where had these girls been during his long exile? Apollo smiled at me, saying, "They learned to occupy each other in my absence."

Artemis sat to Apollo's right, with Timessa to his left. He appeared unusually deferential to Timessa, not yielding as much as showing immense respect. At one point I told him, "I've seen no one as gracious to her as you."

"Being courteous to those who will be celebrated is wise," he said. "Besides, was she not the catalyst?"

"Was she?"

"You came in search. But her song stirred us, awakening longings we had brushed aside, her dance a whirlwind wild enough to stop the birds in the sky and subdue the beasts on land."

"I thought it rather sensuous, at best."

He looked at me with curiosity. "Did you not see?"

Timessa was blushing, glancing between us, more bemused than disconcerted at his words. I said, "I saw Timessa dancing in the rain."

"Her footsteps were tremors, her dance a maelstrom. Hermes

brought you in the storm because there'd be no tourists. We resisted, we resented his decision. We were angry at you as well for your assumptions and intrusion. And then, regardless of our misgivings, we were enchanted when she began to dance."

I glanced at Danaë who shrugged, obviously amused. Artemis added, "Jackson, you alone among us has what Athene calls the Lazarus power. Yet it was Timessa who awoke the sleeping. Give the girl her due."

The girl. Fine. I was outnumbered, still unaware of exactly what occurred. We — she — had revived Dionysos, Ares and now Apollo.

Hephaistos and Poseidon were missing, yet Artemis had implied earlier that Poseidon lived, or at least could be revived. That meant, if one of the five were "lost forever," Hephaistos would not appear.

The other gods had mocked Hephaistos as a cripple, lame after a confrontation with Hera and yet, for a time, married to Aphrodite. They had had no children from the union and she'd been a constant adulteress with Ares, the war god, her secret lover. She never spoke of Hephaistos when I occasionally described my plans, and I assumed she felt no loss. Yet again, I was making assumptions, even that he was lost. Hermes knew, as did Artemis, but they had decided that I, as the presumptuous archaeologist, would have to excavate the truth, stone by stone.

Trying to gauge Artemis's intent, I said, "I sensed them, I heard their voices in the rubble, but could never pinpoint where they were."

She nodded. "Timessa had no need for surgical precision." She turned to T. "Tell him what you did."

"I sensed them everywhere. The island vibrated with their voices and breath. I simply danced the ancient Dionysiakos ..." She glanced at me. "... a dance that honors Dionysos and the gods. The sensuousness you saw was intentional and why Dionysos was the first to wake."

"But why *that* dance?"

"It celebrates the masculine. And its complement, feminine. The old dance was done with phalluses, a prayer for fertility. I remembered it from long ago, and ..." She blushed and looked down. "Well, I've said enough."

Apollo touched her cheek, smiling. "Dionysos and Ares first. And then I woke. Even after your little group had returned to Mykonos, the sands and stones kept moving to your steps."

She looked up at him, acknowledging his words.

"I resisted," he continued, "and then suddenly, I reconstituted. I gathered my lyre and bow, and encountered Hermes waiting patiently. He told me to laugh. It was such a stupid request that I did. Indeed, the awakening was undoubtedly hilarious. After, we spoke briefly. He convinced me that the time had come."

I watched him speak, his perfect skin and classic features captivating. He was reputed to be a master archer like Artemis, his golden arrows said to never miss, bringing instant death. Ἀπολλωνος, a god of truth, music, prophesy, and sun. Too, he was a healer. As god of light, he was called Phoebus, and his golden hair justified his name.

Watching him, I tried to reconcile the obvious conflict between being a master healer and a consummate executioner; I could not. As with so many of the gods, he embodied extremes.

Now that several of these beings had reappeared, I was too aware that I had wanted these virile deities to return, had spent years obsessing over how to make that so, and now sat across from one of the greatest. Apollo turned from me, studying Danaë for the first time. "You too danced the Dionysiakos. Did you know?"

She shook her head. "I barely remembered it. I was copying Timessa."

He smiled tenderly. "Give me your hand —" As he reached across the table to her, Danaë hesitantly met him halfway. Looking into her eyes, he said, "Open yourself."

Danaë closed her eyes, trembling. After a moment studying her, the god said, "Ah, Poseidon's daughter. Your heart is pure, your love for the man beside you is a song. And now you await your father's arrival, praying he is not forever gone."

She nodded. "I have believed I would never see him again."

Apollo stood, taking Artemis by the hand. He looked around at us and said, "You will forgive us. We have much to talk about. My sister will set me straight. There's so much I do not know."

They walked down to the beach and stepped into the wake, strolling hand in hand along the shore until we lost them in the dark. Danaë turned into my arms and Timessa looked away. Aigle and Arlea, the twins, then looked at each, giggling. I said, "Do the two of you ever speak?"

They hesitated, then shook their heads no. At the same moment

Charon stepped onto the patio. We were the last of his guests still at tables, and he said, "Stay as long as you wish. None of you needs much sleep. My only warning is to be aware that Dionysos may appear." He paused. "Now, I have things to prepare. I will see you again at dawn."

§.

Dionysos never appeared. After an hour passed, the five of us agreed to quit for the night. Artemis and her brother were still out, and the sun would rise in hours. The sky had cleared and stars hovered, brilliantly afire. Arlea, one of the twins, pointed overhead and spoke for the first time. "Look! The Pleiades, the sisters, suspended overhead!"

I knew the star cluster located in the Taurus was a common sight here. Before I could speak, her sister Aigle said, "A lucky thing to see!"

Timessa rolled her eyes as if the two were children. "Hardly. They're always up there. Sailors use them to navigate. Big deal."

But the twins spoke simultaneously, "A big deal when they're seen from Mykonos! A really, really big deal!"

We smiled, with Timessa saying, "Okay, okay."

I expected Charon to soon ferry us here to Delos. The Pleiades would be washed away by the sun, by Helios's light, and we would navigate the island's paths with Hermes, not by following stars. We walked the twins to their room, reminding them to double lock the door, then went off to our own. Danaë was preoccupied and we cuddled briefly before she slept. I said a silent invocation that we might encounter her father soon. She had become increasingly quiet since Apollo's emergence. We all knew, based on Artemis and Apollo's signals, that Poseidon was the last, yet he had not appeared.

Danaë seemed brave and determined, and was a fervent advocate for her father. When in the past I had tried to talk with her about his disappearance, she became irritable, even melodramatic, and I learned to avoid the topic.

At sunrise we wandered down to eat. The air was light and the weather perfect. I was aware that if we visited Delos, we would have company. The catamarans would be dropping off the backpackers and day trippers. I wasn't sure what we could accomplish. Regardless, I knew we would agree to whatever Charon proposed.

Danaë remained preoccupied. Timessa playacted her opposite, purposely being cheery, even whistling. I said nothing, trusting T's instincts and counting on their old friendship for insights beyond my own. At one point Danaë turned to her, saying, "Stop it! That's irritating!" Timessa pushed her impishly and balled up her fists. I would be glad when Charon appeared.

Artemis and her brother sat with us briefly, both looking refreshed. She noted that Charon's boat was expandable if necessary, that there were now seven of us, excluding Dionysos, and that the twins were invited. Apollo put his arm around her, saying, "Count me out. I have no desire to return. I'll stay and keep an eye on Dionysos. And I insist the twins stay behind as well. We'd be too large a group to go unnoticed. All those Germans and French kicking stones."

That left four of us. I noticed Charon, who had been standing quietly behind me. He stepped up and said, "I am equipped to carry many."

Apollo waved dismissively. "There will be four. My sister, Poseidon's daughter, Jackson, and Timessa."

Within minutes we were on the beach, with Charon attending to the girls and then starting the engine in the rear. No one wished us well as we pulled away; no one watched. The small boat arced into the sea and cut a straight line toward the eastern slopes of Delos. I observed that we were heading farther south than before, away from the old harbor where the tourist catamarans tied up. Where Charon was headed we'd see no day trippers.

From our direction, I guessed a walk to Apollo's temple might take an hour or more. Charon clearly had other plans. As we steered into a wind, I admired Danaë's profile. Facing the island, her hair back, the shimmering sun on her skin, she was one of the most beautiful women I had ever seen. As if sensing my gaze, she turned and smiled. I raised my voice, "A beautiful day!" and she turned back to face the dark slopes of Delos.

Charon's new destination took longer to reach. We came within a few hundred feet of the shore, then turned, paralleling it and continued south for over a mile until we were near Delos's southern tip. At that point Charon yelled, "Here!" and turned the boat landward, steering it onto an opening between rock outcrops.

I startled, aware that for the first time that Hermes was not awaiting us. Driving the bow into the shore, Charon jumped out, dragging the craft higher and tying it off. He waved us out, hurriedly. I saw no reason to rush, nor did I understand why he'd chosen this location.

Once we were all on land, he pointed. "There, a single trail. Follow it and you will arrive at your destination."

Artemis flashed anger. "Charon, you are being opaque. How will we know when we arrive?"

He scowled and stepped into his boat. "You will know."

I asked, "And Hermes —? Will he come?"

"Only Hermes speaks for Hermes," he said, gunning the engine and turning the boat toward the northeast. We were alone.

Timessa turned to Artemis, saying, "Goddess?"

She sighed. "What we pursue must be down this trail. He will not deceive us. The stakes are high. Any hoax will be punished. He is but a minor god."

Danaë stepped over to me, taking my hand. She said loudly, "Nothing will stop me from finding my father. If I have to go alone, I will walk this path from end to end —"

Artemis smiled. "You will never be alone."

Danaë pulled me along and headed in the direction Charon had indicated. The trail was narrow and strewn with stones. After ten minutes we walked past a field with hundreds of crows; they stood silent, motionless, watching as we passed.

In the next field, separated by a stonewall from the first, we saw sheep, enormous and swaying from side to side in a silent rhythm. Like the crows, they watched as we maneuvered down the narrowing path. Artemis turned to look at me, contracting her eyes, expressing her unspoken concern.

I asked, "Are these creatures a joke?"

"Yes," she said. "Probably Hermes and his sense of humor."

As we hiked south she called back to me, "Do you know the word, ἵππος?

"Like hippos? That's horse, right?"

"Yes, the old tongue. Poseidon was the animal's creator. Some say he conjured the horse from drops of his own blood; others say from his semen. There were instances when he turned himself into a stallion for the usual purposes …"

I laughed. "Isn't he Zeus's brother?"

Danaë stopped and interjected, "Zeus, my father and Hades — all sons of Kronos. After they deposed the old man —"

"How?" I asked.

"Zeus prevailed with endless thunderbolts. Even Kronos could not resist. When he lay dead the three sons drew lots for the sky, the sea and the underworld. Zeus won the sky, and Poseidon the seas and rivers. Hades went down into the darkness to rule the dead."

Artemis added, "Poseidon loved land, although he was given the seas. He and Athene fought over Athens. He lost. There were many territories he took, and many he lost, all in constant disputes with the virgin, Pallas Athene."

"I was raised in his underwater palace off Aegae," Danaë said, "in Euboea." She laughed at the memory. "It sounds watery but he'd sealed it off. We had lawns and gardens and stables filled with horses. The stallions were all magnificent, all with golden manes. We had vast fields to ride them in. Rivers ran from small mountains he'd created, down through the estate and into the ocean floor." She paused, her eyes watering. "When I was ten he gave me a pink conch-shell horn."

"He was kind," Artemis said, "yet, like Dionysos, violent-tempered. He would send floods and storms against cities and towns that angered him."

"And earthquakes," Danaë added. "Yet dolphins danced in joy as he drove his chariots through the waves —"

We resumed hiking. After only moments Timessa stopped, putting her hands on her hips and said to Danaë, "I know what we're doing. Why we're here, why we're walking endlessly." She took Danaë's arm. "But what if we don't find him? What if your father isn't waiting around some bend?"

"Then you'll do your fucking dance again."

Timessa pursed her lips. Danaë shoved her hard. "Understand?"

"Yes —"

Danaë shook her head and turned back down the trail, the rest of us following like ragtag soldiers. After a quarter mile we finally emerged from the dry slopes onto a grassed hollow that surrounded a small cove. The waters of the cove were still; a light breeze stirred the limbs of scattered trees along the banks. A crow swept in from overhead and cawed as it glided by, almost, I thought, mocking us. There was no other life. We were at trail's end.

The cove opened into the sea where Naxos, another Cycladic island, lay some twenty miles south. Artemis reached over to Danaë and said, "Do not despair."

"But there's nothing here —"

The goddess smiled gently. "Perhaps there is."

And at that moment, in the center of the embayment, something moved in the mirrored waters. I thought at first it was a dolphin. Or several. But it was an enormous man, bare-chested, bearded, who now stood, shaking himself off. He held a trident.

Turning sideways to face us, he cried to Danaë, "Get yourself down here, girl!"

She looked quickly to me, grinning, then ran to the water's edge. He strode to her, bent and took her in his arms. She hugged him, laughing and crying as he spun her around.

"I thought you were forever lost," he said.

"Me? I thought I'd never see *you* again!" Danaë squealed.

"I was on sabbatical. Just a little break."

"For 1,600 years?"

"Asleep and content until someone danced on Delos a couple days ago. I got a damn erection just listening to her steps —"

Danaë giggled, slipping out of his arms and dragging him by the hand toward us. Smiling, he looked up and stopped abruptly, half-bowing. "Artemis!"

She cocked her head, smiling cautiously. "Poseidon. How appropriate that you're wet."

"Were you in on this?" he asked.

"No," she said, gesturing toward me. "He started this. Many years ago. He wanted to find you. He did so for your daughter."

"Jackson. Even here on this damned atoll," he said, "we have heard of you. The newly minted god, correct?"

Imitating his courtesy to Artemis, I half-bowed, saying, "Yes, my idea but —" I turned to Timessa. "Her dance. She gets all credit."

He paused, looking at her. "It's said you will exceed us all."

She blushed and he said, "Is it true the Fates are gone?"

Timessa said, "Yes. Jackson watched them die."

He stood a foot taller than me, and with his pointed beard and musculature, seemed larger than I'd imagined. "To have been taken down by an obscure fungus … Stupid of them. Shameful. Were they given rites?"

"Burned on pyres."

"I never trusted Lachesis. She persuaded us to retreat, then secretly left us here."

Artemis interjected, "They dishonored us all. Arrogance, conceit — it was predictable, but none of us believed Lachesis capable of the error she made. She died horribly. As did her sisters, both innocent."

Artemis and Poseidon viewed each other, giving nothing away and buying time. Finally, Poseidon said, "My palace off Aegae awaits. The seas have been soiled in the last century. Even this cove has trash among the shells. Humans have forgotten me. That will change." He frowned. "I have much to do."

He swiveled, taking Danaë by the waist. "Will you come? Your laughter would be a blessing, girl. The horses will need riders, the dolphins playmates once again —"

She said, "Father, I have three sons. And I protect this man with whom I've coupled. I cannot join you, but you are welcome at our home. And perhaps we can visit you?"

"Once I have the palace presentable, you may stay for months. Or years. And I must see my grandsons soon. I erred in following the others to this place. I'll make it up to you."

She broke into tears, standing before him. "First," she said. "you're not going anywhere. Not until we've spent some time together. And you should get to know Jackson. There's so much to talk about." She took his arm. "Don't argue. You're leaving Delos and coming to Mykonos. Charon is a marvelous host and his small hotel has room. You'll stay with us."

The god turned to Artemis and she nodded. "No arguing with your daughter. She plans to keep you above water for as long as possible. Now, let's return."

CHAPTER 17

Epiphany: *The manifestation of a divine being;*
also, a sudden revelation or insight.

We walked a short distance and found Charon, who had
maneuvered his craft onto a cramped landing north of the cove.
When he saw Poseidon, he clambered out of the boat and the two
bumped bellies and roared as if they were Vikings. Poseidon waved his
trident overhead and Charon took Poseidon's face between his hands,
shaking him in joy. Charon beamed. "Apollo, Ares, Dionysos — and now
you, my friend!"

"You *knew* I would return!" Poseidon joked.

"You are the last. I always worry for the last."

Timessa turned to Artemis and said, "But Hephaistos? Is he really
gone?"

The goddess said, "I sense nothing more of him than a tiny spark."
She looked at Poseidon. "Why of all of you is Hephaistos lost?"

Danaë's father became quiet. At first I thought he would not respond,
as he looked over the sea toward Mykonos, his eyes unreadable. Then he
frowned. "When we became quiescent, our atoms were scattered

throughout the island, in the sands, the seasonal grasses, infusing the stones. Yet each atom was still in contact with its brothers and their locale. We were diffused, yet exquisitely networked. That was Lachesis's idea. It was ingenious as we could reconstitute at will …"

"And Hephaistos?" Timessa asked. "Why has he not appeared?"

"You remember," he said. "He was the metallurgist, the smith among us, the ingenious craftsman."

"Yes," Artemis added, "he'd made golden robots to help at his forge, armor for Achilles and others, heartbreakingly beautiful jewelry for the goddesses —" She smiled. "I often wear necklaces he made."

"There was no one like him," Poseidon affirmed, "and when we scattered ourselves about, he spread himself wider than anyone, allowing his molecules to drift out to sea, certain that his ingenuity would keep them all intact. Did I agree? No. As the sea-god, as the tamer of wine-dark waters, I warned him, saying, 'The currents are unpredictable, the riptides will suck your very being away.' But he believed in himself and rejected all advice."

"And?" Timessa asked.

"Even Lachesis urged him to stay on land." Poseidon stared at T as if lost. "In the first great storm that hit Delos, Hephaistos drowned. Or more accurately, too much of him was lost. Or so it seems …

"When the maelstrom raked the shores, he was unprepared. Far too much of his essence was adrift in what had long been the island's calm tides. Then suddenly his atoms were submerged across a hundred miles of sea." He rubbed his eyes, looking away. "That occurred in year three of our retreat. Hephaistos, like Lachesis more recently, gambled foolishly."

T asked, "Is part of him still here?"

"Can you sense him still?"

T nodded. "Like a scent. Or a thin smoke."

"That's all that's left. A scintilla. Too much of the god was lost. The sea is vast. The exquisite network that would have allowed his reconstruction was wrecked in the storm as if it were a spiderweb dashed against a field of wheat."

Charon broke our silence, saying, "Speaking of rough seas, today will be choppy. We should depart. There are provisions at the hotel."

Solemnly, we all boarded his boat, which appeared twenty percent larger than earlier. There was now a second plank for seating. I guessed it was four feet longer and several feet wider than before.

As we sat the boatman gunned the engine and turned out to sea. Poseidon sat beside me, but took Danaë's hand repeatedly, kissing her palm and playing with her as if she were a child. She was charmed, and he behaved as if a bon vivant, clearly relishing our company.

As he held her hand and told jokes, he turned to me and said, "You don't mind?"

I laughed and shook my head. "I have dreamed of this reunion. Welcome back."

He studied my face for a moment, then said, "I know the world has changed. I cannot be what I was once. I count on you and my daughter for advice. Visiting Mykonos makes sense. And Jackson, thank you for all of this —"

As he spoke Charon pointed and sang out, "Δελφισ!" *Dolphins*! Indeed, dolphins jumped and rode the coiling outwash on both sides of the bow, their slick backs shining in the sun. I counted eight, ten. They had come for Poseidon, and Timessa echoed Charon's joy with, "Great good luck!" The sea-god stared impassively ahead but the corners of his mouth flickered in amusement.

We motored closer to the main island and I thought of Apollo, Ares, Dionysos, and now Poseidon. Ares had gone underground, probably already running munitions or brokering rockets for a regional war. Turkey, Cyprus, Iran, Palestine? Numerous countries would vie for his services. None of the gods had morals, but Ares exulted in their absence.

And Dionysos? His overt sexuality offended polite culture, but had infused all countries, however repressed, like a red dye in clear water. A goat-god, he was sex and fertility and violent passion poured in equal measures into a volatile libation. At Timessa's Dionysiakos dance, he had woken from the endless sleep, aroused and unchanged.

I wondered how he could be contained. He would play seducer to the twins, or Timessa, or unimaginably, Danaë. And if rejected he would turn to the next female, or spin his raw charisma on multiple women. The ancient maenads had, by the hundreds, followed him into the hills surrounding Thebes and at a dozen other cities. Divine possession appeared difficult to resist.

I was certain we could not let him roam again as he did in ancient

Greece. His lust was that of an inflamed satyr, a woodland god in the disguise of a young man. His eyes were the trap; once locked on a girl, they played seducers.

As I considered what I had unleashed, Charon cried, "From the island of the dead to la-la land!" Pointing the bow toward the hotel's beach — an act he must have performed countless times — he drove the boat into the sand and cut the engine. For a moment we sat silently, as if to confirm that all was well. Then he leapt from the craft and extended his hand to the women. As each stepped off, he said, "My lovely ... my lovely ..."

Then with Poseidon and me still onboard, he turned and mounted the steps to the café and disappeared. I suggested we find Apollo and announce Poseidon's return. Following Charon up the stairs toward the patio, we immediately noticed changes. The hotel's name had been removed. In its place was a large hand-painted sign that read,

Private

ΑΔΠ INSTITUTE

An iron gate now blocked the narrow driveway that led to the reception area. As we looked, Charon materialized and said, "Too many of us now. Impossible to mix gods and guests. Tourists are gone for good."

Artemis asked, "ΑΔΠ? Alpha, delta, pi?"

He laughed. "Come on, isn't it obvious? Apollo, Dionysos, *Poseidon.* The ADP Institute." He smiled pleasantly. "The institute will be dedicated to the study of old gods. We'll apply for grants and other handouts. I'll make far more money than I ever did before, perhaps get rid of that old boat ..."

"But the hotel?" Artemis asked.

Charon looked stoical. "The hotel has been a front. I've possessed this site for almost three millennium. It actually felt good to give the boot to everyone."

As he spoke Timessa pointed behind him. Dionysos had appeared, grinning and yawning, and he imitated her gesture, pointing back. "My filly! Back from dead-dead-Delos. I've been restless, playing with my thyrsus, wondering if you'd ever come home. Now be a good girl," he said, putting out his hand. "Come please old Dionysos —"

She shook her head. "Never."

"Don't toy with me," he growled.

"You're too old for me," she said mockingly, "and too insecure."

He tensed at the insult. At the same moment Artemis lifted her arm and made a strange sign, flicking her wrist. As she had done years before at the sacred pool in the grove when she caught a man spying, she wrapped the god in thin blue flames. Hot arcs of fire raced along his arms, circled his crotch and burnt his hair in a small explosion. Dionysos crouched, crying, "Enough, enough!"

As he pleaded, she waved her hand dismissively, the flames vanishing. She left him intact. I note that because she had turned the man caught spying into a stag, and the stag had been promptly killed by her nymphs. The flames wrapping the goat-god were simply a warning. She spoke evenly, "The girl is sanctified and untouchable. You know that. How dare you play your vulgar tricks with her?"

With his hair still smoking, Dionysos glared and limped away. Timessa put her arms around Artemis.

Charon cleared his throat loudly and said, "Welcome to the Institute, where the lions and the lambs play together in the fields." He opened his arms, concluding raffishly, "Food is laid out in the usual place. I have rare retsina, olives and ouzo from Athos. Come, my old friends, let's drink —"

Dionysos reappeared halfway through our celebration. His hair was blackened and his arms singed. He made no apologies and said nothing, pulling out a chair beside the twins. Apollo, who had joined us in the café, looked at him and said, "They, too, are sacrosanct. Lovely girls, and mine."

I noticed Apollo's golden bow leaning beside his chair. An arrow was notched and I knew as well as Dionysos that, if released, it would kill whomever it struck. Lachesis had led me to believe that only the Fates killed other gods, and the Fates were dead. I wondered, were Apollo's threats idle? Was I observing simple bullying between the divine?

As before, Charon interceded, saying, "We all are extraordinary and unsurpassed by almost every measure. If — and I speak to all of you — you are to stay here, however briefly, there will be no fighting or assaults.

No one can destroy us but ourselves. And we will not, after all this time, become antagonists."

Dionysos shrugged. As I watched, one of the twins — Aigle, I think — slipped her peplos off her shoulders, pulling it down to her waist and exposing herself. As she did she lifted her chest, staring at the god, her eyes dancing. Her sister, Arlea, giggled. Dionysos said, surprising us all, "Adorable, winsome, but my friendship with Apollo and Artemis supersedes all else." He looked at Charon. "It's true, old friend. I'll behave. Even if I am taunted cruelly."

Aigle pulled her peplos up, pouting, winking at her sister. Arlea shifted her gaze to me and smirked. There was more to the two than I'd guessed.

Apollo shifted his attention from the twins. Looking at Timessa, he said, "You were once a nymph. And now —?"

She smiled shyly. I said, "We're not sure what she is or what she's becoming. Perhaps a philosopher, perhaps a saint."

One of the twins said, "I think a caterpillar with a hundred legs."

I laughed. "Caterpillars turn into butterflies."

T whispered, "Stoppp —!"

Artemis put her hand on Apollo's shoulder, saying, "Yes, she requested her freedom some months ago. No nymph has ever left. Or ever asked to leave. I agreed and she's on her own."

I added, "Nymphs don't do what she did. The Dionysiakos? No nymph is taught those steps, yet she did them instinctively. She is pure and it is not. She raised the benumbed —"

"The salacious pure," Artemis intoned, "rousing the impure from centuries of sleep."

Danaë scuffed. " 'The salacious pure'? Is there such a thing?"

Timessa replied, "Quit using the third person. I'm right here! And they weren't dead. Probably more that my dance was so bad they woke to escape its vulgarity."

We laughed, particularly at Timessa's modesty. Our humor masked our recognition that she was in rapid metamorphosis. Getting her out of Boston had made sense. Bringing her to Delos had been revelatory. Yet I also was aware that she had agreed to walk fashion runways in Paris. Her prestigious gig occurred in days. As she'd said, she might be the girl who launched a thousand slips.

Poseidon stood and stretched. I was amused; the twins watched him open-mouthed. He turned suddenly to them and said softly, "Such beautiful girls. I may steal you from Apollo."

Apollo laughed and the twins looked away.

From the café we could see Delos, its whaleback darkening as the day wore on. I thought of Poseidon's dolphins dancing in joy as we returned. What had Timessa said? "Great good luck!" Yet I couldn't help but think time was playing its own games, and, as always with these beings, the rules were uncertain.

Timessa caught my eye with a brilliant smile, as if she read my thoughts. If she did, that was a first. Nymphs were transparent and gods opaque; the ancient rule was immutable. I looked at her as if indifferent. "What was I just thinking?"

"That you don't have a clue what's up. Or," she laughed, "down."

"What else?"

"That I can't possibly know your thoughts." She was clearly amused. Then as if stating an afterthought, she said, "And now things are reversed. You can't read my thoughts. But I can yours. Oh dear."

CHAPTER 18

When the gods wish to punish us
They answer our prayers.
—Oscar Wilde

Our group broke up. Apollo and the twins wandered off for "lessons." I assumed he meant musical, although after Aigle's earlier performance, I wondered. To my amusement, Charon and Dionysos announced they were taking the boat out. The sea had calmed and the goat-god claimed "salt vapors" would bring him needed equanimity. Charon muttered something about motoring along the shore where they might observe the topless girls, then caught himself: "Still early in the season," he said. "Expect nothing exceptional, my friend." Their odd bond seemed a conspiracy, but I was glad to see Dionysos occupied, however briefly.

Timessa stood as they left, noting she had Paris-related business to conduct: confirmations of her appearance, review of dresses — the designer had made numerous tweaks — and checking her schedule. Several magazines wanted shoots, including *Vogue Paris* and *Elle*. Timessa was becoming a sensation, but her ambiguity about it all was palpable.

Danaë, her father, Artemis and I lingered at the café beside the beach. I sensed that Danaë and her father were still testing connections, gently probing and measuring their interrupted relationship. He was fascinated by her descriptions of Artemis's plans for the tribe's revitalization and of our boys. She showed him photographs. "Have they picked out mates yet?" he asked.

"Our boys? A dozen girls claim each," Danaë said. "Monogamy may be challenging." She smiled warmly. "But it will all work out."

Poseidon stood and took her hand, turning to Artemis and me. "Do you mind if we take a walk? The beach beckons. And I still have endless apologies to make to my girl."

Danaë seemed pleased and I nodded. They wandered down the stairs, opened the new privacy gate Charon had installed and stepped into the sand. They stood for a moment pointing at Delos. A few large rocks were piled to the side, and beside them, a tall stand of phragmites bending in the salt wind. We couldn't make out their words but I heard Danaë's laughter.

Artemis appeared relaxed and, for once, without an agenda. She wore Hephaistos's spiral necklace and leaned back in the wicker chair. "So far it's good, Jackson. I had no idea how this might go. If someone were writing a mythology, the last few days would be epic. The reuniting of the mighty gods. All we lack are smokey sacrifices. But then, today's humans claim to have evolved from that so-called barbarism …"

"There are those who recognize you. The old ways live on."

"Yes, but the tens of thousands who asked for our love have degenerated to hundreds now. Those who believe, who acknowledge we are not characters from tales, are few. I sympathize with the male gods who sighed and slept. And I wonder, now that they are back, what happens next."

"That's my concern, as well. I blundered my way into discovering them …"

"… without knowing what to do with your discovery," she completed my thought. "What becomes of immortals who have slept for almost two millennium, who know nothing of this world?"

"Was it ill-advised?"

She smiled. "Possibly ill-considered. But gods adapt, gracefully or not."

I looked casually onto the beach. Danaë and her father had walked no more than a hundred feet and stopped. He leaned toward her, probably speaking. She backed three paces away, alert to something. Poseidon seemed to swell in size, shook his head from side to side and — in a prismatic flash that lasted a mere second — became a muscled stallion.

The god-horse was black with a golden mane. He pawed the sand beside the sea, rose back on his hind legs and whinnied. Danaë whooped with joy, clapping her hands. Artemis and I stood, startled by the transformation. The goddess said, "What men will do to impress a girl —"

The stallion dipped its head, surrendering. Danaë leapt onto its back, clinging to its mane. The horse reared back slightly and Danaë raised an arm in jubilation. With her legs pressed into the stallion's heaving ribs, they galloped down the beach. Her hair flew and my heart went wild.

She could not have guessed Poseidon's surprise. And I knew her well enough to know this small event made up for years of sadness and sorrow. This was a gift, an extravaganza no other being could bestow. And in Danaë's vast intelligence, she understood exactly what he gave. I smiled to Artemis. "Not 'impress,' " I said. "You are seeing pure love on the grandest scale."

Artemis smiled. "An even better description? Mutual ecstasy."

The horse and rider became smaller and smaller as they flew, then were gone.

The waitress who had been our sole server since our arrival approached us. The obol I had given Charon for each trip to Delos had come from her. With no one else was in the café, she stopped a moment, presenting herself to Artemis, unmoving, her posture impeccable and her arms down, palms open. To me she would have been the perfect kore, a white marble statue from ancient times. Even her clothes echoed the loose gowns of the sculptures.

Artemis stood, saying graciously, "Yes, of course I have known from the start. It has been some years." Our waitress nodded. She appeared to be about twenty-five, unusually virtuous, even irreproachable. Artemis continued, "My goddess, how have you not embraced Poseidon?"

As I too stood, the girl lowered her head. "Charon told me it might all be overload, that I should not reveal myself to anyone until days had passed."

Artemis looked at me. "Jackson, meet Hestia —" She caught herself.

"The two of you met briefly at the sacred grove when we discussed the fate of the Fates."

Then I remembered. She had looked familiar, but had shown no recognition when we first appeared at the café and I discounted knowing her, assuming she was a local girl. Hestia, one of the primary goddesses, dedicated to homes and families, a fierce advocate for chastity. She had been part of the convocation days before the Fates had died. I half-bowed, saying, "My apologies for being fooled so easily."

Artemis whispered, "It was not stated at the time — you did not need to know — but she is Poseidon's sister, and my aunt."

Hestia said softly, "You may already know that my brother and I have not been close since he tried to seduce me. He wooed me endlessly until he finally quit. We have spoken little since."

Artemis said, "Your brother should know you are here. He has reunited with Danaë. His sister is significant, as well."

"Perhaps," she said. "I agree that he should know. What he does then is up to him." Hestia paused and blushed, looking at Artemis. "There is something else." Artemis raised an eyebrow. "Your brother, Apollo, tried to take me as well. I resisted, but he was flattering, always touching me, stroking my hair. It was difficult."

"You were a saucy thing, Hestia. What can I say?"

Hestia looked taken aback by her comment, then whispered, "Yes, fine. I will let them know."

Artemis said nothing. Hestia collected plates and cups from our table, the dutiful waitress, the primal goddess at Charon's estate, tending his hearth and waiting on guests.

I sat on the bottom of the stairway to the beach, awaiting Danaë's return. Artemis had excused herself and I was conscious an hour had passed. I saw them long before I heard the stallion's hooves. Poseidon was a dark mass racing toward me along the surf, a girl clinging to his back, her blouse fluttering in the wind.

Danaë waved and I raised my hand. As they neared the horse slowed, then stopped, lowering itself gracefully. She slipped off its back, patted its flank and skipped to me.

Then with the same prismatic flash, the stallion changed from horse to Poseidon and he stretched, laughing, ankle-deep in the waves. I looked about for anyone gawking, but saw no one. Poseidon had controlled his return flawlessly.

I stood. "You're back."

Danaë promptly burrowed under my arm, saying, "My men!"

"No one thought it odd to see a horse and rider cavorting in the waves?"

"Guess not," she said. "And even if they had?"

She beamed and I knew that taking her to Delos had been inspired. At our estate in Pennsylvania, I wasn't certain her father could be discovered, or would reanimate, so I had gambled, as I had gambled taking Timessa along. These small decisions had proven propitious. Or perhaps simply fortunate, as I no longer believed in luck; every phenomena arose miraculously from primal winds, fire, earth, and water, from spinning electrons, like the scent of a girl's washed hair, the heat of the sun on freckled shoulders, like the song of a golden arrow shot from Apollo's bow. Nothing was accidental.

As I wove these thoughts, taking pleasure in connecting the disparate imagery, Poseidon turned his back to us and, carrying his trident, strode out into the sea. Without a word he sank deeper and deeper, a muscled god now chest-deep in the water. As Danaë saw him disappearing into the sea, she cried, "No!"

In response he wheeled around without breaking stride. "Sea-gods must inspect their seas. I've been no more than ankle-deep since my rebirth. I won't be long —"

Danaë whimpered, "Father!" A pair of sea-blue dolphins emerged, then submarined beside Poseidon's shoulders. Suddenly he disappeared into the chop, into the ancient brine of sunken triremes, shattered black-slip pottery, bones from old battles and ancient sacrifices. She pivoted in my arms, finding my eyes and whispered, "Is he gone?"

"No, he and I are equally in love with you. Anyone who falls like we have does not desert. He'll wander his seas, doing due diligence, checking on his estates, his stables in Aigai — and then return."

She dismissed my assurances, and shocked at his exit, sobbed. "You'll never leave me like he did?"

I lifted her into my arms, thinking of the sea-god. For one reputed to be gentle with those he loved, his departure could have been more felici-tous. I turned and carried her up the stairs to the café. At the top Charon greeted us, apologetic and contrite.

"I knew he was planning that. I should have spoken."

Danaë glared as I set her back on her feet. "Charon! Your silence! You should be ashamed —"

He half-bowed and turned away. I asked her if I should order a drink and she nodded. Hestia stood to the side and I said, "Wine?"

While we waited I said, "Our waitress is not some local girl. She's the goddess Hestia."

Danaë gave me big eyes and stuck out her tongue. "You're so slow. I don't know why I put up with you."

Then unexpectedly, in a compact flush of air and a small flash, Apollo appeared beside us. Simultaneously, Aigle and Arlea materialized, both in cotton frocks, arms linked. Apollo said, "We must talk. May I join you?"

I shrugged. "Always. Poseidon's just gone underwater. Dramatic departure and Danaë's traumatized."

"He will be back." Aigle sat beside him and Arlea took his lap. He slipped an arm around her waist, saying, "No wiggling."

She shook her hips and looked languidly at Aigle, saying, "Okay, okay."

Apollo straightened and said to me, "Have you thought about what you have done?"

I watched him, still amazed at his appearance. His golden hair and eyes were unsettling, and I sensed a sinewy strength beneath his easy confidence. After a pause I said, "You mean the revival?"

"Yes, what you call the revival. We are alone and may speak frankly now."

"Then do so," I said.

"Several of us here are as rational as Plato, as reasoned as Aristotle. But we are matched in number by the madmen you have awakened with your clumsy work. Did you really believe we just called a friendly congress of peers so many years ago? The mighty gods and the virgin Fates, coming together in mutual ennui to sleep on an island in the sea?"

Danaë pulled her chair closer to mine, saying, "Don't be obscure, Apollo. Or insulting —"

He smiled. "Lachesis spread these lies, these inventions, when she awoke a few decades ago. 'All of the mighty gods were bored, tired of fighting Christianity.' Yes, there was a kernel of truth to that. But we also planned the dormancy to put an end to the madness of Ares and, I regret to say, Dionysos, as well."

"You're saying, you engineered a plot," I asked, "to do away with two of the gods?"

"Not to do away with them — I'm not sure we could. But luring them to sleep was equivalent to sedating them." Arlea moved in his lap, smirking and rocking until he squeezed her thigh. "Stop that!"

He went on, "Ares was considering devastating Christendom, an easy enough effort. He could have cleansed the fanatics in a week or so, a country a day until the Levant and Italy were purged. He found them all insufferable —"

"And Dionysos?"

"Dionysos had become a predator, not that any of us ever has had scruples about that sort of thing. But it had become a sickness. He required sex like others require ambrosia. He would take dozens of girls a night, dancing madly in obscure towns, killing anyone who tried to stop his raves. A week before we conferred on Delos, he impregnated four sisters and killed their father and brothers. Then a night later he worked his way through a nunnery. Thirty girls …"

"Couldn't any of you dissuade him?"

"Nothing we said deterred him. For amusement, he also began driving men mad. It was no different than killing flies. As you might imagine, as the exploits of these two became known, sacrifices declined. Entire towns rebelled against us …

"We were under attack rather than worshipped. Ares, always intolerant, tried to punish a small town outside Delphi by burning down its agora."

I asked, "When did this occur?"

"About four centuries post-Christ. I was Delphi's protector, so his attack was an attack against me. Trying to avoid a direct clash, I sat down one morning with the two of them. But Dionysos was a raving fool, his eyes darting in all directions. Poor Aigle and her sister — he tried to take them, the idiot, even as I watched. What was he thinking?"

Aigle shrugged, looking at Danaë. "Whatever," she said. "I caught him before he tore off Arlea's dress. Kicked him in the groin —"

Apollo smiled indulgently. "Frankly, I was about to use my bow when Lachesis said she had an alternative."

"She was there?"

"She was everywhere. But, yes. I had invited her to come. I thought only the Fates could stop the two. She had watched impassively until the moment Dionysos lunged at the twins. Then suddenly, she took Dionysos and the sulking Ares by the hair and threw them off as if catapulted from a crude machine."

Apollo sighed, adjusting Arlea's weight in his lap. "It was at that final summit that she proposed we retreat to Delos. She was persuasive, noting astutely that the withdrawal would solve the terrible publicity, and that in time, when their exploits were forgotten — and when the fires of the new religion cooled — we could return."

Danaë interjected, "But you intended to return on your own terms."

"Yes, not when Jackson Night thought it entertaining."

I watched him carefully, sensing no animosity. "I was driven, at first," I said, "to find Poseidon. That the rest of you were revived is coinciden-tal. My 'excavation,' as you call it, was done for Danaë. I want her happiness —"

As I spoke, Timessa walked into the café. "And I'm at fault as well. You sleepers were easy to find. A few dance steps and you were all breathing heavily."

The twins looked at each other. As if comics, Aigle said to Arlea, "Are you a virgin?"

Arlea said in a singsong voice, "I don't know. Are you?"

Ignoring them, Timessa said, "So what if we accelerated your return? And so what if we have a couple demonic gods goofing around again. If they get out of hand, you have your bow. Do you fear them now that they've been uncaged?"

Her mockery infuriated Apollo. As I sensed him about to punish her — I had no idea how but I knew it was coming — I stood and raised my hands. "Ares would laugh to see you two. We will not fight among ourselves!"

Timessa smiled and said, "Let's count who's here, newly awaken and always awake … You, Apollo and the twins. Of course, Dionysos. Hestia,

Hermes, Charon, Artemis, and Jackson. Ares has gone missing. And there's Poseidon, Danaë and me. Gods, goddesses, a demigoddess, and nymphs. Say what you will, we have a common bloodline and are all a-mortal. Of the thirteen of us, two are savages and one of those two has vanished. By my count eleven of us are sane. Or mostly. Surely we can prevail against two barbarians?"

Silently, Charon stepped into the café, with Dionysos slung over his shoulder. He smiled as if it were obvious. "Had to knock him out. We motored slowly past some topless girls sunning on the beach. He dove out and was on one of them before I could act. She screamed and I clubbed him in the head with my pole. That worked, and he'll revive."

Hestia whispered, "And the girl?"

"Shaken. I paid her handsomely. As well as her friends."

The boatman shook Dionysos off his shoulder, holding him under the arms, allowing him to slump into a chair. His eyes were open but he appeared to see nothing. The twins recoiled into Apollo's arms, and even Danaë pushed herself behind my chair. Timessa, on the other hand, walked up to the fertility god, squatted to observe him closely, then stood, abruptly pushing his chair sideways with her foot. Dionysos slid onto the patio floor, his head hitting hard. She said, "Goat-god or not, he's despicable. He's become a common rapist. To think he once brought joy to women over all of Greece."

"Joy?" one of the twins asked.

"Repressed girls and women, restrained from seeing sunshine, forbidden from leaving their homes without a man — all could find euphoria by following this Dionysos, a god who promised bliss, whose followers found rapture by stepping in his steps, dancing as they did before their days of servitude —"

Timessa pivoted, looking at each of us, then paused, saying to Apollo, "But he's a ruin of what he was. If you won't stop his assaults, I'll do so myself. A quick gelding of the god with a dull, unsterilized blade would end his obsessions for good."

Charon muttered, "What —?"

She laughed. "We must become surgeons who are willing to castrate the monsters we raise. As it is, we are cowering before this beast. Why? Zeus never hesitated to mete out justice when it was deserved! And yet his children wring their hands at the thought."

Hestia stepped up and said, "Get him out of my kitchen. Take him away!"

Charon and I each took an arm and dragged him out, backward toward the hotel. The god's eyes rolled up, his head drooping sideways as he jounced along. Dionysos was bare-chested; angry scratches crisscrossed his chest. The girl on the beach must have fought hard before Charon clubbed him into unconsciousness.

CHAPTER 19

The action of the goddess
was autonomous,
the visages of her authority
obvious, an apotheosis.

When I returned to the café, I motioned to Timessa and Danaë.
"Let's walk."

As we stepped around the prow of Charon's boat, we turned north, following the edge of the surf. Danaë took my hand. T kept laughing to herself.

"What's so funny?"

She said, "I used to be terrified of Apollo."

"And now you're not."

"The goddess would sometimes take us to visit her brother. I'd tremble when I saw his golden eyes, his deadly bow. We would keep our eyes down and never speak."

"Things have changed?"

She said nothing, just looking ahead. Danaë pushed against me and said, "We weren't *all* afraid. I was often there. I remember him playing the lyre one afternoon. The flute-girls were always at his side. It was like listening to Orpheus."

Timessa looked amused and I said, "We have only tomorrow and then Timessa goes to Paris." I nudged Timessa. "We're going as well."

"I'm fine alone." She wrinkled her nose. "What are you so concerned about?"

"Nothing's resolved. I feel some responsibility for this mess we're leaving behind."

T said, smiling, "We geld the mad god tonight, then cage Ares, wherever he is. We give the rest of the awakened duties so they're occupied. We work out an understanding with Poseidon so he sees his grandchildren, and hangs with Danaë a couple times a year … There, I solved it. We'll be done by noon tomorrow and then pack up."

Neither Danaë nor I responded. We were now a quarter mile from the hotel and the sun was low.

Timessa tried again: "Okay, I dance the Dionysiakos backward and their atoms fly apart and they go back to sleep, scattered everywhere. Everyone who's left applauds. Goodnight, Apollo, Ares, goat-god-man, and Poseidon of the sea."

"You're becoming annoying," Danaë whispered.

I stopped. "Let's go back to the hotel. It'll be dark soon and I'm uneasy leaving them back there. What if Dionysos wakes up —?"

"What if —?" T echoed mockingly. "What if?"

We trudged back through the coarse sand. Halfway back Danaë released my hand and put her arm around my waist. At some point she stopped me again and kissed me, hard. Timessa wouldn't slow and continued toward the old hotel. We let her get a hundred feet ahead and she finally turned, yelling, "Well —?"

In the dusk Delos was dark and bruised. On its lower slope, a light blinked twice. I stopped Danaë and pointed. After a few seconds the light blinked again. Then again. The faint outline of the island bled into the darkening sky. The slopes turned sable, transitioning to a warm ebony, then in seconds disappeared entirely. Delos and the night were joined.

Danaë took my hand and pulled me along, the lights of the hotel like motionless fireflies and the sound of small waves an eternal music. I felt more alive than I had in years.

❧

In the café Hermes sat shadowed and silent. Artemis sat beside him. As we climbed the steps, she stood. "Timessa, my brother says you caused quite a scene this afternoon."

T pulled out a chair and sat. "You mean the rapist, the goat-god, caused a scene."

"I mean you, nymph. You're lucky Apollo didn't strike you dead."

Timessa smiled. "Careful. A nymph a year ago —"

The goddess said nothing, looking at me and Danaë. "Sit. We'll talk."

I wondered out loud, "Will talking resolve a thing?"

"Everything happens for a purpose. We're seeking explanations."

Danaë and I sat. Hermes spoke quietly, "A step forward can look like a step back, however bold."

Artemis allowed the corners of her mouth to flicker. "The timid become impudent and the straw-man suddenly wields a stick."

"Enough riddles!" I said. "An old Greek technique. We need resolution. Dionysos might wake at any time."

"No," the goddess said. "I have ensured he sleeps as deeply as Poseidon's seas."

Minutes went by. Hestia came in quietly and set wine glasses around, pouring retsina and putting out olives. I guessed they had been rubbed with garlic; they smelled briny. At times a warm breeze moved through the open sides of the café. When Hestia finished her business, she paused as if she would speak, but instead abruptly turned and left.

Timessa steadily ate, stacking olive pits in a pyramid. Night had fallen and she looked around. "Is this the evening meal. Or hors d'oeuvres?"

Artemis said nothing. Eating another olive, T pushed her chair back and said, "From fossil records some say olives originated on Santorini sixty- to seventy-thousand years ago. Others say that Athene gifted them to the Greeks when she founded Athens." She swiveled to face Hermes. "What do you say, emissary?"

He smiled, recognizing T's maneuver: she was illustrating Artemis's aphorism. *The timid were now impudent.* "The first is science," he said, "and the latter, fact. No one here disputes Athene's gifts to man. Our history is alive because those of us here — however many years have passed — witnessed it firsthand."

T smiled and Artemis watched her in fascination. The girl said quietly, "Dionysos is the youngest of the gods?"

"Yes," Hermes replied. "I had lived many years when he emerged in Thebes, the lovechild of Zeus and Semele. Why?"

"And when word spread throughout our world that a new god was skulking in the fields and woods, what was the reaction?"

"Jubilation from the women in the towns he courted with his silver tongue."

"His songs were empowering?"

"Yes, a seduction," Hermes nodded. "And his dances were solely for the women and girls who danced them endlessly."

"He was a liberator," T intoned. "There were said to be epiphanies."

"Many. There was a purity to him. He was the twelfth of us, a revelatory god."

"And today what would you call him, Hermes?"

He sat silently, reluctant to speak. Artemis interjected, "A madman. None of us disputes that. Athene says he ate *la luna* one night and became a fool."

Timessa said quietly, "A lunatic. There are agreeable lunatics, tender-hearted madmen and women who spend their hours painting the same landscape over and over and giving their fortunes to the poor ... Dionysos is something else, a predator who now consciously stalks the weak — not a beneficent god who liberates."

Hermes sighed. "Apollo explained to you why some of us celebrated the Delos sleep. We thought Lachesis ingenious, and Apollo agreed that it made sense."

"Yet 1,600 years of sleep changed nothing," Timessa said, rolling a new olive in her fingers, contemplating its shape. "This one's like a snail shell, isn't it? A little turret at both ends."

Danaë laughed. "When we were young we used butterknives to cut them apart. We were pretending to be dainty."

"I remember. And hours ago I proposed a knife. It should be just like a butterknife, dull and dipped in fire like a branding iron. A fiery, glowing thing to be slashed like a scythe between his legs. A little blood, a few seconds go by: eternal emasculation."

Artemis stood. "Timessa!"

"Your earlier solution? A failure. Thousands of years for nothing. Mine works."

"It's barbaric."

T retorted, "Is it?"

"We heal ourselves. It wouldn't last."

"It would. The hot knife would cauterize the wound, kill the cells. And you know, genitals are the one part that never regenerates."

"But Timessa, we do not torture our own."

"We do. Prometheus was tormented. Zeus sent eagles daily to eat his guts. And that was merely for giving humans fire." Artemis was pale and Hermes silent. Timessa continued, "I remind you. And ask that you compare Prometheus to Dionysos, the good to the bad. One deserved punishment and the other freedom to rape?"

Hermes's response was almost subvocal. "But Dionysos is the god of fertility!"

"The god of this and the god of that. Who cares?" she smiled. "No one even thinks of us today. We're considered made-up characters from the past —"

To my surprise Danaë stood and said, "I agree. I agree we stop him for good. He terrifies me. I've barely slept since he arrived. He's not one of us. He's abhorrent —"

Hermes said, "You want Charon and me to tie him down, slice him up? I won't."

At that moment Poseidon entered the café; he'd obviously just stepped from the sea. His clothes and hair were wet, his trident shining in the light. "My daughter says he terrifies her. I need hear nothing else. He goes. But he goes underwater where I rule. No one leaves there without my nod. No need to cut him up. He'll be a prisoner forever in my sphere. I have hundreds of stables to clean. And I need a stablehand. Let him charm my horses with his silver tongue."

Danaë applauded. Even Artemis smiled, saying, "Audacious."

Poseidon turned to Artemis. "How long will Dionysos sleep?"

"He wakes at dawn."

"That leaves me time to net him and tie him thoroughly," Poseidon said. "I'll have some dolphins transport him down into the dark sea tonight —" He left as suddenly as he had arrived, striding toward the hotel, the trident slung casually over his shoulder.

Danaë grinned and Timessa followed his back with her eyes. "Refreshing," T said stoically. "No equivocation. A man."

Hermes stood wearily and said in a murmur, "I'll miss his repartee."

"You get off on watching girls raped? Shame on you, Hermes. You should go with the predator," Danaë whispered. "He'll need help shoveling that shit. Shame on anyone who excuses him."

Hestia returned and immediately opened her arms to Timessa and Danaë. "Come here, girls!" They allowed her to gather them and the three held.

Artemis stepped closer to me, saying, "He's not down in Poseidon's palace yet. But only Zeus exceeded the sea-god's strength. Dionysos will be no threat."

I said nothing. She waited expectantly, but I knew too well the stories of hesitant gods, stumbling humans, flawed beings who always wavered until the minuscule light at the labyrinth's end had vanished. By then it was too late. Poseidon was not one to hesitate, but Poseidons were a rarity.

I understood too that the saltwater mist of the dark sea had deepened Poseidon's gaze — the café was the equivalent of a courtroom and the testimony from witnesses sufficient. Only seconds had passed before he assessed the accusations and rendered his verdict. The goat-god was condemned and would be banished.

Perhaps in time the collective memory of his crimes would blur and be minimized as he toiled beneath Poseidon's waves. However, at least within our tribe, his fall might be a caution and similar crimes punished far more swiftly.

As I mused, Danaë broke from her embrace with Hestia and swirled into my arms. Holding her by the waist, I caught Artemis's eye. "We leave tomorrow for Paris. It feels abrupt but T has a show in Paris. We'll attend, then return to the states."

"Good," she said, "but you leave me chasing Ares —"

"Is he your responsibility?"

She looked severe. "If anyone's, he's yours. But I know my way around these parts and you do not. I'll find him."

"And?"

She shrugged. "What I find will dictate what I do."

Danaë slipped from my arm and stepped into Artemis's embrace, saying, "Excuse my earlier harshness, Goddess. I know you didn't know, but Dionysos has always terrified me. His constant slipping between madness and seduction is unnerving … and he so easily lures those around him to his bed …"

Artemis stroked her hair, saying, "Hush."

"I yield to my father's decision. And I rejoice —"

Late the next morning we thanked Charon and Hestia for their hospitality. Charon apologized for Hermes, who was missing (to no one's surprise). As we stood in the driveway I looked overhead at Charon's new sign, AΔΠ INSTITUTE.

"Will you be changing the institute's name?"

He looked surprised. "Why?"

"Apollo, Dionysos, Poseidon …. Using the Δ seems inappropriate as one of the gentlemen will be unavailable. Think of the scholars you'll disappoint!"

"Ah, what would you have me call it, Jackson?"

"You could rename it the AΠ Institute … or," I said thoughtfully, "something even more contemporary, like, Apollo-Aigle-Arlea Institute, in honor of Apollo and the twins." He was unamused and changed the subject abruptly, asking me about the weather in Paris.

Poseidon had promised to visit us, and his grandsons, before the next full moon. Danaë had duly cried in his arms. Artemis finally had pulled her away, saying tears were unseemly and that her father would not disappear again. He assured her that was the case, telling her how lovely she looked, kissing her cheeks and hair, clasping my hand. When he finally left, I was astonished; he moved as if he owned the world. As I watched him stride away, his prowess was extreme. He carried the long bronze trident as if it were a mere stick.

Poseidon had joined us as we lingered over breakfast, as Apollo and the twins played archaic tunes in the sun outside the café. Apollo Phoebus plucked his ivory lyre and the girls alternated between pan-pipes and flutes. The three were quite formal, pausing expressionlessly between tunes, then beginning anew. The music echoed the simple tunes Lachesis had favored years before: one-two-*three*-four, repeated bar after bar. On one solemn piece Aigle sang in a high voice, the words of the song an archaic Greek that I struggled to understand. Midway through, Danaë whispered to me, "A lament for lost youth and innocence …"

An island taxi picked us up before lunch. The waiting turboprop was a small Olympic Air shuttle that took us to Athens. After a brief layover, we flew directly to Paris. During the flight Timessa was preoccupied, constantly thumbing through images of skirts and tops and shoes, which I presumed constituted the designer's Paris collection.

We landed early evening at Roissy Airport and separated in the terminal. Timessa's agency had made reservations for her at a small hotel a block from the show. It had no available rooms, so I called for a room at the Hilton Paris La Defense. We promised to rendezvous for lunch before the show. Timessa left, deep in thoughts that she was unwilling to share. As I observed on Mykonos, she'd become opaque, her reflections no longer transparent to any of us. Yet she seemed at peace. Bright-eyed, she kissed us both and left.

Before she'd gone fifty feet, a man with a camera stepped in front of her and began taking pictures. The camera's flash popped repeatedly. She put her hands before her face and hurried on. He followed a short distance, then stopped, checking his photos. "Paparazzi," Danaë whispered. "She's suddenly one of the hottest models. Perhaps *Le Parisien* will run a shot in tomorrow's edition."

The next morning we taxied to Ellsworth, a brunch spot at the Palais Royal, where Timessa was waiting. She wore dark sunglasses, a scarf over her hair and none of the usual fashion-conscious makeup I expected. "Just want to hang out," she said.

Shoving a newspaper into our hands, she said, "Look. *Le Parisien*." The front page featured her, wide-eyed and glamorous. I recognized the airport background.

She clearly was nervous. The show was to begin in four hours and she was expected to arrive early. Brunch would be hurried. "I have a strange premonition," she said at one point.

"About what?" Danaë asked. "Becoming the next supermodel?"

She wrinkled her nose and looked around the small restaurant. "No, besides, I hate all that."

"Not what you expected when you left us all?"

T laughed carefully. "I miss everyone so much."

Danaë said quietly, "You insisted. No one wanted you to leave."

"This morning feels weird, like there's some peril I can't define." Danaë reached across the table and took her hand. T whispered, "I know it makes no sense —"

I had said nothing, simply observing. But her comments concerned me. I felt nothing; the restaurant was busy and no one seemed to notice us. "It's nothing here?"

"I don't think so," T said. "I just don't know." Again, she looked around restlessly. "Probably just nervous about the show. People seem to be focused more on me than on the clothes, and that's so unfair to the designer —"

"You'll do great. Just be yourself. That's what everyone loves."

We went on like that another ten minutes until she glanced at her phone. When she stood, she said, "You know the address? It's 54 Rue —"

Danaë interrupted, "We know, and we'll be there. Now, go on."

Timessa smiled. She kissed us both and hurried out. Minutes later as I paid the bill I noticed a man sitting by himself. He wore a baseball cap, red shirt and round red designer glasses and gazed at us as if he knew us. When we stood he was still staring. I walked over and said, "Do I know you?" He shook his head, then waved me away. I continued, *"Comprennez-vous Anglais?"* He shook his head again, now looking irritated. Danaë took my arm and pulled me away.

The weather was still cool and we wandered for an hour, favoring the parks and strolling through small shops. Neither of us had seen Paris and were surprised by the number of tourists who, like us, seemed dazed by the architectural diversity and the contemporary structures wedged beside four- and five-hundred-year-old buildings.

At two that afternoon we located the venue, showed our tickets and were told to sit in the second row. The room held well over a hundred people and Danaë whispered, "I recognize almost everyone in the front."

"I don't."

"Celebs, influencers, pop and rap stars. I had no idea."

At precisely ten minutes after the hour, music began, lights dimmed and spotlights lit the door beside a carpeted runway. The designer stepped out and opened her arms to the crowd. I recognized her from the Boston show. With a smile she said, "Welcome to *Viva Skirts and Shirts and Spunk*. This is my fifth year in Paris and I love you guys! I'll host a brief media session after the show." She bowed. "And now we begin!"

Timessa stepped out, her face inscrutable. To my surprise the audience stood and applauded. She paused, then after a moment, took a step. The music ratcheted up, the beat shaking the room. She wore a long silk skirt with criss-crossing stripes and a long-sleeved blouse. The blouse was utterly impractical, I thought, as it had cloth extensions that hung about two feet down from the cuffs. She sashayed down the runway to the beat, allowing the extensions to drift beside her thighs. Near the end she turned and returned. The flight took no more than 45 seconds before she was gone.

This pattern repeated several dozen times, cameras flashing and her changes between outfits taking less than fifteen seconds. The audience was abuzz during the short gaps. I guessed the show was going well and asked Danaë what she thought.

Before she could answer we saw movement in the back. Timessa was midway down the runway when a man stood near the rear of the room, straightening and pressing himself against the wall. He looked casually left and right. I noticed his baseball cap, red shirt and red glasses: the man I'd seen at Ellsworth. A fashionista, I thought. Of course, that explains the staring. He had been focused on Timessa, not us.

But as I watched, he drew a silver pistol. Before I could react, he dropped into a shooting stance, braced himself and raised the gun toward her.

Although models are not supposed to interact with the audience, she must have been scanning the crowd and seen him move. For us — I refer to the divine — time can stop, as it did at this moment, freezing the gunman in place. Timessa half-crouched, her back straight, and, mimicking Artemis's gesture during her confrontation on Mykonos with Dionysos, languidly lifted her arm and made an odd flicking movement with her fingers.

The shooter jerked briefly, then began to disintegrate, head first, his distinguishable parts turning to a grey mist as they lost form. At the end, what had been a body became a thin haze that hovered in place a quarter second, then vanished.

Time began to move again, and T remained stooped, her arm afloat, pointed toward the back wall. As if this were a theatrical moment, she smiled broadly to the audience, straightened and, on her toes, turned in a slow pirouette before continuing down the ramp. The skirt she wore, a raw silk, floated lightly in an arc as she swirled. The audience again broke into applause, unaware of what had occurred.

I thought: Laine's old move, the pirouette stolen from Gaia herself, one that Timessa would have seen dozens of times.

The show ended minutes later to a version of The Stones's *It's Only Rock 'n' Roll (And I Like It)*. Timessa was brought out for minutes of applause. I was still processing the attempted shooting. Why would anyone want her dead? It made no sense. Reading my thoughts, Danaë whispered, "For the last 40 or 50 years, crazy people have shot celebrities. John Lennon, Reagan, two Kennedys, King, Versace — the list goes on and on."

"But why T?"

"Our shooter isn't available for questioning."

"She's lucky to be alive."

Danaë looked out over the milling crowd. "T is supposed to do a couple sessions for magazines in the next two hours. I wonder how she's holding up."

"She took the adoration like a pro."

"Sure, but who knows. She's inscrutable. And Jackson, she just killed a man."

I couldn't shake the image of his face fragmenting, his chest crumbling in slow motion, his torso losing its shape in a swirl of dust. "Indeed. The gunman chose the wrong celeb to shoot. This must have been the danger she sensed at brunch."

"Talk about a premonition."

"And there's something else —"

Danaë grimaced. "What?"

"No nymph does what she did."

"Jackson, she's far from what she was. I'm not sure what she's become, but she's no more a nymph than Charon is just another boatman. Or Artemis some hot chick."

Was the gunman simply crazy? I would be more comfortable knowing he was an obsessive, a fanatic, another madman unworthy of scrutiny. We might never know, although I hoped we would be able to debrief Timessa before we left, before she was swept away in this alternate world. Danaë interrupted my thoughts. "Look! She's coming!"

Within a moment, working her way through the crowd, T stood before us, her hands loose. "You saw?" she asked.

When we nodded she said, "I can't say much here. But I knew minutes before he stood exactly what would transpire, where he sat, his moves, where my foot would be when he rose, even what he looked like before I saw him —"

"He was at the restaurant this morning."

"Oh. Really?" She paused. "That explains my misgivings. How did you know?"

"Noticed him staring at us after you left. The red glasses and shirt. The hat — he looked like he'd never worn a hat."

"What a strange observation."

"A strange man. I confronted him, asking if we knew him."

"What did he say?"

Danaë interjected. "He never spoke and I dragged Jackson away before it got ugly."

"So," Timessa said, "it's all smoke."

I nodded. Several people came up, asking T questions related to the collection. She was charming and solicitous, quick to laugh and full of praise for the designer. Several celebrities asked for her autograph. After a few minutes, a dark-haired woman walked up, touching Timessa's arm and said, "I'm with the *Vogue* team. Can you get away for the shoot?"

The three of us hugged and Danaë and I wandered out, two hours after the show had begun. Timessa had suggested we meet for a late meal at a small brasserie nearby. With hours before dinner, we decided to tour the Musée d'Orsay a few blocks away. It was across the Seine from the Louvre and we guessed the crowds would be smaller there. But when we arrived, the museum was closed. Danaë sighed at the day's unforeseen twists.

I said, "It's a five-minute walk to the Louvre. It's open late."

"No." She quickly spotted a bench overlooking the river, saying, "There!" We sat together, immediately surrounded by pigeons. I took her hand. A small breeze paralleled the river and the sky was overcast. A man sat on the bank on a blanket nearby, fishing with a long, bent rod. An open wine bottle was beside him and what I guessed were remnants of a sandwich. As we watched, a woman in a summer dress pulled up on a bike, dropped it in the grass and joined him.

"It's all so charming," Danaë said.

"I'm looking forward to getting home. Never wanted to come here. And not charmed now that I am."

"My curmudgeon," she said, leaning over and kissing me.

"Hmm, it's not that. I thought we could leave tomorrow and not look backward. I wanted to liberate those gods. Got more than I bargained for, but I get to claim success."

"And we solved a problem we'd all forgotten about. I remember there were rumors about Dionysos. And nymphs were never allowed near him without Artemis."

"Yes, for a time the world was safe. Until I came along. Then it wasn't once again."

"Call it what you will. I bet he's sorry he crossed my father."

"You mean sorry he scared Poseidon's daughter."

"Well, that too —"

"Yes, never cross a greater god."

She said nothing and I continued, "But Dionysos aside, I need to know whether the man in red was a one-off."

"You can't shadow Timessa forever, you know."

"You're right. I probably need to stop."

"She's doing well. Every girl wants what she's got."

"Artemis now has Orthrus following her in Boston. I'd be thrilled to turn in my badge."

"We'll talk again after dinner. Let's see how she's doing. Besides, I need you at the estate. And our boys need you to set them straight."

"About what?"

"About knowing more than we do. They're at that age ..."

She looked no older than twenty-two, fresh and vibrant. Her beauty was remarkable and the constant stares she drew I found a distraction, although she seemed largely unaware. Excitedly, engaging me as she always did, she said, "We'll make love tonight. Maybe all night. I won't sleep at all because you won't allow it. Guests next door will pound the walls! And then I'll sleep well on the flight back! Okay?"

CHAPTER 20

... rationality is simply mysticism misunderstood.
— Peter Kingsley, *Reality*

Night had fallen an hour before we met T at a small brasserie near her hotel. She looked exhausted but ebullient. I sensed she wanted to avoid discussion about the gunman, so we ate and laughed and recounted her triumphs. Danaë was a perfect foil as she recalled in detail most of the designer's collection, and went on with T about materials and textures, the cut of one of the blouses, how several dressers in the back hurriedly had pinned skirts, how one skirt had almost fallen off twice as she strode the catwalk, and how T wished the entire experience had gone more slowly. I largely tuned out their conversation, occasionally scanning the restaurant's patrons for anything amiss or unusual, then replaying recent events.

At some point I heard Timessa's voice. She said loudly, "Jackson!"

I focused on them, aware I had been thinking of Poseidon and the almost impossible physical presence he projected. I had then drifted to memories of Gaia — how she was so different, a sprite in comparison, yet I knew her to be more powerful than he. As I heard T's voice, I looked over to them. "What?"

T said, "I was telling Danaë that the man was a *σατυρος*, a satyr."

"You lose me entirely. The man in red? The gunman?"

"Yes. Had you ever seen one?"

"A satyr? Never. How would you know?"

"Pointy ears under the hat. A poor disguise. I would know them anywhere. I was almost taken by one a millennium ago, but he was clumsy, kept tripping, couldn't run as fast —"

Danaë tittered. "Don't they have, like, a permanent erection?"

Timessa nodded. "Yes, and massive … well, at least long." She smiled. "Jackson, think of what happened. A damn satyr tried to kill me in a stupid fashion show. What? I assumed they still existed, in woodlands and wild places, what few are left, but they haven't been seen in a thousand years. And then one pops up here, his goat ears tucked away in a hat?"

"I know little about them," I said. "I never took them seriously."

T looked puzzled. "They weren't bright bulbs. Mostly drunks, interested in wine and sex." She paused. "And they always hung with Dionysos."

Danaë cried loudly, "That's it! Can't you see? You raised Dionysos from the dead, then conspired to have him put away."

I said, "You mean, he slept, they slept? He's banished, they mourn?"

"My dance." T mused, "Could the Dionysiakos have raised them, as well?"

"Exactly," Danaë said. "You were the catalyst. He returned, they woke. The lot probably was half-asleep in hidden meadows, stroking themselves, comatose, naughty children awaiting his return."

I smiled in disbelief. "Your theory is that they woke and celebrated when Dionysos was roused on Delos. Then they went into — what? Shock when he was banished?"

Danaë smiled triumphantly. "Yes."

"And now these goat-men are stalking Timessa? Why not go after you? It's your father who ended the fun."

After a pause Timessa said, "No, I think the answer's obvious."

"Really?"

She looked at me. "Yes, really. They wouldn't seek revenge on Danaë.

She's a demi-goddess. Can you imagine Poseidon's rage if she were hurt by a satyr? The sea-god would ferret out each long-eared goat, drowning them one by one like rats until the entire race was purged. No, they've chosen to come after me. I'm just a nymph. I was there. I started it all. And I demanded his end."

Danaë looked at her in disbelief. Timessa smiled softly. "They think I'm easy pickings."

"You're almost always surrounded by friends."

"First, they don't care. And second, that's not true. On the runway I was a target. And away from all this pandemonium, I'm usually by myself."

"Makes sense," I said. "I get it, but I have a question."

T smiled. "I know what it is. You want to know what the hell I did back there."

"Uh-huh. The hand-flick, the disintegrating goat-man. You antici-pated his moves before he moved, froze time, and then turned him into a smudge on the wall."

A waiter stopped at our table, and I ordered more wine. Timessa looked around, over her shoulder, scanning the restaurant. Her paranoia remained high. When she turned back to us, she smiled: no threats.

Danaë asked, "Was he a loner?"

"Impossible to have acted alone," T said. "Satyrs are followers. There have been exceptions, but they're simpletons: wine, woodland music and hanging with maenads. They're happiest half-drunk."

Cutting her off, I said, "Wonderful, we agree a lone satyr who has lived for millennia in some lost glade in Greece can't suddenly acquire transportation to Paris, ID, money to buy food, a handgun in a country where they're almost impossible to acquire, and then maneuver his ugly butt through the bedlam in this city to arrive at *Viva Skirts*."

As we spoke a young woman strode up to the table and pulled out the fourth chair. "May I join you?" *Artemis!* Unsurprisingly, she wore a stylish dress, black with a discreet silver necklace and matching earrings. Artemis looked amused, even buoyant.

Danaë jumped up and hugged her, squealing in pleasure. "You said nothing about coming!"

The increasingly stoic Timessa grinned, half-standing in deference.

As the goddess sat, she said, "I am aware of what happened at the show. And I came immediately. I know who is behind this. And you should, too."

Danaë said, "That was quick."

"Remember," the goddess said, "you left me with Charon. Lovely Mykonos. The sun was shining. Apollo was playing with the twins —" She caught her words. "That is, playing music by the pool."

Danaë laughed. "Of course they were."

Artemis appeared annoyed for a moment, then went on. "We joked about the search for Ares. I did not say so, but I expected the hunt to last months, if not years." She looked at us slowly. "But I was wrong. I've already found him."

"Ares?" I asked. He had appeared on Delos for no more than minutes before disappearing. And left angrily. I continued, "It was raining. He couldn't have left a trail."

"Not a trail," she said. "One does not track a god as if tracking deer."

I raised my hands, surrendering. "Of course —"

"He left Delos and went to Thebes."

Timessa asked, "Our Thebes, in Greece?"

"Not Egypt." She turned to me. "Thebes, Jackson, is northwest of Athens, about an hour drive. It is where Dionysos had his coming-out some three thousand years ago, where the young things by the hundreds left the city to dance with the new wine-god."

"Ancient song and dance."

"The girls were debauched, and dissolute. Euripides," she said, "wrote that the women danced in worship and remained pure and chaste. It wasn't true. The playwright white-washed reality."

Danaë said quietly, "Why would Ares go there?"

The goddess said, "Dionysos had agreed to meet him within two days. A sort of homecoming. Then the word got out that the wine-god would be shoveling horseshit for eternity. But too late — the satyrs were already in drunken celebration anticipating his return. Ares knew but said nothing ...

"Reveling, the satyrs lured forty or fifty local girls to what they called a rave, free rap music, intoxicants, dancing through the night, a local band. Not surprisingly, it worked. They threw a party on the outskirts of the city. It grew larger and larger. Forty or fifty turned to hundreds, all girls.

Then, my sources say, a motorcycle gang decided to bust it open and "rescue" the local girls. By then, as the gang arrived, half the girls were being impaled by the goat-men and the other half were hoping to be …"

"What was Ares doing?" Timessa asked.

"You know he understands only slaughter. As the gang roared up, he encouraged the satyrs to taunt them. In moments one of the satyrs hit the gang's leader with a rock. Another satyr attacked a second biker with a bar. Ares's old battle-frenzy began to boil and he induced all of the satyrs — there were hundreds — to join the assault. The Hell's Angels never had a chance."

Angels. Timessa grimaced. "Angels from Hell who ended up in Hades."

"Yes," the goddess whispered. "No one in the gang survived. Many were sexually assaulted either before or after they were battered down. Satyrs prefer girls, but do not discriminate when lust-mad. Ares's infamous howls echoed through the fields. His love of brutality infected the satyrs; their savagery was remarkable. Machetes were found and given to all the goat-men. Even the bikes were destroyed, hacked apart like the bikers. The nymphs based in the area who witnessed all of this only could report blood. One I interviewed kept repeating as she wept, 'A massacre …' "

Artemis continued. "And the girls who had come for dancing were taken in the fields until the sun rose upon the havoc wrought by Ares and his phallic mercenaries. Only then, in the light, did the girls wander back into Thebes, the dawn exposing their torn clothes and bruised legs, their voices hoarse from song and screams."

None of us spoke. Timessa looked around nervously. "And now?"

"Yes, Ares holds you responsible for the capture of Dionysos. He has recruited the satyrs. And he has turned the hunt from himself to you. That's why I came immediately."

I pushed back my chair and looked at the three. "Did he organize the attack on T?"

The goddess nodded.

"And where is he now?"

"A small town a few hours northeast of here. Charleville-Mézières."

Timessa gasped. "Charleville? I have a friend from Charleville."

Artemis glanced at her. "A friend? You mean the wraith, Kore? The eidolon who emails every day?"

Almost inaudibly T said, "I haven't heard anything from her in a week."

None of this was serendipity; it couldn't be. I picked up my wine glass, and slowly spun it in my fingers. I was drinking a table red and placed the goblet before her face. "Artemis, is Ares's blood this red?"

"He was wounded once in Troy. A warrior, Diomedes, was able to spear him in the gut with Athene's help. Yes, he bled red, but immortal blood."

"You were there?"

"Yes."

"Then I will finish Diomedes's work. Ares should not have been allowed to live."

Danaë choked, "Are you crazy?" She turned to Artemis. "Does Jackson stand a chance?"

"They are evenly matched. Except that Ares loves to inflict suffering, which gives him an immense advantage. Jackson is level-headed, not a desirable quality for a fighter."

"Then he can't do this!"

Artemis smiled. "He won't be alone."

❦

Over an aperitif Artemis asked me how I intended to proceed. I responded, "I don't have the slightest idea. But I won't have him sending crazed satyrs to take out Timessa." When she said nothing, I continued. "Why is Ares in Charleville and not some hotel a block away?"

"Because many years ago a poet named Arthur Rimbaud was raised there. The irrational — and I am speaking of Ares — are always attracted to the irrational. And Rimbaud was brilliantly senseless, a deranged and troubled boy. His spirit hovers over the *commune* even today. There is a sad little museum or two in his name. The city is the perfect hangout for Ares. Or so he thinks."

"Will he follow if we change locations?"

"His satyrs will find T wherever she goes."

"Then we need to hide her."

Danaë said, "You and I can shift shapes, look like whatever we want. But Timessa?"

T said, "I can take care of myself."

Artemis laughed gently. "Next time they attack it may be three satyrs or thirty. Like any sentient being, they will learn and adjust. What happened at the show came as a surprise: your self-defense was unexpected. That satyr was one of the most savvy. No one dreamed you could defend yourself."

Timessa again scanned the restaurant. Then she looked at Artemis. "But I was not surprised. At first, hours before, I had a premonition. Then minutes before the attack, even before I'd begun to walk the runway, I knew exactly what would occur. Exactly what he looked like, how he was dressed, what he would do — "

The goddess said, "And did you know what *you* would do?"

"No, but I had no concern."

She shook her head. "You cannot depend on that. Not sufficient. What if your magic goes missing next time? You must defend yourself by knowing each move before you employ it, not count on spontaneity."

They argued for some time, with Danaë casting concerned looks at me all the while. I knew she doubted my ability to take on Ares. And I knew she was logically correct. He had thousands of years of war strategizing, of inducing frenzy and fear, while I had none.

What had I done daring in my life? Disappeared a few acorns from under Laine's nose and pulled off financial coups that made me rich. I could change appearances at will, heal injuries, make objects disappear … but I had never killed a man, let alone a god. In my bravado I was proposing to take on one of history's most brutal warriors. And, as I reminded myself, Ares was also divine.

Artemis turned from Timessa to me, saying, "You are so transparent, Jackson."

"I have tried to be tonight."

"Have you forgotten what you know, what you did in the amphitheatre?"

Of course I hadn't forgotten the trial. It was the tribe's final test of my own supposed divinity. In it I had discovered a latent power: I could effortlessly vanish beings at will. They could be ported to another location. Or, I understood with growing confidence, atomized and forever extinguished. Even Artemis, who had staged the event, was surprised at the revelation on that distant afternoon.

Now I looked at her carefully; we understood each other. "I have hardly forgotten, Artemis."

"Am I, Jackson, immortal?"

"Yes, or as you sometimes correct me, a-mortal."

She smiled. "As is Ares. And did you not make me disappear?"

As I nodded she continued. "And my ingenious jury of a dozen primordial birds? Did you not extinguish them one by one?"

I understood. I didn't need to have thousands of years of war experience, nor wrath and bloodlust overwhelming my senses. I simply needed to face off with him so I could disappear him as I wished. "Does Ares know?"

"About your power? Only rumors, gossip, what little news might have filtered down to Delos as they slept."

"And —?"

"He views you as an amateur, a pretender."

"So he's unaware."

"Largely. If he hears you seek to destroy him, he will relish the fight. And expect swords. Or spears. Or acid thrown in your eyes. Blood and battle, hand-to-hand combat. Something savage, barbarous. Broken skulls, shattered vertebrae. A fight that justifies one of you destroying the other. Or specifically, a short brawl at which Ares destroys the lamb."

Danaë whispered, "Jackson need only vanish Ares?"

The goddess cocked her head. "Yes, and send his atoms to the Pleiades, or to the sun, or across the sands of all the deserts on the earth. Into the stratosphere. Or into the fiery magma of any volcano that awaits a sacrifice."

"I keep forgetting the immortal," Danaë said, "are a-mortal."

Artemis said. "He will not anticipate Jackson's skill. No god has Jackson's power, and it will come as a shock if he is stupid enough to face off."

CHAPTER 21

Same as it ever was.
Same as it ever was.
— David Byrne, *Talking Heads*

My focus shifted from stopping Ares to protecting Timessa and me. Timessa could not return to Boston; the satyrs would follow her everywhere, and regardless of her self-confidence, she was their primary target.

Artemis agreed to remain with us through the crisis. And that night, staying late at the brasserie, I outlined what seemed a logical plan. The plan required flexibility. There were moving targets and unknowns. A broad outline was appropriate — specific details would be impossible. I wanted everyone to be supple, adaptable. Hell, we didn't even know the number of satyrs Ares might employ at the next attack. Nor their appearance. As Artemis emphasized, we never again would be confronted by a man in red glasses.

And Ares would hardly remain in Charleville-Mézières. His next moves would remain a mystery until they were not. We had no insights. Consequently, I was convinced we had to hit the beast on the head, which entailed finding the war-god before he found us. I would never forget his face. The brief view I had on Delos was enough. Yet, like the satyrs, if hunted, he would be disguised: a truck driver, or a professional with a polished demeanor, or a bureaucrat. Our only hope was to find him before he comprehended what he faced.

Artemis would not reveal how she had discovered his location. Timessa probably came closest to knowing when she asked, "Is one of the satyrs an informer, someone you've turned?"

The goddess looked amazed, although I knew she was faking her reaction. "You expect me to admit there is a traitor in their midst?"

In reality, how she obtained her information mattered far less than what she knew. And she quickly agreed when I suggested we drive the next morning to Charleville-Mézières. "Of course," she said. "I know the street. And how he dresses. Where he eats. And the number of satyrs work as guards."

Danaë seemed the least confident of us, wondering if there wasn't another way.

Reassuring her I said, "I'm considering something less than a confrontation. Think of the slaughter in Thebes days ago. Ares incited the minions. If he did so again, we'd see half of Charleville destroyed. But in Thebes, he had time to plan."

"Continue —"

"My thoughts are more … subterranean. Imagine seeing Ares leaning in the shadow of a café, perhaps smoking, squinting as he observes his surroundings and waits on his food. And imagine, in a mere second, seeing his entirety, the eyes in his face, his arms disperse as no more than dust, the soot swirling in a ray of sun. Then even the dust vanishes. All of this happens too quickly for him to grasp the event. And in that moment, his existence ends."

"Imagining it and executing it," Danaë said, "may prove to be different."

"You say Rimbaud scribbled poems there," I said. "Charleville may become the epicenter of celebrated verses once again."

Danaë hugged me, refusing to let go. Then she looked up, saying quietly, "You almost sound arrogant. Confidence is good, but be careful; we have a thousand warnings about conceit."

The next morning we met in the lobby of the Hilton. I refused to let Timessa return to her hotel and found a second room down the hall from us; Artemis agreed to stay with her. Danaë's promised night of love-making did not occur.

I entered the Charleville address in my phone's navigation. The satellite image showed a large apartment building on Rue d'Alsace. As I repeated the address to Artemis for confirmation, Timessa said, "What did you call the street?"

"Rue d'Alsace."

"Kore's city. Her exact street address."

Artemis said, "Of course. We should have known."

I pulled into traffic. We were just over two hours out, presuming traffic was normal. Most of the drive was countryside, except Gare de Reims, a dense city that the old roads would not allow us to bypass. The day was cool. A thin haze, probably from local industry, overlay the unsettled sky. Our conversations were perfunctory and after a half hour of driving, we settled into long silences.

At one point I looked to Artemis. "We know he's in Charleville today?"

She nodded. Danaë reached for my hand and whispered, "Perhaps we shouldn't have all come."

Artemis looked unconcerned. "We'll be disguised."

"As what?"

She said nothing. Timessa, who was beside the goddess in the back-seat, said, "I'd like to be disguised as a goddess. A love goddess. Perhaps Aphrodite for the afternoon."

Artemis laughed. "Then I'll make it so. A love-goddess for the afternoon."

Timessa grinned, saying, "Though it's not appropriate."

Danaë laughed. "The endless trials of a virgin."

Timessa nodded. I remember her crossing her arms, looking out over the farms and muttering, "... *les fermes.*" As we approached Charleville, navigation took us off the A34 onto the N43 and then to the D16 which paralleled La Meuse, a turgid river beside the city. Within minutes we bore hard left and slowed, heading into the small downtown. Artemis said, "Rue d'Alsace is several blocks north. I won't know where he is for some time. We will find an eatery and wait."

After we drove through the city somewhat aimlessly, she pointed to a small restaurant. Amusingly it was called Resto Snack du Mont Olympe. It was cheap and seemed to specialize in Belgian-American. We had coffee and salads, and after a short time, Artemis stood and walked out, saying she would return.

She reappeared after twenty minutes and said, "He is at 22 Avenue d'Arche. An Italian restaurant called La Storia, a five-minute drive from here. He rarely leaves. We can take our time."

Timessa smiled, turning to me. "Do you know of the grand affair between Ares and Aphrodite?"

I admitted I didn't. Much of what I knew about their past came from Chloé, Laine's sister and one of the Fates. That Ares had ever had a lover surprised me.

"That was like a million years ago," Timessa began. "All the nymphs were almost envious, not that Aphrodite was cavorting with the war-god, but that they were both so beautiful. It was like watching A-list celebrities. All of us wanted *news*. We hung on every rumor —!"

Danaë noted that throughout the affair, Aphrodite had been married to Hephaistos, whom she'd made a cuckold, and that the affair had gone on for years. It ended when Helios, the sun god, who'd seen the lovers lying in grasses by the sea as he passed overhead, told Hephaistos.

Danaë said that Aphrodite had had no offspring by Hephaistos, but two sons had resulted from her affair with Ares. They had been named Phobos and Deimos. "In English," she said, "the names translate as Terror and Fear. They served as Ares's wingmen on the battlefield, inciting dread when they darted, screeching like rabid bats over the clashing troops."

Timessa added that Ares was once dashing, even charismatic, and that Aphrodite had been willing to ignore his ignoble rage. "But now," she said, "he's universally despised. Surely Aphrodite regrets it all."

"What was her attraction to Hephaistos?" I asked. "They were such opposites —"

"Aphrodite is an omnivore," Danaë reminded me. "Men, women, girls, boys, the pure and the prostitute. She has an utterly open mind.

What repels you means little to her. As she told me once, she sees the grace, even the glamour, in all."

We saw too little of Aphrodite. Her grand visits were occasional, at best. Her appearance at the estate was in the previous fall, when she was on break from sailing her yacht. She had given her crew time off, and she seemed eager to reconnect, particularly with Danaë and our boys.

The goddess frequently declined my regular invitations; she owned discrete mansions in a half dozen countries, all staffed by lovely girls and young men. Her wealth was immense, and she used the earth as a play-ground. Of all the gods and goddesses, she had survived with grace and — I use the term carefully — light-footedness.

I wondered out loud if she had any lingering affection for Ares. He had, after all, fathered her sons. If so I would not willingly incur her wrath. Artemis assured me she did not. "Their affair was an ancient fling, something that took place before and during Troy. But the end of the ten-year battle ended it all. Remember I told you Diomedes wounded Ares —"

"Yes. With Athene's help."

"When Diomedes's spear got Ares in the gut, he whined and howled. Some men when they are speared rise and fight on; others, cowards in their hearts, fall to the ground, mewling like wounded birds. We were shocked to see Ares cower and then flee the battlefield."

She paused as if to sharpen her words. "He fled to Olympus to complain to Zeus. Even his father despised his whining, calling him a pestilence and the most hated of his children."

Danaë pushed me playfully. "No woman likes a coward who masquerades as fearsome. Ares always prevailed because he was a god and could dominate armies as he wished. But after Troy, we knew his heart. He'd been exposed."

"That battle unmasked him to Aphrodite," Artemis said. "A coward exposed is a coward forever. Diomedes actually wounded Aphrodite first, and she called for her lover's help. Ares swept in, the faux hero, unaware that Athene had placed a protective mist over Diomedes …

"Regardless, when Aphrodite saw Ares wounded, falling to his knees and howling, she felt disgust, contempt. Her loathing doubled when Ares fled to Olympus. All of us who watched were swept with nausea."

"And I assume," I said, "his conduct ended their affair."

Artemis nodded. "Romance withers before disgust."

"Does she know," I asked, "of our discovery on Delos?"

She said no, that his release was not good news and that she, Artemis, would rather resolve the current animus before telling everyone. As our conversation trailed off, Artemis looked at us all and said, "Now, disguises?" She took Danaë's hand, kissing the back lightly. "You, beauty, will become a child, a girl of eight or nine, long hair, sassy dress, blue eyes."

Danaë nodded. "Will I have bathed?"

"Yes, silly, you have wealthy parents who believe you are studying like a good girl at *la bibliothèque municipale*."

Artemis smiled, turning to me. "My warrior," she said. "and our grave executioner."

"Not brave?"

She looked me up and down. "You will be Danaë's playmate, a boy of ten, soiled clothes from a morning of romping in the fields. I prefer a dull face, Jackson, nothing noteworthy. You will be our street kid and Danaë's favorite ruffian, the boy she steals away with at every chance, even at her young age —

"And Timessa … You will be yourself, a delicious decoy. You hardly need to change a thing. I do want you in a dress. Gods, like men, are easily seduced by silk. And an uplifted bosom. There's a small couturier nearby, a startup by a girl just out of school. We will see what she can do."

"And what is my role?" Timessa sniffed.

"Is it not obvious? I want Ares to be inflamed with unquenchable desire. He will recognize you instantly. And in his vast confusion at your unexpected appearance, want at the same moment to both take you and destroy you."

"Won't his satyrs see me as well?"

"All of them will be in shock. The quarry will have come to them. It will appear an impossibility. In their minds the hunt is covert, something known only to them and Ares.

"But you are not to worry. As you lure Ares from his grotto on the Avenue d'Arche, inflamed as he will be, our dirty ten-year-old will release Danaë's hand, which he always holds, and with one of his tricks take Ares out."

I marveled at her plan, only half understanding what she envisioned.

Danaë and I were to be kids. And Timessa a ripened fruit, a siren in the ancient sense. I thought of the ironies — she was a virgin and Ares a pretender on many levels as he was neither a man nor hero-god.

Danaë wrinkled her nose and I knew what would follow. In a small, multicolor flash, she became a girl of nine, her long hair tumbling over her shoulders, a blue pinafore over her white blouse, eyes sparkling at her own audacity. She looked mischievous and said, "Now you, Jackson."

In turn I shifted to Artemis's boy, my jeans and shirt streaked with dirt, my face unwashed. I ran stubby fingers through a head of long hair, then reached over and took a handful of Danaë's tresses, pulling hard. She squealed and Artemis said, "Jackson, be nice!"

I nodded obediently and leaned toward Danaë, saying, "You're such a little girl. Yuck. I guess some day you'll grow up and look like her —" I pointed accusingly at Timessa. "Double yuck!"

Danaë grabbed both my arms, wrestling with me until Artemis cried again, "Kids!"

CHAPTER 22

The truth is always repulsive;
it contradicts your prejudices and conceits.
—Bill Bonner, *author and columnist*

The couturier Artemis had referenced during lunch had a shop a block and a half from Avenue d'Arche, and as Artemis tugged her two kids and Timessa through the front door, the owner smiled. She appeared to be Timessa's age. "New faces. How do you know of my boutique?"

"Oh your reputation grows," Artemis said. She turned and pulled Timessa forward. "My friend needs a dress, something sensual, something that will slay any man who sees her walk, perhaps cause heart attacks when the wind picks up and lifts her petticoats."

"Oh my," the young woman said, "that's quite the request. My dresses mostly are custom-made. You need something immediately?"

Artemis nodded. "She must walk out of here transformed."

"I'm not sure what I have. Perhaps a bit of this and that —" She gestured to Timessa to follow, and they walked to the back. Danaë and I plunked down in antique chairs in the front, making faces. Artemis looked around, preoccupied. She came over to us — we were by now sweetly holding hands — and knelt.

"Jackson, listen carefully. Shortly we will stroll by the restaurant where Ares sits. He is dressed like a banker, in a suit and vest. When you pass the front window, you will see him sitting inside. You will not react and he will ignore you entirely."

"And then?"

"Timessa will be behind you five or six paces. You and Danaë will continue to the corner of the restaurant, stop, turn and await the beautiful girl."

I grimaced, wiggling in my chair and making a face. "You're always ordering me around!"

Danaë pouted, twisting her hair in one hand and nodding her head. We were a team.

Artemis frowned. "Now, listen carefully to what I say. And neither of you is to argue, do you understand? Or I will have to send you home."

We nodded reluctantly. I had been considering kissing Danaë for some minutes, but was certain that a ten-year-old would never kiss a girl. Artemis's admonitions were distracting and I was sure there was still some cunning plan that would allow me to get my hands on the girl beside me. Probably pulling her hair again was easiest, and I knew she would squeal satisfyingly if I did.

Artemis took my arm and said, "Jackson, no! You are thinking like a ten-year-old! You are *not* a boy …" Then she took Danaë's hand. "And *you* must stop distracting him! I need dull and boring children. Perhaps you should hate each other like siblings. However you do it, I need Jackson to be Jackson except in looks."

She was whispering but with great intensity. I pulled myself back from childhood and looked at Danaë: she was a pretty, flat-chested child, someone's half-grown daughter, a schoolgirl in a nameless town. How could she be so alluring?

Artemis continued, her eyes locked on mine. "Focus, Jackson. You will have walked past Ares, maybe even looked into his face. He will appear irritated but will otherwise ignore you. In fifteen feet you will stop, turn and wait on the seductive Timessa to catch up, understand?"

"Yes. What else?"

"If men are loitering around the restaurant's door, they will be his guards, satyrs in today's clothing. Ignore them, even if they taunt you as you pass. Any action on your part will be in error. Just make a face and get by them as you would if you were ten …

"Ares will stand in shock when he sees Timessa. Any man would notice her, but he will be astonished. His prey, through the window only feet away. And looking like Aphrodite. Expect him to rush from the restaurant. When they are face to face, she will say something like, 'Oh Ares, you handsome man,' which will shock him further.

"But then his suspicions will intercede. He will corner her, and the satyrs will, as well. And if you were not there, she would be seized in public, on the street, her lovely dress and underthings torn away. Then when they were finished assaulting her, she would be tortured unhurriedly — satyrs are not satisfied unless their victims suffer grievously — then erased, perhaps dismembered, in the open street, all as revenge for Dionysos's loss."

"You say, 'If I were not there,' but I will be. What am I to do?"

"If I were not clarifying each move, if you knew nothing about the participants and witnessed this outrage on some street, what would you do?"

"Something damned cruel …"

"Go on …"

"First, I'd blind them."

"But they would fight on, Jackson."

"I'd disappear their arms."

She cocked her head. "No arms? I *am* surprised."

"They would be holding her or tearing at her clothes and that would leave them helpless — blind and armless bullies whose actions backfired one sunny afternoon."

Artemis looked at me thoughtfully. "Would that not take longer than merely vanishing them all at once?"

"Yes, but we both recognize the pleasure I'd get from prolonging their pain. A reflection on me and a touch monstrous, isn't it? And yes, I surprise myself."

Danaë, the little girl sitting beside me, still twisting her hair with one hand, giggled. "Or you could vanish their heads. Hmm. Or if you vanished just their feet, they'd topple over. But they could still crawl on their knees, so you'd have to vanish their legs. Then nothing would be left but satyr trunks." She grinned delightedly. "Probably easiest to take off their heads. I'd clap watching them stumble around!"

Artemis stood, looking at us both. "Children, I have read you too many fairy tales. Look at the result! What am I to do with you —?"

As she spoke to us in gentle admonition — and apparent admiration — the couturier stepped out. "Your children are so well-behaved."

"At times they act more like American brats than well-behaved little ones."

Smiling, the young woman said, "I've done my best. There's been no time, but come show off what we've done!"

Shyly, Timessa entered. She wore a dress with layers of filmy, russet-colored material that cascaded down her thighs and ended above her knees. The dress's transparency began with a lace V cut in a soft curve above her breasts. The couturier brought her hands together as in prayer, and said, "Sheer organza layered, as you see, over a dark bustier. Why the bustier? We needed to enhance her breasts somewhat —"

The dress was cinched with a wide silk belt at her waist. The transparent material made her black panties unmistakable.

My reaction was that her pale skin contrasted troublingly with her dress. I say that as a compliment, and I understood for the first time why she had become an instant sensation. She spun left, slowly, in a half-crescent, arms half out, a faint smile on her lips, then returned to the right as slowly and elegantly. Seeing Artemis's reaction, she rolled her eyes and sighed.

The couturier said, "Rarely do women I dress reach this — what shall I say? — perfection of body. Add her beauty and I am able to present a woman who will 'slay any man' who sees her. How much is due to my artistry is debatable."

Timessa's smile dimmed. She said quietly, "Really, Goddess. And you still wonder why I left —" She lifted the hem of the dress above her thighs, throwing it in front of her in dismissal. "Certainly not to become 'a delicious decoy.' This better fucking work."

I noticed that behind Timessa, the couturier was smiling. I could imagine her thinking, *Girls*.

❧

After Artemis handsomely rewarded the couturier, the four of us stepped into the street. Immediately a man driving a sedan slowed and whistled. Timessa seemed oblivious, simply walking north toward Avenue d'Arche, the rest of us steps behind her. After less than a minute, Artemis said, "We turn to the right, and then our destination is a half block down. You'll see the sign, La Storia. From this moment on, we execute."

As a group we turned right — Timessa, a supermodel, Artemis and two children. Artemis stopped us, looking around briefly, then took a hoodie from her backpack, and pulled it on. She scanned the street again, and sunk her head into the shadows of the hood. I knew her eyes but to the casual observer, she would appear an enigma.

I held Danaë's hand tightly. It felt odd walking as a ten-year-old in the streets of an unknown city, and even stranger holding a young girl's hand, feeling her excitement.

Artemis glanced down at me as if she read my mind. Her finger went to her lips: *hush*. She then tapped Timessa's shoulder and nodded. The girl looked up the street and began her self-conscious walk. As we passed a traffic light, a man in a stopped car repeated the earlier reaction, lowering his window and crying, "Hey, *bébé!*" This time Timessa turned her head and smiled languidly toward the car. She was now into her role, a man-slayer, *la fille*.

Just ahead, I saw three men lounging by a doorway. A sign hung over-head but the letters were too small to read. One of the men wore a starched white shirt and all wore hats. We were less than sixty feet away. Artemis looked at me and said, *Yes*.

The lettering on the sign became apparent: La Storia. Leaping fish bookended the letters. I noticed the restaurant's front was a bank of early century ceiling-to-floor windows. One of the men turned and looked at us. Artemis whispered, "As far as I go," and stopped to lean against a building's facade. Who and what she was was inscrutable at thirty feet.

Danaë and I, a nine and ten-year-old, proceeded, slowing impercep-tibly as we got closer to the men. Timessa drifted behind us, probably some fifteen feet. The man closest to us snickered and stepped into the center of the sidewalk, facing us. I gripped Danaë's hand and walked into the street and around him. He slurred, "Is she good in bed, little man?"

Had I been ten I would have puzzled over the barb, although his voice was insulting. Instead, I fought my impulse to retaliate. The other men laughed crudely. We continued walking by the restaurant, pretending to be oblivious.

Then the men noticed Timessa.

She sauntered in a straight line toward them. The man who had blocked me remained immobile. The white-shirt stepped behind him, staring. And the third man wolf-whistled, shaking his head. One of them muttered, "La-la-*laaa*." She was no more than ten feet from them.

Simultaneously, Danaë and I walked by Ares, who sat inside by the front windows. He was unmistakable, slouched sideways in a chair smoking a Gauloises in an ivory holder. His eyes were snake-like, golden and insensible. His face appeared sunburned. As Artemis had predicted, he was dressed like an accountant, a banker in a banker's uniform. I glanced at him and then away. He barely looked at us. *Children.* At the corner of the restaurant we stopped and turned to face Timessa.

She straight-lined into the three men as if they did not exist. The first, the larger man blocking the sidewalk, reached for her and as he did, she rammed her fist into his nose and he reeled back, cursing. His hat fell off, exposing pointed ears. The white-shirt clutched at her as well and she drove her knee into his groin, doubling him over. She wore four-inch high heels and ground one into the side of his head. The third man backed against the entrance and out of her way. She continued her sashay down the sidewalk, pausing only to glance inside the windows for Ares.

When he saw her, he pushed chairs over, shouldering aside a waiter and running to the door. He shoved aside the third man, jumped over the white-shirt who lay crumbled on the sidewalk and shouted, "Stop!" She did so, but her slowing was that of a leopard approaching its prey. Her face was placid, expectant. He opened his hands as if to take her shoulders and simultaneously ordered, "Surround her!"

Several men in hats tumbled out of the restaurant; she was instantly encircled. Danaë and I stood only feet away, ignored in the bedlam. To my delight, T turned and for a split second caught my eye and smiled. Her face was luminescent. Then she wheeled back to Ares, saying softly, "Monsieur Ares, you look handsome in that fancy suit."

He looked startled, confused by her serenity, shocked that he'd been recognized. She cooed, "And to find you here!"

"Timessa?"

She whispered, "Of course."

"Why are you in Charleville?"

"To ask a question … Monsieur," she said, her voice vibrating, "was it you who sent that man to shoot me at the Paris show?"

His eyes darted back and forth; he was oblivious to the danger encircling him, the ring we had set. He stepped back, looking at her sidelong. "You *are* on my most wanted list."

Timessa said calmly, "I've always wanted to be wanted. I thought maybe waking Dionysos would be enough. You know, to turn a couple heads. But after I danced the Dionysiakos, he just wanted sex —"

Ares looked at her carefully. His face softened and he said, "Your beauty nears Aphrodite's." He stepped closer and grabbed a strap on her dress. His last words, spoken as she smirked, were, "And underneath this dress?"

As he began to pull the strap and Timessa instinctively backed away, I stepped forward, shedding the visage of a boy. I took a sharp breath and without hesitation vanished Ares, the glorious war-god, with a single thought. The impression his fingers had left above her bustier disappeared. The entirety of Ares dematerialized in a soft *whoosh*. The torn strap hung loosely at her arm.

I sent his atoms spiraling upward in an invisible column, a reversed tornado that raked the cloud cover at 10,000 feet, spilling his spinning electrons into the frozen crystals, into the pollutants suspended in the thin mantle above Charleville.

The satyrs panicked, looking around. Ares had disappeared. One satyr behind Timessa tried to wrestle her to the pavement. Impatient to be done with his stooges, I vanished the satyr's arms and head; he staggered behind her, slumping to his knees and fell forward. She turned and kicked the satyr's trunk to the side.

Another satyr grabbed her, taking a fistful of dress. Before I could act she flicked her fingers in the same odd gesture I had seen in Paris. He jerked and, simultaneously, disintegrated headfirst, fragmenting downward into pebble-sized bits.

With Timessa still under attack, we destroyed another satyr who partially vanished and partially fractured with an eerie howl as he stumbled toward us.

She looked around, saying in a husky voice, "There will be more. Can't be that easy —"

The door of a building across from us opened and about a dozen satyrs stumbled into the street, squinting against the sun. They crossed toward us like bees from a rattled hive. They had abandoned their hats and disguises. A number were without clothes, their erections obscene. And their tails, hissing as they ran, swung side to side.

Artemis, who I'd momentarily forgotten, stepped onto the sidewalk. She pulled her hood down and her eyes shone. In a quick gesture, she circled her arm overhead as if stirring a galaxy of stars.

The satyrs slowed to a crawl, jerking and lurching in the electrical field that now surrounded them. Howling in pain, they struggled against Artemis's assault. Their skin burst into flame, their tails twitching and fingers melted in the streamer arcs that jumped from one to another.

Impatient, irritated with my own pleasure at the sight, I vanished them as a whole, dispersing their essence as if it were a thin industrial exhaust, letting the wind carry their dust toward the Alsace and the mighty Rhine, washing all evidence of these woodland gods from the city pavement and the cobbled sidewalks.

The skirmish had taken less than a minute. I noted that Avenue d'Arche was oddly empty — no cars or people. I looked into the restaurant; it was deserted. Timessa said, "I made sure anyone within sight or hearing was relocated. Simpler than having to make explanations."

Artemis stepped beside us. "Fifteen satyrs down, one major god. No one since the Fates has openly killed one of us … Congratulations. Jackson, is he really gone?"

"Scattered to the heavens." I paused. "Given the winds up there, his atoms probably are over Tibet by now."

Timessa bent and pulled off her heels, throwing both shoes down the road as if they were stones. "I hate heels," she said. "I'd do the same with this dress but I do love its swish." She seemed unperturbed, even tranquil. When I caught her eye, she said, "Another day in paradise."

"If that, then a fool's."

I found myself trembling and turned to Danaë. She still stood where we had stopped, but, during the brief confrontation, had shifted back to herself. The little girl was gone, replaced by the demi-goddess I loved.

Looking happily at us all, she said, "Let's get out of here."

CHAPTER 23

Yes yes I do. Have the right to be this lush and never ending.
—Nayyirah Waheed, *poet*

With Ares and Dionysos gone, any remaining satyrs (and we assumed many survived, even if not in Charleville), were without a master. Artemis confirmed they would eventually meander back to the ancient woodlands they had populated for millennia. Further assaults against Timessa were improbable, particularly once the word spread about the brief melee.

Artemis was adamant that we inspect Ares's place at Rue d'Alsace. "It's probably a shambles. He was there only a couple days. But we have to know —"

She looked at Timessa and me, waiting, and I volunteered. Danaë quickly protested, saying, "He shouldn't go alone. There may be more."

The goddess just smiled. "Unlikely, but Jackson seems quite capable. You and I, beauty, have to return to the estate. We're done here."

Danaë said, "I'd rather return together."

"You and Jackson? He can follow shortly." She turned to Timessa and said, "And I suggest, given I can no longer order you around, that you make yourself useful. Help check Ares's apartment. You and Jackson. It won't take long. Everything needs to happen quickly."

"Then?"

"Then the two of you return."

Danaë frowned. I knew she was less than pleased. We looked at each other and I said with conviction, "I'll be fine." Then blocking everyone else, she said silently, *When you're back we'll celebrate ...*

The four of us ate a late lunch in a small Charleville brasserie a block from La Storia. Timessa had retrieved her shoes and Artemis gave her the hoodie to wear over her dress. Everything seemed routine. Anyone watching us would never guess the earlier events. Even T was charming at times, falling into her old role as Danaë's lifelong friend.

Our reverie was interrupted by Artemis, who said, "We cannot leave today without discussing Kore."

Timessa seemed startled. "Kore?"

"Yes, she has not appeared throughout this trip. Given she was your shadow for weeks in Boston, I remain concerned."

"It's been a relief. I haven't given her a thought."

"Perhaps," the goddess intoned, "she simply has been lying low. Do you normally sense her presence when she is near?"

Timessa paused. "I've seen her only once, outside that cafe in Cambridge where we met. That was after you'd left with Filly. And no, I had no premonitions, sensed nothing beforehand. Then or now."

"Then, she is able to mask herself," Artemis said. "Which means she could be here. Or in Mykonos. Or Delos. Or Istanbul, if you were to end up there."

I said, "Delos? There were voices of gods, but nothing else."

"Means nothing, Jackson. If she can screen herself from Timessa, who has acquired unusual senses, she can hide from all of us."

I thought of my ability and Danaë's to change appearance. And to block our thoughts selectively, even from the goddess's probing. We could do so without her awareness. We were adept at what we sometimes jokingly called obscuration. Danaë might say to me, wrestling in bed, "No obscuration, Jackson. You're not to hide from *me!*" If we could masquerade, I had to assume Kore, who remained a mystery to us all, could do so, as well.

I said, "So we assume she's been watching. Or following. Or what-

ever. But if so, she's not interfered. Or appeared. I'll take an uninvolved
Kore any day."

Timessa shrugged. "I'm not worried."

Artemis smiled warily. "There will just be the two of you at the apartment. Be alert. We know so little about who this even is. None of us
senses any remaining satyrs — and if they were here, we would know. I
cannot say the same about our eidolon." Timessa twisted a handful of
her hair back and forth. The goddess said, "Even the name Kore is a
fabrication."

I asked, "Isn't it a girl's name?"

She looked at me. "Jackson, it is a generic name for a maiden.
Ancient Greek. No girl was ever named Kore. Calling a girl Kore, would
be like calling a dog Dog. Or if you had a daughter, naming her Girl. It is
not done. It is a descriptive noun, not a name."

Danaë interjected, "It's got to be a clue to call herself that. She's
sending a signal. We assume she's not one of us, but if so, why use
Greek?"

Timessa grimaced. "She could be less than we imagine, a human girl
with a weird name."

I stood. "Okay, T and I will poke around d'Alsace —"

Ares's apartment was on the west side of Rue d'Alsace close to the river,
looking over the Passerelle Bayard. As we stood in the street looking at
the old grey building, I sighed. Artemis and Danaë had left. Ares was
gone forever. But Kore — or whoever she was — could be anywhere. I
found it incredible that she could be here. She'd been left in Boston, as
had Orthrus. I was certain of it. But everything in the last week had been
fantastical. Why not this?

I scanned the windows of the building and Timessa said, "Second
floor. Probably that bank of windows there —" She pointed to a corner
suite. A piece of stained glass hung in an end window, a square with rays
of the sun radiating in an arc of yellow and red rectangles. I thought,
Dawn.

"But," she said, "I don't sense anyone."

"As you shouldn't. Come on, we'll take the stairs."

Like much of Charleville, the building itself was dreary, the stairwell walls faded and the railing as old as the building. We took the steps methodically, cautiously. I stopped several steps before the second floor and T almost ran into me. "Sorry," I said. "I'm trying to decide how we do this. Do I knock on the door? Do I leave you waiting down the hall?"

I looked at her. She was in the same dress, the layers of organza cascading stiffly down her thighs. Even in the dim light the smudge of her panties was evident. The hoodie was draped loosely over her shoulders.

She looked at me looking at her and said, "What?"

I said, "The dress. Genuinely distracting."

"Oh." The lace V above her breasts pointed toward the dark bustier the couturier had said was so critical. I remembered something about it lifting her breasts. Her hair was uncombed and her cheeks flush.

She said, "I can be tempting to any other man, but not to you."

"Okay, I'll pretend there are no provocative girls within a quarter mile. Thank Zeus for little things."

She thumped my chest and whispered, "Once all I wanted was for you to touch me. But that was then. Years ago. You were good and treated me honorably. Don't get all weird on me now."

We stared at each other a moment. I nodded, "Whatever happens, take care of that dress. It's a keeper." She giggled. "Now, follow me. I'll knock. No beating down doors. When arriving anywhere unexpectedly, it's always good to be polite."

The apartment was several doors down to our right. Standing before it I felt no sense of any living thing. The building was silent. Timessa whispered, "Wrong, we're not alone. I sense something. Someone's inside."

I heard music, almost unnoticeable but definite. It rose slightly, then became inaudible, then audible again. An Italian song from the 1950s. I recognized it as one my father would turn up loudly when he was working in his hanger. I heard *Roma* and *amore*. *Bambino*. Timessa nudged me, saying, "Go on, knock."

I tapped twice. When there was no reaction, I knocked again, harder. Then we heard the knob as it slowly turned from the other side. As the door opened we faced a girl, tall, sun-bleached hair parted down the middle and uncombed, much like Timessa's. She held multiple white lilies before her face, hiding, each flower with an orange stigma crowning its swollen pistil — its extended ovary — that thrust gaudily through its center. She watched us in silence, concealed behind the fat, waxen petals. The music abruptly ended.

I wasn't sure whether to speak French or English. Timessa quickly stepped forward and said in English, "Hello. I know you don't know us, but I'm Timessa and this is —"

Cutting her off, the girl said sharply, "Quite a vulgar entrance for immortals. I was hoping for a flash of light, a bit of thunder. Doesn't matter, I suppose."

As she lowered the lilies to her chest, I knew instantly: Kore. Same high cheeks and thin nose. Timessa gasped, frozen in the hall beside me. Kore reached out to her, saying, "Both of you come in —" but T stepped away, avoiding her touch.

Kore swung the door wide and half-bowed, turning the gesture into a curtsy, the lilies swung low behind her back. "I mean it. No hard feelings. No one here but me."

Without thought I put my arm around T's shoulder and steered her into the room as Kore stepped back. The girl whispered, "Where I come from we always welcome strangers. One never knows if a stranger might be a god disguised."

She wore jeans and a crop top, her belly exposed, the straps of the top an odd iridescent pink. Her bare feet were as dirty as if she had been out running in the streets. She motioned for us to sit and said, "We'll talk. Can I get you anything?"

Timessa shook her head, unable to look away. I steered her to a couch and we sat. I noticed the stained glass sunrise in the corner window. Kore said, "Let's play nice. I'm far less than you've made me out to be."

I wondered if Artemis had known what we'd find. Our discussion at lunch had been too apt. Then, I thought, she may have simply wanted to warn us that anything was possible. Kore sat across from us in a chair, one leg tucked under the other, one dirty foot exposed. She smiled, fiddling with the lilies in her hand.

The apartment was furnished pleasantly. To my surprise I noted stylish blinds, bookshelves with numerous volumes, a small table, lamps, cushions, several plants and a number of paintings which, to my untrained eye, appeared original. A laptop glowed on a table to the right. An art nouveau desk lamp was set beside it.

Kore laughed. "I'm not some monster. Both of you relax."

Neither Timessa nor I spoke. I got up and walked over to one of the bookshelves, scanning the titles. There was a law dictionary, a volume on the Peloponnesian war, a book of poems by Ezra Pound, and three slim volumes by Arthur Rimbaud. She said, "I'm in Charleville. One can't live here without owning Rimbaud. Probably a law about it."

"Are you an attorney?"

"Oh, the dictionary?" She paused. "No."

I smiled. "We didn't expect to find anyone here."

Her eyes flickered over Timessa's face. "But I expected you."

Timessa spoke in an almost inaudible whisper. "Whoever you are, you've hovered around me for months. Why?"

"You don't understand."

I watched as Timessa extended her arm toward Kore: the languid cobra's strike. Her fingers swiveled in that odd gesture she used against attackers. I knew what would follow, but Kore put her palms out and sighed. Hers was a gentle gesture, patient and even loving. She said, "Please, don't. And I'm not the enemy you think —"

Timessa said, "What the hell are you?"

"I am," Kore whispered, "just a simple herald."

T hissed, "Stay out of my life."

"I will carry the lantern that lights your way. I exist to proclaim the news."

I interrupted, saying, "Herald? — We need more than that."

She smiled pleasantly. "Yes, such a difficult thing these days … Espresso?"

We declined. She unhurriedly walked into a kitchenette behind us, poured a coffee from a carafe and returned. Her abdomen was flat and she looked extraordinarily fit. "It's a dark roast. Rare around here. The shops all specialize in mild."

I continued, "When I sat with you in Boston —"

Timessa gasped. "You did what?"

I ignored T, who was unaware of the meeting. There was no time to explain, so I continued, "You played the same game then, Kore, dodging questions and after minutes, simply disappearing."

"It wasn't the right time for us to talk."

"And now is?"

"Yes," she said. "Let's be direct for once." She even clapped her hands. "Who would like to start?"

Watching her carefully I said, "*You* would like to start. From the beginning, please." Timessa tentatively took my hand.

Kore glanced down, taking in the small movement. She said, "Fine. Probably the simplest beginning is to correct my name."

Timessa blurted, "It isn't Kore, is it?"

"No, that was a good placeholder. Sort of a clue. But not me." Kore smiled.

I asked quietly, "And your real name?"

"My real name is Eos. E-O-S."

"Eos?"

T turned to me, saying in Greek, "*Εοσ*." She looked amazed. "Dawn."

Kore said, "Yes, *Εοσ*. For tens of thousands of years I announced the coming of Helios, my brother the sun. Day after day. My only breaks were during storms or when heavy fog hung on the sea."

"It isn't possible. And if true, why are you following me?"

"Now I herald another coming, another whose brightness will be even more remarkable."

I smiled, incredulous at her claim. "Are you alluding to Timessa?"

She shrugged. "There is no other."

"Sun, Moon, Dawn —" Timessa whispered, "all were children of the Titans, and all immortals." She turned to Eos. "You are known also as Aurora."

"Yes, we are far older than you. We were born when the natural world was formed."

Timessa went silent, simply starring at the girl. I asked, "And now that you've removed your mask, which do you prefer — Kore or Eos?"

"Kore was a veil. To those who know me, I am Eos."

Timessa continued, more as an aside to me, "She is almost as old as Gaia. They are so ancient that we thought Helios and Eos were myths."

The sudden formality between the two was humorous, except I knew neither girl saw the comedy. Feeling the energy in the room fluctuating I said, "But back to today and our visit here. Why do you share an address with Ares?"

"I don't," she said. "The god is here for just a couple days."

"Explain."

"He has business in Paris. He was traveling from Thebes. We're friends. I mentioned this place as an alternative to the city and he arrived two days ago … There's not a problem?"

"Friends? Ares has been missing for almost two thousand years."

Eos said, "No longer."

"Yes, he reappeared." She watched me, saying nothing. I asked calmly, "Do you know what he wanted here?"

"He says he staged a music festival in Thebes," she smiled, "a great success. And wanted to meet the one I am heralding."

"Just like that. He reappears. And out of the blue wants to meet Timessa?"

"Uh-huh."

"How could he have known about her?"

"Well, I told him stuff."

"What?"

"That she was amazing, beautiful, fun." She scanned the ceiling, glanced away, then looked at her hands. Watching her, I thought of a mischievous child.

"Eos, you're covering for Ares. Not telling us everything. You promised to be direct. And you're not."

Looking impish, she stood and took a few steps to Timessa, standing for a moment looking down at her. Then Eos knelt suddenly and put her head in Timessa's lap. T slowly ran her fingers into Eos's hair and Eos began to sob. To my shock Timessa murmured, "It's okay, it's okay …"

Sitting back on her heels, Eos asked, "Ares is gone, isn't he?" Emotion surged through her face, although I saw her struggle to conceal it.

"Yes," I said. "He planned to torture and kill the one you sit before."

"Impossible!" she cried. "He swore he intended you no harm!" I said nothing. Her eyes bore into mine. "When will he return?"

She did not understand. Perhaps she imagined he'd left Charleville for a day. Or had gone on to Paris without a goodbye.

"Eos," I said, "he's gone forever. Hours ago he attacked Timessa a couple blocks from here. Did so with a gang of satyrs, ripping at her dress, intending to dismember her in some back alley, probably planning to then break her bones one by one until her final breath."

She covered her mouth. "And —?"

"I prevented that."

" 'Prevented'? Now it is you who speak in circles."

"He attacked her. I killed him. I rocketed his essence away, dispersed his fucking atoms around the world. He's not coming back. Do you get it?" My anger surged.

She shook her head no, laughed mockingly, pointing at me. "You're the liar," she cried. "*He* kills. No one kills Ares. Do you think I'm a fool?" Then after a second, she shuttered and broke into tears.

"I'm sorry," I said, "whatever your relationship with him. I had no choice."

Eos whispered, "You weren't aware, but I was there as he re-emerged in Delos."

"No, you weren't."

"I watched as you infuriated him. He was close to destroying you but checked his anger."

"Why would he have hesitated?"

"Because she was there —" Eos pointed to Timessa.

"And then what did he do?"

"He vanished. We went to Thebes."

"We? The two of you?"

"Uh-huh."

"So you were there for the weekend rave?"

"No, I left the day before for Charleville."

"And he told you later the festival was a success?"

"Hundreds attended." She choked. "He was considering producing more, starting in Greece and then expanding to, I don't know, Italy. He spoke of doing one here in Charleville."

"The war-god producing raves? You bought that?"

She had golden eyes, lighter than Apollo's, but lovely. The effect was as if she wore caramel contact lens. Dawn, I thought, the first light of day. She turned to me. "He was charming."

Timessa interjected, "He had to be once, to have been Aphrodite's lover."

"My entire body warmed," Eos said, "when he touched my arm."

"But seductive monsters," T said, "are everywhere. Didn't you know? He was perhaps the first in an endless line."

Eos looked childlike, petulant. "He promised me things." She waited for one of us to respond but we said nothing. After moments she said, "Thebes. Was it the great success he described?"

I said gently, "Hundreds of Ares's satyrs used machetes to kill thirty or forty bikers. Afterward, they raped well over a hundred teenage girls. Several died hours later. Then, as the fires cooled, Ares assigned the fiercest of the satyrs to kill Timessa, charging her with the loss of their beloved Dionysos."

"That's not at all what I heard." She looked between us. "Ares said she was being celebrated for the revival of the gods. That he wanted an opportunity to thank her personally."

"And so," I said, "you cooperated."

She nodded. "And I haven't heard about Dionysos. What do you mean by 'loss'?"

"He emerged from Delos," I said, "in a constant lust. Hermes had to beat him off a girl in Mykonos. He hit repeatedly on Timessa and Danaë. Finally, Poseidon banished him to his stables under the sea. He'll be shoveling manure for eternity. That's what infuriated Ares. The two were partnering. And the satyrs live, as you know, to dance with the wine-god, to debauch the innocent."

She sobbed.

I thought of Thebes and then of the ancient attack on Delos. That day was reported as pleasant, crisp. *Dawn.* Then Mithridates's forces appeared in the crooked harbor. Thebes and Delos and countless other battlefields were identical — Ares wove darkness over all. Even at dawn.

"Dawn," Eos said, "is a harbinger of good."

I said, "Night falls. The earth revolves, the sun appears. Over and over and over. That's all. To assign it good fortune is inane —"

"No!" Eos cried. "I am a messenger. I exist to spread golden light. With light there is hope. I reject any other argument —"

I thought, better to not argue. Our mission was almost complete. Nothing of Ares was left; the apartment's contents were a young woman's. Eos clearly had been used — an ancient story and her antiquity made her none the wiser.

Her idealism was charming, as was her defense of her purpose, but she continued to be elusive about precisely what she heralded. Moments before, she had claimed, "Now I herald another coming, another whose brightness will be remarkable." Timessa was that other whose brightness Eos would proclaim. But what was T becoming? Perhaps even Eos didn't know.

Eos rose and took Timessa's hand. "We can't have you walking around this city dressed like that. We're the same size and I think I have something less formal that you'll like." They went into a back bedroom.

When they returned, Timessa held a single lily to her lips. She wore a short skirt and blouse; the bustier was still obvious, black lace showing above the shirt. Eos had found red sneakers for her and a matching beret. Timessa had transformed from a vamp in frock to a French girl.

But what I found striking was that they had their arms around each other. Eos said something, inches from T's ear, and T giggled delightedly. I felt like I was watching reunited sisters.

T gestured for me to get up from the couch. I stood and she sat with Eos, arm to arm, almost snuggling. I took Eos's former chair, sitting across from them.

"What happened back there?" I asked. "It's as if you two are suddenly fast friends."

"Yeah, well," Timessa said, looking at Eos, who was aglow, "I guess we bonded."

I knew better than to probe too far. I preferred the sweet Timessa to the warrior-nymph. So what if she were now friends with this ancient one?

CHAPTER 24

In the night there were countless
girls's hands taking down the bulls,
tearing trees up by their roots:
all of this for a dark god's kiss —

An hour later the three of us sat in a park overlooking La Meuse.
The haze that had sheathed Charleville hours before had lifted.
Even the river itself flowed pleasantly, its banks lush and mowed. Eos and
Timessa sat on an old bench, arms linked. Occasionally they would grin
at each other, as if sharing a cosmic joke. My irritation surprised me.

I walked to the riverbank. What I had judged that morning as a
turgid waterway was a well-managed, heavily modified river cut in a
perfect arc. I thought of the little stream in the backwoods of my estate.
Laine had called it Pegasus. As I mused, La Meuse drifted by with a sigh
and exhalation.

I turned to the two, saying loudly, "Eos, do you still attend to morning
duties?"

She smiled. "Announcing Helios?"

"Exactly."

"Ask Timessa."

So I played their little game, turning to Timessa expectantly. "And your word on this, T?"

"She does, but not in the old ways. Now she just wakes, opens her eyes and illuminates the world. Every morning."

"Steady work," I said.

Eos smirked.

"We should get an early dinner," I said. "Who wants to join me?"

They stood, Eos saying, "There's a neighborhood place around the corner. Baklava, tzatziki, gyros … Follow me."

At the restaurant we jammed into a small booth. When our food arrived, Timessa spoke to Eos shyly, "You know, I thought I invented you. The goddess corrected me and said you had planted yourself in my mind. That was good, Eos. Pretty sly."

Eos smiled.

I asked Eos what had motivated her to shadow Timessa. "I mean, one day she was a nymph and then suddenly she has an obsessive follower. Why?"

"Jackson, you're always drilling deeper," Eos said. "Can't things just be?"

I pondered her question a moment, looking at them. Timessa was expectant, interested in how I'd respond. Finally I said, "Not in this case. Like Artemis, I seem to be called to shield this girl. I'd be thrilled to let her go, but can't figure out how."

T cried, "Jackson! That was mean."

I looked at her with amusement. "You know what I'm saying."

Eos scrunched her face. "About a month before the goddess released her, while the tribe still debated her request to leave, I had a premonition. Up to that point, I'd never heard of her. Why would I have? She was just a nymph."

"You're mean, too," T groaned.

"My premonition was that I would be called to trumpet something bright, something that shone like polished gold. That I would be a harbinger of something radiant."

"Your vagueness still bothers me," I said.

"As in, what am I heralding?"

"Yes, that." I turned to Timessa. "And you. You're like a calyx, girl, a whorl of softness that protects the bud of gorgeous flowers."

She smiled and in a lighthearted voice said, "That's not me."

"Yes," Eos said. "Jackson's right. You're opening."

Timessa blushed. a fiery flushing of her cheeks and neck. She said, "I want a hand, from each of you." Eos offered hers first, and T lifted it to her lips and kissed the back. Then she repeated the gesture with me. "Thanks, both of you." As she set my hand down softly, she swiveled and lightly kissed Eos on the cheek. "My eidolon, transformed to guardian angel." She caught herself and said to Eos, "Angels. Was that you —?"

Eos smiled, "The allegation! What angels, Timessa?"

"Months ago I dreamt about an angel. In it an angel conveyed the great truths of all time to me. Whatever it said, I couldn't understand a word —"

"I am tasked with waking you, then announcing your awakening. At times I have moved heaven, then I have moved earth. That particular night I used a bit of heaven."

"But there are no angels!"

"Nor," said Eos, "is there a heaven above earth."

"Then why that?"

"One never knows what will cause an eruption." She put a finger on Timessa's lips. "I have tried innumerable tricks. And until you fully spread your wings, I may try more."

"Can we be friends like this?"

"Be explicit, little one."

"With you tricking me?"

Eos looked weary. "Dark approaches. Unlike the two of you, I sleep as long as night skulks the skies. I now have little time."

"Answer my question, Eos."

"If I must answer, yes, my tricks are over. How can I be both antagonist and friend?"

"Then Kore is gone?"

"No more emails or letters or confrontations. I embedded Kore and now must, perhaps while you sleep tonight, remove her, alpha to omega."

I interrupted their parries. "Eos, will your decoupling interfere with Timessa's transformation?"

"It would go on without me. I was not the catalyst; we don't know what sparked the change. We never know. A subtle selection takes place beyond our understanding. Perhaps Gaia herself selects who will become the next grand butterfly."

Timessa put her face in her hands and we sat quietly. A waiter came over and took our plates. A Moroccan, I thought. He returned and left a bill, looking at Timessa. In French he asked, "She okay?"

Eos nodded. "*Ça a été une longue journée.* It's been a long day."

T dropped her hands and smiled broadly. As the waiter left, she hugged Eos, looking at me with a smile. Eos looked pleased, but spent. In a half day she had lost Ares and bonded with T. She said, "I am expected to maintain distance ... What is that dog-thing's name, the one that follows you in Boston?"

"Orthrus."

"Yes, like Orthrus. I am to observe, and bark at you at times to keep you wakeful."

"Eos, you're now my favorite dog."

She smiled. "The two of you are to stay at my apartment tonight. There is nowhere safer. But I'm crashing as we banter." She stood. "Here's a key. I know you won't go to sleep for hours. I suggest you sample some of the local wines. There's *le bar* a block away. And Timessa, you'll turn every head in that skirt."

She leaned over and kissed T's cheek. I said, "Not me?"

Eos gave me an annoyed look but kissed my cheek as well. "Be quiet when you come in," she directed. "Jackson, you get the couch. Timessa sleeps in my huge bed. I'll see you both at sunrise."

She left.

෬

Eos had recommended *Boîte*, a small nightclub that was tucked down a side alley and which was almost empty when we entered. I was grateful, for Timessa remained a magnet. Even though I appeared to be no more than a few years older than her, men in their 20s and 30s approached us wherever we were, ignoring me and saying to her in French, "Beautiful and sexy both .... Are you free tonight?" or some similar variation of the local pickup line. She always responded, "*Je ne parle pas Français.*"

That evening we were left alone. Two other couples sat nearby, both older than us. We took barstools at a square formica-topped table and sat for minutes without talking. Although Eos had recommended their wine, I ordered us brandy. T threw hers back in a single hit.

She said, "Nice," exhaling with a long sigh.

"It's even better if it's sipped."

"I'm exhausted."

"Bet you never imagined today."

"Let's see," she said. "This morning I sauntered down Avenue d'Arche, causing heart attacks at every corner. Then we took out fifteen satyrs and a major god. Within another hour or two I met my nemesis, Kore, who turned out to be Eos, who claims to be a herald of some unknown and glorious thing I may yet become. Then the two of us bonded. And I thought killing that satyr during the show in Paris was a big deal."

I signaled the bartender for more. "You're aware that when you left Artemis, your beauty seemed to double. There's probably a law against that. I should send you back to running bare-assed in the woods."

She laughed. "Getting me out of those tunics helped."

I made a point of scanning her chest. "And accoutrements like that black bustier do no harm."

"You're not hitting on me, are you Jackson?"

I smiled. "Not a chance."

She said, "Just checking."

"Much of this started on Delos in the rain."

"As I did the Dionysiakos?"

"The dance that raised the gods. I tactfully call it a revival, but it's closer to a resurrection. I set the scene but you danced the dance."

"And Eos says she watched."

"Eos, Hermes, Danaë and I. Immortals in the rain. And I haven't thanked you properly."

"I did nothing."

"You brought great joy to Danaë. For that I'm grateful."

She giggled. "And joy to the twins who reunited with the mad Apollo."

"The only madman in the group was Dionysos."

"I think," she said quietly, "that we're all quite mad."

I looked at her without expression. She returned my gaze, then waved me away with an exasperated grin. I smiled, saying, "What will you do when we leave France?"

She looked surprised. "I have a job."

"Modeling."

"Of course. Boston may not be a good base. I may have to move. New York, Milan?"

"And you'll spend your time sashaying on catwalks, and looking angry in every photo shoot?"

"Might lead to a movie gig. That happens, you know."

"Yes. Fame and fortune. Just what you sought."

She looked away, then her eyes filled with tears. "Jackson, what the hell am I becoming? A little twist of my wrist and foes disintegrate. And without effort I've become a sensation."

"Honestly, no one knows."

"I feel it too. The changing. Sometimes when I lie in bed I feel a little river rippling through my veins, making changes here and there. Am I really some chrysalis —"

"— metamorphosing?"

"Yes. And it's embarrassing. I'm beginning to feel like an object. You, Artemis, now Eos — everyone is watching. Waiting."

"You're a pleasure to watch."

"What if I turn into something vile, some odious bug?"

"We send you to the stables. Hard labor for eternity."

"No thanks. I'd run into Dionysos."

"Then you'd better become that bright and brilliant thing Eos talks about." She sniffed and jiggled her empty glass. "Just remember your old friends when you transform. We stroked your back and sang you to sleep each night."

"And there's Josef," she said. "My landlord, the industrialist's grandchild."

I shrugged. "With the money you're pulling down, no need to stay there."

"It's a pleasant house, but you're right." She paused. "Should I give notice?"

"He's a hermaphrodite."

"Kind of exotic," she said.

"The French would say, *outré*. What was outré once is orthodox today." I knew she was still a virgin, that she'd never broken her vows to Artemis. Sex, like anything forbidden, was inevitably fascinating.

She read my thoughts and said, "You and sex. You're like Freud. Everything originates from some sexual thing." She laughed. "But then, what do I know?"

She showed the second brandy more respect, aware that I was still sipping my first.

"Timessa, at some point you began to select when to be transparent, and when to block thoughts. And you've largely gone opaque. We both know nymphs can't do that. Are you conscious of blocking us?"

"Of course."

"Can you open to me, now?"

"Yes …" She opened her eyes wide, then reached across the table and touched my cheek. As I watched her, I felt a flood of emotions, millennia of experiences, events, exploits, a wild nymph running with Artemis and her friends.

Minutes passed as the sensations and memories pummeled me, and finally I shook my head. "Enough, enough."

"There's more," she said. "I'm being selective. I've forgotten nothing. Everything I've undergone, all I've come across."

"My lifetime is one percent the length of yours."

She smirked, "You've just begun, Jackson." She watched me, then teared up again. "I guess I block everyone now because I don't know who I am or what they'll see."

"A self-confidence thing?"

"As in, lack of —"

"Exposing yourself, even to those who love you, can be perilous."

She nodded. "I guess. Particularly when you don't know who the hell you are."

Our conversation wandered after that. We avoided anything painful. She inquired about the boys and which nymphs they favored, rolling her eyes as I named names, saying, "Not her!" After a while, I stood. We exchanged looks and left for Eos's apartment.

A light wind blew down the sidewalks, papers kicking up and tumbling down the edges. At times I could smell the river, its wet, organic

funk far heavier in the dark. As we approached our destination, the river
— now only paces away — murmured steadily as it moved through the
long arc of its channel, its presence portentous, premonitory.

Timessa took my hand, clearly unconcerned in the ambivalence of
Charleville's night.

CHAPTER 25

She was violet-crowned —
γαρυφαλιά, the common gillyflower
found all over Athens
even now.

I woke to sunlight. Gold flooded the walls and etched long, narrow shadows off tables and chairs. Curtains had been opened. Rising from the couch, I sat and scanned the front room.

Eos and T entered the kitchenette, already dressed. Coffee was in a carafe and croissants on the side. Eos suggested we eat in.

We talked softly, conversations subdued. Eventually Eos turned to Timessa. "I told you yesterday about this and that — things like premonitions. But I need to tell you more."

Timessa smiled and said, "I want to hear it all."

Eos paused, saying, "You look happier today."

"Not happier, but … yes, happier, I suppose."

Eos touched her cheek. "There's more about me. Let me begin …"

I wondered if I were intruding, and volunteered to walk the river while they talked. Eos insisted I stay, emphasizing she wanted no secrets.

Then she settled back and said, "This will take a few minutes. I'll be going back centuries. Don't be angry when you hear, but the first time I 'heralded' someone's coming was for Dionysos."

Timessa looked startled. Eos quickly continued, saying, "You probably remember the story. He was conceived when Zeus took Semele. She was the daughter of the king of Thebes. Hera, Zeus's wife, was enraged and tried to destroy the girl. She tricked Zeus into doing her dirty work. Semele was lost, but Zeus saved the child who became the wine-god."

"And where do you come in?" T asked.

"Zeus hid the child. Hera tried repeatedly to kill Dionysos. Zeus kept hiding him, disguising him as a girl, then as a goat. Even when he was grown, Hera pursued him wherever he went. Dionysos wandered the world, but accumulated followers everywhere he went …

"At last, in his guise as a liberator, he returned to Greece. That's when I was recruited to herald his coming. Many had been poisoned with the belief that he was a foreign god, even an Egyptian. My job was to smooth his path, spread the message of his revelations and the glories of his wine. I was assured he was a gift to women."

"Was he?" Timessa asked. "Artemis would not allow any of us near."

"Perhaps. For a time. I left his entourage when the god became too big a star. I was no more than his star-making machinery. And I had succeeded at my task."

"Had he changed?" T asked.

"He had been married briefly in the earliest years. Not to a divine girl. When his wife, Ariadne, died, he changed."

"Dionysos," Timessa muttered. "liberator, then monster."

"Yes, I left him shortly after …" Eos smiled softly. "The years before that were exciting. And that was the first time I had held a lantern for an emerging force. There have been many times since then."

"For other gods?" Timessa asked.

"Never another god. Since then I've worked with humans. Until you."

"Eos," she said, "elaborate. I love your stories but I'm confused. How could you herald humans? They never change. They're what they are when they're born."

"I was assigned a different, but similar, role." T watched her expectantly. "I became a muse, inspiring the great to greatness."

Timessa giggled, and turned, punching me in the arm. "I was once a muse!" she said. "This one made me *his* — I mean his muse — and I inspired him, right? That was in the days before Lachesis lost her mind. And before Danaë came along." She still smiled broadly. "So Eos and I are both muses!"

The goddess of dawn said, "I knew that about you. I thought it was sweet."

"I posed occasionally half-nude. But mostly he wanted me to just sit and wouldn't even let me talk."

I shrugged. "I explained I wasn't an artist, that I needed her for *financial* inspiration."

Eos snorted. "Uh-huh."

All of us laughed. Then Eos said, "I served as a muse to Ovid, Orpheus, Sappho, Phidias, Euripides, and Sophocles, artists and musicians, writers and even architects. Not everyone wanted me. For instance, I briefly worked for Leonardo. Was he appreciative? No. He considered me distracting. I moved on. Yet most men and women drank from my well —"

She took a deep breath. "In Boston I appear as a violin prodigy. It's how I support myself."

She continued. "I have many violins. I was a muse for Niccolò Paganini from about 1810 on. He was the greatest violinist of all time. I worked with him, invisibly, for decades. When even he thought he had achieved greatness, I pushed him harder. Many at the time accused him of selling his soul to the devil. It wasn't a demon that inspired him …"

"You played even then?"

"Yes, I was fortunate as I learned to play on his Stradivarius."

T said, "Amazing."

"In the last year I've given concerts in the Harvard area as a wild girl. Keeps me in money. And I've found I can cause all the girls watching to break into tears if I end my performances with a reading. Romantic poetry." She smiled. "Have you heard of the French Symbolists?"

Timessa shook her head. "I was a science major."

"The Symbolists included Baudelaire, Verlaine and Mallarmé. I knew them all. Most important, I worked with Rimbaud here in Charleville, before he fled to Paris. Then I followed him there. I remained in Paris until he shot Verlaine. That was about 1875. When he fled to Africa, I decoupled. I simply couldn't go to Abyssinia." She smiled, and continued. "I guided him during his school years here in Charleville. It was then that I acquired this place."

T said, "You've lived here for more than a century?"

"I have of course traveled worldwide since. I've just never released the apartment. It's served as a good retreat. Rimbaud's ghost still lingers in the city alleys like a faded handprint on a wall. Because of my time with him, I knew each of the Symbolists, their histories, poems, stories, and mistresses. So now in Boston, when I finish playing the violin, and complete reciting my short poems, at times I will speak of these things. Students are amazed that I know far more about Rimbaud and Baudelaire than their professors."

"Aren't you afraid of exposing yourself in some way? Perhaps accusations that what you know is impossible?"

"Not really. Scholars are easily proven wrong. And it's an amusement."

I interjected, "What are some recent inspirations, artists you've influenced since Rimbaud? Anyone famous?"

She smiled. "I've spoken too much about myself. I wanted T to have more insight into who I am. And I've gone on too long. But, yes. One or two more names, then we plot our moves." She poured more coffee for us all. "I should note that like Leonardo, Picasso rejected me. Too protean, and he liked his muses to be lovers as well. Not my thing."

She frowned. "Have you heard of Auden, an English poet?"

Timessa said quickly, "No."

"Well known to scholars. We worked together briefly, but he was a dry, humorless man. He needed help but I moved on." She winked at me. "Ah, here's another one I presume you *haven't* heard of ... Scarlet Rivera?"

We shook our heads. The name meant nothing. Eos smiled. "She's an American violinist. She shot to fame when she recorded albums with Bob Dylan."

"Dylan?" I blurted. "Saw him in concert, when I was merely Jack — years ago. You were Rivera's muse?"

"Yes, Dylan discovered her in New York. He was driving around, saw her walking with a violin on a street in SoHo. He invited her to a recording studio, and got lucky as she had perfect pitch. She was a virtuoso, but petrified of failing. So I merged with her quietly that day and inspired the better work. She played a sort of gypsy violin when she was with him. She can thank Paganini. That was me ..."

Timessa whispered, "I'm charmed by these stories. To think I rejected you —"

"My error. I was more aggressive with you than anyone before. And remember: I've not been your muse." Then she said emphatically, "I'm your herald. As dawn announced the sun, I will soon advance your way."

T said, "I wish you'd drop that formal shit. You don't even know what you're heralding."

Eos stood. "We should get dressed. I've gone on too long." Eos took T's hand. "You need something to wear. Come on —"

I sensed that nothing remained for us in Charleville. Ares had intended his visit to be token. He had come — and would have gone as quickly. As it was he'd never terrorize anyone again. He and his select corps of satyrs: all scuttled like rotten ships.

Ironic, I reflected, that Apollo and Laine had conspired to eliminate both Ares and Dionysos — and had done so at least temporarily. Their solution had lasted for 1,600 years. And then I came along. I may as well have uncaged prehistoric wolves.

As T and Eos dressed, Danaë and I texted. I kept news minimal, but she already knew about Ares's demise. Artemis no doubt passed along the news via her network, but I didn't press the issue. We would have time to talk when I returned.

Eos came out, dressed casually. She sat beside me and said, "Timessa will be another minute. If you have no objections, I'll return with you."

"To Boston?" She nodded. "Of course."

❧

From my viewpoint, our trip to Paris, then to back Boston was uneventful. From Timessa's I suspect it was otherwise. During the flight she expressed her discomfort in returning to Josef's apartment, and her dismay at the "provincial" nature of the city's fashion scene. Eos noted that she was renting "a beachfront villa" near Revere Beach on the harbor — then admitted that "villa" was an exaggeration.

I don't know if Eos's disclosure was an implicit offer, or whether she simply was being conversational. Regardless, within a short time Eos had agreed to share the apartment, even conceding that the spare bedroom looked out over the water.

I distinctly remember Timessa turning to me during the flight and saying, "In the thousands of years I've lived, I've never really *felt* immortal. But something has changed. There's a new sense of ..." She struggled for a moment. "... authority that has swept me. I know that sounds ridiculous. It's like I have an increasing sense of power."

"Or sovereignty," I said.

To any outside observer, I sat beside a stunning girl in her early twenties, who acted like any girl her age. She paused, "There are moments when I feel like I fucking rule it all."

I smiled. "When I was almost at the end of my own transition to ... to what I am, Artemis warned me to watch myself. There were times when I was as high as a drone, drowning in my own sense of power."

"Am I that obvious?"

"No, you've contained it well. But when it all seems to come too easily, that's when you watch your ass."

"I'm *not* describing pride," she said. "I'm being factual. I feel *power*. I felt it when that stupid satyr at the show pulled a gun. I had no idea how I'd take him down but I knew I would. And I did. I was *aware*. The act itself was almost an afterthought —"

"Yes, I know. Nothing premeditated, yet everything solved impeccably."

She reached over and squeezed my hand. "Yes, flawlessly. Nice to have you to talk to, Jackson."

I asked her, "What's that fancy hand-flick you do? The one that turns targets into dust?"

"I just suddenly knew how. The goat-man pulled the gun, and the finger twist was there. No idea what I was doing. Small swivel and he disintegrated."

"You did it again when Ares and his minions attacked."

"Yup." She made an elfish grin. "Was just checking to see if it was still there."

"I'm glad it was. There were three of us doing wizardry. Not sure what would have happened if it were just Artemis and me ... if you'd backslid into being a nymph again."

"Oh, nymphs can kick ass, too."

"That wasn't kicking ass. That was subatomic, that was neutrons colliding with a cyclone." As she nodded, I continued. "If we go back a few days, another impulsive — and flawless — thing you did was the rain dance on Delos."

"The Dionysiakos."

"A dance to wake the stones."

"A dance to raise the dead." Her eyes sparkled.

"And the hand-flick works in reverse. Sends the living into death. Lovely polarities."

"Only one thing troubles me about that," Timessa said. "Not only did I feel no guilt as their bodies shattered, I felt … triumph. I liked what I saw."

"Consider that a warning against conceit."

"I was taking lives no differently than Ares had the day before."

"His was bloodlust; yours was self-defense."

She leaned over and kissed my cheek. "We land in a couple hours. I'm closing my eyes."

In Boston later that night, a driver took them to Eos's Revere Beach house while I returned to our small Eden outside Philadelphia, the mansion lit up awaiting my arrival. Danaë and I talked for some time, then retired. As the sun rose in golds and fire, I thought of Eos, wondering. And I sent word to Artemis, requesting that she join Danaë and me for dinner.

She arrived wearing her ancient attire, a thin tunic with gold trim, a leather band hitched tightly below her breasts. Her face was serene. We stood as she sat.

"Jackson, I know the basics of what occurred after I left. But I admit to being taken aback at Eos."

"Who has been masquerading as Kore."

"We always believed Eos and Helios and all of the ancient ones were simply myths. Gaia seemed the only one still animate."

"Even stranger is that Eos and Timessa now get along like old friends," I said.

The goddess watched me without reaction, then said, "It's all happened too fast."

"Yes, T has even moved in with Eos, who has quarters overlooking the Boston harbor."

"This is after she spied on Timessa for months?"

I said, "Senseless, isn't it?"

Artemis shrugged. "And what is your assessment of Timessa's state?"

"That she is no more a nymph today than a butterfly is a caterpillar."

Artemis shook her head. "It is astonishing."

"You mean a nymph turning into something else?"

"When Lachesis played with your DNA, when you became a-mortal, your change was intelligible. She jiggled your chromosomes and, given her expertise, what occurred was straightforward. Timessa's changes are something else."

"Yet they seem organic."

"Indeed."

Danaë interjected, "Immortals do not evolve. What we are when we're born is what we remain. Is there an instance in our chronicles of anyone transforming into something else, something more powerful? Because that appears to be what's happening —"

Artemis shook her head. "You know that even our births so long ago were a brief biological paroxysm. There was a short outbreak of a-mortals, then the spasm ended. It was like a breath being exhaled for a few seconds. It's not happened again. We've been endangered for millennia."

"Then out of the blue there was me. And now Timessa."

"And we don't know yet," Artemis intoned, "what she'll become."

"You must have a gut feeling," Danaë said.

"A premonition?" Artemis said. "I do. But it's fanciful."

I shrugged. "Share, however absurd."

"Fine," she said. "Hermes threw it out when we were about to leave Mykonos. I laughed at the suggestion."

"And —?"

"It involves a primordial goddess — one that once ensured favorable crops. That granted fertility. That rearranged the stars if it suited her."

Danaë made a sharp inhalation. "An ancient fertility goddess?"

Artemis went on. "Far before our time, several goddesses were worshipped as such. In the Mediterranean there was Eileithyia, or Iithyia. She was present when Athene was born and like me, was in Zeus's lineage. Eileithyia was the goddess of childbirth, the one women prayed to when they wished to become pregnant." Artemis continued, "And another power common to early goddesses was the ability to generate crops. And to wither them when the goddess felt maligned ... I sense Timessa may contain both. And more."

Danaë looked at Artemis in disbelief. "Are you saying she is morphing into Eileithyia?"

The goddess said, "No. But there was a goddess who predated Eileithyia."

"And so predated even Eos?"

"They coexisted. She dominated pre-bronze cultures. That was the time women ruled men. Not like Amazons, but ruled throughout the world. Everywhere and without exception."

I asked, "What happened to this early goddess?"

"Do you mean," Artemis said, "did we supplant her?"

"I suppose. I'm not sure I know what to ask."

"Nor do I know how to respond. Her cult dissipated as we appeared. She was still worshipped in Crete, Delos, Sparta. With Demeter, she founded the Elysian rites. Then she appeared to slowly vanish as Zeus increased his hold on things."

Danaë, who was steeped in the tribe's history, said, "Goddess, I'm confused. You're saying there was a goddess before Eileithyia who ..." She grimaced. "... encompassed in herself the powers of fertility and harvests?"

"Yes, and although she went missing, her spirit has lingered. When hunting I often have been aware of a presence, as if a ghost. A rarified ether. Yet that inkling of the past has never revealed itself as more than an impression of what was once immense power." Then with the slightest trace of drama, she said, "Until now."

Neither Danaë nor I spoke, startled by her implication. Finally I said, "T is a work in progress. I presume you agree."

"I agree that I am not certain what she is. I have limited evidence, so you are hearing my hypothesis."

"Which you say was first suggested by Hermes."

"Which he said was affirmed by Apollo. We have all sensed it. What is the word you use? Chrysalis? She is something-that-is-coming, a pupa, a being in transition."

Danaë whispered, "What will confirm your suspicion?"

"Timessa alone determines that." Artemis paused.

Danaë asked, "Did this goddess have a name?"

"The few who know refer to her simply as ..." Artemis hesitated. "... the Great Goddess."

"Just that?" Danaë asked.

She smiled. "She has appeared in many iterations. Triple Goddess, Cybele during the Roman period, Rhea before that. It's all speculation — they do not know and we should not concern ourselves with names. My interest is in this being's possible re-emergence."

Danaë looked stunned. "You're saying Timessa may have become a vessel for this ... ancient Great Goddess?"

"Unwittingly, I believe. It's all happening quickly."

CHAPTER 26

Of the Great Goddess I cry,
The glorious goddess with gleaming eye,
Brilliantly inventive, heart relentless …
All tremble at her gentle kiss

W as Timessa embodying or assimilating a prehistoric goddess? I couldn't help but link my quest for the male gods — and their re-emergence — to the her own transformation. Was it coincidence, or a conscious force moving boulders aside? Artemis raised possibilities. Yet we may have all been conflating events.

As Laine once lectured me in the early days, we are bound by invisible ropes and cables and lines. We struggle against them, but few of us ever are freed. Now we were witnessing Timessa as she unraveled a millennium of bonds that had defined her since birth. She was born a nymph, and had known nothing but running in the wild until now. Over a period of a few years, she was given unusual freedom, first to attend Vassar, then to assist Laine and the Fates to prevent a catastrophe (which we now considered Laine's fraud), and finally, at her request, to wander outside of our safety net to "find" herself.

What she had found so far was remarkable, as her dance on Delos had awakened four of the ancient gods. Further, she had been pursued by Eos, who felt a calling, yet unexplained, to be her "herald." And in her pursuit of a conventional career, Timessa had become an acclaimed model who, during a show in Paris, had discovered yet another remarkable power.

She was evolving. The transition was preternatural. Now, Artemis hypothesized that T might be exhuming the primal energy of a far earlier being known as the Great Goddess. I thought her conjecture was implausible.

But these were our private discussions. In Boston, Timessa immediately re-entered the whirl of fashion shows. In the first days after her return, she sent Eos, in disguise as a friend, to Josef's for the few belongings she had left at his house. He could not have guessed that Eos was the infamous Kore. Packing Timessa's clothes and books took her minutes, and Eos left.

I was startled one morning as I skimmed a major newspaper to see T featured on the front of a style section showing a new line of dresses. Rather than effecting the usual angry or vacuous expressions so expected of today's models, she stared with astonished eyes and a beguiling transparency. When I showed Danaë, she said, "Her appeal is that she hasn't sold her soul. She's a perfect mother's daughter."

"You mean she hasn't told her mother to go to hell."

"Yes. Fashion models today are anti-enticing. She, on the other hand, projects something irresistible."

Several weekends after their return to the states, Eos persuaded T to take a short road trip to western Massachusetts. She knew trails near the Hoosic, a large river. She said that the sound of the water over riffles there was like a thin, wild mercury song. Timessa laughed at the description and agreed that too much time had passed since she had run among trees and meadows. The idea of a day-trip seemed delightful.

Yet even Timessa had not anticipated the disquieting event that ended the long day. They hiked a portion of the Appalachian Trail between Cheshire and Mount Greylock, reveling in the changes in topography. The weather in late spring was ideal and neither girl was bothered by the black flies that seemed to swarm everyone else.

By three that afternoon they were just a few miles from the trailhead.

They stopped briefly, alone at an overlook to a floodplain beside the Hoosic. Eos guessed that the flat plain had been planted with hops that now emerged in an unvarying blanket of spring green. The afternoon sun — brother Helios, Eos smiled — swept over the unending plants, with black shadows darting like speckles among small, countless gaps in the crop.

T was not cognizant of what precipitated her action. Without forethought she raised her arms, a languid and unassuming gesture that vaguely mimicked the ancient goddess greeting — arms out, palms open, a hieratic move usually intended to acknowledge equals. Instead, facing the swath of floodplain, she frowned, narrowing her eyes.

Eos told me later that she gasped as acres of hops withered, browning as T shifted from side to side. Timessa stopped breathing, simply experiencing waves of sensation as she willed the crop's demise. Within a minute the greenery was ruined as she remained poised, palms out, breathing. Havoc soundlessly rippled over the plants.

Timessa then fell to her knees, bowing her head. She knew what she had done and knew that no event had precipitated her action. Yes, wish, she thought: I wished it all to happen. I was irritated at the field's intense greens, angry at its radiance and its purity.

Then as suddenly as her temper rose, she grieved. Facing the field, Timessa said, "I'm like some quicksilver wind."

"Anger?"

"Yes."

"Then you must mend what you have broken."

Timessa looked at her, and understood. Yes, she thought, I can do that, too. Scythe, then restore. Destroy and repair. Whatever I want. She was giddy, and repressed her comprehension. *Just act*, she thought —

Legs wide, she raised her right fist and slowly rolled her fingers out into a five-digit star, lifting her hand high and crying, "Eeiiiiiii—!" demanding the radiant field return. She imagined a sinuosity of green along the river's plain. As they watched, the field rippled with new colors, waves like a spontaneous flush shifting the chromas from browns to yellows to pale viridescent, then suddenly, finally, to a bright emerald as robust as the field she'd destroyed.

Eos could feel her heart pounding and said simply, "Yes. Yes, Timessa, yes."

Both knew that this was grand, even memorable. T turned to Eos with luminous eyes and laughed cautiously. Then without hesitation, she looked up the path, raised her palms, opening them and browned a half dozen huckleberry bushes lining the trail. Just as quickly, she turned her hand into a star and the bushes regenerated, forcing out hard buds which opened fully in seconds. Then she closed her hand and brought it to her chest. The two linked arms and quietly descended the slope.

On the ride home, neither spoke. Timessa tried to analyze what had occurred. She knew her actions and the results, but nothing more; she could measure the power but not the source. T felt her entire body humming, her nipples hard and her stomach taunt. An odd electricity ran through her thighs, up her belly and tingled in her scalp. She laughed occasionally. But mostly she studied the landscape, trying, after she had failed to make sense of anything, to drain her mind of thought.

By the time they were within view of Boston's harbor, Timessa was inexplicably happy. They crossed the Zakim Bridge and wound north off the highway toward the beach. Eos reached over as she drove and put her hand on T's thigh. Her touch was warm, and Timessa was flooded with a golden wash, a tranquility she found remarkable.

Eos said quietly, "The changes will continue. She who makes them is as ancient as I."

"And her name, Eos?"

"I called her Great One, but she has had many names. Lemnos, Cybele, the Great Goddess, Ishtar, the White Goddess, the Triple Goddess … She is an ancient deity, one who eradicates and creates, who exterminates and procreates. She is from the old time of matriarchy, when women ruled."

"I have heard of that time, but never of her."

"She vanished in the same era in which your goddess, Artemis, appeared."

"Vanished," Timessa said. "Like the male gods?"

"No. I think not. They atomized into the sands of Delos, an act of self-delusion. Her retreat was far earlier, and was one of solitude. Now she seems to have swept back like a she-eagle. Perhaps she has been awaiting the right vessel. Perhaps Gaia is involved. But I speculate —"

"You scare me."

"I shouldn't. Your gifts protect you."

"What were hers?"

"She granted fertility. She guaranteed robust harvests." Eos pulled into her driveway and cut the engine. "She was moody — gracious one moment and angry the next, irritated suddenly, then unimaginably compassionate."

"She had temples and worshippers?"

"Many."

"What would happen when she was angry?"

"She would turn fields to dust and wombs to empty casks."

"I was angry hours ago. The green was too intense."

"Yes, then you grieved when it was gone."

"And I made it grow back."

"Bountifully."

Timessa felt energy whirring through her limbs, crackling like an ancient song behind her eyes. She closed them and saw fire. A vast wild-fire stretched across a field of grass, leaping and releasing a roiling, orange smoke. She turned to Eos, saying, "I need time alone. Thank you for being a companion on our getaway."

She touched Eos's shoulder and went to her room. There, she lay on her bed, trying to quantify the ebullience she felt, justifying its serenity with the enraged fire that–still burned through her veins. Indeed, her thighs were feverish, her belly hot.

Timessa covered herself with a sheet, struggling to quantify the changes. She wondered if she should confer with Artemis, seek her guidance. Surely, she was unaware of all this madness. When she had seen her in France, it all seemed far simpler. How could she destroy vast fields, then regenerate them as easily? No one she knew had such might.

Her mind wandered, recalling the years she had been cuddled by the goddess before sleep. She had become dependent on being held and stroked. This night she struggled to sleep, alone and harried by many unknowns. To think she had pleaded for this, begging Artemis to release her into the world.

A room away, Eos sat, measuring Timessa's metamorphosis. In addition to celebrating dawn, she was a muse, but now felt far closer to an acolyte, someone to light Timessa's altar candles as she advanced along an unmapped path.

As midnight approached and Timessa struggled, Eos knocked on her door. T whispered, "Come in."

Eos sat on her bed. "Close your eyes, Timessa. I'll stay here until you sleep."

"Eos, did worshippers of the Great Goddess offer sacrifices?"

"Of course, as nymphs do today to Artemis and other gods."

"And her anger rose when sacrifices were absent?"

"Yes."

Exhausted, T turned on her side and closed her eyes. She felt charged particles still flowing through her muscles, energy hissing through her bones. Eos stroked her side, ran her fingers through her hair, imitating the soft massages T had received from Artemis when when she was a child.

Eos's fingers felt like a breeze. Timessa no longer saw fire sweeping through the fields of switchgrass. Now a full moon was overhead, roped to the dark night by hundreds of stars. From somewhere she heard the laughter of girls. She sighed and within minutes slept.

Weeks passed with little change. In the meantime, Timessa made friends with models from her agency — all of them angular and lithe. The agency favored rawboned girls in their mid to late teens. Timessa, who appeared about twenty, became an older sister to many. She found it a bit difficult to relate, but her reticence increased her mystery, and her increasing fame drew them to her for camaraderie. To be seen after-hours with Timessa added to any girl's allure.

Her poise and exotic beauty made her a magnet. As much as she remained aware of the superficiality of it all, the adulation built her confidence. Her friends steadily increased, and Eos began to think of them as T's wolf-pack. And Timessa herself was reminded of Artemis with her gang of nymphs, amused at the analogy and pleased, imagining herself similarly.

Eos was delighted to see her grow, although she wondered if Timessa were repressing the momentous events from the hike. She stroked her on rare evenings when she couldn't sleep. The physical changes, the slip-streams of crackling energy, now seemed subdued.

As a result, Eos retreated as overt muse. Pressure on T would not accelerate her evolvement. And as dramatic events dimmed around Timessa, Eos appeared at several Harvard poetry fests, playing hyped versions of Vivaldi violin pieces on an 17th century Guarneri. She had acquired the instrument when she was Paganini's muse from an apprentice boy desperate for cash. That was more than 200 years ago and she could still see the boy's flushed face and excitement at receiving the gold ducats she slipped him one night.

During this lull Timessa flitted in and out of the villa, seemingly ignoring Eos. But Eos rarely let her out of sight, attending shoots and comforting her when emotions flared. Eos was aware of Timessa's eruptions, her increasing tendencies toward sudden anger, followed by immediate anguish at her own outbursts. Those around her forgave her, yielding to her celebrity. Within a three-week period, she appeared on the covers of *Allure*, *Elle* and *Marie Claire*.

Eos recognized that the changes in Timessa were not due to the seduction of fame, but rather to the Great Goddess's influence. And she knew Timessa's volatile emotions would be a challenge to control, particularly as the Great One continued to forge T's demeanor. Although she understood, Eos had no insight into what the goddess ultimately intended.

One of the models who most adored Timessa was nicknamed Lucky. She had married when she was seventeen and, regardless of her burgeoning career, was increasing desperate to have a child. She was approaching nineteen, and assumed her career would end within a few years. Her husband worked as a coder for an IT firm in Cambridge, and was pressuring her to wind down her modeling. But she couldn't get pregnant, largely because, she believed, she was necessarily underweight. For a year she had followed medical advice, recording her cycles and monitoring ovulation; they had sex during the recommended interval; her husband's sperm count had been checked; and she underwent a preconception checkup — and testing confirmed them both as healthy.

One quiet afternoon four of the girls gathered at Eos's. Although it was early summer, no one could risk much sun so they avoided the beach across the street, and hung out in the living room. Inevitably T asked Lucky if anything had changed in her quest, and she said, "Nope. Guess I'm just unlucky."

Timessa said, "You're still so young. You have years to try."

"That's not how my husband feels. He wants kids ... and I guess, so do I."

"Lucky, you're not even twenty. When we've all retired from this madness, you can gain some weight, act like a normal girl, lay off the wine for a few months, take some vitamins. Everything will turn around."

She sat beside T, and suddenly burst into tears. "That may never happen."

"Of course it will."

"I've failed!"

"At nineteen?"

"Over the weekend I even considered, I don't know, suicide. Joe was out and I thought, 'Get a rope.' He'll find me and probably be relieved. Then he can marry some normal chick who gives him kids."

"Lucky!"

She leaned into Timessa, sobbing uncontrollably. Eos watched the group from the kitchen, curious. Timessa put an arm around the girl and stroked her hair. Lucky slowly quieted. T said, "You're going to be fine."

And Lucky whispered, "No, I'm not good enough. He hates me and I understand —"

Timessa took Lucky's face in her hands and turned her head so that she couldn't avoid her eyes. "That's not happening. I'll not allow you to fail."

"I have already."

Timessa tugged her into her arms, leaving Lucky's stomach exposed. She put her palm over Lucky's belly, gently making circles. As she did, she said, "No thoughts ..."

"What are you doing?"

"Opening you, turning you into a golden thing ..."

Rather than laugh Lucky appeared awed. "Your hand is hot. What's happening?"

"You'll see." Lucky nodded, unquestioningly.

The other girls sat forward on the edge of their chairs, staring in disbelief. One of them said, "Your hand's emitting like, a yellow light."

No more than a minute passed and T said, "There. Tonight make him love you. You'll be pleased."

Lucky nodded dumbly, convinced that something had occurred. She blushed, stood placing a hand over her stomach and said, "What in the world?" She looked dazed, stumbled backward and left in a rush. The others stood as well, unwillingly to question what they'd seen.

When T and Eos were alone, Eos said, "Quite the performance."

"Spontaneous."

"Another faculty: gifting fertility."

Timessa looked at Eos. "Was that it?"

"Yes, another dominion you can claim. Fertility in the fields and in the womb."

Timessa looked away, examining her palms. "This hand turned hot. She was right. I could see a golden light emanating from my fingers."

"A shimmering."

T paused. "Eos, I opened her for sex. Yet I've never even slept with a man."

"Nor will you. It is not your way."

"My way?"

"The Great One cannot cross that line."

Standing, she said angrily, "I'm not a goddess!"

Eos shook her head. "Neither of us knows your path. But you are following the Great Goddess's footsteps, walking her trail, guided by her at every step."

T whispered, "Very dramatic."

"Your changes are what are dramatic, not my words."

"Fertility? Maybe. But I am constantly fighting destructive impulses, as well. How will I restrain my anger?"

"With your powers will come mindfulness."

"Oh, I'm aware. I'm also afraid of lashing out. And I have no wish to harm anyone I know."

"You are not to worry about those you know. It's the others, strangers, supplicants who are at risk."

"Really?"

"There are, of course, exceptions —"

"Words! I'm sick of them! And of you!"

Without warning Timessa's nostrils dilated and she turned on Eos. As she did so she raised her hand. The wrist-circling was languid, as if impelled through a viscous fluid, and Eos knew exactly what would come.

She fell to her knees and cried, "Timessa! No, not me!"

CHAPTER 27

*For centuries
she issued edicts through her priestesses,
held dominion until new gods
declared her temples felonious.*

Frozen by Eos's anguished cry, Timessa dropped her arm.

Eos remained kneeling. After moments T said in a half-whisper, "Well, I won't be able to appear in public if that occurs with any regularity."

"Nor will you have me around."

"Is it possible to disintegrate a primal goddess?"

"It is."

Dominion, she thought, my bounds are falling away. Power: it surrounds me. Force: I simply call upon it. And compassion? It comes and goes. There's where my work lies: I must find control.

Then she strode from the house, ran across the street, and stopped on the beach. The Atlantic was choppy, the late afternoon sun on her back. She walked into the waves up to her thighs, wondering if she could reverse the tides, drain the harbor. She raised her arms in the ancient goddess greeting — palms out —acknowledging the equality of the oceans and seas, the tides and riptides, the dolphins, the slick grey sharks and bottom-skimming eels.

Couples out for a walk passed her as if she were invisible. The sea was darkening as the sun set and she felt the sand moving under her feet. None of it mattered — not the stars or sun or the helical planets whirring overhead. She was alone, unnoticed yet able to command whatever she wished. She looked down at her hands: transparent, limpid, like a girl's slip, as were her arms and legs. She had become diaphanous, barely detectable, yet containing galaxies.

Then she noticed before her, from the waves, a man slowly emerging, growing taller as he strode toward her from the sea. He was tall and fit and accompanied by porpoises. She knew instantly: Poseidon.

He wore nothing and carried a trident. He too was translucent; she could see through him into the salt spray. He stopped before her and examined her quietly, then reached over and touched her arm: yes, she was a material girl, yet ethereal. He stepped back and said, "All is happening quickly. For millennia we were quiescent. Now we stir with increasing speed."

She realized he included her when he said *we*. Poseidon was speaking of the gods, and including her in his declaration. Nodding, she continued to hold up her palms in the old greeting. He mimicked her gesture, smiling.

"You struggle accepting who you have become. Or are becoming."

His eyes were scintillating, and she lowered her arms, saying, "Sea-god."

He stepped closer, then shockingly, dropped to a knee. "My oceans and seas, tides and riptides — all are yours."

"No," she said. "They are ours. We are two moons, binary." As she spoke she wondered where her words originated. They flowed as sponta-neously as her powers. She was being put to use by a greater being. Or so it seemed, as she stood matched with the mighty Poseidon, vaguely aware that his porpoises hovered at his knees, their grey eyes fixed on hers.

He stood. "Equal is more than I expected. I thank you. All of us greet you. We have lingered in the darkness for far too long. That is ending. Think of me and I will come. Apollo, Artemis, Aphrodite, Athene, Hestia, Hermes — Jackson — all of us are at your service, Queen."

Queen. Yes, if she were honest she owned that title. Absurdly destroying and creating. Waving her wand. Or perhaps Dionysos's phallic thyrsus. A fertility queen. But she had earned none of it. And she understood nothing going on. It was all like a massive wildfire that had sprung from a spark. And if she were a queen, where was her king? Eos had implied earlier that she was to sleep with no man. Perhaps her king was gone, sacrificed to guarantee rich harvests. She remembered a saying that made her shudder: *Almost all kings lose their heads.*

Poseidon said, "As the days pass, you will grow to understand. You are like my seas — eternal, timeless."

"As vast as your oceans."

"Even before my time, it was said you were like the amaranth, the plant whose flower never fades."

Timessa knew the bloom. Its leaves crown many of the columns in Rome. "Ἀμαραντοσ?"

"Yes." He bent and reached into the seawater, grasping a shell, straightening himself and offering it to her. "And here, for you, a nautilus."

The shell was small and flawless. "But they are not found in these waters!"

"They appear where I wish."

She smiled, the shell fitting her palm perfectly. "Of course. I am honored."

Poseidon stepped back, descending back into the sea, his translucence masking him from all except the girl who stood watching him descend. He turned and dove into the black waters, the porpoises leaping twice before diving in his wake.

⚘

When she returned to the villa, Eos waited. Timessa nodded, slumped onto the couch, and said, "Headache."

"You know why?"

Timessa shrugged. "How could I know? How can I know anything? Everything just happens —"

"Let's think."

"Sure, Eos."

"When you ran with Artemis, you acknowledged her gifts?"

"Acknowledged?"

"Showed appreciation."

"You mean worshipped? Just say it, Eos."

"Call it veneration."

"I don't know. We showed devotion. How could we not? She provided everything."

"What form did this 'devotion' take?"

"Rituals, small festivals, celebrations. You know."

"And what were the rituals?"

"The usual. Rites of dedication. The old ones — you must know them all. Lustral branches being waved, barley tossed into the wind. We prayed for her blessings." Timessa caressed the curves of the nautilus shell. She placed the shell over one of her eyes as if it were a monocle.

"And how," Eos asked, "did these 'rites' end?"

"A treasured animal was slaughtered. Sheep, a ewe, birds — she favors woodcocks and doves."

"Call it what it is: sacrifice."

"Of course. θεσια …"

"Yes, thysia. And these rituals are a form of adoration?"

"I've said so."

"For the many things she provides."

"Eos, where are you going with this?"

"Goddesses are venerated for their gifts. And gifting is reciprocal. The one who benefits thanks the one who gives."

"I suppose."

"What do goddesses do when they're not thanked?

"They withdraw what they bestow."

"So the relationship," Eos said, "is complementary."

"This is stupid. Of course. If they are not thanked, or if they are not respected, or if they are mocked, they retaliate."

"Perhaps they become grumpy and irritated."

T shrugged. "I wouldn't know."

"Perhaps they get headaches."

Timessa looked at her. "Eos, are you saying —?"

"You are vexed, whether you know or not." She sat across from Timessa. "What did Lucky do when you blessed her?"

"Blessed her?"

"You and I know you opened her. You granted her fertility. She knew it, too. And what happened next?"

Timessa covered her eyes and sighed. "She left."

"No, she didn't. She said, 'What in the world?' Then she fled."

"She was scared."

"She showed no gratitude."

"I asked for none."

"Goddesses never ask. They expect."

"Would you be happier," Timessa asked angrily, "if she'd fallen to her knees?"

Eos paused, deferential but certain. "That *you* must decide."

Timessa rose and looked out a window. Then she turned to Eos. "You have claimed to be my guide. That you felt a calling. That you are the goddess Dawn — our revered Eos. And that you clearly see far beyond what I can see."

"Are you questioning who I am?"

"No, but I'm irritated you see what I cannot."

"Like a light that heralds the new day, I illuminate your change."

"You speak like some religious text. Drop the gobbledygook."

Eos bowed her head.

Timessa stood before her and said, "Look at me."

Eos looked up, saying softly, "We have all said you are a chrysalis. There were small signs it was happening. That was then. Now the shell has split, dawn has broken. It's morning, can't you see?"

"No," she said uneasily.

"You are shedding the membrane that bound you, blinded you for so long."

"And what have I become?"

"What did Poseidon just call you?"

"You knew he came?"

"Of course. The seashell you hold is his calling card. And his offering."

"He called me 'Queen.'"

"Yet you resist."

"What did he mean?"

"I think you know."

"Clarify it for me, Eos." Her statement was a command and Eos looked away.

"It was the Great One's name. The Great Queen. I haven't heard it used since ancient times."

"And I am becoming her?"

"There has been a transference. It has been coming in pulses, a sacred heartbeat."

Pacing, Timessa said, "I'm just a nymph who's blessed to have become a model. I wanted out of Artemis's restraints. I wanted freedom, nothing more."

"One does not request or seek bestowals. Neither is this honor some handout you rebuff. You have *become*, do you understand? You still must assimilate the gifts and modulate your emotions. And I tell you, you will never recover the old happiness you knew. That was a nymph's life, but not a goddess's way."

"I know so little."

"You must still test the extent of your powers." Timessa looked confused and Eos said, "The Great One has been patient. You were tapped long before you understood. It is why you had to leave the tribe, why you sought what you believed was freedom. When you said you needed to find yourself, the Great One drove those desires. Now what you *become* will play out bit by bit."

"I feel powerless."

"To stop it, yes. But otherwise, what you feel is raw power. Hardly powerless. Am I wrong?"

Timessa trembled, shedding her humility. Eos was right: her change was real. "There are times when I feel I know the truth of every mystery. Or can cure the heartbreak of every girl. Or crush the evil in all men's hearts —"

"You can. And far more. All of us see it. It is why Poseidon appeared. Artemis will come shortly. And others. All to pay respects."

Timessa laughed, not manically. Or with self-importance. Instead her laughter was a slash of the raw emotion Eos had described — pain and wisdom and growing acceptance.

CHAPTER 28

The Great One, helmeted,
armored, resting with her staff
and golden aegis. Glorious sea-
eagle sprung from Gaia's mind.

Over succeeding weeks when she had afternoons off, Timessa took long beach walks. Poseidon never reappeared, although she was convinced that Artemis watched her on occasion, always a lone figure hundreds of feet down the shoreline, a half-phantom who vanished by the time she neared. Once T waved but got no response. Perhaps Artemis was unwilling to meet because Timessa almost always brought friends.

Four or five and even eight girls would accompany her, half in swim suits and the others in summer garb. Timessa didn't care; she increasingly felt a sense of supremacy that she struggled to repress. Her consequent mystery — she felt compelled to reveal less and less of herself — combined with her fierce confidence and fame made her increasingly beguiling. The wolf pack (or as one of them characterized it, "Timessa's bitches") grew in its own desirability. Few models wanted to be excluded from the tight circle of beautiful girls who orbited Timessa's world. Her walks became events, and the gang of thin girls in mod beach gear attracted Boston paparazzi.

One late afternoon when she ventured out by herself for a brief run, a woman stood alone on the shoreline, watching her approach. Within 300 feet Timessa knew: it was Artemis. She slowed to a walk. At about fifteen feet, the goddess put up her hand as if to stop her and Timessa paused. They stood apart and as T tried to catch her breath, she felt Artemis's scan. The goddess wore a linen tunic that might have passed for uninspired beach wear; her face was implacable, her eyes anodyne.

Waves lapped at her feet. A discolored gull swept by crying as if a hoarse crow. All the while Artemis watched. Then in her vast silence, she nodded once and vanished, leaving T alone and breathless.

Several weeks passed and Timessa participated in a private showing on Martha's Vineyard off the coast of Cape Cod. Her agency flew three models in. The show was attended by a dozen women who either were themselves celebrities or simply wealthy residents. When Timessa opened the show to polite applause, she immediately noticed Artemis sitting in the front. She wore her usual clothes, a white blouse and black skirt complimented by a gold necklace. Her legs were crossed and expression bored; she held a notebook and pen, tapping the ballpoint restlessly. T wondered how she had talked her way in.

Their eyes met but neither acknowledged the other. The goddess sat through about ten minutes of the show, got up and left — and did not return. T was piqued but unworried. She found it an annoyance, at worst. What was Artemis seeking that she hadn't already determined? For her part, Timessa simply was biding her time, awaiting the next shift; she was certain the Great One had not completed her work.

Back on the mainland that weekend, T invited Lucky to visit. The girl had pleaded to see her and came alone, which itself was unusual, and the two sat together. Eos offered drinks and Lucky declined. She seemed deferential, and finally blurted that she'd missed her period. Then she began sobbing. T held her for a moment and Lucky apologized, explaining unnecessarily that her tears were joyous, that she had only Timessa to thank, that she wasn't sure what had occurred that night but she had conceived because of her.

Timessa knew all of this before the girl spoke. Lucky reminded her of the way deer stared at Artemis, open and trusting. T said, "Close your eyes, Lucky," and she did. T touched her cheek with her palm, letting heat ripple up her scalp. Within seconds Lucky's mind emptied, then slowly filled with a blotched red, pulsating sky. Then a dark horizon rose within the matrix, and on it, or behind it, a rising fire. Mesmerized, Lucky's lips opened and her shoulders slumped. Timessa allowed the fire to recede, the red sky to soften into pinks, then blues.

When T moved her hand away, Lucky opened her eyes. Her only option, she knew, was to bow stupidly, which she did, pressing her palms together as if in supplication. "Oh Timessa," she said, "whoever you are, thank you for what you've done."

"Yes."

"I know this will sound ridiculous," the girl said near the end of her visit, "but I have a friend who can't. Her man's upset and so is she. It's become really bad. Could I bring her by —?"

Timessa instantly understood the risk — first there'd be two girls, then a flood — but she nodded, curious. Was Lucky's pregnancy a one-off? "How old is she?"

"Twenty-four."

"Tomorrow," she said. "I'm between gigs at two. Bring her then."

After Lucky left, Eos handed Timessa wine. She smiled. "Experimenting?"

"At Vassar we were taught to call it corroborating."

"Multiple identical tests with the same results are publishable."

"Something like that."

The next day Lucky and her friend, Colleen, came a few minutes early. The new girl clearly was not a model and was introduced as a friend of Lucky's older sister. Colleen had been married three years and been under the care of a women's health center most of that time.

After small talk that led to Colleen's confession that she feared she might be permanently infertile, Timessa said, "Sit beside me."

Colleen looked alternately doubtful and bashful. She said, "Lucky says you put your hand on her belly."

"Yes. Lift your blouse a bit."

The girl looked over to Lucky, then pulled her blouse out of her jeans and held it just below her bra. "Here?"

Timessa nodded.

She smiled to reassure the girl. Before she made contact she could feel heat throbbing through her fingers. She placed her palm on Colleen's stomach, gently circling, imagining spheres, fiery wheels turning entire worlds. A golden light radiated from the back of her hand and the girl gasped, "Oh my god."

Timessa said, "Hush. Are you ovulating?"

"Yes."

"Then take advantage of your man, tonight, tomorrow, the following day —"

"Completing the circle ..." Eos whispered.

After several minutes, as the heat receded, T lifted her hand. "Tuck in your blouse." She turned to Lucky. "That's all the time I have. Will I see you at the shoot tonight?"

Lucky nodded, animatedly asking Colleen if she had felt the heat. The girl breathed, "Yes, yes, it's still down here —" touching her belly and standing unsteadily.

Suddenly Timessa was swept with exasperation. The girl had said, "... still down here." What a stupid, thankless thing to say, she thought. Angrily she rose from the couch and waved them away, with an obvious irritation, a headache rippling through the back of her skull.

Eos gently pushed them from the room, saying, "She needs to be alone." Without saying more, the girls left the house, looking at each other.

&

One evening when the wolf pack, increasingly called T's gang, met at Eos's before an afternoon beach walk, T had them sit on the floor facing her, saying, "I've got something really cool to share."

They sat expectantly, almost childlike. One of them said, "We're so fortunate to have you as a friend."

Timessa smiled, her offer impromptu. She acknowledged to herself the spontaneity of it, which probably meant another opening, a shift dealt like a random card from the Great One. She no longer knew what to expect, but she accepted each mutation.

Opening her arms, she said, "I'm going to touch each of you. As I do so, close your eyes."

Walking from girl to girl, she quickly touched their cheeks, her caress softly emptying their minds, replacing jumbled thoughts with the blotched red sky she had revealed to Lucky. Each girl's sky was a firmament that pulsated softly, a red scrim illuminated by dim lights. A dark horizon arose upon the crimson matrix, and behind it, distant fires across the skyline, fierce and hot like endless pyres.

Within seconds all the girls were breathing restlessly and sighing. Of the dozen, three fainted and several wept. Others rocked on their haunches, or lay on their sides. Timessa knelt, scanning their faces. She allowed the fires to burn until she was certain each girl was purged. Passing minutes gently purified their thoughts. When she was sure all were unburdened, she stood.

"Girls," she whispered. "eyes open."

As one, the girls blinked back into a new consciousness, happier than they could remember, light-hearted and free. One asked, "What happened?"

Another responded, giggling, "A little shot of euphoria?"

Earlier on their way to Eos's, one of them had bought beach parasols from a shop in Chinatown and gave them out. They tumbled as a group into the sun, waving them and frolicking onto the beach. Timessa stayed behind, watching from the front windows as they ran into the surf.

"They seem a happy group," Eos said. "Anesthetized and far more malleable."

"Not that. Freed from worry."

"Before long, they'll be dancing in the woods like Dionysos's maenads." She paused. "Can't you see? They're too happy. A millimeter away from the same frenzy as all of his girls. Soon they'll be tearing apart dogs and cats."

"You're being crude."

"Why the magic?"

"Just came to me to do."

Eos looked at her carefully. "No headaches?"

Timessa shook her head. "Feeling pretty sunny."

"You need to check your impulses, whatever their source."

"Meaning I could be misled?"

"You should think for yourself." Pausing she said, "Gaia expects you to begin to show discretion, not just leap when told."

Timessa gave Eos a light push. "I escaped Artemis only to be captured by a greater one?"

"It was she," Eos smiled, "who sent me to you. As it is she who compels me even now to be your guide."

"Okay, I get it. But these girls —" She waved a hand toward the beach. "— are suddenly happier than they dreamed possible."

Eos followed her gaze onto the beach. "Look: two men with cameras beside the seawall. They're stalking Boston's supermodel."

"Yes, a problem."

"So far the word has not spread about your tricks with girls — fertile hands, hallucinations. When — not if — it does, you won't be able to expose yourself so easily. Photogs will be flying in from everywhere."

Timessa shrugged, but she knew Eos was correct. Her public adventures would be ending quickly. She knew that other models had become reclusive, and she could see that happening to her. Sunglasses, brimmed hats, frumpy clothes, cheap accoutrements. The paparazzi — mostly stringers for local papers — were not simply an annoyance: they were an inflammation. Twice she'd caught herself on the verge of making the two men waiting by the seawall across the street disappear.

"Too many sharks," she said, "already know where I hang."

Her experiments had proven Eos's concerns to be true. She could raise dead gods, kill men as easily, destroy and recreate crops, and grant fertility. These extraordinary skills, once publicized, would create an uproar, a worldwide sensation. What had she been thinking? She'd become sloppy. Artemis would judge her unfit to wear the Great Goddess's crown. Yet the Great Goddess herself kept dealing new cards.

She looked up and saw her gang about to cross the street. As they waited on cars, the two men leapt off the seawall, crouched and started taking photos. To T's surprise, one of the girls must have anticipated the blitz, as she had a handful of sand and threw it into the face of the closest man. He stumbled back, clawing at his eyes, while the other cursed, trying to grab the girl.

Timessa watched no more than a second, observing the second man as he gripped the girl's wrist, pulling her toward him. She shrieked, twisting away. Another girl started pummeling him.

Timessa flicked her wrist languidly, and the man began to dissolve from the head down, swirling into dust, his camera clattering against the road.

The first attacker was still blinded and the girls dashed across the road and into Eos's house. They shouted excitedly to each other. "What just happened?"

"Did you see his head dissolve?"

The girl who had been grabbed said, "He had my wrist and then his hand disappeared! Then his arm!"

Another cried, "Then his legs! I saw it all! Like I was watching some sci-fi flick!"

"And we left the other twisted on the ground!"

"Fucking crazy!"

Their adrenalin was high, mixed with nervousness and fear. The peace Timessa had conjured earlier was gone. She herded them back to the living room, commanding them to sit. Going from girl to girl, she touched their cheeks. Their harried breathing slowed. Each relaxed, and as seconds passed, T teased away their memories. When she returned their consciousness, they were the same happy group that had spilled out onto the beach.

As Timessa snuffed out the moments of danger ricochetting in their minds, Eos turned to the front window and erased the memories of the man sprawled on the ground. When he regained his sight, he was irritated to find his friend had abandoned the shoot. *Great friend*, he thought, curious when he saw the camera lying in the gutter.

The camera body was scratched. Why would he have dropped it? But at this point he could remember nothing and couldn't fathom why he found himself on Revere Beach. A seagull circled him and landed on the wall, clicking its head inanely.

The men had gone there for something, some promise. They were a team, always tracking celebs, in search of images that might go viral or sell for a couple hundred dollars. Yet there was nothing here. He knew no one of importance would be caught in such a place.

Frustrated, he pulled his phone from his camera bag and called his friend: no answer. He saw their truck across the boulevard and, suddenly, deeply tired, crossed toward it, tapping his pocket for the car keys.

CHAPTER 29

In that flow, time is neither
subject, object, nor measurable,
not scalable, dimensional or other:
rather some bird tossed into the aether.

Acknowledging that their privacy was lost, Eos ordered an eight-foot tall perimeter fence. Timessa bought a car; Eos's sedan was inadequate, the windows transparent and anyone inside the vehicle far too visible. She chose a silver SUV with quad electric motors and quick acceleration. The windows were heavily tinted.

Eos persuaded her to hire a driver. Although Timessa drove well, her income easily allowed the indulgence. The owner of one of the firms she called, after hearing her concerns, suggested she hire a man who could double as security. He specialized in hiring former military. Could she come by to interview personnel? Timessa said she would send a friend.

On the first interview Eos hired a full-time driver, a young man who had completed five years in an elite army unit, then moved into private security. According to Eos he looked young, which she found appealing. And another asset, highly unusual for ex-military, was that he was gay.

"But not overt," she told T. "Narrow waist, Broad shoulders. Won't hit on anyone."

"His name?"

"John Tomas. Deferential. He starts tomorrow. When I saw the list of his awards and commendations, I concluded he was perfect."

"Regardless," Timessa said, "he'll be on trial the first couple months. Anything weird and he's gone."

At the end of the week, after hours of being on her feet, Timessa wandered alone into a small coffee shop a half-block from the GIA agency. Models were a common sight there; no one bothered her. As she finished a latte, she noticed a tall, blond man walk in and look around. When he saw her, he strode up to the table.

He was dressed casually in khaki pants and a blue button-down shirt, and his skin was flawless. She looked into his eyes. His pupils shifted from brown to golden as she watched, and when he smiled, she stood, saying, "Apollo."

"Divinity."

She sensed no mockery. "Please sit."

He looked around again, as if to assure himself they could speak privately, then sat. "You look well."

"Thank you. No twins?"

His eyes flickered and he studied her carefully. "The two amuse me but are not good travelers."

"You look particularly handsome," she said.

"Yes," he smiled. "But then I always do."

They said nothing for a few moments. She waved to a waitress and asked for a refill. Apollo indicated he would pass. "Water?" she asked.

"I'm drinking only an obscure wine these days. A light retsina from Naxos."

She smiled pleasantly but did not speak. He casually opened a palm in the ancient hieratic greeting. Timessa did the same and they touched fingers. He closed his eyes at the touch and said, "Yes. I remained doubtful. Poseidon assured me several weeks ago, but I needed to confirm."

She ignored his insinuation, tired of always talking about herself with these beings, of her changes, of the Great One. Instead, she asked, "And how's Charon?"

Apollo pursed his mouth. "Bored, I think. The Delos visit was a high point. He misses you. And the others."

"And Hermes?"

"I haven't seen him much. He seems to travel constantly."

"We should call a reunion. Artemis's estate in this countryside. Large, private, with all the amenities. You and Hermes, Charon and Hestia, Poseidon, of course. And Artemis."

"And Aphrodite and Athene?"

"Everyone. A gathering."

"And what would be your role?"

"Facilitator … But perhaps you come to lecture me?"

Like Poseidon and Eos, he suddenly was deferential. "Not I. Not I at all. Your gifts are considerable, mine trivial in comparison."

"In comparison?" She almost laughed. Her gifts greater than Apollo's?

As if reading her mind, he said in a whisper, "Most of us are mere fireworks. Sure, we live for millennia. Our powers are extraordinary. But not in comparison, Queen. You make broken girls well. What's the old word —? Fecund. You make things flourish, give birth to … life."

"Or I make fields barren. I destroy."

"Indeed." He bowed almost imperceptibly. "And from reports I have received, you extinguish those whom you find irritating."

"You exaggerate. I cull only those who threaten."

"Of course."

To her shock she found the conversation increasingly tedious. Had he, like Poseidon, traveled great distances simply to assess her? Who was he to judge? Then she caught herself: she sat across from Apollo, one of the greatest of the ancient gods. She said politely, "You haven't said what brings you here."

Anticipating her concern, he said, "Not to measure you. I come to caution, even warn you." She said nothing, and he continued. "Has Eos told you about the old ways?"

"You need to be specific."

"Has she told you about what guaranteed the harvests every year?"

"I guarantee what I wish."

He looked at her, deciding how to proceed. "I am not the first to call you Queen."

"No, Poseidon was first."

"Do not all queens have kings?"

She remembered again. *Almost all kings lose their heads.* Where had that come from? She stared into his golden eyes. "I am told I shall not sleep with men."

"I am not discussing sex. I refer to ceremonial matters."

"There is a certain monotony to all of this," she sighed. "No one wants to speak directly. Do *not* bore me, Apollo."

"Then we shall be direct: the Great Goddess takes a new man every year."

"You make no sense."

"A new man, who just before the harvest, is reaped himself to make way for the next, always to ensure a bountiful yield."

"This man — her king?"

"Temporarily."

"And he is culled?"

"Sacrificed."

"How?"

"Sometimes the Great One wields a knife, sometimes the knife is used by one of her priestesses. The king is killed, cut apart, and his pieces scattered in the furrows of the fields. And then on the same day, a new king is chosen."

"A new man volunteers?"

"There is no greater honor. The new king is anointed — divine oil is smeared on his forehead." She listened without emotion. "Then one of your surrogates — usually the youngest priestess — mates in the grasses before appointed witnesses. Which consecrates the joining."

"Never the queen lying with the king?"

"Only in the earliest years …"

"History. Like dust blowing down alleyways. Why do you tell me this?"

"Because you will reinitiate the practices. Not around witnesses like these," Apollo swept his arm around the coffee shop. "But watched by nymphs and demigoddesses and divinities."

"No, I will change the practices. There will be no kings."

"Gaia created this sacrament. She has awakened the Great One, who in turn has selected you from all of us. A nymph raised to the greatest of goddesses. We glory in your acclaim. And you will find that you will begin the old rituals again."

"So you say."

"What the Great One wishes has always occurred."

Timessa stood, glancing at a clock. "I'm back under lights in ten. Can you stay for dinner tonight? I'll tell Eos to expect you. We'll continue this discussion then."

"My pleasure. Where should we meet?"

"Here, at six. My driver will pick you up."

He nodded, stood and she left.

That night at Eos's, the three discussed events at Delos: Dionysos's outrages and Ares's unremitting bloodlust. Apollo noted Timessa's unusual strengths, emphasizing that the Great Goddess was a force of life for crops and fertility.

Eos, stood, pouring wine. "Yet what you, Timessa, are remains unclear. The Great One has transferred her essential gifts. But you have others, including great beauty. All of that said, you clearly do not have her memories. Apollo has had to tell you stories of what occurred and what is expected."

"The Great One — what did she look like?" Timessa asked quietly.

Eos smiled. "She had red hair that fell below her breasts. Her cheeks and lips were the color of mulberries and her eyes violet, like yours. Her nose was aquiline. She, too, was tall."

"How did she dress?"

Eos said, "White gowns, always tied by ribbons at her ribcage. She went barefoot, followed by young girls wherever she went."

Timessa smiled, thinking of her gang. "Was she flesh and blood?"

"She ate like we do," Apollo said. "She slept briefly just before Eos lit the skies."

Timessa hesitated, then asked, "Was she virginal?"

"I never heard stories of her coupling." Eos went on. "Her kings were all young men. Boys, really. Twelve, thirteen, fourteen. I cannot imagine her lying with any of them."

Apollo affirmed her opinion. "She was a celestial object, a burning force — not a sexual thing."

Timessa scrunched her face. "And the sacrifices every year? Why an annual king?"

"Their deaths symbolized the end of seasons. Celebrated her gifts. And, I suppose, guaranteed succeeding harvests. She had to be appeased."

"Appeased? With human sacrifice? Was it her idea?"

Apollo smiled. "The ritual? As I mentioned this afternoon, Gaia mandates these things. All of the ancient ceremonies were created before my time." He turned to Eos. "You're the oldest of us. Do you know more?"

"The Great Goddess was revered throughout the world when I emerged. I was told her ceremonies reflected the galactic harmony ..."

They fell into silence. After awhile Apollo said, "I like your new car. Silver. My first chariot had a similar panache."

Eos said, "Timessa, you haven't commented about John."

"The driver? I like the car. I can squeeze in half the gang and still have room to put up my feet."

Did she have an opinion about him? He was difficult to characterize. As Eos had said, he was narrow-waisted and muscular. She could imagine him as a killing machine; his face was unsettlingly cruel. She had tried briefly to engage him in small talk but he seemed disinterested. If he knew she was one of the country's top models, he gave no clue.

"And you approve of him?"

"Do you care?"

"Of course. Johnboy wants to please."

Timessa flinched. "Johnboy?"

"My nickname. I don't like John."

Timessa restrained herself; she instantly sensed deceit. What was Eos doing? A fury rose through her. She felt herself exhaling a ferocity like that she'd felt beside the Hoosic River when she'd burnt acres of hops with a gesture. Yet a part of her mind was placid, more alert than emotional.

She stood and walked up behind Eos, placing her hands on her shoulders. "We've shared a Johnboy in the past, haven't we?"

"Have we?"

"Remember the script, Eos? The one you sent months ago, back in the days when you called yourself Kore? Kore Serowik. I think the script was titled, *Not Her Man*."

"Oh, that."

Timessa felt outrage. Yet calmly she said, "You called him The Boy. Or Johnboy. He was gay. Under the influence of an older man."

"A coincidence."

"Fine. Boy or John or Johnboy. I don't like the Johnboy you hired."

"Timessa, he needs to stay."

"You're disguising your thoughts, Eos. You're always open and now you're not. Do you think I don't know?"

"I like this kid. He likes you, as well. And the similarities between the script and this —?"

"Yes?"

"I'll say it again: coincidence."

Apollo looked at them and stood. "Should I leave?"

Timessa smiled graciously. "When I was at Vassar, I learned the word *mendacity*. Do you know the word, Apollo?"

"Untruthfulness?"

"Yes, precisely. Eos, who sits before us, first appeared to me as an old girlfriend named Kore. Of course that was impossible because Kore was someone I invented, a fantasy. Just a momentary invention, someone I conceived, considered and then rejected as too absurd. Then behold! Artemis tells me Kore has planted herself in my thoughts, twisting them so that I would believe she was my invention.

"Then my invention non-invention appears without explanation. And keeps reappearing. My herald, Kore. Or is she Eos?"

She motioned to Apollo to sit. "She sent texts, emails, letters, and finally a movie script. All more and more complex and unsettling. Kore, whom Jackson and I later discovered by 'coincidence' in Charleville. This was after we had taken out Ares and his satyrs. Eos pleaded ignorant to everything."

Apollo glanced at Eos, who appeared indifferent, even disengaged. She sat looking out a side window, her mouth tight. He said, "I'm fascinated. Elaborate, Queen."

"We suspected she was conspiring with Ares, hiding him in her bolt-hole in Rimbaud's hometown. She convinced us she wasn't. Nor was she

Ares's girlfriend. She was just plain ol' Eos, the primal goddess of dawn, hanging out by 'coincidence' in Charleville. Why Charleville? Because she loved Rimbaud. Don't we all? And we found her in the very apartment Artemis had identified as Ares's."

"Jackson accepted her as Eos?"

"He accepted that I, as a naive, nymph-becoming-something-else, embraced her as my friend. And here we are."

Apollo turned to Eos. "These are serious aspersions."

"I think Timessa's tired," she said. "I care only about her health. She gets like this. Sudden emotions, a tendency toward anger —"

He said, "Deception, Eos. We may, as you are doing, block each other's probes, but we rarely do so. The moment you asked Timessa about this 'John,' you sealed yourself."

"You exaggerate."

"Hardly," he said. "You mask yourself even now."

Timessa interjected, "Where is Johnboy at this moment?"

"At home."

"'How are you so certain?"

"He told me."

"A former military special ops, at home, feet up with his glass of wine."

Eos said, "With his lover."

"And," T said, "how old is Johnny-boy's lover?"

"It's Johnboy. And his lover's an older man."

"Who," Timessa said, "in the script was called simply Older Man."

Eos shrugged. "Isn't it nice, Timessa, when things all make sense? They haven't and now they do." She paused, then said, "It's as if the planets …" As she spoke Apollo's eyes turned a molten gold and she froze, her mouth still open, one hand caught midair gesturing.

He looked at T and said, "Sorry if I surprised you. We were about to experience an Eos incantation, something foul. I couldn't tell exactly what, but I didn't want to waste the energy repelling it."

Timessa stared at Eos, half-surprised. "Thanks, you anticipated me by a heartbeat."

"You sensed it, too?"

"Of course." She studied Apollo, then looked at Eos. "What did you do?"

"If she were a machine, she was just deactivated. She's not, of course, but the effect is the same."

"Apollo, is she who she says she is?"

"Finding out is partly why I'm here. I knew you were doing well; Poseidon affirmed that. But I also knew much of what Eos claimed was pure concoction. And that you were at increasing risk."

"Why did you suspect?"

"We haven't seen Eos since the earliest days. Dawn was mechanical. She wasn't needed. The sun — mighty Helios — rose and set without her. Then suddenly she appears."

"She said she was chosen by the Great One."

"And if by some other force —?"

"I've become my own force, Apollo. I think I may be beyond danger. I know that sounds vain."

"None of us is invulnerable. Remember that —"

She smiled charmingly. "Yes, sir. Now, what do we do with her?"

"Much of what I've heard tonight is new to me. Johnboy, and an older man. Who are they?"

"Characters in a movie script she wrote. In it I was Laetia, half-forced to marry the gay Boy, who had an older man-lover. None of it made sense at the time. And of course she was masquerading then as Kore."

"Then this setup has been in the works for awhile."

"Evidently."

He asked, "This house is hers?"

"Yes, her 'villa'."

"And the car we were driven in?"

"Mine. In the driveway. And I drive."

He frowned. "She is definitely immortal. Even now her heart beats like a small bird's, at least ten times faster than any human's. I could leave her like this for weeks."

"But when she revives —?"

"I have to determine who she is beforehand."

"Apollo, I can't stay here tonight. However impervious I may feel, knowing she is sitting here, mouth open and eyes glazed ..." She looked around the room. "Give me a few minutes to pack a bag. I'll drive us into the city. There's a hotel you'll like."

Within a few minutes, T appeared with a bag, looking solemn. She nodded to him, and he checked Eos's eyes. "We're good."

She backed the SUV into the boulevard and drove them into Boston. Beside the Charles River, on the Boston side, she pulled into a new hotel on Storrow Drive. He looked up at the signage and laughed. "The Apollo Doubletree."

"I thought you'd approve."

She registered them, met him for a late dinner and they talked til the restaurant closed. He avoided all discussion about the earlier events, all references to Eos and Johnboy and movie scripts. As they conversed a woman played a harp from a low dais in the front of the room. Occasionally he flinched. "The lyre is a much more elegant instrument. And she's killing the higher notes."

Before they parted she texted the driver, John, telling him not to return, that his services would no longer be required. She gave no explanation for dismissing him, wondering out loud to Apollo if the boy would check in with Eos in the morning and begin to investigate when there was no reply.

It crossed her mind when she was in her own room to simply vanish the entire villa. Doing so would eliminate Eos and end whatever threat she represented. Still, Apollo seemed intent on discovering more about her. For now she would defer.

She was certain she was virtually invulnerable and hardly needed these complications, let alone a god's protection. And she was also certain Apollo would be disappointed if she took the easy way.

He was a *thaumaturge*, a wonder-worker. He was golden Apollo, Phoebus, Artemis's brother — and she would allow him time. Or at least a day.

CHAPTER 30

There, too, the long track
of day that carves records in her eyes
is not recordable —
is unmeasurable and without reprise.

E arly in the morning, John, or whoever he was, replied to her text.
My client is Eos, not you.
Until I hear otherwise from her
I will continue my assignments.
Text me your location.

She showed Apollo, who said, "He won't hear from Eos. But we can't risk him finding her inert. Do you have obligations this morning?"

"Yes, a shoot at ten."

"Then I'll take care of her on my own. And I won't need a ride."

She understood. He would simply appear. "What do you have planned?"

"I'd love to book her at Charon's hotel for a couple nights. But my powers don't extend that far. I'll find something closer."

"How about here at the Apollo?"

"No. Even with a Do Not Disturb sign on the door, imagine a cleaning woman's shock upon entering the room."

She giggled and Apollo smiled. "Respond to the text. Tell him to meet you at the house in 30 minutes. I'll take it from there."

She texted the driver, *I'll be at the house at nine.*

They parted and within seconds Apollo stood in the room where Eos sat suspended. She had not moved; her eyes were dim and mouth slack. He spent a few minutes searching the house and found nothing of note. Eos lived simply. There were no books, pieces of artwork or plants except for T's Bravo photograph, which he set aside.

A strange habitation, he thought. When Apollo returned to the room where Eos sat, he pulled a chair out across from her and spoke as if she were conscious. "So, Eos, as you must know I usually shoot arrows into anyone who menaces my friends. You're lucky. I intend to let you live until I've unraveled a few knots. And then, whether you survive will depend on what I find."

He looked around, aware he now had roughly ten minutes before the driver arrived. He stood. "What shall I do with you?"

Then he knew. Artemis was hours away, and Jackson's Pennsylvania retreat the perfect holding place. A few days in the countryside would be appropriate for one as pale as poor Eos. She'd have nymphs to watch her, and an array of divinities to help him deconstruct whatever walls she had built. He closed his eyes a moment, connecting with his sister. Then his eyes turned molten again. And at that moment, in a small flash, Eos vanished.

He quieted himself, breathing slowly, then looked out a front window. An old sedan pulled up to the curb and a young, athletic man swung out of the car, a baseball hat backward and low on his head. John was early and stood looking down the driveway. Apollo knew he expected to see Timessa's SUV. He hesitated, then strode to the front door and knocked, crying, "E-o!"

Apollo stepped to the door, silently, opening it suddenly, his eyes a molten gold. At the same moment he stepped aside and crouched as the boy jabbed his fingers toward Apollo's throat. The god dodged and drove his elbow into John's side, aware of shattering ribs, watching as the man stumbled violently into the doorframe. But he recovered, seemingly unfazed at Apollo's counterattack.

Extraordinarily low pain threshold, Apollo thought. And he couldn't read his thoughts. This being was far more than a former military operator.

Apollo vanished and reappeared twenty feet away and two rooms from the door. His bow materialized in his hand, notched with a bronze-pointed shaft. As he pulled the arrow to full draw, John entered the room. Without hesitation Apollo released the arrow into his chest, stepping aside as he staggered and dropped to a knee. "Fuck!" the man hissed. "What the hell?"

By that point he was spitting blood, trying vainly to pull the arrow from his chest. Apollo stepped forward and shoved him with his foot. John slumped sideways, blinking hard, breathing raggedly, and Apollo said, "Who the hell are you?"

As Apollo spoke he saw a goat-tail half out of his pants. And noticed long ears partially hidden in his hair, the tips tucked into the hat. How could he have not noticed when John drove them here? He had not been introduced, and not given the driver a glance, an unusual oversight. And apparently Timessa had detected nothing herself.

"Are you one of Ares's men?"

The satyr lay on his left arm, an increasingly large stain covering his shirt. His blood was nearly black, and he coughed repeatedly, then rolled onto his back, groaning sharply when the weight of his body pushed the arrow backward and partially out of his chest.

Apollo's shaft had pierced the satyr's left lung a half-inch from his heart. His lung filled with blood darker than Poseidon's deepest seas. He was drowning. As Apollo watched calmly, the satyr hissed, "Ares is gone." Then after coughing at length he said, "Who are you?"

"Phoebus Apollo."

"The archer."

"Yes."

"I wasn't told." His legs began to spasm. "The god with the golden bow."

"Your mission, goat-boy?"

"To disfigure the girl. Scar her face. A splash of acid in the eyes."

"Why?"

"She danced Dionysos back to life, then in days, condemned him to a humiliating fate."

"Why would Ares have cared?"

"Dionysos's last word as Poseidon dragged him underwater was *revenge.*"

"Are you operating alone?"

In the silence Apollo drew another arrow. The satyr watched indifferently, unwilling to respond. Their eyes locked and the god released the shaft into the satyr's heart. The impact was startling — bones broke, his chest rose momentarily, then sank as he gasped. An oxblood-black fluid pumped from the wound. The pulsing ceased and the satyr shut his eyes with a lazy smile.

🐌

There was little to preserve at Eos's home. Apollo left the house with Timessa's prized Bravo photograph and a bag of clothing he found in her room. He crossed the boulevard and sat on the seawall, watching the morning waves break and roll away. Quieting himself he contacted Timessa: *I suggest you immediately raze Eos's grounds. The house, what's inside, everything. Afterward, I'll meet you at the coffee shop near your offices.*

He wondered if she could execute this from so far away. Hearing a small *tunk*, he turned to look at the house and watched as it crumbled slowly, almost soundlessly into a blurred rectangle of soot. Apollo stood, marveling at her power: she had projected seven miles. His request had been a test; he had assumed she would drive to the beach, perhaps even see the house before being able to obliterate it.

He didn't bother to recross the street. Instead, he scanned the ocean, following several seagulls as they wheeled overhead. Unseemly birds, he thought, their grey wings the color of the heaped ash of Eos's house. He looked around, ensuring no one was watching, closed his eyes and vanished.

Twenty minutes later as Timessa walked into the coffee shop and sat across from him, she said, "Kore's movie had another character, Amy. Eos's cover letter said I was Laetia, and she was Amy. It was all predicted. Me, the boy and Kore-Amy, who's now Eos."

He listened quietly. "How did it end?"

"The movie? I killed the boy."

"Not like this morning."

"No, in her movie *I* killed him. You didn't appear."

"Tell me you didn't use a bow and arrow."

"A knife." She grimaced. "Drove it into his stomach and then pulled it up inside his ribs."

"And did Amy die as well?"

"No," she said. "She fled with the older man."

Apollo glanced around. "For one specializing in nightmares, Eos seemed such a pleasant girl … Artemis was right. My sister detected disloyalty, or double-dealing, but discounted her instincts. She said you seemed so enamored. And none of us knew Eos well enough to judge."

"What will you do with her — with Eos. Or whoever she is?"

"We will talk to Artemis. She's now on the estate. Even though I've locked Eos down, her mind may be functioning at some level."

Timessa nodded. "Plotting."

"Doubtful, but we don't know." He paused. "And there's another party we haven't considered. Could be as dangerous as the boy."

"The older man. The satyr's lover."

"Yes. Or so you say the script went. He may be satyr number two. The boy's handler."

"I hoped Charleville would end it."

Apollo smiled. "Apparently Ares's ghost lives on. Any chance you know where they live?"

"You're suggesting we visit?"

"Of course."

Within minutes they were driving to Somerville, a city a few miles north of Boston. As they idled at a traffic light, Timessa said. "It's a small apartment on Prospect Hill."

"How do you know?"

"I know. How would *you* find the address?"

He laughed. "Might take me more time."

"We're about five minutes away. Do you have a plan?"

"Sure. Remember how you and Jackson made a team?"

She smiled. "So we're winging it, aren't we?"

After a pause, he said, "Exactly."

A few minutes later, they pulled up to a triple decker. She whispered,

"The apartment's on the second floor. Entry is through the front door, ground floor. Then there's a flight of stairs."

He said, "Can you sense anyone?"

"Yes, an older man."

"Age?"

"Fifty, fifty-five. And Apollo, something else —"

"What?"

"He's half-dressed. No hat, loose pants, tail and ears obvious. And he's watching a movie."

"Then he doesn't know."

"Not about the boy and not about us."

"Okay," he said. "Let's go introduce ourselves."

As Timessa turned off the SUV, she realized confrontation was needless. She visualized the inside of the apartment as if she stood in its center.

She was instantly aware that she could manipulate the very particles and molecules, the atoms that made up the walls, the couches, the widescreen TV, and every other object in the apartment. The sense of dominion she had experienced over the last months surged; it was accompanied by an outpouring of joy, and she turned to look at Apollo. Her eyes shone; he knew.

In a rush she sensed her control of the satyr himself. He would become a danger only once he knew. Now, unguarded, he was easy. She and Apollo would not go up the building's stairs, making noise as they ran, alerting the man. Nor would they take down his door in a sudden act.

Instead, she would stun him silently, then expunge the entirety of the unit. Doing so would be a riff on the wrist-flick she'd used in Paris, and again so effectively in Charleville. It would be more discreet than the blunt force she used earlier on Eos's house.

She sensed Apollo's agreement. As she focused on the apartment, he said, "Proceed. It's brilliant."

She released an instant concussive force within the unit. The silent blast originated in front of the man who was sprawled low on the couch and drove him back into the cushions, flattening him against the wooden frame and shattering his spine. In almost the same moment, Timessa loosed — or as she visualized it, liberated — the molecules, then the

atoms, that composed the forms of every object in the room. Her loos-
ening included the flesh and bones of the satyr, fragmenting the minute
galaxies of his electrons, splintering his cortex and nervous system in an
almost imperceptible flash.

The assault was so sudden that he was never aware. One moment he
watched TV and the next he did not exist.

The attack took a tenth of a second and in the end, only walls
remained. A light ash filled the apartment, and light from the southeast-
erly windows illuminated a thin dust which hovered like a dry fog
throughout the space.

Timessa opened her eyes, scanned the building as if to confirm her
work, and said, "There's no need to inspect."

CHAPTER 31

Never allow yourself to mistake outward appearance for reality.
—Huang Po, *Taoist monk*

"Jackson?"

I turned and saw Filly, who, when Timessa left, had become Artemis's main nymph. She found me in the back gardens of the estate where I often walked when I needed to think.

Without pleasantries she said, "Come. Artemis told me to find you."

I called Danaë to join us. We wound down the trail to the amphitheatre. Filly had first taken me there years before when I attended the so-called trial. Purportedly held to determine Laine and Chloé's guilt, it instead confirmed my own startling changes.

Today, Eos sat on a simple stool in the center of the space, fixed in place. Her eyes were unreadable and lightly yellowed as if lacquered.

Someone had propped a painted sign at her feet which read,

Eos, Goddess of the Dawn
or Not?

I thought it unusual for Artemis to allow such mockery. Timessa, Artemis and Apollo stood before her in the afternoon sun. Walking up to the small group, I asked, "Conclusion?"

Apollo said, "To read her I have to wake her."

"And when that occurs," Timessa said, "she may prove to be either a monster Eos or the charming Eos we all thought we knew."

"Or," Apollo said, "not Eos at all."

They were debating. I realized my trip to Delos had not triggered any of this. The dance between Eos and Timessa had begun months before, and the awakening of the gods was merely a sideshow, however impressive. That said, without my archeological push, Apollo would not be standing beside me. And without Apollo, Eos might not have been rendered so easily insensible. These elements loosely strung together, yet we were still pawing through prehistory, uncertain whether any of what we knew would cohere.

Artemis wore her usual tunic, and Apollo had shed his khakis and button-down for a tunic that matched hers. Years before, when Danaë and I were joined, I was honored to wear his gold-fringed chiton. I had offered it to him when he appeared earlier in the day and he replied, "No, now it's yours. Consider it my thanks for what you've done. And who you've become."

His sister asked again if he could tap Eos's memories without waking her formally. "No," he responded. "And waking her seems unwise. Yet leaving her like this leads us nowhere. I need to consider options. Perhaps I'll try something later tonight —"

We left Eos with several nymphs. Having guards seemed unnecessary. I wondered who had painted the sign at her feet. One of the nymphs? There was a latent cruelty that accompanied their a-morality, and they certainly had no sympathy for the fallen. If Eos emerged from all of this somehow redeemed, they would duly honor her. If not, she would be forgotten. And if she were not the legendary Eos as she represented, her end would be abrupt. The gods tended to act rapidly once facts were clear. Misrepresentation of divinity — and daring to mislead real divinities — was never forgiven. I knew of no mechanism for appeals.

Hours later we gathered at the sacred grove, Apollo announcing he had new insights. A nymph played a pan-pipe as we arrived. The after-noon sun was low and the sky pink. Torches were lit and the roiling flames gleamed off the waters of the pool. We could have been in some sanctified thicket thousands of years earlier. Timessa wore a white archaic gown. Danaë, Filly at her side, Apollo, and Artemis had all changed into similar dress.

I remained in awe at being in Apollo's presence. One-on-one he was inspiring; here, among these immortals, his charisma burnt with an unusual light. His golden eyes flashed as he stood and said, "Before our time, before the Olympians emerged as new gods, the lands of the Levant and the forests of that region for hundreds of miles to the north of the Mediterranean were ruled by women. The villages and towns, the tribes and clans — all matriarchal."

Artemis interjected, "Men deferred to women for key decisions."

Apollo nodded. "Property and wealth passed from mother to daugh-ter. All celebrated their fortune, as this also was a time of peace that lasted from generation to generation. War, if use of the word is even appropriate, consisted of small skirmishes, arguments over food or mates."

"At times women," Artemis said, "allowed their men to wield spears, but the victors without exception knelt to give thanks to —"

"— The Great Goddess," Apollo interjected. "All acknowledged that fertility, bountiful harvests and great health flowed from her as if an endless gift."

Timessa watched, her face inscrutable. Her eyes, shrouded, shifted from Apollo to Artemis. Once she caught me observing her and smiled. She appeared immensely self-possessed.

"This period," Apollo said, "lasted far longer than our own. Our legends indicate the Great Goddess ruled for forty- to fifty-thousand years. I say that in comparison to our own several thousand."

Danaë leaned forward. "Yet when we emerged, she was no more than a myth."

He nodded. "Yes. Her earthly retreat, like ours later, coincided with the transformation of human society from female-led to male. Waves of Germanic, Vandals, Goths and Gaul tribes, all patriarchal, invaded her lands over several hundred years. The long peace that assured prosperity and safety ended in the destruction that was typical of that final millennium. All of this occurred just before our birth."

Artemis added, "And these people that the Greeks called barbarians brought their own gods. Men ruled tribes and towns, and wealth passed from father to son. The Great Goddess was spurned by the invaders and ridiculed by the priests who supplemented the priestesses."

Apollo noted, "We emerged into the chaos of the so-called Mycenaean period. Zeus, and then later my sister and I, with others, muscled out many of the invaders's gods. Between 1350 and 1150 BCE, the region was swept by geologic change — droughts and earthquakes, volcanoes — as well as an unheard of culture of war." He paused. "Although you know this history, it is bears repetition."

Timessa said nothing, her eyes dark. Artemis glanced at her and said, "All of us thrive on adulation. Worship is reciprocal. A goddess gives and the recipient gives thanks. When the praise goes, the gifts do, as well. As patriarchy prevailed, the Great Goddess withdrew — as we withdrew sixteen hundred years later when the region was swept by the Jesus cult."

Apollo gestured emphatically. "The Great One never expired."

His sister spoke quickly, "Nor have we."

"But the point of my recitation," he said, "is that Eos — the one we now discuss — like us, was a creature of the chaos. She preceded us, serving Helios in the earliest days. She was a minor divinity, rarely worshipped and rarely mentioned. We knew of her, but paid her little mind."

Artemis smiled. "Given the last half year of her meddling, we suspect her ego was far larger than her importance."

I said, "A disgruntled goddess?"

"Exactly," she said.

Apollo added, "Since we met earlier in the amphitheatre, Artemis and I have decided that our captive is the real Eos, and not a poseur."

"But," Artemis added, "we cannot determine her intentions."

Timessa spoke for the first time. "It's no secret that she's been trying to influence what has been happening to me. At first, as Artemis alerted me, she manipulated my thoughts, claiming to be someone she wasn't. When caught lying she backtracked and claimed instead to be my herald, or as she said, 'I carry the lantern that lights your way. I proclaim the news,' as if I'm a messiah. Which I am not …

"We have caught her in deceptions repeatedly. There was Ares in Charleville —" She caught my eye. "Jackson, you and I were initially convinced that her presence was a mere coincidence."

"The two of you," I affirmed, "bonded too quickly."

"Yes, she was charming. But catching her in Boston with satyrs is despicable. Setting me up to be disfigured by one is unforgivable."

I leaned forward, looking between T and Apollo. "I see no path to redemption. She has lied time and again. She was caught red-handed when Apollo confirmed T's driver to be a satyr hitman. All of this was Eos's doing."

Apollo sat for the first time and gazed at Timessa. "One thing she said was accurate: 'You are breaths away from absorbing the full energy of the Great One.' It is likely that when that occurs, you will have been granted the entirety of her powers."

Timessa stood abruptly, her gown spiraling gently. "Enough speculation! Time to wake Eos."

Apollo slowly nodded. "Yes, of course," he said, but then warned, "She will try something to avoid her fate."

❧

We left the grove for the amphitheatre. Eos appeared not to have moved, and the guard-nymphs confirmed our suspicion. We formed a triangle before her. I looked overhead at the settling darkness. In the gray dusk a single contrail overhead formed a diagonal from one edge of the theatre portal to the other. Danaë caught my eye for a moment, then nodded toward Eos.

Apollo said softly, "I'll wake her now," and shut his eyes.

Eos jerked as if touched by an electrical wire, then after trembling momentarily, sighed. As she inhaled she raised her head, eyes open and looked around. Timessa stood behind me and to the side, her gown moving gently in a faint breeze that seemed to circle her alone.

Eos smiled lazily, saying, "My Queen, you look beautiful. Have I seen that gown?"

Then she turned to Artemis and said, "Ah, Artemis!"

When Artemis said nothing, Eos looked at me in silence — I detected only contempt — finally rotating to Apollo. "Return me to my house. I'll never bother anyone again." Then her words became slower and slower. "There are ... so many ... loose ends ..."

Apollo spoke evenly, "Eos, your house is gone. It was obliterated after I killed the driver."

She cried, "What?!"

"We eliminated the older man as well."

Eos's face contorted. Then she wept, covering her eyes. We stepped back, watching. As suddenly, she inhaled slowly, audibly, and looked at Apollo. "You monster. Both ... were fine men, ancient ... spirits from ... an ancient time."

"Satyrs," he said. "are at best contemptible."

She scanned our faces. Artemis said as if revolted, "I tire of this."

"You were always merciless," Eos said.

"You deserve no mercy," Artemis said coldly.

"Just release me. I'll move on."

Apollo said, "Why, Eos?"

"Why what? Are you asking me to explain myself?"

"Yes," Apollo said. "Why would the goddess of dawn plot against one of us?"

"Is it not obvious?"

"No."

She pointed at Timessa, shrieking. "Fools! *She* is the threat! Not I. Progress and innovation arise from war, from anger and conflict! Not from women's love! If allowed to flourish, she would bring back ... harmony.""

Artemis whispered, "You *are* mad."

"No!" Eos cried, "The Great One was silenced once. A blessing. Are you blind? She cannot return — yet she is. She's re-emerging before our eyes! It cannot be allowed!"

"Were you planning to have the driver kill her suddenly?" Artemis asked.

"Oh no," Eos said, "the opposite. After he disfigured her, in her fury, she would cast him out. He was to be her first ancient, annual sacrifice."

Timessa said, "What?"

"Do you pretend to forget?" Eos asked. "The old ways demand a king's sacrifice. Every year. The boy was to be the beginning. I hoped she'd enjoy gutting him with some cheap knife ..."

Eos continued, "That little game with the boy was all for you, Timessa. So that you'd taste blood. So that you would not forget the violence that lies deep in the Great Goddess's heart."

"Did you believe that we would mate?" Timessa asked.

"Doubtful. The boy would have been as disgusted."

"Ah," Timessa said. "Laetia and The Boy."

"You failed to see. The boy was a king to be harvested."

"To what purpose, Eos? Why would I do such a thing?"

"You're as much a fool as Apollo. For mere slaughter. For blood! To disrupt goodwill!"

"I would never," T said.

"Oh, you would have," Eos countered. "I was your counselor. The one who whispered in your ear, who would have kept alive the violence in your heart."

I interrupted. "Charleville. You and Ares were not casual friends. You were a pair."

She looked at me in disgust. "Yes, Jackson, he was a superb lover. And you were so easily fooled."

I said, "Your apartment was, as Artemis guessed, his bolthole."

She laughed. "However briefly. Both of you wanted to believe the opposite. So easily misled."

Timessa said, "Go on, Eos. Elaborate."

"You killed Ares. Unimaginable. An assassination. From that, two of his finest satyrs swore allegiance, swore they'd pursue you to till the end."

"An end which came rapidly. For them," Apollo said.

Eos looked furtively to each of us. She had not tried to escape, but she must have sensed she was seconds from a terrible denouement, a terminus she might yet escape.

She spoke slowly. "In Athens many years ago, in its shining moments when temples were rising and its people ruled the seas, I was counsel to the priestess for Athene Polias. Hers was one of the most distinguished offices in the world, a life tenure ..." She smiled. "Her name was Lysimache, and her brother was temple treasurer. A brother-sister team. The post was hereditary and the girl was from the best of families. But her beauty was not matched by her brains. She needed help. That's where I came in ..."

Timessa interjected, "Enough!" Turning to the three of us, she said, "Shall we end this now? And who among us will have the honor?"

Eos spoke more rapidly. "I organized temple celebrations, ensured sacrifices were appropriate to each holiday, guaranteed crowds, ensured that her clothing was the finest, and checked her brother's books so he wouldn't skim silver from the goddess's purse." She raised her hands, half imploringly, half in despair. "I wanted nothing less for the Great One who stands before me now!"

"Except," Timessa said, "you gave false counsel."

"I feared you would return the world to matriarchy. Matriarchy is tranquility. Peace is passivity; passivity is the end of imagination and invention. Don't you see? Harmony is a fallacy."

"And you dare call us fools," Timessa said.

Eos shook her head. "I state the truth. Αλεθε."

Night had now fallen and her face was illuminated by torchlight, the fiery brands held by nymphs behind us. In the flickering light, her eyes were anxious. Timessa whispered, "Everyone be aware. Shield yourself. She has the ability to erase thoughts."

"But," Eos said, "I haven't acted. All of us are friends."

Apollo began to circle Eos, speaking as he walked. "Sister," he said to Artemis, "are there not laurel trees on these grounds, and particularly in the sacred grove?"

"Yes, we preserve them carefully. The leaves are evergreen, a symbol of immortality."

"And," he said, "the laurel is sacred to me, is it not?"

"Yes, I honor that which is sacred to my brother."

He stopped abruptly and asked, "And the laurel is sacred to me particularly because …"

One of the nymphs giggled. "Because of Daphne."

He turned to the nymph. "Yes, the lovely Daphne. That was so many years ago." He stepped up to her and said, "Recite the story, nymph, since you seem to know it well."

She blushed and looked to Artemis. The goddess nodded and the nymph said, "The love god Eros, Aphrodite's son, pierced you with his arrows. In moments, you glimpsed the naiad, Daphne, and wanted her. In your fever you pursued her through the woods. She cried out to her father, a river god, to help her get away. In desperation he —"

"— turned her into a laurel tree," Apollo continued. "What a stupid thing to do. I would have shown her eternal love."

Timessa said, knowingly, "Was Daphne released?"

"No," the nymph said. "She couldn't move. Her feet had turned into roots."

"Could she speak?"

"Her voice was silenced forever."

T smiled, "So she couldn't move. Or speak. Could she communicate in any way?"

Apollo shook his head. "No, she is as mute as a statue. To this day, after millennia, she remains immobile, her fingers rustling leaves."

The nymph said, "The story is one we often tell."

Apollo groaned. "After, in her honor I awarded laurel wreaths to victors at the Pythian games."

Artemis said quietly, "Brother, do not dwell on what took place so long ago."

"It remains fresh. I blame Eros, and Daphne's father. Gods do not always act wisely. I did not, nor did he."

Timessa nodded. "There were once laurel forests throughout Greece. The climate was cooler, more humid. Now they are a rarity, found like satyrs only in mountain glades. Perhaps an extra laurel beside the sacred pool would be a pleasant thing, a reminder of what once was …"

Eos cried, "No —!"

Apollo's voice rose. "Yes … As Artemis's nymphs pass this new laurel tree on their daily tasks, they perhaps will nod and say to no one in particular, 'Ah, that even Dawn could be turned into a tree!' "

He swiveled toward Eos, clinching his fists, saying quietly, "We have wasted much time."

She began violently shaking her head and stood for the first time, raising her hands to the sky, or perhaps in a plea to her brother, Helios. But the sun had set. From her open mouth it appeared she would speak. Instead, she howled piteously.

Apollo's eyes were molten as Eos trembled, gasped and raised her hands.

CHAPTER 32

Her despair, despair: she looks down
at her legs, aware they glow.
Transparent skin now so sheer her bones show
through like porcelain.

Timessa woke the next morning, recalling her dream from the night before. It began with a *Dionysiakos*. She whirled and circled and at the end of the dancing found herself breathless in a field of uncut grass. This was no dream planted by Eos. This was one from another source.

An hour before dawn, dreaming in a vast transparency, she found herself on that same wide meadow, on the same blanket on the same pleasant day with what appeared to be the same angel that she'd dreamt a half year earlier. They sat together, the angel's exquisite hair blonde as always in these dreams. She remembered the butterfly from the earlier dream and at that moment saw one dart through the asters scattered through the field.

T was in a summer dress sitting sideways beside the angel. The angel stroked her back and sang gently in a language she wasn't sure she knew. After awhile the being stopped and said, "Timessa, Timessa, look at me."

As Timessa did, she realized that this was no angel. She was instead a glistering, radiant little girl. When T later told me details, I knew it was the same girl who had flittered teasingly through my dreams back when Chloé and I believed we were in love. Later, after a long year, the same little girl, in blue dress and ribbons, danced gloriously at the coupling ceremony for Danaë and me.

Timessa had never dreamed of her before; the little girl's visitations in her soft translucence were always to gods and goddesses. Now the girl appeared to the former nymph as well, laughing in delight at Timessa's astonishment.

T feared saying her name, afraid that doing so might shatter the gravity, the meaning of the dream. Still, the little girl watched her in amusement, nodding, tugging at T's hair and dress, finally making funny faces to counter T's disbelief. The little girl whispered, "Say my name."

Timessa could not speak, and the girl poked her gently. "Say … my name."

She nodded, aware this was just a dream, and so said, "Gaia."

The little girl giggled, stood and did a slow pirouette, then bowed. She said, "You have been on our minds for some time. And," she giggled, "our expectations have been met."

" 'Our'?"

"Of course. The Great One found you in a gaggle of nymphs many years ago. Together we have prepared the table."

"You have been involved?"

"With the Goddess. Now she passes the sacred keys to you, her successor."

And the little girl laughed, clapping her hands. Oddly, she cried, "High five!" and the two slapped palms. Then Gaia cartwheeled away and vanished in a small flash.

In another dream, almost immediately after the first, T sat with Josef in his back garden; a screen of ivy up a brick wall shielded them from a crowd on the street. She could hear voices crying, "Show us the sacred One!" and, "We are hers!"

Then she and Josef stood in his angel room, with the collection stacked in varying levels. Josef was in his usual robe, standing beside an angel with opened wings. He exhaled audibly and said, "These are not what they appear."

As she looked at him, she saw movement among the angel statues. One, then another, changed in small white flashes from seraph statues to marble, stylized figurines of women. None was taller than ten inches, and each was carved with tight legs and rounded stumps for arms. Flash after flash changed more angels to marble figures, all small, with small breasts and incised genitalia. The statues appeared quite phallic, she thought.

Reading her mind, Josef said loudly, "Explicitly."

"What are these?"

"Cycladic in origin. All from about 6,000 to 2,000 BCE. Archeologists once called them idols, but they are not."

"So they are ..."

"Statuettes of the Great One. Each a representation of the One, the Queen. I call them my Cycladic girls."

" 'Cycladic girls'?"

"Found on the islands south of Athens."

"How were they used?"

Josef untied his silk robe, exposing his breasts and opening his hands in an odd, welcoming gesture. He said, "By women. The Great Goddess was careful to protect those who carried representations. She gave them blessings. Made them fertile. Ensured each found secret pleasures in the dark of night."

As his voice trailed off, the room filled with a dense smoke. Josef was no longer there, and the dozens of marble figurines walked themselves backwards as Timessa reached out to touch one, then another. After a few frustrating seconds, she woke.

When Timessa saw Artemis later that morning, she linked arms with the goddess and they walked slowly to the grove. Artemis pointed to a new laurel that had appeared to the left of a small grouping. It stood about Eos's height and was moving slightly in the summer breeze. To her surprise, T felt nothing. She spoke dispassionately: "Each of us must be prepared to change."

Artemis was silent. They turned back to the village. On the way Timessa told her fragments of her last dream, how Josef's angels had turned into figurines. Artemis asked about their appearance and T described them: small, marble, almost Cubist in appearance. She said, "He called them Cycladic."

"Do you remember what the word means?"

"I guess I didn't pay attention when we were taught. I recall circle, κγκλοσ."

"The Cyclades are the islands that encircle Delos."

"And the epicenter," Timessa intoned, "Delos, was the sacred isle of your birth."

"And my brother's."

"The little statues looked familiar. Have I seen one before?"

Artemis smiled. "You've forgotten. When you were young, you played with one. I think I can find it when we get back."

"Funny what children forget."

Again they walked in silence. In the village the goddess went into a long hut built for girl's play. T waited, watching the usual bedlam of nymphs in the village. She looked overhead: a hawk circled, and T thought, *We are the epicenter.*

In a few minutes, Artemis returned and opened her hand. In her palm was a white Cycladic statue, six inches long and polished from a millennia of rubbing. She offered it to T, who smiled. "Now I remember!"

"There were many years when you wouldn't let any of the other girls near it. Others liked to cuddle bears. But you adored this statue. Do you remember what you named it?"

Timessa was embarrassed. "No. Was it something stupid?"

"You called it, Queenie."

She nodded. It was all flooding back. *Queenie.* The marble in her hand felt cold; she began to rub it gently and it warmed. Timessa smiled and Artemis said, "Would you like it? The two of you bonded long ago."

Queenie. She slipped it into a pocket, feeling the silky hardness and the heat, imagining thousands of Cycladic women and girls so many years ago, each cherishing a similar figurine. She closed her eyes, trying to recall details of her childhood. Why had she alone been attracted to this?

As she opened her eyes, she saw Orthrus sitting near them in a shadow, its anodyne eyes languid and unblinking. She looked at Artemis. "The beast!"

It was two-headed, barely breathing in its praetorian focus. Timessa squeezed the goddess's arm, asking, "What does it see?"

"You know. Everything."

࿐

Timessa had asked if she could visit with Danaë and me before returning to Boston. She came by the house mid-afternoon. Danaë hugged T for minutes when she arrived. Both wore sundresses as if they were vibrant twenty-two-year-olds on any summer afternoon. T removed her huge sunglasses and stepped inside.

I ushered her into the room with the Phidias statue. She charmingly curtsied before Aphrodite, saying, "The world's rarest piece of art."

I found it hard to be as light-hearted, knowing what Timessa had become. But the two went back unimaginably far. And Danaë deferred to no one. Me? I admit to caution. I had seen T's anger rise without warning. She was formidable. Still, I was pleased to be considered a friend. As we sat I asked if she would return to modeling.

"You're prescient. It's what I want to talk about."

"You have no need to work."

She smiled gently. "It could be argued I have no need for anything."

Danaë asked, "Where would you live?"

T frowned. "Apollo and I enjoyed the Doubletree. You haven't seen it, but there's a penthouse with a great view of the city. Looks out over the Charles. But it feels pretentious."

I said, "Josef?"

"Funny. I dreamed of him last night. We were in a room filled with dozens of little Cycladic statues." T reached into a pocket and pulled out Queenie. "Like this."

Danaë said, "Timessa, it's Queenie!"

She looked embarrassed. "The goddess retrieved it for me this morning. Now it's mine. Again." She held the statue by the waist and pretended it was walking from left to right. As she did she pursed her lips, saying in a childish voice, "Little Queenie's going home!"

"Why go back to modeling?" I asked. "And how will you reconcile the grind of work with … let me say this tactfully … what you've become?"

She looked at me quizzically. Then I saw a trace of anger. "I am what I've become. And I am not."

Danaë laughed, deflecting T's irritation. "As your friend I can safely say you're not bewildered, but rather, mystified."

T smiled. "You mean, not dumbfounded, just demented!?"

Danaë nodded. "Wine?"

"Yes, always."

Danaë rose and looked at me. I said, "Water. Thanks."

With Danaë in the kitchen, T leaned forward and said, "Jackson, the truth is, I'm terrified."

"I understand."

"You probably don't."

"Then I apologize for assuming I do."

"I don't mean to sound harsh."

"How can any of us fathom what you're experiencing?"

"Yes. There are times when I am all too aware of myself."

"And?"

"You've seen glimpses. But it has become far more vast. I know so much …" She paused. "Not facts like history, but matters of control, distortion, creation. I can project myself and destroy from great distances. I can exploit resources, or guarantee a doubling of crops. I can make barren girls ovulate."

"The fertility goddess lives again."

"Perhaps, yet how ironic that I've never slept with a man."

Danaë walked in with wine coolers and water. Timessa said casually, "Danaë, I was just saying I'm scared. I guess that's it. It's happened too quickly. A year ago I was a nymph, restless, looking around — but still just another girl."

"Just another immortal nymph."

She sniffed. "Shut up."

Danaë said, "I suspect it's not possible for us to advise you. Not really." She looked at me. "Jackson?"

"Logically, she can't go on in two roles. The modeling is frivolous, even meaningless. The other dictates life and death. How can they be reconciled?"

Timessa pointed at me. "That's it. And worse, I'm reluctant to use the powers I seem to possess."

Pretending to pout, Danaë said, "Aww. Exotic beauty, extraordinary fame and the added burden of becoming a Great Goddess."

Timessa's eyes flickered over her and I wondered for a moment if Danaë had pushed too far. Timessa stood and wandered over to the Phidias. "May I touch?"

I said, "Of course."

She ran a hand casually over Aphrodite's breast, circling the marble nub of nipple with her thumb. "I've never understood the attraction of one woman for another. But this statue could change my mind."

"Be careful," Danaë said. "Rumors are if a girl merely touches the divine statue, she'll never want a man."

Timessa smiled. "Her breasts are definitely provocative." She opened her lips, leaning forward as if she might taste a nipple.

We should have laughed but we didn't. Timessa watched us, finally saying, "I don't want to sound like the long lost Lachesis, but I can't stand the concept of virginity." She swiveled to me. "Stupid man, I threw myself at you for weeks, but you didn't care."

Danaë's eyes were dark, but she said nothing. T continued, "But that's why I trust you today."

Before I could respond, Danaë interjected, "Do you have perimeters? Is it allowed for you to love?"

"It's very simple. I am not supposed to sleep with men."

I said softly, "As the Great Goddess I suspect you can fucking do what you want."

She laughed. "That's why I love you, Jackson. You're frank. What can I get away with? Let's not forget, Orthrus watches all."

Danaë smiled. "He used to watch Jackson and me. Months before we joined. We'd escape to that little shack in the woods. He'd hover nearby, watching. But we didn't care."

Timessa restlessly waved her hand as if brushing away an irritation. "I think I'll return to Boston, at least for awhile. I have dozens of girls who seem to count on me. It's like my own nymph gang. Gorgeous girls who all crave love."

"You're aware," Danaë said, "that Sappho had a bevy of girls who followed her around. That's when the rumors about *her* began!"

"I'd forgotten. Sappho's Academy on Lesbos."

"A girl's school. Only beautiful schoolgirls may apply."

Timessa laughed. "My exact criteria." Then she paused. "I still a few months at most before I assume authority."

"You know that with certainty?" I asked.

She looked at me. "Yes."

Danaë wondered, "What will you do?"

"There will come a time when I disappear."

Danaë said indignantly. "No!"

"Not from you, but from humans. I understand celebrity. We crave adoration, but idolization becomes suffocating. If I'm not careful, humans will turn me into a cult figure, a beautiful guru, an object of worship. And they will want to ensure I never change …

"But it won't happen," she continued. "Before then I'll disappear."

"What do you mean by 'assume authority'?" I wondered if she knew what she was talking about.

"I will expect," she said as if I were an idiot, her voice suddenly imperious, "reverence, adoration, praise. And if homage does not occur, I will withdraw largesse."

Danaë whispered, "Homage?"

"Offerings."

"Like sacrifices?"

"Maybe. Eos mentioned the Great One having her counterpart, her king, killed annually. Each year a new young man, each eager to see his predecessor dead, each unwilling to believe his fate would be the same."

"You are not to sleep with others," I said, "yet you might take a 'king' each year?"

"The boys were symbols. I'm sure they imagined nights of glorious goddess sex. If I'm to believe sex is glorious …" She shrugged. "But instead they got stand-ins, my surrogates. Then the lucky boy was harvested each fall."

Danaë and I looked at each other.

Timessa said, "What?"

"When you 'assume authority,' " Danaë said, "you will have more power than Artemis or Apollo."

"I already do."

"Then, quoting Jackson," Danaë said, "you can fucking do what you want. You won't be bound by any of the ancient rites. You won't have to take boys in a fake coupling and then take their lives. You can take what you want as sacrifices, if that's what you demand …

"Think about it, Timessa," she went on, "you could ask for cupcakes or silver coins. Or demand worshippers blow kisses to you on their knees."

"Or like the minotaur," T said, "I could require seven boys and seven maidens from every city, every year."

Danaë made a face. "Well, strike an old friend dead if you wish, but as a mother with sons, you suddenly terrify me. I don't think any of this is funny."

Timessa circled the Phidias statue as she spoke slowly. She cupped the statue's breasts from behind. "Then don't mock me. Sacrifice is never frivolous. You, Danaë, have made hundreds yourself. You have done so to placate the goddess, to stay in her graces. The sows and ewes and wood-cocks we sacrifice cost us dearly. And the goddess would be insulted if her nymphs used meaningless things. In the same way, I will be infuriated if I am spurned."

Danaë stood and said, "It's been good visiting."

"Am I being dismissed?"

Danaë said nothing and Timessa said, "Indeed, I am," and left.

CHAPTER 33

*She lowers herself to lie
in the din.
A crow above her in a pine
wings away with a cry*

Timessa waited one more night before returning to Boston, but slept little. Perhaps her afternoon visit with us sparked another change, an incremental shift. She left agitated, an outcome I suspect she had not expected. I'm certain we increased her disquiet, the opposite of what she might have sought. Old friends are often unduly frank.

After Timessa visited with Filly for hours that same night, she left the comfort of the small village to lie under bright constellations in a field between Artemis's encampment and the sacred grove. Like bright pearls tossed into hot tar, the evening's stars seemed to bulge from the firmament. She imagined each returning to primal seas in celestial tails of yellows and spinning reds.

After making a bed in crushed grass, Timessa lay on her back in her clothes, conscious of the fires rippling through her muscles, roaring down her nerves. Were the stars moving, or was this another trick of Gaian gravity? Was the summer wind that moved through the estate pushing stars from west to east? Or up and down?

She had no interest in answers, content to feel the heat in her thighs and belly. In time the heat became an intrusive smoke, moving up her neck and finally into her hair.

Fire: she had tasted it before and knew she now glowed in a luminous fusion in the dark.

After watching planets and tumbling meteors for hours, she closed her eyes. She had been afraid to do so earlier. Now she surrendered, her eyelids feverish. She felt charred, imagining her bones blackened like coal or bleached like porcelain. Who knew what game the heat would play? Perhaps it was as fickle as one's heart. She knew she was the Great One, Queen, Ishtar or Cybele, a goddess set afire under stars. The old Timessa burned away, and the new goddess she was becoming burned as well. Both old and new were ablaze, alight, smoldering as if lying opened, thrown onto a bed of hot coals that had never cooled.

With her eyes shut, she saw the field of uncut grass from her angel dreams. It too lay under stars, in the dark, still and pregnant with an unspeakable anxiety. Then almost instantly, it burst into flames, the initial flare starting in the center of her vision and spreading sideways until the entire horizon was afire. She knew its name: conflagration. And knew it had come for her. Not others, finally for her. Would she sacrifice herself to the firestorm? She had nothing else to give. She was all there was.

She might demand as much from those who wanted gifts. There was nothing more than all.

She felt the heat, the flames approaching—rising higher toward the stars and wheeling galaxies, blistering her lips, searing off her blouse and linen skirt. All of it was lost in smoke. All, all. All of it afire as even her under garments burst into flame.

Unintelligible voices sang in an odd perfection with the crackling fire-brands and singed grasses, with the half-mad ewes and lambs and oxen that now surrounded her bed. As she opened her eyes she saw woodcocks circling overhead, hundreds, more than she had ever sacrificed. She was startled to find fat sheep sitting on their rumps at the corners of her bed, watching her with small red eyes. She looked from side to side for a knife, thinking, *Blood*. Thinking, *All of these await my blade*. All, all ....

But the smoke began to curl and circle and thicken so much that the woodcocks fled en masse. She propped herself up on her elbows. The fat sheep were gone, the ewes had turned and were entering the fire single file, marching into an oven. As she watched they burst into flame, one by one by one, vanishing in constant white flashes.

Suddenly empty, she felt around for Queenie. The statue lay beside her, yellowed in the heat, and when she gripped it, the marble sizzled against her skin. She laid down again, laughing at her emptiness, her gains and losses, the fires that still flared occasionally down her legs, the small earthquakes shuddering through her chest, the silence that filled her, the electrons within molecules suspended in mid spin. Old and new were in a secret pact, a silence of dominion. Sound and light were immaterial.

Her breath sang in half-exhalation; otherwise the world was mute. As she lay reveling in her state, dawn broke. She smiled into the few stars that still hung above her, aware that Eos, now nothing more than a laurel, would not be missed, not by Helios or any other divinity. Dawn had become an automata. Day occurred without its dawn, the sun moving on its great ecliptic without a god dragging it behind his chariot.

Eos: even as a minor goddess, Eos was a measurable offering, a worthy thing to be lowered onto her altar. Eos, a sacrifice made to her, to the Great One. To the goddess who lies now as if a reveler on duvets in the grass. A first sacrifice: Eos.

The sun began to turn her a rosy pastel. She felt the light across her eyelids and opened her eyes. The field of grass stirred in its verdancy, each stem, the millions of rough stems, all deep green. All, all. All of the blades singing in the golden light. In the sacred, golden dawn that was a dawn without Eos.

In a half-rapture of her own making, she felt a presence, rolled on her side, and looked into Apollo's face. He stood fifteen feet away, his eyes a molten gold. He watched her without greeting, as if a sentinel.

Timessa sat up and spoke loudly, almost shouting. "I spent the night on fire. The world was flames. The air whirred with woodcocks. The ewes burned and the sheep surrounded me like oarsmen, steering me from here to somewhere else."

A faint smile flickered at the corners of his mouth. Like Poseidon weeks earlier, he dropped to a knee and said, bowing his head, "Oh, Queen."

ॐ

In Boston Timessa checked first with her agency. Her absence was excused; no questions were asked. Was she now available? She confirmed she was.

She inquired about the extent of her funds. Her income was handled by a private wealth management bank in Cambridge. Her account manager quoted amounts on hand, and suggested creating a trust. Her earnings, particularly given the short duration she had worked, were impressive. And she had to thank Artemis who had provided the initial capital, itself enough to cover her projected expenses for years. Timessa knew money itself was unnecessary, but it facilitated her passage while she worked. She asked the manager to prepare the necessary papers. The fund would be called The Stones Speak Trust.

She also texted her gang — the wolf pack — suggesting a meetup that night. They hadn't gathered in over a week. In minutes she had a dozen confirmatory texts. Wine, seltzer, sodas, crab cakes: everyone would cancel other obligations and meet her at the Storehouse, a quiet venue in Cambridge. It offered light jazz and bragged about its lack of sports TVs.

Her final challenge was housing. The Apollo would work for a short time, but she needed something else. She checked in at the hotel, showered and began to email confirmations for a half dozen shoots around the region.

Within a day she would be busy again. And after all, fashion seemed a perfect way to kill a month. Still, she wasn't sure she would last that long; her two days at Artemis's had convinced her that changes would quickly run their course. Yet she acknowledged she thrived on the adulation. She imagined the girls on their knees, heads bent. And she admitted her need for exaltation grew in parallel with her powers.

She thought, *veneration and command*. The concept played on social dynamics, and hinged on control. She remembered a phrase from a history class at Vassar: command and control. An ugly term, military, but it could as easily refer to a religious hierarchy. An officer assigned tasks to effect certain goals. She, the Great Goddess, would exercise control and in return, worshippers would offer veneration. Daydreams.

She slipped into a casual dress and brushed her hair. Her cheeks were flush — mulberry red — and her hair lustrous. Watching herself move in the mirror, she was startled at her cheekbones, her heart-shaped face. Exotic was an insufficient description. Perhaps for the first time she saw herself as others did. Her beauty seemed to have grown with her power.

Yet wasn't it all vastly egotistical? No, she thought, not egotistical, logical. She was what she was.

She hadn't asked for this, but she accepted it. All of it.

And yes, when she took control she would demand acknowledgement. And thanks for whatever she bestowed. If she was to sacrifice, so would they. The process was an ancient feedback loop. The religious instinct was cooked into human DNA: power was acknowledged, great power venerated.

With a final look in the mirror, she thought, *Until thy sacred coming out, thou art simply biding time.*

At the Storehouse she found the function room she'd reserved already full. Sixteen girls had come, several new to the gang. They were wild-eyed seeing her, giggling and touching. She paused with each, stroking their cheeks or giving them light kisses, complimenting their clothes or hair, asking about their recent gigs. Drinks and food were served, and she was aware that several of the girls fought politely to be closest to her as they ate.

She drifted through the evening, giving just enough attention for each to feel exceptional. Near the end of the gathering, T stood and spoke, the room slowly quieting.

"None of you is older than twenty. Some of you are far younger. Who here is just fourteen?"

Two girls raised their hands. She smiled and asked, "Do your mothers know you're here?" To giggles they blushed and looked away.

"And how many of you are a year older, fifteen?"

Five girls, all lanky, long-lashed and wide-eyed, raised their hands. She maintained the lightness, smiling again and said, "And *your* mothers — did you have to sneak away?" All laughed or nodded, one confessing, "My mom's waiting in the parking lot. But she loves you, too!"

Timessa continued, "And the rest of you then are sixteen to twenty. Look around at yourselves. You're all beautiful. High cheekbones, narrow faces. Big fat lips!" To general laughter she said, "But each of us has a slightly different look. I have this stupid curved nose —" She tapped her straight nose, and one of the girls cried out, "*Vogue* calls it aquiline!"

"Yes, they're sweethearts. But we each have a slightly different look. And we think we're all different inside, as well. We like to think we're unique. 'There's no one like me,' right? Or, 'I'm exceptional. I'm even a model!' And on and on. But there's more we have in common. For instance, we all want love. And admiration and families. And a long life."

They watched her, smiling. She continued, "For instance, when I was growing up, I couldn't sleep without being held. I'll bet a couple of you needed cuddling too, am I right?"

The girls all nodded, rapt at her talk, eager to know what she'd conclude. "Another thing we have is our little gang —"

A girl cried out, "TB's gang!"

Timessa pretended to look bored, saying, "Timessa's bitches?" She pointed at one of the younger girls and said, "Honey, you're not old enough to be a bitch." Everyone laughed.

Timessa was conscious of her patter and its effect. Too, she admitted that their adoration mattered. Immensely. The adoration had not risen to veneration, but parties like this were a warmup, a trial to hone her prowess. She asked loudly, "Shall we bring this to a vote? Make the gang's name official?"

A chorus of yeses rose. Timessa raised her hand. "Wait? Are their other names? Anyone have something cooler we can call ourselves?"

They all shook their heads. She shrugged. "Okaaay, girls. Let's see hands for 'TB's gang'."

The unanimous "yes" vote was followed by applause. Then one of the older girls called out, "What's the gang gonna do?"

"Hmm," Timessa said. "Uh, hang out with me?!"

She was surprised when everyone jumped up and ran to her, forming a cluster of hugging, laughing girls. It took minutes to give each an embrace as several cried when held, and others thanked her profusely, muttering things like, "I'd be lost without you," and "I've never been so happy —"

The gathering had run less than two hours when she called its end. "I'll be in a new place soon, one with lots of space for get-togethers. Until then, the Storehouse works. Now, everyone sleep well! No dark circles under eyes!"

CHAPTER 34

So shalt thou feed on Death, that feeds on men,
And, Death once dead, there's no more dying then.
—Shakespeare, *Sonnet 146*

A lone in her suite at the Apollo, for a second night Timessa couldn't sleep. This late evening was no different than the previous night at the Pennsylvania estate, except the mad, tumbling stars above were hidden from view by sheet-rocked ceilings, sheathing and wires buried in the walls. Too, the wildfires on the horizon of her mind were barely embers. The ceiling as she stared was a bitumen grey, and if she tried, she could see black clouds moving over it from one side to the other like distant horses across a beach.

For a moment the ceiling was a cyclorama with dark palls dancing between pencils of light. Ah, she thought, our old friend, Helios. And for a second she thought of Eos, wondering if the night's breezes were rustling her and if her leaves would tremble when thunder shuddered the sacred grove. Once Artemis described thunder as a metal gong being struck by a dragon's tail. Would that send fear down Eos's delicate trunk?

As she lay on her back, she was aware she rarely missed an entire night of sleep. Without at least four hours, she knew she'd be a wreck. Now she was in her second sleepless night, and although vaguely aggravated at her loss of routine, she wasn't drowsy. In fact, using a word of one of the photographers she knew, she felt wired.

The more she reflected, the more the loss of sleep became merely a curiosity. She knew that none of the gods and goddesses slept more than an hour, and even that was, they claimed, unnecessary. Without anticipating the possibility — or even imagining it — she was mimicking them even in this capacity.

She swiveled and sat up on the edge of the bed. For minutes she practiced mindful breathing, then stopped, aware that she already had become conscious of every breath, aware that her autonomous system was conceding more and more control to her active mind. Too, she recalled the gathering at the Storehouse, how she had been able to follow every girl's thoughts and movements. Sixteen hyperactive girls with wildly different thoughts, and she had been aware of everything, factually and emotionally. Could she have done the same with fifty girls?

Queenie lay on her bed stand. T picked her up, saying, "Are you sleepless, too?"

Queenie's porcelain skin was comforting, strangely regal. Timessa stroked its short belly and touched its incised pubic Y. The statuette felt warm and she smiled to herself: she and Queenie were reunited.

She had been tempted when the gang's name came up for a vote to suggest Queen's Club, but it was obtuse, would have required explanations — none of them called her Queen or anything similar — and the girls were insistent that the gang's name reflect her own. And, she thought, there was a trace of bad-girl by using Bitches.

Holding Queenie she looked at its expressionless face and, in a little girl's voice, rocking her head side to side, said, "Sorry, Queenie. Your time will come."

She perched the marble icon between her breasts. Now when she looked at the ceiling, nothing moved. Yet she inexplicably thought of a winter day thousands of years ago when she'd seen the Acropolis covered in a blanket of silvery snow. The event was a rarity, and dozens of girls had danced through the marble entranceway, over the wide stairs, past the Erechtheion and up to the polished head of the stone plinth. Their footprints were shaped like small boats; several of the girls laid on their backs beside the Parthenon and make snow goddesses with their arms and legs. What she most vividly remembered was a heavy grey sky and snow falling on her face.

Now as the sun rose she checked her schedule, noting that studio work began at two. She had the morning free. On impulse she checked with the hotel's concierge and asked if they could recommend a real estate agent to find something discrete, a Boston pied-à-terre. By ten that morning she was viewing Back Bay apartments and by noon had selected a renovated townhouse. Near the river, it was furnished and immediately available, and she decided to take immediate occupancy. A minimum lease was a year, although she tried to negotiate six months. In the end she shrugged: the location was lovely, money irrelevant and her future unforeseeable. The move itself took less than an hour; her belongings consisted of clothes, small sundries and the Bravo photograph.

Then she was quickly caught up in the frenzy of constant shoots. Within weeks she appeared on two European magazine covers. A Japanese crew flew in to photograph her wearing a designer's men's line; in the next Tokyo issue of *Eyescream* she appeared on the cover, wide-eyed and expectant. The *Boston Globe* referred to her in a Sunday special as Boston's cover girl.

She continued to decline swimsuit and lingerie shoots. She increasingly affected transparent, slightly bewitched expressions. Her agency turned down requests for interviews: she would say, "My photographs speak for themselves." Critics called her look "twitchy" and "restlessly intelligent."

As her notoriety increased, so did her agency's concern for her safety. To her irritation they echoed Eos's earlier opinion, insisting on a driver and security. A stalker incident — a man claiming to be an old school friend — had interrupted a morning shoot, and an investigating officer from the Cambridge police told her that more incidents were inevitable. Days later T received a kidnapping threat. Although it proved to be a prank, the incident led her agency to insist she protect herself. However reluctantly, remembering Johnboy, she went along.

Consequently, within a few days she was under full-time watch. GIA selected an operative who had worked with the agency before. Her new driver-security was a woman in her mid-30s, solid, and seemingly disinterested in her as a personality; she was a professional ex-cop unimpressed by T's celebrity. Timessa wondered about the woman's effectiveness, until the agency showed her CCTV footage from six months earlier in which the woman had protected a client.

In jumpy, pixilated footage, the woman broke one attacker's neck and stunned another with a groin kick. A third attacker fled and the woman pulled a pistol from a shoulder holster and fired twice, saying almost inaudibly, "Last one's down, as well."

Consequently, T approved of "Joan" and Joan approved of Timessa's SUV, although she insisted on tire upgrades and bullet-proof windshields. Timessa knew she had to play the role of a typical helpless model loose on the town. At the least, being driven would be a luxury.

Within a week Joan became ground transportation for many of the gang. Six or seven of them would pack into the SUV after work and be dropped off all over the city, their mothers usually waiting outside as if the SUV were a school bus. As the last onboard, Timessa sometimes would direct Joan to take her to a quiet beach to watch dusk darken the eastern sky. They would sit silently until stars appeared, and even then, T would say, "Another 30 minutes." Joan never queried her or made small talk; whatever T wanted, as long it as fit into Joan's definition of safe, went unquestioned.

One evening Timessa went Back Bay partying with two of the older girls, one seventeen and one nineteen. The Pink Rendezvous — a lounge near her apartment — catered to women and was a quick walk from the Copley Plaza. Locals referred to it as "The Pink." They ordered wine, with the two girls flashing fake ID. Joan had asked to be excused to run errands a mile away and T agreed to text her when ready.

T felt unusually anxious, watching patrons come and go. Tiring of the conversations as the evening wore on — at the end the girls were complaining endlessly about a certain art director's attitude — Timessa texted Joan, noting they'd be waiting outside The Pink. She paid and the three left the lounge.

The evening was cool and cloudless, the street a throwback to an earlier century, the sidewalks a burnt slate and the narrow road cobble-stones. Gas streetlights flickered disarmingly. One of the girls wondered when their driver would arrive

Then they noticed two men standing about fifty feet away. The two were on the same side of the street, nicely dressed and appeared to be ignoring the girls. Timessa, though, knew better. Their thoughts were transparent; the two had been waiting for anyone exiting the lounge who might be an easy mark. As she watched, the men turned toward the girls, the taller man saying loudly, "Waiting on a ride?"

She said flatly, "Don't need help, thanks."

"Aw, lonely girls."

Stepping closer, the men blocked off access to the lounge. T had seen this before in Charleville; the street satyrs had moved as one, raptors smelling blood. The men's thoughts were simple, predacious, smiles twitching. The two girls stepped behind Timessa. She wondered where Joan was — should she act or wait? One of the girls flicked on her phone and said loudly, "Time to turn on the video?"

T said in a low voice, "Put it away."

As she spoke the shorter man said, "No, turn it on, baby. I'll show you moves you've never seen —"

The street was empty — no cars, taxis, casual strollers. In the strange silence, Timessa took the elbows of the girls and started to lead them away. Where the hell was Joan? Long shadows streaked the sides of the old buildings. A grey trickle of water ran down the street gutter. A dark alley lay to their right. She suspected it was a dead end.

The girls traveled no more than ten feet when T stopped. The men had steadily gotten closer. She swiveled and faced them, knowing already that they intended to push them into the alley, the taller man taking the two younger women and the other grabbing Timessa.

She raised her arm, her palm out. "You're making a mistake."

"Oh baby, even your voice turns me on —" He reached for her and she stepped back. These men were pitiful; she felt no threat. Their swagger was bluster. Her concern was for the two girls, as she couldn't defend her little gang without revealing far too much. She looked up and down the street for her driver, still amazed at the absence of pedestrians or cars.

At the same moment the men grabbed the girls. The taller man simply took their blouses, bunching them in his fists, pushing the girls backward. The other man pushed Timessa hard, shoving and then swiveling her toward the alley.

She easily read his thoughts: back alley, no lights, slap girls, stop screams, clutch throats, choke, fear …

She did several things simultaneously, first becoming immobile, unyielding, while smiling at her attacker. Her face was pleasant and her smile adorable, as delighted as any young girl's, and he looked bewildered at her strength. As he gaped at her, she paralyzed his thoughts and locked the cognitive functions of both girls and attackers. Their faces went blank; the men dropped their arms, slumping slightly. Concurrently she dialed back the memories of the girls to the moment they stepped from The Pink.

Now whatever she did with the men would be a private matter. The need to act quickly had ended. Touching her pants pocket, she felt Queenie — the figurine was as hot as a knife blade pulled from coals. Timessa's smile disappeared, and she drew Queenie out, holding her by the legs and impulsively pressed Queenie's expressionless face into the man's forehead. He flinched as the fiery statuette branded an oval between his eyes, his skin sizzling briefly. She turned to the second man, who stood slack-jawed between the girls.

Timessa noted her own lack of emotion. Both men were violent, neither particularly different from the hopeless satyrs. These two were hers now, with one man already branded for life.

Looking down at Queenie, at the eyeless glowing head of the small icon which burned impatiently, T pushed the top of the figurine into the second man's forehead, causing him to cry out stupidly as the coal-red marble burnt another oval. She wrinkled her nose at the smell.

Now each had a third eye, an evil-eye like those painted on the prows of ancient ships, except theirs would not ward off evil, but rather warn those who saw them that evil approached. The ovals would be warnings the men would see in any mirror on every day.

Timessa put her Cycladic warrior, now cooling, back in her pocket and gathered her girls, slipping her hands under their arms and steering them to the street. As she did so, the silver SUV rolled into view: Joan. As the woman saw the three, she pulled the vehicle up, leaping out and saying, "My apologies. A fender bender over on Commonwealth slowed traffic to a crawl."

Awakening the two girls, T watched as they blinked, looking around half-dazed. The older one said, "Brain freeze! Thought we were gonna wait on the ride. And it's here."

"No questions," Timessa scolded. "You're easily distracted."

Both girls smiled and they tumbled into the SUV. It was time to take them home and T decided to say nothing to her guard. As Joan accelerated away, T glanced into the alley at the men and freed them both. She saw each straighten and touch their foreheads.

Joan turned to her. "Home with these girls?"

Timessa nodded. "Yes. So ends another night."

CHAPTER 35

Whoever knows that nothing depends on anything has found the way.
—Bodhidharma

On a warm summer night, Timessa understood: the changes were complete.

How she knew didn't matter. Her childhood entanglement with Artemis was snipped. The tribe — all her friends and the various goddesses — still existed unchanged, but her reliance on them was over. Flooded with a sense of sovereignty, Timessa now was her own empyrean, her own unapproachable heaven. The knowledge, as bright as a nova, came cascading into her like a final constituent part, an immutable gift. Although she had been expectant, the realization caused a certain incredulity. Yes, fine. Smiling to herself, she acknowledged there was nothing left to anticipate. She was all. And she was dazzled in the realization.

Lying in her bedroom, washed in the amniotic fluid of her deliverance, she felt she had emerged from millennia of uncertainty, skepticism and dependency. The polarity between a moon and its planet had switched. She now was the earth and no longer a satellite. Or she was a comet entering the atmosphere, ignorant of the very ecosphere she pene-trated. Carried for so long in Gaia's belly, she never imagined this autonomy.

With a sense of being ridiculously infinite, she stood and walked to the bank of windows in her room. The Charles River, a dark snake of rippling silk, twinkled solemnly in its bituminous silence. Stars, their brightness suddenly unobscured by the city's lights, hung in inexhaustible numbers, swaying overhead in the slight breeze blowing off the harbor to the east.

Then, like a warm breath, she felt a presence. As she turned from the windows, she laughed. A little girl sat in the center of her bed: Gaia, in her blue dress, was cross-legged and sparkling, luminescent in her joy. When their eyes met, the goddess giggled. Timessa said, "It took so long for me to get from there to here."

Gaia smiled. "A great goddess requires great gestation. And so we have had great patience."

Timessa bowed slightly. As always Gaia was slightly translucent; the yellow bedcover shone through her as if a scrim. T walked closer and sat primly on the bed. "Goddess," she said, "what comes next?"

"You will know."

"A mission will emerge?"

"There may not be a mission. You are not a vocation. And this is not a calling."

"Then?"

"The Great One simply is."

Timessa understood. Or she thought she did. She sat before Gaia feeling vast, boundless in energy; a small smile flickered on her mouth.

"Why have I been chosen?"

"You were destined even as a child."

"Did Artemis know?"

"What did everyone you knew say about you?"

"I was teased as being innocent. Filly called me special."

"And Artemis?"

"That I would be made whole by love."

"And she said nothing more?"

"That my beauty would serve your purposes."

"My purposes?"

"Yes. I never understood. We almost never argued. I wasn't willful like some of the girls. But once, a year or two ago, I disobeyed and she said, 'You are not really mine. You are Gaia's girl.' Then she turned her back and left."

Gaia said, "She has always known that I would call to take what's mine. But she never quite understood."

"I am still confused. You are saying I belong to you, not Artemis?"

"Of course. Artemis simply never knew your destiny. And the Great One who preceded you has not disappeared or died. She watches. And she knows that in today's world, great beauty and great innocence may succeed. Repugnance and ancient cynicism will not. She could not shake her world-weariness. She had seen too much. In many ways, she failed."

"Failed?"

"Yes. In time you may understand. There are challenges ahead. Regardless, she wished her successor to be gracious and beautiful."

"Was the Great One not beautiful?"

Gaia studied her face thoughtfully, considering her reply. She finally said, "The Great One defers to you." Gaia sighed and smiled gently. "You have advantages she did not. How you use them in this world will be yours to determine."

"So it's a trick of the eye."

"One that works for your chosen métier."

"Modeling? But I do it because it amuses me."

"No, you model because you desire adoration."

Timessa flushed. Yes, Gaia knew, but that was far from all of it. There was more. "Yes, I crave veneration. But there's more."

"More as in adulation, adoration, homage. We need these things."

Timessa slowly nodded. What Gaia said was true. TB's Gang was a small reflection of it. She liked the awe in the girl's eyes. Not admiration — awe. And liked their absolute, manifest love.

"You will have to maneuver in this world," Gaia said. "You are no longer under Artemis's shield. Now, you protect. And those you shelter must offer thanks."

"You refer to sacrifice?"

"Your conundrum is this: with the loss of belief millennia ago came the end of oblation, the ending of that tradition."

"Which I still covet?"

"Not covet, require. Do not deny the truth."

Timessa's word choice had been indelicate. "Yes, my needs are primordial," she said. "Yes, *require*, not covet."

"But remember," Gaia said, "what you need is attainable."

Timessa reached out to the goddess. She felt a heat coming from the little girl, one that seemed to reflect clustered stars and a compaction of galaxies, the compression spawning an inexplicable power and equanimity.

She bowed her head. Thought was inappropriate; her sense of sovereignty extinguished the need to evaluate. What she was now breathed in the energy of the entire cosmos. There was an immeasurable infinity. She was now the Queen. The Queen had arisen once again. The Queen. Power now, as in the past, streamed through a woman's eyes.

They touched fingertips and Gaia's body began to vibrate. In a small flash of amber light, she was gone and — for the first time in her absence — Timessa felt no loss.

❧

TB's Gang, as it grew in numbers, became TB's Girls. For a brief time, probably no longer than a month, some members moved to call it The Gathering. Timessa disliked the connotation and steered it to simply The Girls.

The Girls functioned almost as a secret society. Only select girls could belong. T chose the members. In time, the group grew to more than 170, then 200.

The early adherents, who numbered no more than a dozen, soon referred to each other as the disciples. Inevitably, friends of friends in Boston recruited girls from New York and Miami, then San Francisco and L.A. All were models. Their average age was seventeen, and all possessed Timessa's lanky, photogenic aura. All exuded an outward confidence, but T knew better; their insecurities did not escape her. None was as confident as she appeared.

In a serendipitous moment, the mother of one of the girls, a jewelry designer, showed Timessa a necklace she'd made, suggesting it function as an indicator of membership. The gold necklace held an oval pendant, a wafer-thin replica of Queenie's head. With T's blessing the medallion became the group's official symbol, and each girl had to pledge secrecy to its meaning. For many girls it became their most precious belonging. All understood that if they violated the group's precepts and were expelled, the necklace would have to be returned.

Because of its increasing numbers, The Girls became loosely organized. Structure was inevitable. At 350 members, T appointed several girls to function as part-time communication and scheduling staff. She created a website that could be accessed only by password. Timessa called all of this "building the bones," and the girls loved the stability. The group published an occasional newsletter — *The Girls* — and Timessa wrote a monthly column.

When the clique was opened to girls worldwide, a flood of new models joined, many from France, Scandinavia, Italy, England, and even Greece. Vetting the new girls became difficult, and T appointed representatives in each country to approve applications. Within six months the nascent Girls numbered in the thousands.

As in the earliest days, Timessa's charisma united them. Many of the girls openly cried in her presence, sobbing if they met her eyes. And as frequently, the girls inexplicably would break into laughter, giggling at shared jokes and insider allusions. But emotional outbursts occurred only when T was present; if she were absent from a meeting, they would sit sullenly, or at best, quietly, holding hands and sighing until she appeared.

As The Girls grew in influence — at least upon the girls's lives — Timessa said less and less, communicating by touch, girl by girl. Sometimes she would simply place a hand on a girl's neck. Other times she would kneel, and touch forehead to forehead with the younger ones, putting her hand over theirs, smiling as she touched. Whatever the contact, when it ended, each girl felt filled and fulfilled, tranquil and joyous. Belonging affirmed that each was significant and that modeling, however frivolous, had connected them to amazing friends.

All the while, T maintained her frantic schedule. Using Gaia's word, she called it her *métier* rather than career, aware she might escape — or disappear, as she had described it to Danaë at the estate — at any moment. Modeling was extraordinarily lucrative. As one of the country's supermodels, she made millions in her first year. Yet there were days when she was under lights, affecting the wonderstruck look that now was her trademark, when she wondered what a Great Goddess was doing in this charade. Nothing was genuine; all was invented. She was shilling for what? Riches, flattery?

Gaia had said she would know. Yet what she knew was that she was remarkably adept. Ambitious. That she generated adulation, even idolization, from almost everyone she encountered. And she knew she did not want to decouple yet.

A social critic in the American edition of *Vogue* wrote after a rare interview,

The extraordinary Timessa, who goes by that single name, has illuminated the relatively staid world of fashion with her unprecedented charisma. As Vogue's *readers know, in less than a year she has captured four covers on this magazine alone, and appeared internationally on covers from Japan to Germany. Is it incautious to speculate that Timessa, who has sprung from obscurity, is now the world's most famous face?*

During my forty-five-minute interview with this young woman, I admit to being seduced by her charm. Yet "charm" does not describe her fully, for Timessa elicits a certain wonderment from even the most hard-boiled of us.

So what was it? Was I overcome by her beauty? Seduced by her perfect symmetry, which exists as a paragon even within her field?

I think not. Her allure is something else: intangible, even magical. Yes, I used that word. She is a presence whose force might propel armies (I think of Jeanne d'Arc) or lead multitudes over hills and valleys to some eventual rhapsody. I imagine her in a sensational dress — lets mount her on a horse, as well — waving a sword and pointing ahead.

In addition to her recherché appeal, she crackles with a raw intelligence. In our short time together, we spoke of Lawrence Durrell, Matisse, Sophocles, an obscure economist from Denmark, and the loveliness of the Maeander River in Turkey, which she claims to have sailed. Our conversation segued briefly to an obscure priestess in ancient Greece, and then to current politics. Her intellect appears as remarkable as her energy.

Timessa claims to have no love interests. When I asked directly — tactlessly, I admit — she said, and I quote, "I'm a big sister to the girls I work around — the models who are up and coming. Who has time for love?"

If Timessa calls for volunteers for her next campaign, I offer myself, no matter the hills and dales we might traverse. All bow to the reigning queen.

Of course *Vogue* knew nothing of The Girls, of the extraordinary circle she'd built. Timessa was simply a highly sought-after supermodel with whom a journalist had scored an interview. Yet he too was seduced, as were all who spent more than a few minutes in her presence. *Blessed*, or *privileged* or *honored* were the common accolades that followed routine encounters.

Within the tight secrecy of The Girls, she was increasingly acclaimed for her apparent — and baffling — ability to make the infertile fecund. The two older girls whom she'd "opened" months before at Eos's beach house were now large with child. They had excitedly shared their news with anyone struggling. Since then Timessa had periodically laid hands — she despised the term the girls used — on a dozen more who had struggled with pregnancy. One of them, after becoming expectant within weeks, half-jokingly referred to her as the Fertility Goddess.

Girls from the club began to fly in from Europe, purportedly to visit New England, but in reality to have Timessa make their bellies glow. When she made contact, they felt heat throbbing through her fingers. She placed her palm on their stomachs, making circles, spheres, wheels of fire over their somnolent, torpid wombs. Golden light radiated from her hand and unfailingly, the girl would gasp in an orgasmic shudder.

When it was over, Timessa would ask the same question: "Are you ovulating?"

As the girl nodded, T would whisper, "Then take advantage tonight, and again tomorrow night —"

After minutes the heat would dissipate, the girl would touch her belly, standing unsteadily and, invariably, Timessa would be swept with post-event emptiness, even irritation. The girl would awkwardly try to half-thank her benefactor, and T would angrily wave her away, the inevitable headache beginning to stir in her skull. As the girl was rushed away, Timessa would close her eyes, drowning in a small nausea, demanding to be alone.

In time she understood that the goddess-girl relationship was not reciprocal. That was its failing. She, the Great One, the Triple Goddess, would fill empty vessels with an exquisite elixir, and the recipients barely acknowledged her gift. They viewed her touch as a benefit flowing to those in The Girls, whereas, T knew that her touch was a divine intercession, a gift of life that in all instances left them full — and left her exhausted. Their high-voiced, young-girl thanks and downcast eyes were never adequate, their gratitude paltry in comparison to the gift.

What did she want? What would stop the rise in her anger? Gaia had said she needed oblation, and then corrected herself. Not oblation, as that could be anything — white scarves, or the white-flowered narcissus, or a bottle of cheap white wine. Or even coins as thanks. All wearisome, none of it invaluable.

She wanted nothing white-washed. No, she wanted sacrifice, and when she was being honest, blood sacrifice.

She, Timessa, was an old god, a primal thing. Old gods required crimson. High sacrifice necessitated fresh blood, steaming entrails.

Sacrifice: she thought of Artemis's altar, the stones stained blood-red, cochineal at the notch that allowed the blood to spill onto the cinnamon-colored ground at the base. She remembered the poisonous daffodils surrounding the place of worship, the flushed faces of the nymphs as sheep were slaughtered in the goddess's name.

There, after the killing, they would strip the meat to the bones, revealing shining white cartilage penciled with red sinews, coral ribbons. Smoke from the burning flesh would darken with sparks.

And somewhere, watching, would be an immortal crow with its ruby eyes, overseeing the sacrificial festival — watching the blood splatter the girls's ochre tunics, caking their ankles and coloring their feet. When satisfied, it would flutter skyward to report its observations.

Sacrifice, blood. And in the end Artemis, or Athene, or Apollo, would be satisfied. Now, as the one who had supplanted them all, she too required the old oblation.

CHAPTER 36

In the dark basilica on the burled
wooden wall hung a Black Madonna —
a cross-eyed Isis, long cheeks, exotic fauna:
guardian of the passage to the underworld.

Timessa ended the fertility rites. She had blessed almost two dozen girls, brought joy into their lives and, in the end, felt used. In parallel she withdrew further from the gang's activities. Now when The Girls met, she stopped speaking formally, her inspirational talks over. It seemed sufficient that she simply appear.

To her amusement, touches and smiles satisfied them. Dozens would gather and as the meetings began, Timessa would wander in, appearing preoccupied and inattentive. She would stop before certain girls, pensively looking into their eyes, then move to the next. She was becoming a beloved enigma, and with the slightest look, capable of inducing panic or euphoria, alarm or exuberance in those she engaged.

On occasion, her touch caused girls to lose consciousness. T might pat one's cheek, or brush one's lips with a finger, and uncontrollable emotions would surge through the girl; it was as if a hot wind had chosen the girl alone out of dozens, lifting her up into the season's stars, or exposing her to the fickle eddies of consciousness.

Yet, on the whole, the experiences were pleasant and frequently seductive. The girls vied for Timessa's attention, unaware that the sensations she imparted were often erotic. Most of them were as naive as T. Sexuality was a mere concept, a romantic abstraction. Married or partnered girls understood, but remained silent. Naming sensuality for what it was seemed out of place, its mention ill-advised. If Timessa's touch appeared to cause an occasional girl to shudder, the others watching shuddered in empathy, or smiled silently.

T's decision to curtail the fertility sessions shocked many. Hysteria overcame girls who had planned to seek her help. Although they were a tiny percentage of the overall membership, they lobbied for her to resume.

A girl from Italy posted a video on the group's website in which she pleaded to Timessa to change her mind, and as the video ended, wept. Her vulnerability was heartbreaking. The video became a small sensation and a point of confusion among the girls. If Timessa could "open" those who needed help, why would she not?

In response, Timessa wrote a blog titled, "Guiding Light: A Fantasy," in which she invented a dialogue between a goddess and a naive girl, a parable, a fairy tale.

Guiding Light: A Fantasy

A girl who appears to be about eighteen sits across from a goddess. Both are beautiful. They are in a small grove beside a stream. The goddess has a radiance that causes to girl to squint when she tries to look at her directly.

The girl says, "Goddess, you have changed my life."

The goddess smiles, saying, "Our lives are intertwined."

"I, like many of us, was lost until you came."

"You were never lost. You simply needed to be shown."

"And you have done so, my Queen." Looking at the goddess was challenging, as the light emanating from her seemed to grow.

The goddess sighed and said quietly, "All of us go hand in hand. But we must retain the balance."

"Balance?" the girl asked.

"I refer to gifts, largesse, offerings."

"We always sing your praise."

The goddess said, "If I were to give you an immense gift, one of inestimable value, would balance be maintained if you simply thanked me and walked away?"

"Well," she said, "perhaps I see. Just thanking you might not be enough."

"When gifts are exchanged, particularly among valued friends, shouldn't gifts be of equal worth?"

"Sure. You mean like, if I give my best friend an expensive necklace, she should give me something as valuable?"

"Perhaps not at the same instant. Surprises among friends are a pleasantry. But in time, the giver of the greater gift expects something of equal value. Lopsided giving makes us all uneasy, even angry over time."

"But isn't that selfish of the one who gave the greater gift?"

"Explain," the goddess asked.

"I suppose I mean, what if the giver just … likes to give big presents?"

The goddess smiled pleasantly, saying, "Let's discuss love, instead."

"Yes," the girl said. "Our love for you is unending."

"Unending?" The goddess shifted in her chair. "What if your love is insufficient?"

"I don't understand."

"What if the love I give is greater than the love I get?"

The girl, twisting her hands together, said, "You mean our love has been too little, has been, like, self-seeking?"

The goddess turned and pointed at the stream. "Isn't great love that is unrequited something like that stream? In a drought, when the sky gives too little rain, it stops its flow."

"I think I get it," she said. "You're saying that you're the stream?"

"And the river. And the sky."

"Oh. Like it flows again when the drought ends."

"Exactly." The goddess's light grew more intense. "One-sided love never lives long. What is given must be returned in kind, or the lover turns her back. Gift or bestowal, love or offering — balance must be maintained. We see it everywhere. In the stars and in the tides. Harmony underlies life. Imbalance destroys the gods. Must I go on?"

The girl cried openly, shaking her head. "How do we know how much? How do we measure how much to give?"

"Gifts must be comparable. Frivolous gifts antagonize. Frivolous love forces the lover to withdraw."

"Is that why you have been so distant, Queen?"

"Consider my words."

"Then our gifts must equal those you give ..."

———————

T recognized that the parable was too direct, but she was through with subtlety.

What the blog dodged was what form gifts should take. Nor did she use the word *sacrifice*. Instead, she had side-shuffled, using euphemisms like love. And balance. Harmony and symmetry.

Regardless, she stood by what she wrote; saying she demanded primitive sacrifice would have collapsed the group. Without exception, this so-called modern society considered animal sacrifice a barbarism, a Greek word now used against the ancient Greeks.

Symbolic sacrifice, low-cost and cheap sacrifice — those had become substitutes for the authentic. Civilization had lost its fire. Tokens and metaphors were stand-ins. All was hidden. Animals were killed in factories. The dead were no longer washed and clothed for burial by loved ones. Death was distant. She smiled, knowing the mere sight of blood caused many to faint.

She knew, too, she was now cursed by her transformation. She might as well have been reborn as a howling, demented Fury, one of the Erinyes. As it was, as the Great Goddess, she now had to navigate in a feeble, effete world. Millennia ago recipients of her gifts knew how to respond. It was known then that gifts required appropriate thanks, and that spurning a goddess was disastrous.

Somewhat to her surprise, the posting caused the immediate resignation of about fifteen percent of the girls. Their parents found the piece "disgraceful" or "embarrassing." They assumed Timessa was seeking money, and that she was doing so by using guilt. That she was pressuring the girls whose lives centered more and more around the activities of The Girls. Few saw the post for what it was.

"Models," one parent wrote T, "are under enough pressure without this. Why don't you simply charge to belong to your little club? Shaming them with this is manipulative."

Another wrote, "We viewed The Girls as a sort of support group. But you're just another scammer, aren't you? Grubbing for money and masking your hustle in terms like love. Screw you, cover girl — our daughter loved you once, but now she's out."

Timessa had drawn a line: she needed the ancient way, the most ancient of ways. A gift of gold required a reciprocal gift of gold. Her gifts were immense. The girls, if they needed her touch, would have to show her greater thanks. And those who were childless would have a far higher burden to express their gratitude, as Timessa's gift was that of life itself.

❦

A week later at the Storehouse, after touching or hugging everyone, she held a brief Q & A session in response to many of the girls admitting they remained confused about her post. And there was awareness from buzz on the forum that some girls had quit the group. She had those present sit as she stood before them. Hands went up and Timessa pointed at one girl, then another.

The first question was benign, even silly, and it broke the tension in the room. "Cool dress you're wearing. You know it doesn't match the color of your eyes?"

Timessa laughed, grateful for the girl's wit. She pointed to another and said, "Now, all of you attack dogs, ask me something serious."

A younger girl said, "Okay. Like that girl in the story, how do we know how much? I mean, how much love?"

"As the goddess in the story said, 'Gifts must be comparable.' "

The girl broke into tears, as so many of the girls were prone to do. "I won't know. And then you'll hate me, won't you?"

Timessa said, "What the story meant was that gifts have little meaning if the giver makes no sacrifice."

The girl looked puzzled. Another waved her arm and T looked at her, saying, "Yes, Clarissa."

"Everything we do is like a sacrifice, right? I don't want to do that shoot next week, but I'll sacrifice and show up anyway."

T smiled. "Okay, all of you. No one seems to understand. First, let's talk about today. And then we'll leap back a couple thousand years ..."

She looked across their faces. They were enthralled; she knew her allure was as strong as ever. "Let's do girl talk. What's a sacrifice you make each month?"

The common reaction was to shrug. One of them cried, "It's a sacrifice putting up with Mom! That's like every day!"

"No," Timessa said. "I'm thinking differently. Something more serious. We all have periods. Every month. What happens when we do? We sacrifice our blood, don't we? It's messy. We give so we can be renewed. Something precious is gifted, so to speak, and in return we ovulate. We're opened —"

"Opened like you do to girls who can't have babies?"

"Sort of," she said. "But that's different. When we have our period, blood begets ovulation, which means ovum are released, priming each of us for life."

An older girl whispered drolly, "You mean priming us for getting screwed."

Everyone laughed and T said, "We're not going to talk about getting 'screwed.' That's sex ed and sitting through that in class is probably sacrifice enough."

The girls smirked. T knew many of the older ones were sexually active, and she appreciated their silence. She caught the eye of one girl who was married, and they exchanged knowing smiles.

Clarissa waved again and Timessa nodded. Clarissa said, "In your story the girl calls the goddess, 'Queen.' Should we call you Queen?"

"Am I a goddess?"

Clarissa hesitated, then whispered, "*I* think so."

A girl in the back shouted, " 'Queen' is prettier than Timessa!"

T shook her head. "We'll not go there now. The story was just a parable. Pretend. We were talking just now about periods, right? Those are real. And that's a modern sacrifice we're all familiar with. A blood sacrifice. And when we suddenly can't give that sort of gift, we have screwed up insides and sometimes become infertile. When it's really bad, we become barren."

She scanned the serious faces. "Now let's go back in time. Another type of sacrifice occurred long, long ago. Gods and goddesses gave everything to people — rich crops, fat sheep, health, children, wealth, good weather — and in return they demanded gratitude. The highest gifts people could give were livestock — sheep, ewes and even oxen, which were killed by priestesses and offered on altars as sacrifices to the gods."

Many of the girls made faces. A few muttered, "Yuck" and "Gross."

T went on. "But no one gave it a second thought. No one said, 'Gross.' Why? Because they recognized the immensity of the gifts bestowed, and knew thanks were necessary. And in time the gods and goddesses — the recipients of these sacrifices — became expectant. If they did not receive thanks, they became irritated. Or worse, angry."

A girl cried, "What happened if they got mad?"

"Earthquakes, famine, rivers drying up."

"Like that stream in your story."

"Exactly. Women struggled to have children. Men lost wars and became slaves instead of warriors."

A younger girl waved her hand. T nodded and said, "Yes, Thea."

"How do you know all this?"

Timessa winked. "I'm lucky, Thea, to have known a couple goddesses when I was growing up." She said it lightly, "And they clued me in on this stuff."

Thea said simply, "Wow," and a couple of the other girls said, "She's just kidding, you idiot!"

Timessa waved her hand dismissively. "That's enough for tonight. We'll talk about this again."

A girl in front frantically waved her hand. "One last question!"

"Yes, Miriam?"

"My mom read what you wrote and didn't want me to come tonight. We had an awful argument. But I'm here …"

"Yes," Timessa said. "As you may have heard, some girls were told not to return. But I want you to know two things. First, those of you here are brave. You are strong enough to withstand anyone's criticism. When you're confronted by those who don't understand, you push back —

"Second, throughout time, the truth has stung those who would rather live daydreams. Delusions are safe. Many people surround them-selves with make-believe …

"If you encounter people with such reactions, just indulge their exas-peration. Don't agree. But don't argue — it will do no good." She paused and looked into the eyes of each girl. "Now be gone. Be beautiful. Our Girls club will never be harmed by angry talk."

She was taken aback as several of the girls cried out, "Okay, Queen!" and, "We love you, love you, love you, Queen!"

As her eyes swept the faces of the forty girls there, she saw Filly standing against a back wall in a sweatshirt and jeans. Philippa was Timessa's oldest friend, a nymph like she had been. Her hair was tied back in a ponytail and she smiled.

Timessa had not invited her. Months had passed since they'd said goodbyes at the Pennsylvania estate. The only explanation for her appearance was Artemis. Filly walked through the cluster of girls, saying, "Excuse me, excuse me," as she pushed her way closer. Finally she broke through and the two touched fingertips, their old greeting.

Solemnly, Filly said, "I have my girls down at Jackson's estate, and here in Boston, you have yours."

CHAPTER 37

Women and children starved in Chalcedon
(now greater Istanbul). Who remembers?
Not the imams. Or the Orthodox. Xenophon
sent his calvary away and he, too, lies in ashes.

Filly rode in the back of Timessa's SUV, silent as Joan sped and braked, accelerated and wove through late traffic toward the Back Bay. Backseat car rides always nauseated her. "How long before we get there?" Filly whined.

From the front seat, Timessa turned and said, "A few minutes. There's a second bedroom. I've decorated simply. My place'll suit you. How long can you stay?"

They had roomed together during their years at Vassar, sleeping like soldiers in the same narrow bed. But they had dropped out three years ago. As Timessa drifted away from the tribe, Filly had taken charge of the hundred nymphs at the estate, freeing Artemis to pursue her interests. Now Artemis had reassigned her, sending her to Boston, into Timessa's world.

Filly said, "I'm to be your assistant."

"Says who?"

"The goddess."

"No, you're my friend."

"And your confidant."

"Not Artemis's spy?"

"Spying would be futile."

"Why do you say that?"

"She says you have surpassed her in …" Filly looked at Joan. "… all things."

"I'm just a cover model."

Filly snorted rudely. "Of course. I hear you've done well."

Later that evening they talked. Filly set down a brandy snifter, saying, "I think I prefer wine."

"I have that, too."

"It's all here, isn't it? White?"

"Or red."

Filly said, "White. But red reminds me. I meant to compliment you. I liked your analogy in your talk this evening. Periods. Sacrifice and periods — I'd never thought of that."

"Yes, I needed something bloody that they could relate to. The girls are all so squeamish."

"It's cultural."

"Worried mothers. And it all worries me, as much as them."

"As in, animal sacrifices may prove difficult to sell?"

"You don't understand, Filly. Since I changed I've realized nothing else feels right. The Great Goddess's entire persona has permeated what I was — and now I'm her, with little bits of the old Timessa. But increasingly her. And she expects animal offerings …"

"How do the girls presently show gratitude?"

"With a 'thanks.' Or, as you saw tonight, 'We love you, Queen.' By the way, 'Queen' is something new."

"I read your blog. You were doing everything but begging them to call you that."

"Poseidon was the first to use the term."

"But I'm confused. If you're now largely her, don't you have immense power?"

"You have no idea."

"Then you should be able to change what you once demanded. Whatever she was, you can be something new, something *you* create."

"It's not that simple," Timessa said. "She blankets me, smothers me. Can't you see? It's like I'm coated in ground bone marrow. Propitiatory blood —"

"Propitiatory?"

"Blood spilled to please me. Propitiatory. It binds me to her like glue. It doesn't wash off. Can't you smell it? It's an ancient stench. It's like being downwind of a slaughterhouse."

"No, I can't. And you look the same."

"I'm not."

Filly smiled cautiously. "The goddess has said there's a wrist-flick you do. Attackers are ... gone."

"That's nothing."

"Then why security?"

"Joan? As long as I play in the material world, my management insists I employ protection. There have been a couple incidents."

"I can't imagine you needing her."

"I don't. But here, modeling, I have to appear to be like every other girl."

Filly grimaced. "The Great Goddess was an immense presence. Her powers encompassed those of all the present gods. She was sovereign. Are you sure you've become all of that?"

"Yes, certain. As are Gaia, and Apollo, and Poseidon, and Artemis. Everyone is startled, but no one asks how it could be." For the first time, she laughed. "Except perhaps you, my old friend."

Filly half-bowed, her hands together. Smiling she said, "And so, if you're all those things, what are you? I'm bewildered."

"Quoting Gaia: 'The Great One simply is.' What that means I think is that I'm meant to discover what I am, at least beyond the obvious. Beyond the propitiatory blood —"

"And then I show up. Will I complicate it all?"

Timessa reached her hand out to Filly. "There's no one I trust more. And I'm glad we still talk."

"Me, too. And I have ideas. My years of working with all the nymphs might help." She paused. "A question I've wrestled with ... How do you reconcile modeling with goddess work?"

"Easy. Beauty is a reflection of the perfect. Women are beautiful. Isn't it obvious? There's no contradiction." Smiling, Timessa looked at the time. "Something you should know," she said. "I no longer need sleep. I often go days without a nap. But it's time for you. We'll talk more when you wake tomorrow —"

❧

Over the next week, Filly went everywhere Timessa went, meeting with art directors and attending shoots. She helped with her personal items when they did an early morning shoot on Nantucket, and carried gear when T and other models did a beach series for *Vanity Fair* in Maine. Filly was always introduced as Timessa's long-time friend, and even was included in a New York City shoot when the photographer decided they looked like sisters. She was briefly flustered when asked to sign a release, and wrote with a flourish, *Philippa d'Artemis*.

When she occasionally complained to T about feeling constrained by the city, Timessa would smile. "You must look inside, Filly. There is your countryside."

One of the older girls in the club approached T after a weekend gathering, upset over her older sister's inability to conceive. Timessa declined to help, reminding the girl that the so-called healing sessions were something of the past. But the girl persisted.

When Timessa refused again, the girl proposed that T visit, noting her family lived on a farm in western New York. Her sister's husband, a hobbyist pilot, would pick them up and fly them to a local airfield. The entire flight was less than two hours. And she noted that the family was prepared to handsomely reward Timessa.

Timessa said, "Elaborate."

"Nothing is more important to Juliette," she said. "They are willing to sacrifice everything for a child."

"And 'everything' means —?"

"They'd give you their farm. They'd start over from scratch if they could just have a child. She's been to every clinic in the country for four years. Nothing has worked."

Filly leaned her head on T's shoulder and whispered, "You should go."

Timessa said, "No, I go nowhere. She can come here."

That evening Filly questioned Timessa, but her inquiries were rejected. The best she could get was, "I'm evaluating, re-evaluating. Thinking, Filly."

Two nights later Juliette and the girl arrived at T's townhouse, along with Juliette's husband. As the three stood at her doorway, Timessa was abrupt. "Not him."

After a moment of awkwardness, the man shrugged, saying, "Text me when you're done," and walked away.

Timessa herself turned and left, leaving Filly to lead the two women to the living room that looked out over the river and into Cambridge. "Here, sit," she said. "She'll return."

She offered them nothing to drink and watched while they sat, exchanging glances. Juliette was dressed in a loose pair of linen pants and a blouse cut just below her waist. She had the build of a ballet dancer and was nervous. She looked at her sister and whispered, "Why not Peter?"

Her sister shrugged. Filly interjected, "Be quiet while you wait."

Timessa entered, her hands up at her shoulders, palms out and fingers loose in an ambiguous greeting. She wore a gown that started at her neck, tightly collared in a purple band. It flowed down in thin cotton pleats to her ankles, and appeared to imitate Artemis's formal wear, even cinched with a polished leather band just below her breasts. Pausing, she lowered her hands to her hips. "Juliette?"

The woman said, "Yes. Thank you so much for seeing me."

Filly was startled at Timessa's radiance. She felt an unexpected frisson at the sight of her friend, and she reached for a chair arm to steady herself.

Standing a short distance from the women, Timessa spoke, her voice oddly deeper and melodious. "You have traveled far."

"Peter, my husband, is a pilot and owns a Cessna. We landed in an airfield outside the city, I think called Hanscom, and caught a ride in."

"Tell me what you want." T's statement was a demand. The girl blinked, uncertain of how to proceed. Timessa said again, "Transparency."

"I'm unable to get pregnant —"

Cutting her off, Timessa said, "Do you have some abnormality?"

"You mean physical? All the doctors say I'm fine."

"And your husband?"

"Normal, apparently healthy."

"How old are you?"

"Twenty-three." Juliette looked down, nodding. "We've tried every-thing." Then she looked up suddenly at Timessa. "Forgive me, but we're willing to do almost anything. Pay you anything for help."

"Your sister says you have a farm."

"Yes, several hundred acres. It's not as large as we'd like."

"And what do you grow?"

"Barley, groats, and a variety of amaranth."

"Amaranth?"

"An archaic grain. It's favored by advocates of slow-cooking."

Timessa smiled. "You know its Greek meaning?" The girl shook her head. Timessa said, "Unfading."

"Oh. Local restaurants love it."

"And you have farm animals?"

Juliette looked puzzled. "Yes, chickens, a half dozen cows. Oxen, ewes."

"And the oxen. What color are they?"

She smiled, surprised at Timessa's queries. "They're both black. The older has won some ribbons from 4-H."

"Horns?" she said.

Juliette nodded. "They're both nice boys." She paused. "I never imagined chatting about farm animals."

Timessa gestured to Juliette's sister. "Off the couch. She needs to be on her back." The sister rose and stepped aside. T engaged Juliette again, saying, "Now lie back. Unzip your slacks. I'll need access to your belly."

In a moment Juliette was lying down, her head sideways, her eyes on Timessa. The girl said, "What are you going to do?"

"Nothing until you agree to payment."

"We'd agree to about anything."

"If I succeed, I want your oxen."

Juliette gasped, covering her mouth. Lowering her hand she said, "I'm to give you both?"

Timessa nodded, keeping her eyes on the girl. Juliette said, "Both." Then she frowned, "But they weigh almost a ton apiece."

"I don't plan to pick them up. But first let's see if I can help." Timessa knelt beside the girl, raising her blouse and placed her hand on her belly. "No talk. Close your eyes."

Timessa imagined a cascade of soft fire, an outward flare, the same superheated vibrancy that she had experienced during past openings. She made ovals, gentle waves of invisible fire over the girl's listless womb, sensing its response. A topaz light radiated from her hand and after minutes, moaning, Juliette shook in a long, orgasmic shudder, crying, "Oh yes, oh my god!"

Then, moments later, she apologized and Timessa simply smiled, saying, "What you felt was just a confirmation."

When Juliette quieted, Timessa tapped her arm and whispered, "You are opened. Your child will be a girl. Her health will please you."

"What did you do?"

"Are you ovulating?"

Juliette nodded, and Timessa told her what she'd told all the girls before. "Then take your man, tonight, tomorrow night —" With large eyes the girl nodded.

"The oxen. Your thanks to me. When you have confirmed your pregnancy, I will know. We will assume two missed periods is sufficient proof. When that date comes, your husband will build a large table outside from field stones. Then you will lead the oldest of the oxen to the spot. I need no more than one initially. You will decorate the ox will ribbons and paint its horns gold. It must come willingly, as it shall if you are calm and speak sweetly as you walk it there —

"At the altar —" She corrected herself. "— table, you will take a knife and open its throat with force. The blood must be caught in a bowl. When the bowl is full, you are to lift it overhead and cry, 'O Great Goddess, I give my eternal thanks.' Then the blood is to be poured over the stones, and the meat from the oxen roasted and eaten by the two of you in thanks."

"I'm to kill my ox?"

"*Mine*. The bones after the roasting are to be buried on the farm. And when you deliver your child, when the girl is thirty days of age, you are to repeat the task with the other, identically, step by step. If these tasks are not performed exactly as I say, the child will die. Now repeat my instructions."

However shocked, Juliette recited Timessa's orders without error, her voice trembling. Filly noticed she kept wiping her eyes against the sleeve of her blouse.

Timessa stood, looked down on the girl and said, "Now go. Nothing about this evening is to be repeated. If word gets out about this, what I have done, or what I require, your family will experience untold suffering. And no child will come."

"I would never tell a soul."

"Gifts," T said, "cannot be scorned." Then she swiveled on Juliette's sister. "You, as well. Any discussion of this with anyone will doom your sister's pregnancy. And your participation with The Girls will end."

Timessa's radiance had not lessened. She turned and left.

CHAPTER 38

So-called Golden One, Great Goddess of the hawks
bloody raptor bearing thunderbolts
(as etymology refers to the mind of god),
born malicious, armed, purple-eyed.

Timessa's headaches did not follow. Or were at least delayed. Juliette's "healing" and the pact they made appeared to have deterred her usual neuralgia. Yet later that night, to Filly's questions, she said, "But if the oxen are not sacrificed, my anger may be uncontrollable. Their farm will be destroyed."

"No middle ground?"

"None. My gifts cannot be spurned."

"You can choose not to give gifts."

"If I am asked and promises are made, I may act. When I do, the recipient is at great risk as I must receive appropriate thanks."

"Nothing in-between?"

She shook her head.

In fact, she increasingly understood that, if she could be patient, a number of these girls would embrace the old ways. If their needs were great enough, and her demands clear, the institution of sacrifice might be introduced again. It also occurred to her that she could manipulate conditions, creating the circumstances that would bring humans asking for her help. A years-long drought, a subsequent loss of crops, repeated pestilence rolling through upscale piggeries — any of these might bring mortal to their knees. Again.

Scientists would blame insects, sanitation or climate change, dismissing any suggestion that an ancient goddess might be at play. In an ironic way, she thought, their hubris would give her cover to reintroduce the old. And as T, the fashion sensation, she knew that humans were, at their core, eager to idolize.

After Filly had gone to bed, Timessa lay on the couch where she had opened Juliette. On her back, eyes open, she imagined the verses, chapters and volumes of what would become her recreated society. At some point she knew she would have to be beneficent. Disasters were an aid, but she would have to limit them. She laughed to herself: *If not careful I could become high on sacrifices, addicted again to veneration.*

Yet what she was doing was necessary, was *de rigueur* for the Great Goddess from the beginning of time. Civilization, as defined by contemporary denizens, was now whitewashed, bleached of its old vibrancy, plundered of passion, cleansed of blood and, worse, rampant with self-declared victims.

Culture, bifurcated by tribalism, individualism and crumbling religions, was a devolvement from the days when she had been celebrated universally. Then, women governed, and it was right and just that goddesses adjudicated law. No one debated right and wrong. Women bled; the normalcy of blood sacrifice was indisputable. There was joy and serenity and a feminine self-confidence.

At about six she heard Filly waking. Her old friend walked in, a leopardess even half-awake. She wore nothing but panties, her hair in disarray. The nymph said, "I dreamed of you last night."

"Indeed?"

"We were in a vast field. I stood behind you and young women led oxen one by one into a hollow at the field's edge, a sort of amphitheatre."

"And?" Timessa asked.

"You had called for a hecatomb —"

"The sacrifice of a hundred gold-horned beasts."

"Yes. A horrible drought had struck the land. Famine was everywhere. You were the women's last resort. A glorious sacrifice was the only out."

"Was the sacrifice successful?" She continued staring at the ceiling, turning a lock of hair in one of her fingers.

Filly paused. "Yes, Queen. The sacrifice succeeded."

Timessa snapped her head around and glared at Filly. "Did you just mock me with 'Queen'?"

Filly's eyes clouded. Timessa saw the fear and watched the girl step back. "No," Filly said. "It was acknowledging what is true. You are the One."

Timessa stood and pulled Filly into her arms. As they held she kissed her forehead and blew gently on her neck, running her hands over the girl's bare back. Then she placed a hand above Filly's left breast. "Your heart beats as mine. You are not to fear. I protect you. And I love you as my age-old friend."

She looked at Filly, at her beauty, her freckles like tiny, russet stars, and thought, *I challenged her sincerity. The friend I trust as much as anyone ...*

Timessa whispered, "We have a busy day. Our formidable security, that single woman, Joan, comes at seven. Let's get dressed."

Weeks went by, T's routine rarely varying. In the evenings, long after Filly fell asleep, she recovered more memories from ancient, archaic times. Whereas in earlier months these memories were no more than impressions, now she possessed them in their original scents and textures, their heat and emotion and color. They first would appear as a fire on a long horizon, approaching in the dark. Their smoke would thin, and the old moments become clear.

What was dim became, over many weeks, vivid again. And as she filled herself with the Great One's experiences, her own memories became increasingly nebulous. The new being she had become looked back on her years with Artemis as soft reminiscences, the moments muted and indistinct: she had once been a nymph, but was now a colossus.

Mysteriously, hints of the sweetness — the swirling, unanchored naïveté of the nymph — remained, no less tangled in her very being than the Great One's tentacles. Yet, Timessa often felt the honeyed purity of her youth slipping away, a hollowness in its place. And too frequently, she showed only the dark eyes of the Great Goddess to those who gazed upon her.

§&

One evening as Filly and T sat quietly in the townhouse, Filly asked almost inaudibly, "What *should* I call you?"

"What do others call me?"

"You know. Although many of the girls have taken to using 'Queen.'"

"I have many names."

"We're old friends. What name should *I* use?"

"Perhaps just use T."

Filly bowed her head, and T stood, taking her by the arms and lifting her to her feet. "You too are a-mortal. Yet we must be honest. Artemis has given you to me. You are mine and are as transparent to me as glass, your every thought as bright as a flower's bloom."

Filly nodded, saying simply, "Yes."

T lifted the girl's chin, forcing their eyes to meet. "Filly, are you aware of your own beauty?"

T knew she wasn't. Nymphs are not self-conscious. They are beings made to adore others, for following goddesses, however they are asked.

Filly looked at her with wonderment, still unable to fully reconcile the immensity of change she saw. As their eyes met, T bent and kissed Filly lightly on her mouth, feeling her yield. She allowed the kiss to linger, the energy to flow from her into the girl. The kiss was the same as those Lachesis used to tame T's own wildnesses so many years before. At that moment it served one purpose only: to fully bind Filly.

The girl fainted. Timessa caught her, lowering her to a chair, running her fingers through the girl's hair until she regained consciousness. When Filly woke, Timessa said, "You alone are not allowed to worship me," yet she knew her admonitions would be ignored.

For Filly's adoration was abounding and indisputable.

§&

Juliette missed her second period. For days she walked in bliss, aware of the new life she carried, overwhelmed by her turn of fortune. Then, dutifully, she turned to her promise, telling Peter to build a stone table in the back beside the barn. She somehow knew its exact dimensions — it was to be thirty-two inches high, twenty-four wide and thirty-six inches long. She would broach no suggestions from him as he progressed. Building it took hours, and when he had finished, she sent him into town to buy gold paint and festive ribbons. Her oldest and favorite ox would go down within the day.

She sensed the goddess near. The very air she breathed seemed infused with hyper-vivacity. Mindful of her obligations and her oath, she fittingly washed the ox, preparing the massive beast for its ceremony. She and her husband painted its horns, and crying softly, wove the red and yellow and white silk ribbons into its coarse fur, singing softly as she allowed time to pass. Then in a wave of unexpected joy, she led the ox to the altar at the barn's edge. It walked beside her, placid and serene.

In Boston, an hour beforehand, Timessa canceled a long-planned shoot and instructed Joan to drive them to Horseneck Beach, a grey sand spit south of Westport. The afternoon was overcast with a cool wind and the beach almost barren. Joan was told to wait. Filly took T's hand and led her out to the ocean's edge, and they walked slowly along the surf.

Filly only vaguely understood, but sensed the immensity of what might occur. Timessa said nothing, her entire body vibrating as she stepped through the foam and wrack, waiting, light-headed. Gulls wrangled overhead, but their racket quieted, their voices becoming melodious. And as Juliette suddenly wielded her sharpened knife on the farm far to the west — the ox falling on its knees before the knife — the goddess was swept with a rapture she hadn't thought possible. Ankle-deep in the tide, she was radiant. The gift had been reciprocated.

Filly stepped back, awestruck at the goddess's luminosity. "Yes?" she asked.

"It is done. And the blood is on the stones."

She turned toward the ocean. A ray of light wavered lazily through an opening in the grey sky, falling like a wavering spot on the raw salt waves. She did not need Poseidon to appear or Artemis to approach from a distance. She needed no Apollo to drop to a knee and gaze on her with his golden eyes. She now was impeccable, with or without their eyes.

She found that during shoots she could turn on a new radiance at will. Doing so lent her a luminescence that no photographer could explain. At first, agencies would attribute her looks to the photographer's lighting choices — soft boxes, gold and silver reflectors. Or to digital filters and post-processing. But as photog after photog returned similar results, art directors realized their model's incandescence was unique. In fact, Timessa's brilliance was unmistakable to anyone who watched her work. Directors, dressers, assistants, and artists agreed that her eyes shone with a never-seen vivacity. Their modeling sensation had become a graceful conflagration, a sensual firestorm who burned across advertisements with an easy and enviable self-assurance.

Fashion houses fought for her representation, and magazines that had clamored for her face on their covers now broke all of the industry's tacit rules: in an unprecedented move, *Vogue* featured her on its cover for four consecutive months; *W* devoted eight pages to her in issue after issue. Her status as a supermodel escalated and her face eclipsed that of any Hollywood star.

Timessa was beyond a household term; she suddenly defined a universal beauty that defied a cultural countermovement toward inclusion of diverse facial types and ethnic groups. Scholars opined that for the first time since the 15th and 16th centuries, one female face characterized an ideal across all cultures. Even diversity activists stood down; no one wanted to oppose the juggernaut that became known simply as *T*.

During this period of media frenzy, she continued her work with her quasi-secret group, The Girls. The club of young models expanded in number, and almost every fashion center had an active branch. Milan became Europe's epicenter, competing amiably with Paris, New York and L.A. In Asia, a club in Tokyo vied with one in Singapore. Using video conferencing, T stayed in weekly touch with her girls. When she was in Paris, Berlin or Beijing for work, she met with local affiliates. Membership grew.

Nursing her evolving creation, Timessa knew the girls were, in every sense, her devotees. Nothing had changed from the earliest days. When in her presence, the girls would be near hysteria, open to almost any suggestion and eager to embrace them. T's energy seemed endless, infusing each girl with her soft fire and enthusiasm, her touch a thrill.

During this time, Filly began to implement a strategy to initiate a select group of the older girls into what T called "The Old Ways." Filly quickly abbreviated the phrase to TOW, which avoided inevitable questions from parents about the locution.

When asked, girls would say, "TOW means pulling us along to be more like her," or, "T can tow me anywhere!"

It seemed benign enough. Those selected considered themselves elite among an already chosen elite. At the onset, Filly selected only six girls for the honor, all from the New York-New England region. Their ages varied from sixteen and nineteen.

The TOW initiations would be incremental, a leisurely persuading, as Filly viewed it, one that would play out over months. From Filly's experience with Artemis's younger nymphs, gradual always trumped abrupt and slowly was surely. Girls learned best when introductions were sweet talk, not commands. So she approached the TOW project similarly. Filly had fused with the girls, and T frequently deferred to her suggestions.

And Juliette proved to be a surprising ally. Her farm was Filly's perfect training ground, as it exposed the girls to grit and manure, births and disease. Almost all of them were urban children, sheltered from old agricultural realities. Filly knew they needed this exposure before she could take them further. They began making weekend trips to the farm, all of it a grand adventure.

Reinforcement and encouragement from Timessa helped, as well. She mentioned casually to the small group that Juliette's farm was similar to the environment she had known growing up. She was emphatic that what she called *jouissance* flowed only from fully knowing all extremes. Farms mirrored reality, and she wanted them to see shadows as well as sunshine, mud as well as pearls, donkeys as well as dogs. Or as Filly said once, "Dirty jeans, not fashion." The girls nodded sagely, as if they completely understood. Not one of them would have changed a thing.

These weekend trips usually were overseen by Filly. Timessa often was out of town at shoots, which suited Filly. T was a distraction and focusing the girls was far more difficult when she accompanied the group. Juliette was inducted into The Girls and became Filly's accomplice. Other than Filly and T, only Juliette understood.

One of Filly's first goals for the initiates was to synchronize their periods. All of Artemis's nymphs had done so millennia ago. Harmonizing periods: it had proved a simple thing. Ceremonially, as Artemis's nymphs celebrated the sacred days with pride, all wore the same burnt-red panties. No one remembered when the tradition had begun, but the goddess indulged the girls, amused at their camaraderie.

Now Filly wanted the TOW girls to mimic her nymphs. So she began, to their horror and embarrassment, by telling them the tradition. She didn't speak of nymphs, instead describing a tight-knit group of girls she'd known. Her explanations were met with giggles and side glances, yet the thought had been planted. The power of suggestion, she knew, was immense.

She explained, "You now are all like sisters, sharing everything. What one does, the others do. What one thinks, the others know."

When a girl would say, "But I like my privacy," Filly would respond, "Even twins have privacy, but their actions are reflexive and their thoughts often synchronized."

The girls were skeptical, but within three months, to their disbelief, they began and ended menses identically. In a solemn but silly ceremony after the first time, Filly gave them all the same red panties to wear in coming months. "You're to wear them during. No one outside of us will know, and you don't have to explain a thing."

"What if my boyfriend asks?"

"Tell him you're having your period. Be indignant. He'll be so surprised at your response, he'll just say, 'Oh.'

"You know the term 'blood brothers'? Boys pledge to each other by cutting their thumbs and pressing thumb to thumb, sharing blood. We girls are more finely drawn. No sliced thumbs: red panties will suffice."

The TOWs nodded, absorbing the unexpected lessons. They did feel closer, almost inseparable. Their hugs when they saw each other lingered, their looks were knowing. Truly, they believed that their shared secrets would make them forever entangled.

CHAPTER 39

On a weekend at Juliette's late in the summer, Filly — using a chicken — demonstrated how to kill.

She didn't treat the event as mechanical. Death, she said, wasn't something perfunctory. She first asked how many of the girls had seen something die; no one raised a hand. "I suspected," she said. "Remember that death is not romantic. It's often violent."

She held the chicken by the head against a wooden block and brought a hand-axe down on its neck. To the shock of all nine girls watching, the body fell free onto its feet, lurched in an awkward wobbling oval, then leaned sideways and inexplicably ran away. The girls screamed.

To the those attending, Filly's point was amorphous. Yet by this date, all of them had been exposed to days of raw-boned basics — planting, harvesting of hops and summer squash, tending to sick cows, raking stalls and scattering hay. They were exposed to biting donkeys, rabbits killed by raccoons and Juliette's obscenely fat sunflowers growing out of horseshit behind the barn.

Juliette was now five months pregnant and showing. She'd allowed them to view horses coupling in a back meadow in the sun. To these coddled girls, everything on the farm seemed either fecund or in decay. None of it mirrored anything they had seen before.

Juliette now called the stone table where she had killed the ox her "altar," pointing to the bloodstains on the stones that rain only deepened. When the girls visited, she made them pause as a group before the small structure, standing in a strange silence as if the edifice were consecrated. Once she said, "This was built for T," but she never elaborated. The girls accepted the mysteries, converts to Filly's equivocal doctrines, enthusiasts as long as they were assured they were Timessa's special girls.

The girls agreed that Filly's enthusiasm (and Timessa's blessings) brought them back for the long weekends, made them more intimate with each other than before. Timessa had met with them more than once for what she described as a "special" dinner at the Storehouse where she had identified them now, her TOWs, as "indivisible." She assured them they were capable of anything. She promised she had selected them because of their adeptness and dedication to her ideals.

Timessa's celebrity became a constant aggravation, complicating the TOW mission. Her original security, Joan, was increasingly unable to cope. Far too many aggressive autograph seekers and fans demanded selfies with the world's most famous model. The agency contracted with a larger security group. By midsummer three formidable men surrounded T wherever she went, an intimidating phalanx. Her SUV was replaced with a larger, reinforced version. All the men were — ridiculously, she thought — ex-Seals. Unlike Johnboy, all were professional.

She needed none of them, yet was surrounded as she went from place to place. Her agency wanted her to move to a more secure location, but she insisted on remaining in her townhouse. As a compromise, security was assigned outside her door and at entrances. She agreed that, on the face, it was justified. In a period of three months, she had more than a dozen rape and death threats; police arrested stalkers almost every month.

The security costs were enormous, but her income easily offset the expenses. In less than a year, she had become one of the five highest paid women in the world. *T* — the celebrity T — was mentioned on the news as frequently as the president. Journalists were mad for stories and her baffling past only made her more alluring. She was referenced as *The Enigmatic T* or *The World's Most Inscrutable Woman*. She had millions of followers on social media, yet seemed disinterested in celebrity-making necessities.

Rather than constantly priming her social accounts, she let her agency post occasional photos culled from back-scene shoots. She disdained selfies. No one understood her detachment, yet the professionals around her saw that, ironically, her apparent disinterest increased the public's hunger. Many considered her a savant, not only beautiful but inexplicably savvy.

In reality, she simply didn't care. None of it mattered except to launch something she still could not fully define. Yet she knew that an immense wheel was turning, its gears becoming polished once again, the pitting and gunk of quiet, lost millennia discarded as the wheel's speed multiplied. She felt its hum and knew its motion as a validation. She knew, too, this world she walked was fraudulent. Women were debauched, propagandized and diverted from the old ways. Fashion, her own impure undertaking, was as corrupt as all else. Sports, academia, religion, entertainment, politics, and finance — all of it was a vast public diversion.

T thought of Juliette, whom she had visited once in the last three months, impressed at her deepening understanding. Juliette seemed unaffected by the noise of nearby cities, the distractions and seductions. Filly reinforced T's assessment, noting that the girl seemed steps ahead of her instruction, always nodding and anticipating. Timessa called her Juliette of the Sunflowers, as the plants had proliferated behind the altar by the barn. "Ox blood," Juliette concluded. "Horseshit and ox blood, a sunflower aphrodisiac."

Yet Juliette's bluster was underlain with worry. The farm had seen little rain that summer and lay in paralysis. Their cash crop was two-thirds less than previous summers. She agonized over paying the next month's mortgage.

The weekend Timessa visited, she wandered out into the back meadow as the sun began to rise. When she left her guest room, the sky still sparkled with stars. She could see them revolving in a vast oval, a river of lights cascading in their slow sinuosity through the darkness. She thought of Eos, once the harbinger of dawn. What had corrupted her?

The eastern edge of the horizon bled a thin pink. She sensed a presence and turned: Juliette, in a nightgown, smiling. She half bowed, "May I join you, Queen?"

Timessa reached out and drew the girl against her. Juliette's swollen belly was warm and the double lives of mother and daughter precious. Juliette said, "I know you leave soon. I have a surprise, if you will indulge me ..."

T nodded, knowing immediately. She asked, "And the dozen girls who are here: won't they be terrified by what they see?"

"They're having their periods," Juliette intoned. "I will make reference to blood, how it all flows in a sacred river when offered in your name."

A half hour later, the small group gathered at the altar. T knew that all wore identical red, their camaraderie evident as they linked arms and waited expectantly, unaware of Juliette's plans. Filly had said that Juliette planned a special sunrise moment before the goddess left, that they would share in the event, sisters to the stars and sun, observers of the Old Ways — TOW girls, exceptional and indivisible.

Timessa stood fifty feet from the group, in a hooded gown that hid her face. She felt herself vibrating, her atoms pulsing in the yellow light. A silver knife lay on the altar surface, and Juliette appeared from the barn with a fat lamb in her arms. The animal could have been a favorite dog, content as she carried it to the structure beside the girls. Pausing by the stones, she set the lamb down. It stood docilely, and she turned to the girls.

"We gather together in the new light to thank the goddess." Juliette bowed her head toward T. "The one," she said, "we call Queen. Your lives are full because of Her. And you are alive, more than others, because of Her." The girls became quiet. "And I am full with child because of Her. I have told you of this consecrated altar. It is Hers. Yet I have not told you what occurs in this sacred spot when we give thanks."

Juliette took the lamb by its scruff, lifting it off its front legs. As she did she raised the knife above her head, crying, "Oh Goddess —!"

Then her knife arced down.

Watching from a distance, Timessa's reaction was identical to when the ox was sacrificed: flushing, flooding sensations through her belly, a sense of an empty, rolling ecstasy, followed by an indolent fullness. It was what Filly had described: a sacred river of red, a thing of inexplicable tenderness.

As the lamb's blood pulsed out, she pulled her hood closed and circled away. She thought: *There is nothing left to see.*

Filly held a bowl, capturing the blood, then lofted it high, singing, "Our blood, given monthly, is like this lamb's. It is thanks. And we are grateful for gifts received."

She poured the blood over the altar, then stepped back, facing the stone block, bowing and holding herself in obeisance. To Juliette's surprise the TOW girls pushed forward excitedly, gathering closely around the altar and the fallen lamb. Filly held the bowl out, and several girls ran their fingers through the sticky crimson. A girl a row back raised her hand, waving frantically to Filly.

"Can you let me do it next?"

"The sacrifice?" Filly asked.

The girl nodded furiously. "Oh yes! I'd be good."

Another girl raised her hand. "Or me!"

Filly said, "Perhaps next month —"

Then another cried, "Yes! Let's do this next month — !"

As Filly tried to control them, Juliette felt exhaustion. When she had sacrificed the ox two months earlier, she had felt a similar fatigue. Moments after it had collapsed onto its knees, she collapsed as well, the dirt beside the altar cutting into the skin of her legs. Now she was merely wobbly. Still, she braced herself against the altar, honored to have wielded the knife again. When she looked around for the goddess, she saw Timessa walking away, through the burnt grass, uphill toward the main house. Juliette was certain her thanks had been received.

Filly had taught her the word for sacrifice: *thysia*, θυσια. Juliette would have to teach the girls. And there was another, equally important expression — the phrase, be thankful, χαριν εχω.

Gifts and thanks were one. Favors, blessings were reciprocated. She knew enough to recognize that thanks was never praying. Praying was pleading, begging. *Thysia* was contact, goddess to recipient, beneficiary to divinity. Juliette did not merely hope for contact; she knew the goddess's touch directly. She was grateful. And the goddess's gift — the sweet proof — was the child she bore.

❦

Timessa stopped at the other side of the barn, out of view of those at the altar. She saw drought-bent grass around the buildings of the farm. Even the century-old trees looked singed. Simply walking up the slope toward the house had raised dust higher than her knees.

So, as she had when standing before Eos on the Hoosic River so many months ago, she raised her right fist and slowly rolled her fingers out into a five-digit star, lifting her face into the sun and crying, "Eeiiiiiii—!"

The clamoring girls in the back froze as they heard the sound. Filly smiled and turned, looking over her shoulder toward the house. One of the girls whispered, "That was Queen, wasn't it?"

Filly nodded, saying, "Yes. She's speaking to the earth."

Standing between the house and the barn, Timessa imagined a checkerboard of green fields along the dirt roads that bordered Juliette's farm. As she watched, imposing her vision onto the land, the umber meadows flanking the stables rippled with light, the burnt chromas of grass shifting in seconds to a pale viridescent, then to a bright emerald of straightening hops and corn and grains, all now waving lightly in a soft breeze. The dry loam that held the roots in a death thrall turned moist.

Timessa's eyes were luminous. She reached into a pocket of her gown, stroking Queenie as if she were an amulet. The Cycladic marble was warm, as silken as the inside of her thighs. She knew at that moment her very existence was a perfection, her moves and bliss and ecstatic atoms impeccable. What she did was inimitable. She knew without arrogance; everything now aligned.

Conscious, too, that a single verdant farm centered within a hundred square-mile region of drought would draw scrutiny, Timessa extended the lush viridescence away from the farm, tapering its edges out over a distance of miles into the browns and caramels everywhere, blending the new growth naturally into the thirsty crops of Juliette's neighbors. The multiplication of stalks and leaves made a thin susurration like a choir's song.

When the rustling softened, she went up to her room. She quietly shed her gown and dressed in jeans and a plain pullover, packed her few things in a pretentious Vuitton suitcase someone had given her, and checked messages.

From the dozens of texts, she knew tumult would begin again on her return to the city, the first six days alone booked with shoots and interviews and a short promotional video for a prestigious sedan. She sighed, wondering whether to continue with any of it. Yet still, she believed the raw fame, the colossal, international wave she rode would prove to be an accelerant, fuel for the Great Goddess's mission. The time to vanish was approaching, but the timing was not now. Work remained. Disappearing — and reappearing — would come in time.

Free of thoughts, she looked out a second-story window. Juliette and her husband were walking the lines of lush crops and Juliette was in tears. She must have sensed T's observation as she turned and waved wildly. T smiled, amused Juliette could see her at that distance. As a continuing gift, T would ensure that moderate rain fell on the region through the harvest season. And she would return in a month to assure her work endured.

She texted her security detail. The armored SUV and her defenders were quartered minutes away at a nearby farm stand, close enough for an emergency and far enough to ensure her privacy. The vehicle would arrive with the bus that carried the girls from the city to the farm. Timessa alerted Filly that they were leaving, and ambled down to wait.

As she walked into the sunlight, several of the girls saw her and ran up. "Queen, Queen! We have an idea!"

She smiled. For her entire life she had been surrounded by similarly ardent girls. Nymphs were always ebullient, and now these girl-models were, as well. "Yes?" she said. "I want to hear!"

The girls became shy. T pressed them, saying, "Out with it. You can't be so keen and then not tell."

The oldest of the group said, "Well, as Filly thought would happen, we're all synchronized.

"And Juliette has just shown us θυσια." She pronounced it with an awkward Greek trill, avoiding the word sacrifice. Perhaps, T thought, they haven't conflated the two. Perhaps Juliette had simply said, "We call this thysia, θυσια."

A younger girl, Evie, interjected, "So we think that when we have our periods, we should have θυσια as well."

"They are both sacred moments of blood," T said. "All mammals are the same, all females bleed."

Evie had a smoky voice and a fashionable split between her front teeth. One of Timessa's favorites, she said, "It all makes sense. But we were never told."

As they spoke Filly walked up. "Transportation's here."

Evie interrupted, insistent. "Should we call it θυσια? Is that what you want?"

Timessa smiled. She still had not shaken off the languid fullness, the warm flooding in her thighs. Looking out across the now green fields that flanked the clearing, she felt deep pleasure.

The girl said, "Queeeen!"

Touching Evie's shoulder, T said, "θυσια is an ancient word. It's a good word to know, but it has lost its ancient meaning. What we now do each month, we'll call The Observance."

"Observance?" the girl asked.

"As in being aware. Marking the sacred time of the month. Celebrating, confirming. Observing."

The girl said, "I like that."

Timessa pulled her close for a quick hug. "Good. Now, no more questions."

CHAPTER 40

She pulls her shirt tight, eyes as black as olives.
Charlotte Corday d'Armont with her kitchen knife.
He sits in silence and she rises, the blade high,
and strikes beneath his clavicle. He cries,
"A moi, ma chere amie!"

The shift was subtle. She knew it. Ancient sacrifices, relabeled, to be called Observances, the ceremony itself The Observance, taking place when the TOW girls were in monthly bloom. The real object was not to celebrate their periods, but to create a ritual for thanks. The thanks, however undeclared, would be to T. And however amorphous to the girls, its purpose would be an offering, in the old sense, in every respect. Yet Timessa knew there could be no reference to *sacrifice*. Sacrifice would be sublimated into the observance, its dark roots buried in the new ritual.

In touch with thousands via The Girls and her fashion network, and followed by millions on her social media accounts, Timessa was still an island. She would not be subsumed. The sun on her atoll shown as if through lemon shavings, its rays filtered through sulfur, its chromas a smoky cadmium. Regardless of how the girls viewed her, Timessa was now the Great One, Ishtar of Babylon, the White Goddess, the Triple Goddess of primeval Europe, Cybele of Anatolia, or simply, the Great Goddess. They were all one, the same deity with different names. Her face flushed with a purity that never fluctuated, her subtle inflorescence a constant revitalization. She was a flower opening endlessly in a startling radiance.

Eclipsing Hestia, Athene and Artemis, she supposed she had absorbed the entirety of their powers. Yet there was Aphrodite, the love goddess, the one of sensual pleasures. Timessa knew no intimacy with the carnal, and her transformation had included no insights, no revelations. She knew sexual pleasure flowed from physical touch. Yet, as much as she was once obsessed with sex, now that she had veered into divinity, desire seemed an amusing memory from a decade before. Yet in all her fullness, there was, she admitted, an emptiness.

On her return to Boston, she reviewed reports from clubs around the world. Membership in The Girls was now approaching fifteen hundred. She instructed Filly to end inductions. She reasoned if it became known that she no longer accepted new girls, the value of membership for those already members would increase. There were growing calls for her to expand the elite TOWs, but she was uncomfortable doing so. The Observance was in its infancy, and she recognized its potential for controversy.

Soon or later one of her TOW girls would excitedly tell her mother or father about The Observance. In the girl's innocence, she would try to explain how the cycle of thanks meshed with her own monthly cycle. Perhaps she would praise Juliette and speak of the brave lamb, and its killing. The parent would say with indignation, "That's horrible. You watched them kill a lamb? And Timessa went along with that?"

The girl would break into tears. Timessa knew this culture too well to believe The Old Ways would be viewed as anything other than barbarism. Arguments that modern slaughterhouses and abattoirs were far worse than the occasional killing of a lamb would persuade few. It mattered little that millions of animals were killed monthly in the great machine. Slaughter under the auspices of livestock industrialization was viewed as a necessity, and killing to give thanks an abomination. False virtue was a sanctimony, a deceit — yet the speciousness of it all was viewed as evolution, progress from a "barbarity" T was now reviving.

None of the girls yet understood the necessity of the ritual; only the divine could know. And that meant only Filly and T, although she was certain Artemis was aware. The TOW girls? They were no more than Timessa's — Queen's — enthusiasts, swept into her charisma and fame. She had charmed them with terms like synchronicity and sacred. Now their periods were special rather than an irritation. Yet they could not be expected to grasp T's divine needs. Without primal, sacrificial blood — which was the Great Goddess's addiction — she could not continue to give. And they would not receive.

The ritual was better left clandestine. Before the girls left the farm, she had sworn them to secrecy. She knew while doing so that secrets were fragile, and that the girls's loyalty, however sincere, might be abandoned under attack. Yet their oath might buy some time.

Perhaps she was wrong and the dozen girls more capable than she guessed. Children as young as eight and ten could be warriors. Or for girls, lithe Amazons. Self-sacrifice, a subset of *thysia*, was a requisite of idealism. She might yet be surprised.

She foresaw a wave of unimaginably bad publicity if one girl cracked. She wasn't certain that she cared. Whatever came she would adapt.

After an uneventful month, the TOWs trekked out to Juliette's, purportedly to see her swollen belly and to get away from the city once again. She was fewer than two months from delivery. In what was now late summer, the caravan sped west, out of Massachusetts and into New York; it included the girls in their van, T and Filly in the black SUV, and a tagalong vehicle for backup security.

Ten girls had signed up for the five-day retreat, all TOWs, including Evie and other top models from New York and Boston. They were eager, sharpened by the knowledge that they might re-enact events at Juliette's altar. None could explain their sudden fascination with ... blood ... It had become as seductive as the prospect of sex. None of them had killed, but they had watched Juliette, watched her long knife rise and fall. Several had been horrified, even sickened, but others wanted the experience, knowing Juliette might yield her weapon to them if they whined like little girls.

A fulvous sun, like an aging daffodil, hung delicately in the southern sky, followed the caravan as the girls whispered among themselves, giggles punctuating the excited discussions. They were a gang, tireless girl-cubs in synchronicity. Several briefly flashed each other glimpses of their panties, their smiles maniacal and challenging. All were committed, daring each other to flinch or repudiate their vows. None could.

On arrival at Juliette's, they spent the first hour wandering her fields, admiring the richness of her crops. She mentioned that they'd had rain the night before, and that precipitation had been almost every other third night after months of drought. Her husband showed them the growing flock of sheep, noting they had birthed a half dozen lambs since mid summer. The girls had little patience for these details, these obvious preliminaries. The farm's fortunes became quickly tedious to them. Walking through fields of hops and corn felt like a preface. All wanted more.

A friend of Evie's, Louisa, took Juliette aside after the group returned to the house and asked, "Will we get to offer thanks?"

"You mean," Juliette asked, "perform The Observance?"

"Yes!"

"Soon. Perhaps," she said with amusement, "at dusk."

"With a lamb?"

"Is that what you want?"

"Very much."

"Then," Juliette said, "you will get to pick the ewe."

"That's a girl lamb?"

"Of course. Late this afternoon we'll go down together and pick one out."

"Can Evie come?"

Juliette took her shoulders gently and asked, "Are the two of you close?"

Louisa nodded. "Besties, I guess."

"Then bring her along."

Most of the girls, after carrying their bags into the main house, took naps in their rooms, weary from the long road trip, aware that the evening promised a rare magic gifted only to TOW girls on Juliette's farm. In the flaxen heat, they laid on their beds without undressing, gorgeous creatures caught in the amber of late summer, their arms and legs akimbo. As they napped, the sun descended imperceptibly.

Timessa dismissed Filly and wandered from the house toward the barn. There she lingered to watch the sky. Breathing the immensity of the lush countryside she had created, she unwound, feeling a primordial vibration begin in her spine. She paused, measuring the hum, thinking it akin to a plucked lyre string.

The shudder wound downward, becoming snakelike, lowering itself, circling her waist, then constricting itself at her hips and — poised like one of Dionysos's thyrsi before her heat — filled her effortlessly. As it did so, seizing her in its splendor, she gasped, taken by its strange invasion. Still, she knew she remained sovereign — this lover could be extinguished at will.

Was this the lovely enslavement Aphrodite celebrated? Or was it something more mundane? She didn't know, had never been subjected to such sensations. Allowing the violation to continue its play, she asked herself what invisible serpent could have the temerity to ravage a goddess? The impunity was startling. Closing her eyes she felt its vibrations against her cervix, its warmth filling her hips in its magnificence. She gasped for breath, awaiting a nothingness that she felt approaching, a vacuum stalking her with its soft heat.

Flames rose on the horizon of her consciousness. The beast approaching was oblivion. And as she struggled against its touch, she trembled at its end, the vibrations winding down, down …

Enough! she thought: she would not be obliterated.

꙳

Late that afternoon, after a shared dinner at the house, the girls were instructed to change into clothes appropriate for an Observance. Dusk was twenty minutes away. While they changed into short gowns that mimicked what Timessa had worn a month earlier, Juliette took Evie and Louisa down to the flock.

"Close your eyes. Empty yourself." Juliette put her arm around Louisa as Evie stepped up to the low enclosure, saying, "Now, Evie, choose carefully."

The girl opened the gate, slipping in amongst the flock, touching first one, then another. The low sun washed the lambs with a salmon light, their coats flush with a coral phosphorescence, their black eyes on her as she moved deliberately. After she selected one, saying, "Here's a sweetheart!" Juliette picked it up, lifting it above her swollen belly, saying, "Once we get away from the flock, I'll put it down. You'll see — she'll follow us back to the barn."

The girls nodded and Juliette said, "Now go. You have but minutes to change. Then join the rest of us in the back."

The dusk's western light was a mauve-rose, the horizon to the east a dark band of oxidized mercury as black as the lamb's eyes. Juliette's husband had mentioned rain would sweep in after midnight, grinning as he spoke. Filly watched him in silence, wondering what he thought about all the girls and about Juliette's miraculous pregnancy. He was stoic, speaking rarely, yet supportive. He usually disappeared into the back of the house, aware that the gatherings behind the barn was female-only. Juliette would have made that clear.

Now before the altar, Juliette wore a gown loose enough to accommodate her swelling. Filly stood beside her and the two looked out over the ten girls. Their energy played over their faces like flames. The ewe singled out earlier stood placidly beside Juliette, untied, its eyes unreadable.

"Today, tonight, at dusk —" Juliette whispered, "we make Observances."

"The Observance!" one of the girls cried.

"Yes, exactly."

"But," Filly interjected, "one of you must step forward. We will not lead the thysia tonight. One of you will instead."

Looking around Evie asked, "Where is Queen?"

"Nearby, watching." Filly stated. "Now, which of you will guide us through tonight's event?"

Evie waved her hand. "Me!"

When Filly nodded and Juliette reached her hand out to the girl, Evie stepped forward, asking, "What happens first?"

🙚

Timessa lay on her back a short distance away in a field of hops. The plants grew in long rows on tall slanted poles ending far above her head. Virescent in the sun, and now a deep jade as evening fell, the crop was lush, the leaves vibrating in a low communal hum that mimicked the thrumming of Timessa's thighs. There, among the harvest-to-be, she was safe, hidden from sight, yet close, close enough.

Moments before she had experienced an effervescence, a thin shuddering that repeated itself with a richness she hadn't thought possible. Although she was ignorant, still clouded by a nymph's naivety, she knew the shuddering was orgasmic. She thought, lying with her arms spread and hair carelessly cast over the grass, the experience might be a precursor to the thysia. And why not? She was a bird on the wing to an unknown grove, the shrubs heavy with a fruit she'd never tasted.

And, she wondered, was this sex, this taking by an invisible thing, a non-thing — an unnamed thing? Or was it, frighteningly, parthenogenesis? Yet she had no wish to conceive. Women once did so, their ovum lighting up without a man, in the time of matriarchy. But, she thought, parthenogenesis was born of desire, a desperation like Juliette's, the primal need to procreate. She, the Great Goddess, had no such desire.

No, this was a spontaneous, unprompted supernova. It could not be colored otherwise. Weeks before she had wondered about Aphrodite's art; this surge of foreign sensations was Gaia's delayed reply. She imagined Gaia whispering, *This, Timessa, is a woman's sense of sex.*

Gaia, the trickster, pulling veils aside. Yes, yes, yes, she thought. *Gaia.*

Minutes later, as she sought some normalcy, a return to the time-space flow in the confines of the farm, the girls's voices began to penetrate the field where she lay. She remained on her back, shifting her consciousness to the small theatre beside the barn.

There, beside the altar, Evie whispered, "What happens first?"

Filly said gently, "You will know."

Evie looked out excitedly at her friends. She spoke in a voice unlike her own: "Who here has not washed their hands?"

Two girls pointed at themselves. Evie nodded and said, "Go. Return when you are clean."

Then she spread her arms, her palms open and fingers splayed. Quietly, she said, "We are one. We attend The Observance because we love our Queen."

One of the older girls cried, "And we give thanks."

All of them responded, "Thanks!"

Evie went on, "She has enriched our lives!"

Louisa sang out, "Abundantly!"

Like a small chorus the girls shouted, "Abundantly!"

Evie paused, her eyes glittering. "The one we call Queen is more than someone we admire." She turned to Filly, smiling knowingly. "Her old friend calls her Goddess!"

By now the girls who'd been dismissed returned. Evie looked at them, saying, "Your lives are full because of Her. And you are alive, more than others, because of Her."

The two broke into tears, nodding in acknowledgement. The girls became quiet. Then one with glossy black hair said, "We're the fortunate. We are the few who understand —"

Another girl cried, "— that Timessa is more than a supermodel!"

There were cries of "Yes!" and Louisa stepped up beside Evie, turning to her friends and said, "She is a goddess, no matter how crazy that sounds. Look! She made this farm green again. And Juliette carries a child because Timessa decided it should be."

The girls were all holding hands, or standing with their arms around each other. One cried, "And we give thanks."

All of them again responded, "Thanks!"

Evie sang, "And we are all a river of blood. We bleed her sacred blood!"

The girls cried, "Yes!"

At that juncture Evie took the ewe by its neck and lifted it off its front legs. Louisa swiveled and grasped a long knife from the altar, handing it to Evie. The girl's eyes rolled backward and she cried, "Oh Goddess!"

In the field of hops, still on her back, Timessa trembled as before, the same flushing sensation from the month earlier flooding her thighs. This new wave was not oblivion. Instead, this was reciprocity bred in an indolent frenzy.

She was a queen in thrall, ravaged by the simplest of acts: Evie's enormous gift.

Evie struck down and the ewe flinched, its blood pulsing as its eyes emptied of life. Its cone of vision narrowed. Darkness fell. A great wind blew through its cranium, emptying its senses.

Filly bent with her silver bowl, collecting blood. A strand of her hair fell forward into the bowl and she snapped her head back, her hair freed of the crimson wash. She pulled her lips back into an inexplicable grimace, showing her shark's teeth, white scimitars in the dim light, then rose and poured the blood across the stones.

Timessa thought: *There is nothing left. It is done, a gift of blood and bones.*

CHAPTER 41

Light, concocted from spun
gold, falls across her chest,
a thousand gradients, zones
of light finessed —

That evening, an hour after the sacrifice, Juliette played piano for the girls. She was a surprising virtuoso, able to play anything anyone requested. She'd never mentioned her skill.

No one spoke of or to Timessa, who sat in a corner chair, translucent in the incandescent light, half there at best. When a girl would turn and look at T, she saw a sheer form with burning eyes, a frightening, gossamer female whose form seemed more luminous than real. After a half dozen songs, Queen stood and, with all the girls watching breathlessly, simply vanished. It was as if she were a celestial object, no more than ice, dust and gas, consumed in the plant's atmosphere.

Upstairs, irritated by her unnecessary drama, Timessa sat on her bed, listening to the noise from downstairs. Juliette continued to play and when she paused, half the girls broke into a cappella, others dancing in bare feet, all giggling at their ingenuity.

Timessa's room, though, was dark. She had closed the curtains, and stretched out on her back as she had done beneath the hops in Juliette's rich fields. She could feel the earth breathing, the stars over the New York countryside pulsing in a cosmic tide. Minutes passed and someone knocked lightly on her door. She knew instantly: Louisa.

Timessa debated whether to acknowledge her, but after a moment, whispered, "Come in, girl."

Louisa quietly opened and closed the door, standing waif-like and immobile. She was still in her Observance gown, late summer ivy woven through her hair. T could see her eyes as she looked around the darkness. Timessa said nothing and the girl sighed. "You're really angry at me, aren't you?"

"For what?"

"I just know you are."

Timessa sat up and put out her arms. "Come here."

Louisa slowly padded barefoot to T's bed, her head down. When she was close she felt the goddess take her gown at the waist and tug her down until she was sitting pressed against T's side. Queen whispered into her long hair, "Don't speak."

Nodding, Louisa sat, barely breathing, afraid to move, her heart racing. The goddess stroked her lightly, her fingers moving over her spine, pausing to trace a rib around her waist, blowing gently into her hair, keeping her close. The goddess's touch was warm. In Timessa's arms she was fine. Nothing existed except the goddess's fingers.

Timessa whispered, her lips near the girl's neck, "Why have you come?"

"Needed this …"

Yes, she knew. As the goddess stroked her waist and hips, the girl suddenly sobbed, overcome by a vast opening, a cleft parting through high grasses, an aperture through which she saw a golden light wavering, far away. Then she felt Timessa shifting, forcing her onto her lap, touching her gently while Louisa cried softly.

"Queen," she finally whispered. "Who are you, really?"

Timessa's fingers fondled the girl's hair, brushing her scalp. "You know who I am."

"No, you're more than what you say." As the girl looked at her, T pulled her head closer and kissed her forehead. Louisa purred, "Tell me Queen. Tell me who you are."

Timessa gripped Louisa's head in both hands and whispered, "I am ancient, beyond your comprehension."

"No," the girl said, "you're hardly older than me."

"I go back tens of thousands of years."

Louisa shook her head from side to side, smiling. She knew Queen was teasing her. But Queen continued, "Once long ago, I was the Great One. A goddess who ruled over all."

"Ruled?"

Continuing to stroke Louisa's hair, Timessa said, "A time when women ruled over men. You cannot understand, child."

"I want to."

"Yes, I know —"

Louisa continued, "What's your real name? It can't be just T."

"The one all of you use."

"Queen, not Timessa?"

"Queen is the oldest of my names. When I began modeling, Timessa worked."

Louisa put her forehead between T's breasts and said plaintively, "Will you always love us?"

"Love?"

The girl whispered, "We all love you."

Someone knocked on the bedroom door. Louisa shrugged, saying in a little girl's voice, "Oh, probably Evie."

Timessa told her to enter. Evie, dressed the same as Louisa, stepped in. Looking at the two, she said, "Not fair. You've had Queen to yourself."

Louisa smiled. "So what?"

"We do things together," Evie said.

"I was freelancing."

Timessa motioned for her to come closer. Like she had done with Louisa, when Evie was within reach, T grabbed her gown and pulled her down. She found Evie's ribs and tickled her. The girl thrashed and squealed, but to no avail as Louisa doubled the attack, pinning her down.

While Louisa continued to restrain Evie, Timessa shifted from tickling to stroking her cheeks, saying, "Aw, poor thing. Caught between two monsters, helpless, helpless. This'll teach you to interrupt —"

Evie felt light-headed in the dark. She felt an immense tenderness as the goddess opened her petal by petal, her affection for Queen and Louisa overflowing as seconds passed. Then, she too, like Louisa, began to cry. "Oh Queen, do you know what I did this afternoon?"

"The ewe?"

"But you weren't there. I looked!"

"You're wrong. I watched."

"Juliette chose me for the thysia."

"Are you glad?"

"I was euphoric."

"The blood, yours and the lamb's?"

Evie nodded, her head buried in T's neck. "Yes, and I gave thanks for you."

"Do you know why?"

She paused. "For all the things you've given us?"

"Yes, I can grant you many things but you must thank me in return."

"With thysia?"

"Yes, thysia , θυσια. And you must all be thankful. Never forget the old phrase that Filly taught you both, χαριν εχω."

Evie whispered, " 'Be thankful,' right? But we are!"

"Χαριν εχω is the old way. Always thank the one who gives."

Like a small bird, Louisa pried Timessa's hand from Evie's side and lifted it to her mouth, kissing the top. "Evie gave thanks at dusk. I hope to be the next to wield the knife."

Timessa cupped the girl's cheek. "You as well?"

"Oh yes!"

Timessa looked at them impartially. "It seems so simple. Rapture comes easily. You've had a taste. There will be more. Now it's late. You need your sleep."

Louisa and Evie spoke simultaneously, "Can we stay here tonight? With you?"

Timessa shook her head. As the two girls watched, she appeared to become translucent again. Only her eyes were full, her irises a violet-black. She pushed them away. "Go," she said.

Inexplicably, both felt immense love. The emotion was a honey that left them moving slowly, heavy-limbed and half-faint. They would have done anything she asked.

Timessa stood, less translucent than moments before, steering them with a mother's force to the bedroom door. As Evie opened the door, T touched Louisa's shoulder. "At dusk tomorrow *you* will choose the ewe, and do the thysia like Evie did tonight. Then two girls will understand. Now go, and get your rest."

℞

In the morning of the second day on the farm, Timessa met briefly with her security team. They reported they had stopped an intruder the night before, a man in a car who pulled into Juliette's circular drive. As he got out carrying a camera, they had tackled him, gagging him first and then handcuffing him. He carried no ID but a wallet in his vehicle had several business cards. His name was Cherry Calloway and the cards advertised photography services. A line on the cards read, "We capture the world's celebrities." The firm was based in New York City.

Timessa observed, "A paparazzo."

The lead man said, "There's been some buzz on social media. Rumors you were holed up on some farm near here. We've been following it. He must have figured it out."

"What started the rumors?"

"Someone local spotted our vehicles and knew Juliette was a friend."

"And this man, Calloway — what did you do with him?"

"Left him with some bruised ribs. Not much else we could do except warn him about trespassing. And that if he was seen again there's be no second chance."

She praised their work and dismissed them. Surveillance would continue. She knew she was impervious to any attack, but there were others to protect. The parents of several of the girls had been persuaded to allow the trip on the basis of the extraordinary protection.

The day passed quickly and at dusk the thysia was again performed. Timessa watched from the nearby field. As Louisa wielded the long knife in an almost identical ritual to that of the day before, T trembled, undergoing the same sensations, the same deep pleasure flooding her and causing her to cry out silently. The indolent fever she felt was intense, rippling through her belly. As Louisa cried, "Oh Goddess," plunging her knife down into the ewe, Timessa gasped.

Long moments passed before she fluttered her eyes. When she did she saw Gaia, squatting beside her without expression. Gaia's body as always was lightly vibrating. She appeared ephemeral, even more translucent than Timessa the night before.

This ardor, Timessa, at the moment of thysia, is a woman's alone.

"Is it like sex?"

What you feel is more intense. What humans feel at orgasm is a ghost in comparison. You are a goddess. All sensations are greater.

Then Gaia vanished. T lay for minutes unmoving, as still as a fallen branch. The first planets and stars began to appear overhead, Venus, Vega, Rigel, Mars and Sirius blinked on, one by one. A summer breeze caused the palm-sized leaves of the hops overhead to rustle. She shuddered, aware of a second fluttering in her belly and thighs, conscious that the very atoms of her body burned.

As the stars spun like mobiles — fiery dots suspended on wires in the cold phosphorescence — she laughed. Her voice was radiant. She imagined she could still see Gaia's eyes, inscrutable. To the girls nearby who knelt before Juliette as the thysia ended, vibrations swept over them like a wave, a throbbing undercurrent that left their limbs tingling.

Evie, who stood beside Louisa at the altar, cried out, "That's it! Our thanks for her gifts is accepted!"

CHAPTER 42

Exploits, exploits. Still, she was simply, Goddess,
a divinity without a lover, labium majorum
sealed, pureness
in her constant hum.

Occasionally, Timessa thought of Eos, who had surrendered her divinity. Vanity had not brought her down. Not pride, or hauteur. Instead, her blunder had been defiance of the gods and duplicity. She was one in a long line of divinities who had over-reached.

T rose before the sun, dressing and quietly leaving the house. Juliette's farm had a small promontory southwest of the barn, a high meadow shaped like an island from which she could see over the fields. In a white knee-length dress — a gift from her agency — she strode barefoot up the narrow trail, mounting the rise. The sun was just coloring the horizon's edge with an orange band no wider than a knife's blade. She turned to face it, light-hearted and light-headed.

Juliette's house was still dark, the girls sleeping. They were still children, however glamorized. At this hour she could savor the recent events, replay Gaia's surreptitious visit, and anticipate the thysia that would be performed again at dusk. She had already chosen a third girl to conduct the ritual, one younger than Evie and Louisa. She had already memorized the nascent ritual.

Now, in the quarter-light of dawn, Timessa bent beside blue asters on the hilltop and, picking a dozen, wove herself a crown of flowers. *Gillyflowers*. Straightening, placing the wreath on her head, she smiled. The sun's orange band had widened, and the delicate clouds on the horizon pulsed.

Then she heard a faint chop-chop-chop in the distance. As the sound grew — a mercurial thrumming of silver blades against the still air — a helicopter appeared, dark, dangerously low and skimming a line of trees. She knew that it wasn't airborne to spray farm fields or conduct inventory; it was coming for her, toward her as if a blunt projectile. At its speed it would arrive in seconds. As it closed on the promontory, she read, Curtis Copter, stenciled in fat block letters on its side. She could feel the downdraft from the blades. The pilot was wearing a red jump suit and helmet; he looked grim.

Watching as the copter hovered, she saw the side door facing her swing open and a safety bar project from the helicopter's body. A man leaned from the copter, clutching the sidebar with one hand and a large camera with the other. He raised the camera and shouted over the din, "Smile, Timessa!"

The copter's backdraft caused her to shield her face with her hands while stumbling sideways. Dust spiraled up and into the blades. The photographer shouted, "Hands down, beautiful. You'll spoil the shots!"

Artemis used to call these things whirlybirds. T remembered the goddess — decades ago before the second Great War when they still were sheltering in the foothills of the French Pyrenees — making one crash when it hovered suddenly over the small tribe of nymphs. Timessa had been a part of a hunt. She remembered her utter fear at its appearance. Artemis would not allow them to be discovered and, in instant reaction, had merely nodded her head and the blades froze, the machine falling from the sky. There had been no repercussions, no search parties, and they simply avoided the shattered aircraft on future hunts.

The whirlybird hovering over Timessa was now rocking side to side, causing the dust to tornado upward. Her dress was orbiting over her hips, her hair awhirl and her long legs exposed. Through the haze she saw the photographer grinning — leering, she thought, successful in his petty hunt. This was probably Cherry Calloway, upping the stakes. She knew her startled face would appear in some tabloid. Worse, the farm's location would be trumpeted, reduced to a red dot on a newspaper map. She imagined an arrow pointed at it, a headline screaming, *Timessa's Hideaway*.

"That's it baby! Gotcha, baby. Now give me a grin —"

She raised her hand to him, palm open, a motion he construed as a concession, even an encouraging wave.

He yelled, "Yeah, baby! Love you, too."

Then with a faint smile and wide eyes, she flicked her wrist. The helicopter's structure slowly began disintegrating. Cherry, if that's who he was, disappeared first, his body and camera fragmenting. An instant later the copter began to tilt. She saw the pilot's arm lift as if to stop a blow, then vanish.

A sudden silence: the helicopter and the men had vaporized. What remained was suspended in an odd rectangle of soot, a thin smoke in a strange, wine-red geometry. She briefly watched the metallic cloud drift west as it dissipated. Then, in seconds, the helicopter was gone.

Timessa smoothed her dress down her thighs, straightening the pleats and clearing dust off her arms. The Dior would have to be dry-cleaned, and she would have to shower. Her hair felt gritty, but she felt nothing else. Unlike the effect of the thysia, this small incident left her passionless; she supposed no one would even know because the rude event had been brief. Extinguishing the threat had been no different than brushing away a gnat.

Then she felt someone. She turned. Standing several hundred feet away, leaning against the main house, Juliette and Louisa stood watching. Juliette had covered her mouth with her palm. Both were motionless. They clearly had seen at least part of the encounter. She put up her hand, calling out, "Stay where you are," then quickly walked toward them, her eyes shrouded.

❧

Moments later she sat in Juliette's kitchen with the two. They had not spoken since the incident. T looked at Juliette and commanded, "Get me a coffee."

Juliette nodded. Timessa noted that Louisa was in tears, trying without success to suppress her shock. T touched her cheek and the girl flinched, pushing away.

"Okay," Timessa said. "Let's talk."

Louisa said, "We saw everything. You just killed two men. Maybe there were others inside that thing."

"There weren't," she said. "Just a pilot and photographer."

"Then that's two."

Juliette handed T a coffee, her hand trembling, and said, "There'll be cops here soon. We'll be destroyed. Everything lost. Why?"

"No," Timessa said. "none of that will occur. They filed no flight plans. They flew too low to be on radar. It was all covert, a celebrity hunt. No one was to know. And consequently nobody does."

"Our neighbors," Juliette said. "Someone will have seen it coming."

"Perhaps, but when it hovered over me, I made it invisible to anyone else. The moment it stopped and that man swung out taking photos, there was nothing for anyone to see. It simply disappeared."

Louisa said in a tiny voice, "Did you really blow it up?"

"Not 'blow it up.' I broke it down into atoms. Then broke the atoms into electrons. Then let the breeze do its work."

"That's horrible," Louisa said.

"Why do that?" Juliette whispered. "From what I saw they were just taking pictures."

"Yes," T said. "Pictures that would have made your farm a target for every crazy in this country. Pictures that would have destroyed everything we've built here. For years people would have been knocking on your door, asking about me, about what you knew, what you could say — "

Louisa shook her head, whispering, "Atoms, electrons. That's impossible. What did you really do?"

"What I did when I ended the drought here. The way I shot green through every withering plant for miles around."

Juliette said, "But those men —?"

"Gone," she replied.

Juliette whispered, "I still don't understand. How could you have killed them?"

"How could I have made you full with child, with a daughter who will be as beautiful as her mom? Is this any different?"

"One is life and one is death. You know that!"

"How soon you forget. Here we sit on your farm, Juliette — you experienced years of drought. And I have made it sing with life."

"This is different."

"No," Timessa said. "You rejoiced when I saved your farm, didn't you?"

"Yes ..."

"And you rejoiced even more when I made you full with child."

Juliette nodded, in tears.

"You were infertile. I gave you life. Now when I take life, you are shocked?"

Timessa's face was impassive. She was as enigmatic as the experience of death is to one who is left holding the cold hand of their beloved, conscious that an indefinable essence has abruptly slipped away and that no intervention, no sorcerer's magic, can change the fact. Timessa's face indicated that she saw no difference between the living and the dead, that Juliette's arguments were naive.

More so, Juliette saw in Timessa's eyes only cold observation, a night sky with cold stars — a night sky usurping an astronomer's role, the night watching the astronomer ... Too, she saw in Timessa's eyes, inexplicably, the eyes of a deathless horsewoman riding her white mare.

Then, Juliette understood. She fell to her knees, shaking her head frantically, clutching Timessa's legs. "Oh Goddess," she cried. "I'm suddenly terrified."

Timessa ran her fingers through Juliette's hair. "No more will I leave you, than you will me. We are one."

Juliette sobbed, her face between Timessa's thighs. Louisa in turn nodded sagely, saying, "It's about balance, isn't it?"

T said, "So you think you understand?" Louisa nodded again. At the same moment they heard footsteps. Several of the other girls ran into the kitchen, rubbing their eyes.

"Oh!" one cried on seeing the three, "early birds!"

Juliette lifted her head, her face wet with tears. As she wiped her cheeks, she said, "We have been up with our goddess. It's been good to have some time alone." Then she looked at Timessa and said, "And so the day begins."

CHAPTER 43

Here's to theories of elasticity: first, sotto voce.
Then, hands on her curves, her antonyms; flora
beside fauna; passion (unanticipated); and the distance
between words. (And the lights of Borealis aurora.)

J amie was the third girl, the one Timessa had designated to follow Evie and Louisa. A year younger than the others, she was a complete convert. As eager as the others to wield the long knife, she had instantly married the concept of merging her blood with the lamb's — she understood that uniting them was a consecrated act. One gave meaning to the other, she told Filly an hour before dusk. Beyond that, she admitted, praising her Goddess — celebrating Queen — made her terribly excited. That the blood from her periods could be as sacred as a purified lamb's felt intoxicating.

Late in the afternoon she selected the votive ewe, a black-eyed, half-year-old lamb. Its eyes were expectant and Jamie picked it up, handing it awkwardly to Juliette, who took it in her arms. "We consecrate it," Jamie said, "as our gift tonight."

Juliette nodded. "Yes," she said. "But it is the goddess who consecrates."

Nervous but exhilarated that she was next, Jamie spent the thirty minutes before the ritual changing into her gown and brushing her hair. She brushed far longer than necessary, standing like a sprite before the full-length mirror, looking at herself as if at a dark sea, the waves of her long hair mesmerizing. She imagined them under moonlight.

When Evie came to get her, the older girl hugged her and said, "Try not to become aroused when you strike with the knife. The blood will feel as if it's burning your thighs, even if a drop never touches you."

Jamie looked at her, chagrined. "Louisa told me. I can barely stand the thought."

"Have you ever been with a boy?"

She hesitated, finally saying, "Yes, sort of, halfway, once."

"This is more intense than anything like that."

Jamie said nothing, nodding solemnly. They walked down together, Jamie grateful that Evie took her hand. Out in the flat between the house and the barn, the ground was damp — a mid-afternoon shower had appeared as if an atmospheric anomaly, its steady rain centered over Juliette's farm and her immediate fields. After a quarter hour, the rain turned to a warm drizzle, then ended. A faint scent of ancient lilacs lingered in the air. The pastures and the rolling meadows sparkled, a mist rising toward the sun.

Near the end of the shower, a truck stopped on the road in front of Juliette's house. An older couple, probably locals, sat watching the microstorm. They lowered their windows, staring as the rain pummeled the precise dimensions of the farm, conforming to fence lines and fields. The road and truck remained dry. Neither spoke, and after a moment, expressionless, they slowly drove away.

Now as Jamie scanned the area, watching the blue-grey vapors rise off fields, she thought of a word she'd learned in a botany class: *evapotranspiration*. It wasn't perfectly analogous, but she liked its jumbled syllables. And it felt like what she expected to feel soon — things merging and releasing, inhalations and exhalations — a dance of living things with the dying, even the arousal that Evie had mentioned. Fire, water, earth, and air: all a jubilation.

Evie was dressed in a gown identical to hers, and it occurred to Jamie that Evie herself could be the sacrifice. She imagined her bent over the altar, her white throat uncovered — then pushed the thought away, afraid that the goddess would know and find her impure. Yet the image of blood on Evie's gown — Filly holding her down firmly, the bowl under her neck — kept reappearing, and she was relieved when they rounded the back of the barn.

There all the girls waited, their excitement palpable. Jamie straightened, releasing Evie's hand. Confidence flooded her as she saw Juliette in the front, the ewe tied beside the altar.

She strode to the front and Filly handed her the knife. Turning to the group, their faces shadowed in the fallen light, Jamie took the blade, raising it overhead and cried, "Oh Goddess!"

As with every observance, Timessa waited in anticipation in the secrecy of the fields. This third night she silently merged her consciousness with Jamie's, making the words of the thysia spoken by the girl precise. The ritual was coalescing into a liturgy. Jamie sang, "We give thanks."

All of them responded, "Thanks!"

Jamie cried, "And we live in the river of life, in a river of blood. And what we bleed is sacred to what is sanctified!"

The girls cried, "Yes!"

"We are girls, and we are blessed!"

"Yes!"

At that moment Jamie, like others before her, took the ewe by its neck and lifted it high. Her eyes rolled backward and she cried, "Oh Goddess! For you we give thanks!"

When the girls had returned to their jobs and homes, Timessa met her professional obligations in multiple shoots over successive days. Juliette had received no queries regarding the helicopter; the local community paper noted in a brief paragraph that Cherry Calloway, a celebrity photographer, had been reported missing in the area. Otherwise, as Queen had predicted, the incident might not have occurred … except that Juliette and Louisa had been awakened by the copter's chop and watched the goddess destroy the machine and its occupants with a flick of her hand.

Timessa gave it no thought. She liked the phrase Louisa had used at one point as they sat in the kitchen — The Lord giveth and the Lord taketh away.

The nights in Boston were sultry, the air the briny tang of a dying summer. Her late night discussions with Filly were unfulfilling, yet she knew the nymph was devoted. Timessa — or as Filly now called her alternately, Queen — was aware that her uneasiness was due to the duality she had chosen. One dimension was as supermodel, the other as divinity. Reconciliation remained a challenge.

One afternoon while Timessa idled in her townhouse between shoots, security buzzed her cell: she had an unannounced visitor, a man who identified himself Josef, as an old friend, and that he carried a large package. She asked for them to text her a photo. Yes, it was Josef, waiting on the street. Amused and curious, Timessa allowed him upstairs. What could he possibly want?

At a knock, she opened the door. He looked identical, his hair slicked back, a rectangular box in his arms. "I had to show the contents to get past your army downstairs."

"Pleasant to see you."

"Yes." He paused, watching her. "It's been months."

"Close to a year."

"When you left, you just walked out. You never even gave notice."

"I sent you a check, paid you in full. You're not here to hit me up, are you, your hand out, like everyone else?"

He smiled easily. "No. I have a gift to give you. I planned it a year ago, then, poof! you were gone."

"Yes, too abrupt."

"So," he said, "thanks for letting me in. I know you've become a big deal."

"I suppose. These things are ephemeral."

"You mean fame is fleeting?"

"That's what they say."

"I've always been curious about one thing." He frowned. "What happened to Kore? The girl tormenting you at the time."

"Hmm, let me think — she became an ancient divinity, then a laurel tree."

"I always appreciated your sense of wit. I suppose," he said, "that's a good segue to why I came."

"I do want to know."

"I dreamed about you several nights ago. Probably triggered by the magazine spread I'd seen at lunch."

"Which?"

"You were on a beach modeling fall clothes."

"*Vogue*," she said. "It was an early morning shoot. Capes and hats by Chanel."

"That's it. Six or seven pages." She said nothing and he continued. "One shot particularly reminded me of the gift I had planned to give you. So I thought I might try again."

"You're being mysterious, Josef." She couldn't tell him she knew why he had come, what he had brought. She had trained herself to pretend otherwise. No one was comfortable unmasked.

"In one shot you were shown in semi-profile." He raised his hand as if molding clay, twisting his fingers expressively. "You reminded me of an angel in my collection. I've always thought it was intended for you."

"Is that's what in the box?"

"Yes," he said, hesitating. "You may remember it. I realized one day it's you, your face, your profile. Not some artist's idealization. Even the odd way you cock your hip when you stand ..."

She smiled indulgently. "Show me."

Pausing a moment, he shrugged and opened the box, pulling out an object swathed in yellow tissue. It appeared to be about thirty inches long. Somewhat dramatically, he unraveled the tissue and held the angel out in his arms. It was the bronze piece from the 15th century, the one cast by Donatello himself, circa 1440. Josef had not said so, but she knew that once its attribution was affirmed by experts, it would be worth millions. She wasn't sure how to respond. The statue meant nothing to her, and everything to him.

"It's bronze," he said. "I have that aged cherry case for it with a marble base. It's got glass doors, remember? If you like the angel, I'll bring the case at a later time." Timessa reached out and touched the angel's cold, polished head. He continued in a hushed voice, "The halo is beaten gold. Most of these statues are men. Not this one."

"It does look like me."

"It does."

She said, "If it's an angel, why doesn't it have wings?"

"It's unique. I'm not sure. But with the halo, it must be divine."

"Josef, why are you doing this?"

"Some things that we acquire, we acquire mistakenly. The longer I've owned it, knowing this angel was you, or an amazing impersonation of you, the more it's felt wrong for me to be its owner."

He was serious, and would not be dissuaded. She thought of her own dream in which Josef had taken her into his angel room. There all his angels, instead of being heavenly messengers, were small Cycladic statuettes. Not long after that, Artemis had given her Queenie, her childhood toy.

She reached into her pocket, Queenie's constant refuge, and pulled the statue out. "Here," she said. "It's small but if we're showing off, you might be interested."

He held it gingerly, asking, "It's real? Do you know what you own?"

"Yes," she said. "A goddess gave it to me."

He smiled at her exaggeration. "These are all Cycladic, from the Greek islands. Idols or icons or representations of some goddess. They're ancient."

"I know what it is. And this one personifies the Great Goddess, the most ancient of goddesses."

Josef looked at her as if to elaborate or correct her understanding. But he hesitated. "Have you had an expert examine it? Perhaps someone at the Fogg or the MFA?"

"Yes," she said. "One of the world's top authorities has confirmed its age and origin."

He handed it back, saying, "It seems to be warming in my hand."

"She does that at times." Timessa smiled. "I call her Queenie. Now, with your gift, she'll have a friend."

They looked at each other for a quiet moment. He said, "I've overstayed."

"Josef, who made this angel statue?"

He shrugged, "Whoever, they knew what they were doing."

Not once during his visit had he said, *Donatello*.

❧

About eleven that night, Filly sat on the couch examining the angel. Her first reaction was that one of Queen's admirers had commissioned the bronze. But T insisted that wasn't the case. "It's a gift," she said. "Very old."

"It can't be. It's a perfect likeness of you. And it doesn't have wings."

"But it has a halo."

"Hmm, so do you."

Timessa smiled and ignored her, except to note that Filly should handle the figure carefully. "It may be worth a fortune," she said. "Wipe off your fingerprints when you're finished."

After a few minutes, Filly turned it upside down, poking her fingernail along a seam on the base. "There's a tiny button," she muttered. "I'll bet the bottom opens."

Then as Timessa watched, Filly pushed on the clasp and a metallic hatch swung open with a rasp. "Old or not, the spring still works," she said triumphantly. She shifted the base toward a lamp to see inside. When she tilted it up, a gold florin rolled out into her lap. "A coin. And there! Something else —"

She extracted a paper with writing. Words in calligraphy. Timessa stepped closer. "Can you read it?"

"I'm guessing it's Italian." Filly read,

Mi sono svegliato una notte dopo un sogno. C'era una ragazza. Brillava di luce. Lei era un angelo senza ali. Il suo nome era Temesina. Quindi l'ho fatta qui, questa statua, per ricordarmi per sempre della sua bellezza. —D

"Lousy pronunciation," Filly said. "But I bet 'Il suo nome era Temesina' means her name is Temesina. Which, Goddess, is a pretty good match for Timessa."

"No. The statue is about 600 years old. I wasn't posing as anyone's model in the 15th century. I was Artemis's girl."

"Who was sneaking out into the woods at night to rendezvous with some sculptor."

"Ha. You were my best friend. You know I wasn't."

She looked at Timessa without comment, finally asking, "Who is D?"

"The signature?" She shrugged. "We'll have to get the note translated. One of the girls in the club is Italian."

"Vani?"

"Yes, take a photo of the note and email it to her tonight. Explain nothing except that I need it translated."

Filly found her phone and snapped an image, sending it out.

Within twenty minutes her phone chirped. It was Vani, who lived in Florence and was a charter member of The Girls. It was 5:30 in the morning there. She wrote, "Couldn't sleep. Funny writing. It's old Italian but it pretty much says,

I woke one night after a dream. There was a girl. She shone with light. She was an angel without wings. Her name was Temesina. So I made her here, this statue, to remind me forever of her beauty. —D

Vani went on, "Very romantic. Someone sending Timessa notes?"

Filly thanked her without elaborating and turned to Timessa. "It's my bedtime. Want to tell me more?"

Timessa shook her head. The Donatello sat on an end table, with Queenie propped beside it. On a back wall, Bravo's small photograph, *Obrero*, glowered. T looked at them all, then at the new statue, struggling to reconcile apparent facts with an impossibility. And why, she thought, had Josef suddenly appeared? The Donatello was his most valued possession. She read him thoroughly; she also read his sincerity: he believed the statue should be hers, and so it had become.

CHAPTER 44

The cedar groves groan lightly.
Stones vibrate, rivers throb,
Snakes sway,
as two doves, heavy
in their sorrow, lift away.

The river, the river, she thought — a discarded cobra's skin, its scales glittering below numberless city lights. The docile Charles wound darkly along Storrow Drive. Her memories of her millennia of servitude to Artemis were vanishing, she thought. Knowing felt no different than what she had felt during the disappearance of gods, satyrs or men who dared challenge her.

After Josef's departure, events accelerated. As in a nautilus shell's geometry (where the spiral becomes tighter as it winds inward to its heart), daily phenomenon became breathtakingly delicate. A vast celestial movement of gears and cogs seemed to be driven now by an immutable song. She imagined it was Gaia's aria, like a cosmic whale's call that remained perfect in its pitch, an impeccable hymn that hurried her impending ascent.

Over the last months, The Girls, whose membership had been curtailed at T's request, initiated a dozen new girls into thysia. The ritual coalesced into a formal liturgy that Juliette and others transcribed, and published as a pamphlet. Timessa — or Queen, as most of the girls now addressed her — approved the text.

She also set certain rules that prohibited all mention of The Girls on social media, to include photographs or videos for any purpose. Any mention of the group to any nonmember was forbidden. Their monthly celebration became more sacred, something for which all gave thanks, for their love for T united them.

Yet Timessa herself still wavered. She vacillated about her sovereignty. She could obliterate men and inanimate things, but could she do so with armies of men? She granted fertility. She could break the back of drought with a simple thought; but could she overlay a differing climate for hundreds of miles, or even thousands? The six square miles over which she had granted precipitation at Juliette's farm? Insignificant ….

What had her predecessor, the old Great Goddess, done in the distant past? Had her power extended farther? Her memories, increasingly T's, encompassed pastoral landscapes and pre-agricultural societies. At that time, fields were cultivated by humans, not machines. They lived in small groups — a typical clan might comprise thirty to fifty individuals. The group would traverse known travel-ways seasonally, often moving multiple times a year to follow the migration of wildlife, or the fruiting of shrubs and trees.

It was over these distinct groups that Queen, 40,000 years ago, ruled without question. Men were hunters and, more importantly, inseminators of women, always subservient to the females who, at best, tolerated them. Regardless of gender, all deferred first to the goddess, and second, to small councils of women who were bearers of the Goddess's wisdom. When weather shifted precipitously, when cyclical drought affected crops, the Great One merely tweaked atmospheric conditions over areas no larger than the New York farm.

The manipulations were practical and discreet. And her need to protectively eliminate threats was similarly circumspect — she would kill rogue wolves terrorizing a small encampment, or destroy marauding lions. All these projections of dominion were necessary and strategic, comparable to raising the water level of a small pond, as opposed to the elevation of an ocean.

Now, again tasting dominion, the archaic Queen-cum-Great Goddess faced a different world. As she looked onto the city from her townhouse, she felt sorrow, not for the multitudes, but for the captured river that snaked between Boston and Cambridge, its velocity anathematized by revetments and armored banks.

She watched a lone boat, pointed west, as its passed the Harvard boathouse. On its prow she read, Curtis Cat. The helicopter at Juliette's had been stenciled, Curtis Copter. Coincidences, she knew. Humans used the same words repeatedly. None of this was significant. The boat's iron hull was rusted and it flew a single, square red flag over the wheelhouse.

On a whim she wished the boat to a stop, freezing the massive engine in its rear. As she watched, after a minute it turned sideways and began to drift east with the outgoing current. Simply observing, thoughtless, she made the engine restart, aware of the two men onboard who patiently maneuvered the boat back into the channel. Stop, start — her play was effortless.

§

Some days later on a weeklong shoot outside Marrakesh and south of the Oued Tensift river, Timessa observed a region of vast plain between the site and the Atlas Mountains to the south. The sinuous Oued Tensift river braided delicately through a wide floodplain, although most of its channels were dry. The art director had chosen the Moroccan location for its fierceness and aridity.

Berber rugs — Boucherouites, Beni Ourain and Ourikas — sourced by local Bedouins were used as backdrops for the new Versace collection. A tall, waxed-cotton tent became T's living quarters. The crew of a dozen stylists and markup artists constantly complained about the dry heat; even for September, the temperatures were hot.

A local guide noted that the Oued Tensift's flow traditionally increased in early fall as rains swept in from the distant mountain range, but the storms were cyclical. The river was now a shadow of itself. The region, almost a million acres in size, lay in a drought that might have been, Timessa thought, designed for a Great Goddess's play.

Late on the evening of their third day, Timessa stepped outside. The brightness of the stars reminded her of the stars she admired when she roamed the back hills and wildlands of France and Spain so many years ago. Now, in Morocco, in the Arab wasteland that fashion houses found so picturesque, she quietly stood in the cool night. Temperatures dropped 30 degrees within hours of sunset.

The encampment was heavily guarded—the same Bedouins who furnished necessities were infamous for cutting the throats of those who slept. Although she felt no threat, one of the guards walked deferentially toward her.

"Mademoiselle," he whispered, "dangerous for *la fille* outside at night."

She nodded to the man. He wore a long robe, embroidered in cross-hatched stitching. The long barrel of his rifle glinted in the light of lanterns which hung off poles beside the tents. "I won't wander far. Thank you for being here."

He shook his head as if muttering *women* and retreated to the edge of the tents, using his hand to signal to another guard. Then he disappeared into the dark.

Light-headed, almost ecstatic, Timessa sensed the immensity of the sands, and smelled the thin, tea-colored river a hundred feet to the north. It ran silently as if in fear of revealing itself, a stallion running low with its mane tucked into the shallows of its neck.

Stepping into the center of the camp, she raised her hands toward the arid skies. Anyone aware of her gesturing would have seen her fingers glowing in a soft phosphorescence, the color of her eyes echoing the gold of Apollo's eyes. She reached up toward Venus, Vega and Sirius, which were as hushed as the Oued Tensift itself.

But the stars and planets observing her were no different than Orthrus — mere recording machines, anodyne in their glittering analysis. A small, brilliant comet arced across the sky. The goddess closed her eyes and envisioned clouds filling the night sky, rain sweeping in off Madeira and Isla de la Palma — storms black with Poseidon's salted rains boiling east off the Atlantic and swaggering into the Moroccan plains.

And so storms arose. She could sense sheets of rain, miles away, slanting at odd angles, occasional pencils of light dividing the tempests as the slow, soaked beast bellowed ponderously over Safi, Sebt Gzoula, Grand Casablanca and Settat.

Opening her eyes, she saw thunderstorms to the northwest, the stars blacked out. That was quick, she thought. *Breakneck*. Lightning, zigzagged bolts of blue and silver, crackled across the advancing front. As she whirled her hands overhead, the art director stumbled from his tent.

"What the hell? There's no bad weather predicted here for weeks. What the fuck?" He noticed Timessa standing in the open and said, "Thunder wake you up, as well?"

"Quite the show, isn't it?"

"Better not last long," he said. "We didn't come prepared for anything like this."

A thin rain began, light at first and then increasingly heavy. The raindrops were sticky, hot lead shots half-ricocheting off their arms and onto the stretched poplin of the tents.

The director looked around. "Better lift by dawn," he muttered and returned hurriedly to his tent while the Great Goddess stood under the deluge. Her mere wish had affected the climate of an area greater than ninety thousand square miles. The area was thousands of times greater than the microenvironment of Juliette's small farm — the area where she stood greater than the entirety of New England.

She smiled at her authority: her dominion extended far beyond what she'd dreamed. The appellation *great*, as in *Great* Goddess, was, she thought without emotion, apt.

She understood. She knew of no corollary with any other god's power. Pivotally, her brief weather experiment in a little-populated country was more than instructive. For months she had been waiting for an instinctive and obvious moment. This, she thought, was a deflection point. Morocco. She could hear the Oued Tensift river beginning to rage.

CHAPTER 45

Red dawn sky
and a scythe sweeps horizontally,
crackling through the fields of poppies:
rabbits and voles scatter for their lives.

The Moroccan shoot ended early, an induced washout. The rain, far more characteristic of a rare African hurricane than of the usual fall storms, forced the crew out days before scheduled. The last daylight hours were spent with Timessa posing in the deluge, the entire Versace collection soaked in fashionable dishevelment.

While photographers shot under umbrellas, she waded in the rain along the bank of the far-higher river, clothing clinging to her body, the director desperate to return to New York with modish, even outrageous images. Perhaps the world's most popular model, caught in shocking conditions, would succeed as well as photos of her against nomadic rugs and desert backgrounds. Besides, he rationalized, regardless of his client's request, deserts were so *National Geographic*.

Timessa was unfazed by the chaos. On the return flight, she contemplated her experiment, and its results. On the plane's Wi-Fi, hours from

North America, she received an encouraging text: Juliette had delivered a beautiful baby girl. And the farm a week earlier had harvested its most abundant crops.

When she arrived in Boston she called an international meeting of The Girls, tasking Filly with details. All members worldwide would be invited. The goddess demanded that no publicity occur; contact among members would be electronic.

Filly could choose the venue, depending on demand. Imagining an open amphitheatre, the goddess encouraged Filly to rent an appropriate field. Perhaps Juliette knew of something in her vicinity.

The event was scheduled for a weekend in early October. Filly promoted the event as the group's most important yet; it would be formative, a happening that might never happen again. After listening at length to latest Timessa's instructions, Filly asked, "What will transpire? Describe, at least for my benefit, 'formative.' "

"In time. But surely you know my transition is ending."

"Or, has ended."

"Yes." She gestured for the nymph to sit, and joined her on the couch. Looking into Filly's eyes, she asked, "How often are you in touch with Artemis?"

Filly looked down and said, "She asks me nothing. And I provide nothing."

"I'm surprised."

"What would be gained? You have surpassed us all."

"Yes." Timessa paused. "By Gaia's machinations … I have been hammered like soft gold into something else."

"Into a resplendence," Filly whispered, her eyes wide.

"I'm glad to be a part," Filly said. "To have watched."

"To be an essential part."

"Will I be sent back to Artemis?"

"Is that your request?"

Filly sat in silence, finally turning to look into T's face. "No. We have been together for so long."

"Forever." Timessa stood. "I may withdraw. Or at least disappear from this life. I have been thinking of the old hills and valleys we once traversed in La Porcheria."

"The river valley in Sicily. It's become developed."

"There are places enough to hide a few of us. And Sicily was once a Greek domain."

"If allowed, I will be at your side."

T offered Filly her hand and pulled her onto her feet. "Good. I will wind down this fashion thing I wandered into so thoughtlessly. In the meantime, organize my little gathering of girls."

§⃟

Timessa formally notified her agency, GIA, that she was terminating her contract and her career. All modeling would conclude within 30 days. She demanded that, for the last month, her day rate be doubled. Although pressed she gave no explanations. Marriage, illness, simple burnout? She said nothing.

Impulsively, the evening of the day she notified GIA, she deleted her media accounts. One had more than 140 million followers. When they simultaneously went dark around 3 a.m. EST, there was a worldwide outcry. Media assumed her accounts had been hacked.

She left her private accounts intact. She also left the website for The Girls untouched, sending a private message to members that their group was secure. She also wrote the TOWs, *Ignore whatever you may read. Our worship, our thysia, remains intact. Together we are strong.*

By the following day, media outlets led only with T stories, and wild speculation. She was followed by paparazzi whenever her SUV left the underground parking garage and was forced to double her security. She was deluged with requests for interviews. The street outside her town-house was clotted with frantic reporters. Mobile transmitting trucks with antenna towers sat with their engines idling. A police detail controlled traffic on the narrow street.

Vogue, W and other leading magazines offered her extravagant sums for a concluding shoot. After repeatedly refusing all requests, she accepted a single, half-day contract with *Elle*. The magazine proposed to call the secret session "The Last Shoot" and include the cover.

As part of her negotiations, T insisted on wearing only clothes by a designer no one knew. Although she said nothing, it was the couturier Artemis had selected in Charleville, the young woman who had turned her into an unexpected sensation to lure Ares in his final moments.

Timessa had not forgotten the girl's eyes and husky voice, or her demure carriage, which had been offset by an immense confidence.

Inexplicably to *Elle*'s fashion editors, T further insisted on wearing the designer's strange concoction: a sheer organza-layered dress over a dark bustier cinched with a narrow silk belt. T knew Artemis would be amused. And the Charleville couturier would become a worldwide sensation upon publication. T's modeling fee exceeded millions of dollars, a sum no magazine had ever offered talent.

In the meantime, Filly began organizing The Girl's extravaganza. The same day media broke with news that T was ending her career, Filly emailed and texted all members, and within minutes began receiving confirmations of attendance. Acceptances came from members in New England, then from all over North America, then Europe and Asia. Filly's invitation, coupled with worldwide media coverage about T's retirement, left the girls apprehensive. Six weeks was short notice, but other obligations were cancelled and flights scheduled.

The stalwart Juliette found a farm several miles from her own to accommodate thousands. The property — Vanishing Valley — had been in the owner's family for generations and periodically was rented for concerts. Filly hired a New York firm specializing in large events to manage logistics. They would arrange for an appropriate sound stage, tents, food, first aid, transportation for select participants, registration, and other necessities.

Yet there was an underlying sense of panic from Girls members that Filly found difficult to quiet. The private forum on the website was rife with speculation, each official post followed by hundreds of comments. At best she could reply, *Queen's first allegiance is to The Girls*. Or, *By stepping away from modeling she'll have far more time for us*. Still, she couldn't quell their anxiety. T's abrupt retreat had been unexpected. Each of the girls aspired to her success. How could T simply walk away?

Too many of the forum comments alluded to a fear that Queen was ill, perhaps dying. At one point, days after the news broke, Juliette posted on the forum that Queen had never been healthier, using a word that T had always discouraged: the girls should have greater *faith*. Even so, Juliette herself wondered what the young woman she knew to be a goddess was conjuring. The gathering became singularly anticipated, the entire membership anxious for Queen's reassurance.

Coordinating the event details became overwhelming and Filly recruited two older nymphs from the Pennsylvania estate. Within days of the announcement of the gathering, more than a thousand girls had signed up. Although the venue was fenced, ensuring complete protection of the attendees would be paramount; consequently, Filly assigned security selection to the same New York firm she'd hired earlier.

Although Juliette was preoccupied with her new daughter, she was asked to select a dozen ewes for a private TOW Observance. Doing so would thin her herd by a third; regardless, she promised to select the finest.

Timessa continued to wind down her schedule, confining her remaining shoots to locales near Boston and to photographers she knew. Although GIA offered to renegotiate fees and increase her benefits, the agency was unable to persuade its highest earning model to reconsider.

In less than a year, Timessa had appeared on thirty-six magazine covers in fourteen countries. Countless media outlets had printed millions of words describing her beauty, hair style and clothes. The industry's initial response to her announcement was that no one since Greta Garbo had simply disappeared. Many asserted that it was all a ploy by her PR firm, that she would return to dominate fashion before weeks had passed.

On receiving T's notice, Seneca Ibsen, the agent who had discovered her in the Cambridge cafe, mounted each of Timessa's covers in expensive gold frames, hanging the lot in a prominent block in the agency's lobby. The frames were hung in four rows, nine covers per row. Below them in large, seriffed golden letters was a single word: TIMESSA. No client could avoid seeing the display or misunderstand its message: GIA had found and managed the world's most famous woman.

Seneca's parting words to Timessa on her final visit to the agency's offices were, "I don't know how you can do this to me."

CHAPTER 46

Bird goddess roosting in her olive trees,
wings as swift as any hawk.
The Great One, reveling in asymmetries.

Ten days before The Last Shoot, the *Elle* spectacle, Timessa flew the Charleville couturier from Paris to Boston. Her name was Iole Bouchard, but she, like Timessa, went by her first name only. Freckled and wide-eyed, Iole had trained in Paris and Milan, and apprenticed for a year with a Frenchman who had worked closely as a young man with Coco Chanel. In his late 70s, he became her mentor, himself famous as a designer. It was he who steered her away from becoming a mere employee at one of the major fashion houses. "You are too good," he said. "Open your own shop. Great things come to those who forge great art. In time, you will clothe goddesses."

Wearing immense round sunglasses, T picked up the girl at the airport and drove without her usual security. She had eluded her guards, driving a rented Jaguar. As they wound back into the city, she wanted time to talk. "We'll eat at a seafood place I know," she said.

As they drove Iole described her late teens and early twenties.

Timessa said nothing when the couturier said, "You must know: I also do this because I like women. I like to dress them. And love them. Not men. I hope I don't offend you."

Then the girl yawned, her hand over her mouth, giggling at herself. "Long flight, I guess. I've never been to America."

"Yet I've been to Charleville."

"Tourists come occasionally to see the museum. Rimbaud, He was a crazy boy, I think. That's what they say."

"I wasn't there for that."

"I know," she said simply.

Timessa glanced over at the girl. She sat with her knees high, her bare feet on the Jaguar's dark leather seat. "What do you know?"

"Oh," she laughed. "I know the things I know."

The couturier's thoughts were open. Timessa had made no attempt earlier to probe. Now she did and she, too, laughed. "So you know Artemis. Old friends. Secrets, secrets."

Iole looked at her. "Am I that obvious?"

"Perhaps. I see we have much to talk about." Timessa pulled the sedan into a parking garage. Before they got out, T turned to her. "If anyone asks, my name is Rita. I waitress at a small place nearby. My sunglasses don't come off. If anyone asks for an autograph, we walk out. Get it?"

The girl giggled. "I do. But can't we make a scene?"

"No, let's not." She smiled. "No scenes, my new friend."

As they took an elevator up to the restaurant level, T slipped her arm into Iole's. "I, too, love girls. You'll see."

The restaurant was dimly lit in yellows and mauves. Massive aquariums were filled with exotic fish. 1960s lava lamps bubbled softly in the foyer. One of the restaurant's hostesses, a thin girl in black, took them to a table.

Iole asked, looking around, "Private enough?"

T nodded. "Yes, no one will notice. Just two young women out for dinner."

They both ordered a rosé and while they waited for entrées, Timessa described what she envisioned for the *Elle* shoot. The two bantered back and forth. After some minutes, T said, "Tell me about Artemis."

"But you seem to know."

Timessa placed her hand on Iole's and said, "If we are to be friends, you should know that nothing you think or have experienced is unknown to me."

"So I am just that transparent?"

"To me. To no one else."

"Strangely," she said, "I find that comforting."

T smiled. "I see that you met her when you were seventeen."

"*Oui*, Artemis saved me when I had fallen hiking."

"A forest in central France. Dark woods, late afternoon. Your girl-friend had gotten ahead of you, out of sight," Timessa said.

"I twisted my ankle and went down. I remember I was wearing a skirt I had made, gathered nicely at my waist, I might add!"

"And as you went down you hit your head on something."

"When I woke, my head was in Artemis's lap."

"A lucky French girl."

"She was just a young woman. With kind and endless eyes."

"Until she put her hand on your ankle."

"I expected to scream but her hand was … warm."

"And in moments, Iole, you were well again."

"She said, 'Stand, girl.' And I did. It was as if nothing had happened."

"And then —?"

Iole laughed. "But you know! She told me to follow her. That she had a retreat where I could stay until the morning."

"And you met her hunting companions."

"Fifteen lovely girls."

"She was making her periodic contact with nymphs in that region."

The girl blushed. "I suppose. I fell in love with them all."

"And how much time passed before you knew?"

"That Artemis was the *goddess* Artemis?"

Timessa looked into her grey eyes, knowing her every thought. "Yes, that."

"You are testing me."

"Not really. I love stories and those around me live in great fear. Of me. I rarely hear the truth. Now, go on. How long before you knew?"

Iole moved the corners of her mouth up, almost smirking. "One of the nymphs called her Goddess. I said nothing, thinking it was like a nickname. But then when I looked for the long scratch on my leg, I found nothing. How would you say? It was away. I looked up and she was smiling."

"She said the oddest thing," T whispered. "Something like, 'Iole, your eyes are honeyed like Apollo's.' "

"Yes, she said his are golden. But mine are grey."

"Grey-gold." Timessa paused. "Then she asked if you were thirsty, and when you said you were, she snapped her fingers and a glass of water was in your hands."

"*Oui*, with ice. I trembled."

"One of the nymphs—"

"Philippa."

"Hmm, you know her?" Iole asked.

"Yes, you will meet her again tonight."

"Oh my, Timessa!"

"… You were speaking. One of the nymphs, Philippa —"

"Yes, Philippa said, 'You are in the company of the ancient goddess, Artemis.' I asked stupidly, 'A Greek god?' "

"This is such a sweet story," Timessa said. "The goddess never told me. I might have been along, but she chose Filly to go that time."

"Filly?"

"Filly, Philippa."

"I see. The next morning all of them walked me to a nearby village. On the edge of the forest when we saw a search party and gendarme, they vanished."

"But," T said gently, "she has always stayed in touch."

"Several times a year. She was an early patron when I started selling. And —" Iole broke into tears. "She gave me the funds to start my little shop."

"And then," Timessa said, "one afternoon I appeared."

"*Oui*, with Artemis. You were so beautiful. And there was a boy and a girl."

"Jackson and his sweetheart, Danaë. Neither was really a child."

"Four of you …" she smiled.

The waitress brought entrees. Timessa used the opportunity to scan the room. "You are aware that when the *Elle* spread appears, you will be overwhelmed with requests?"

"I like my quiet shop. I create what I wish. If women want to buy, I sell. If they walk out without a masterpiece, I shrug."

"Nothing will be the same."

They looked at each other. Iole said, "Yet when you called, I said '*Oui.*' And I have come. I am here to make *you* masterpieces."

Iole felt Timessa's eyes and blushed again. Odd, she thought, as T reached across the table to her, pressing a single finger to her forehead perfectly between her eyes. Iole shook bravely, not allowing her gaze to drop, even as heat rose through her arms and chest.

Timessa's finger felt like a weld of hot wax, sending a pulse of electricity into her belly and legs. She felt her breath waver, then saw a dark horizon of flames. A flare started in the center of her vision and spread sideways until the entire skyline was afire. Yet, during the seconds the vision lasted, she felt secure. Exhaling, she blinked and saw T before her, at the table, her hands folded together, smiling.

Iole said, "You took me somewhere."

"I wanted you to see where I play."

"Oh my, Timessa. What a lonely place."

"Yet there delusions are destroyed. Impurities are burnt away."

"Is it like death?"

"For some. For you, no. There was nothing there to purify."

"I do not understand."

"Iole, you are … unalloyed." T paused. "Okay, a poor choice of words. Perhaps it's better to say you contain none of the internal demons so many struggle to overcome."

"I'm just a seamstress," she whispered.

"You remind me of another girl I knew so long ago."

"Who?" she asked.

She lifted the glass of Perrier beside her wine. "I had not expected this when I invited you, but you are refreshing, Iole, like this glass of sparkling water. Pristine, cloudless …." Timessa was amazed at what she had found. Iole was immaculate. She found herself looking at the girl's neck, imagining herself gently tasting it, then shook herself back into the moment.

"Who was this other girl?" T asked rhetorically. "She, too, was French. Jeanne d'Arc — a girl as limpid as you. Her crystalline purity terrified men."

Iole looked down. "But she went up in flames."

"Flames are not your fate."

Even Artemis had never been this direct. Iole felt embarrassment. "But Timessa, I am not pure. How can I be? I like girls and seduce those I want. When I want. I'm really a bit of a raptor."

T smiled softly. "I do not refer to sex."

Inexplicably, Iole experienced a lightness similar to what she first felt when she lay in Artemis's lap, opening her eyes into a speciousness she never imagined. Trusting Timessa as thoroughly, she said, "I know from Artemis's comments that you are ... how did she say it? Something 'remarkable.' And there is your fame, which did not exist when I dressed you in Charleville. Can you explain?"

"Explain Artemis?" She laughed. "She was my goddess for millennia."

"I meant, explain yourself. Who you are."

"Then, I was a nymph like Philippa. One of the goddess's girls."

"And now?"

"A being called the Great Goddess has returned." She paused to assess Iole's reaction. Sensing only curiosity, Timessa whispered, "She ruled the primeval world long, long ago. The Great One, or the Triple Goddess. Or she was called, as many call me now, Queen."

Iole smiled. "You may call me Io."

"A nickname?"

"My mother said Iole was from the English word *violet*—you know, iole without the v and t."

"And not," Timessa asked, "from the English, violence?"

"No!" she giggled. "My baby eyes were violet."

CHAPTER 47

Pulled to the guillotine in a tumbril,
her assassin's scarlet shirt wet from summer rain,
she stands against the shouted insults, while
girls sing a sad refrain.

Io said, "Shall I, too, call you Queen?"

Their tone had become serious. Timessa had flown Iole to Boston to design dresses for her final, effervescent splash, not to search each other's souls. Yet the girl was remarkable. Timessa had not known Artemis to take in a human girl as if she were a nymph. This one had been saved, healed, then funded sufficiently to start her little shop. Why? Although she could assess Io to her bones, she puzzled over Artemis's choice. She was missing something.

"Tell me," she whispered to Io, "about the girls you say you like."

"If I am so transparent, why must you ask?"

"There is more than is transparent."

Io giggled. "Not much."

"Then you shouldn't hesitate."

She shrugged. "*Oui*, like what I like? They are always medium tall, slender. I like small hips and breasts. Fitting girls who are almost women is … felicitous?'"

"Pleasing."

"Yes, I can grasp their hips and their ribs without anyone objecting." Her eyes sparkled. "Do I offend you with my words?"

"No, not at all. I'm always curious."

"I will go on if you wish." Timessa nodded and Io said, "When I fit a girl, I always know if she is aware of what I want, or if she daydreams of a boyfriend. If she trembles in my hands, then my heart sings."

"And if you sense she likes your touch?"

"I spend more time than necessary. Usually she will, after I am obvious, sigh or make small sounds. A month ago, as I stood behind a girl and cupped her breasts to check the fit, whispering compliments as I held her far too long, she turned and kissed my mouth."

Timessa felt an immense warmth for this girl, as foreign as she seemed. She didn't want the conversation to end, although the restaurant closed soon. "I have only heard stories, seen couples mating in the woods, watched once five years ago when one of our goddesses was stung by lust."

"But you say you have lived so long. You must have had many, many lovers in those years."

"Nymphs are virgins."

"You are no longer a nymph."

They stared at each other. T said nothing. Io smiled and said, "Can I confess something?"

Timessa knew suddenly. Why wasn't it transparent before? Yet she nodded. "Speak, Io."

"The goddess, Artemis, told me she had saved me for you."

T was shocked, but showed nothing. She said with levity, "And what would I do with you?"

"What you wish," she said. When Timessa said nothing, she continued, "When you called me, I was awaiting your call. When you left Charleville without saying goodbye, I wondered if the goddess was wrong. But when you called last week, I knew she was not."

"Was not what?" She felt stupid asking, but wanted to hear Io's response.

"Was not wrong that your hand would stroke my neck. That you would whisper I am yours."

"Iole!"

"That you would touch me ... like I touch others. That your touch would be forever and that I would never look on another."

Timessa felt no irritation or displeasure, annoyance or wrath. Instead, she felt alternately warm and confused. Io spoke without complications, and T knew the girl invented nothing. Artemis had apparently planned this, and hidden it from T. Timessa reminded herself to breathe; her skin felt unusually delicate.

Io said, "You did not know?"

"I am a goddess. I need nothing like this."

"You need me."

"No," she said, shaking her head.

To her shock Io reached over and took her hand. "*Yes*. You need me more than thysia."

"How could you know *thysia*?"

"Artemis. She says thysia is an artificial thanks, that instead, I will fill you with love."

"That's absurd."

Timessa could barely find her words. Struggling, she removed her sunglasses to see Io clearly. The girl was neither beautiful, nor was she plain. She, like the girls Io claimed to favor, had slender hips and slight breasts. Her hair was chestnut and she looked uncommonly healthy, her cheeks the color of raspberries.

As T studied her, Io smiled, absentmindedly stroking the top of T's hand with her thumb, unaffected by what had so startled T.

"Perhaps I have said too much, *oui*?"

"I can see into anyone's present, but not into my own future."

"No need. You *can* see me and ... Goddess, no need to look ahead. Now you know."

Timessa stood, slipping her sunglasses on. She offered Io her arm and said, "Come. I want to take you home. Filly will be overjoyed to see you again."

Both were silent as Timessa drove to the townhouse. She wondered briefly where the girl would sleep. Filly would share and do whatever she was asked. But Timessa slowly convinced herself that Io should not be treated as a nymph, which she wasn't. She was something else, something bright and independent. Once Timessa allowed herself a glance at the girl, the frisson was unmistakable. Irritated at herself, she couldn't shake her sense that Io's appeal was partially her gracefulness. Yet purity was there, as well. Then she thought: she is meant to sleep with me — absurd. She instantly rejected her intuition.

Maneuvering through the light traffic, she practiced emptiness. That lasted seconds and she glanced at Io again, the girl turning and meeting her glance with a soft smile. With a light French accent Io whispered, "Hi, you."

Timessa thought, *There's fragility. And I find that … fetching, too.*

Fetching? She caught herself — what was she becoming? She, Timessa, was no longer of the material world. She found no one beguiling. Not in that way. How could she? Since she had transformed to something of spirit, becoming something immutable, physicality had held no interest. In the fashion world, she was surrounded by beauty and by attractive girls. None of them had turned her head.

Sex, she assumed, was not for goddesses. Yet that wasn't true. In the car with this girl, she thought of Apollo and the twins, of Aphrodite and her insatiability. Many of the gods had had affairs.

Her thoughts were choked, emerging at half-speed and without the certainty that she usually possessed. *Lovely Io.*

By the time they pulled into the parking garage, her resistance had fragmented. Pulling into her space, Timessa turned off the car and looked at Io. The girl said, "We are equally smitten, Goddess."

Her expression was gentle, yet Timessa sensed something else. The girl whispered, "What you feel is desire. I have always found it to be quite divine."

T avoided further touch. Her confidence was shaken, yet it returned as they stepped out of the Jaguar. Security surrounded them and she had to yell at her lead man to back away. "She's a friend!"

Her anger dissipated as Io slipped her arm into hers. The girl spoke softly. "Let's find Filly. I can't wait."

As they entered the townhouse, Io saw Filly, exclaiming, "Philippa!"

and they embraced. After minutes, the three wandered into the living area and sat. Filly looking back and forth at the two. In no more than moments she blurted, gazing in fascination at Timessa, "Oh my, you're in love!"

Love. In love with Io.

Yes, perhaps Filly had been less than subtle with her comment, but T could not deny the assertion. With only the slightest emotion, she replied, "Not impeccably stated. You could have done better. But, yes, it appears true."

❧

Both Io and Filly were up past their bedtimes, and Io had not slept on the flight. At around one in the morning, after briefing Timessa on the extravaganza's progress, Filly volunteered that Io was welcome to sleep in her room.

Io looked at T, who said, "That is not for me to say." She paused. "Io?"

The girl smiled and pointed at Timessa without speaking, as if where she would sleep should be obvious. Filly nodded, shaking her head. "Wait 'til Artemis hears," she said. "I'm elated. I think she'll be as thrilled."

Io interjected quietly, "She arranged this, like five years ago. She knew then."

"That's impossible," Filly said. "No one knew Timessa would become this so long ago."

"Okay, Filly," the girl said, "whatever you say. But I think Artemis keeps a lot of secrets."

Smiling — after all, she could not refute Io's statement — Filly kissed each on the cheek and left.

The goddess stood, taking Io's hand. "Let me show you the view of the river."

The old cobra, the Charles, its slick skin glittering below the countless city lights, wound beside some of the world's most famous universities. For Timessa the sight was always emotional. On one hand, she admired the vitality of the city. On the other, she never shook her knowledge that all of these beings would be dead in time, many in mere decades, some in far less time. The human life span was frighteningly short, and she had seen so many perish in the millennia she had lived.

Io pointed into the distance. "That building across the river. What is it?"

"Part of the MIT campus. Harvard is to the north. Boston University is on our side, not far upriver."

Timessa gazed into the night. The city's lights flooded the sky and few stars could be seen. The night was like a gauze reflecting the lights into the streets and roof tops. Less than a week ago, she had been certain her transformation was complete. Gaia seemed to imply it was so.

Who was this Charleville dressmaker? As she had said to the girl, she could not foresee the future. But she also knew Io had been correct: simply looking into Io's eyes seemed to show her destiny. *Iole.* And when she looked there, she drowned in the love she saw. All of this was so new.

Io said, "Are you resisting me?"

"No," T finally said in response. "I am not."

Smiling, the girl said, "Good, because I'm crashing. Show me where we sleep."

We. She had brought a small carry-on. When Timessa took her to her bedroom, Io dropped the bag, throwing herself into the middle of the bed. On her back, arms angled out like wings, she sighed, "Nice." It was the same thing Iole had said twenty minutes earlier on seeing the Donatello.

Timessa watched her from the doorway. The girl wore a cotton dress of her own making. It was blue, a simple piece, zipped in the back, scalloped at her neckline and ending at her knees. The effect was 1950s sweet. Timessa thought, *My own schoolgirl,* wondering how she had allowed this beguilement. How could she not have foreseen this and stopped it cold? Not only had she anticipated nothing, she appeared at Io's mercy.

A voice, perhaps Gaia's, whispered, *This is love.*

Timessa walked slowly to the bed. Although Io was in her early twenties, she appeared sixteen or seventeen. As T watched, her eyes closed, her lips parted and she began to snore lightly. What had she said? "I'm crashing." T wondered whether to undress her but did not. She was self-aware enough to fear touching this girl.

Iole. The lovely Io.

To her surprise she was swept with serenity. Ridiculous to be afraid of anything. Ridiculous to resist her. With the slightest hesitation she reached out and stroked the girl's neck with her fingertips. She caressed the skin above her collarbone, then touched her cheek. Like Filly and others she knew, Io was awash with golden freckles that began at her hairline and descended gracefully by the dozens, schools of diving fish, until they disappeared into her dress.

Bemused, Timessa bent and kissed the girl's eyebrows, then her cheek. *Iole.*

The girl half opened one eye and whispered, "*Goddess.*"

CHAPTER 48

Recall the birth of Isis. Years
later, her brother's fingers up between her legs.
After, every night like swans entwined.
Then the birth of some thing *divine.*

Girls. She was surrounded by them.

It had always been. She was born generations earlier into a galaxy of girls, nymphs who grew and, in time, ran effortlessly with the goddess of the woods and bow. The paradigm of dozens of girls, gathering to give thysia to Artemis, never ended. They were bound as one. For the goddess gave each their lives. They were born for her, a gaggle of precious girls who would, in return, give their lives for her if asked. This grouping was, inarguably, the quintessence of a goddess's coterie, the commonality a coupling of gift and thanks, love and gratitude.

Timessa recognized she unconsciously had recreated the archetype with The Girls, the elite of the already glamorized beautiful that this celebrity fascinated culture worshiped so openly. Whereas Artemis surrounded herself with dozens, Timessa's gathering totaled thousands.

Still, both women had built an ecosphere whose overt assertion was that men were a lesser gender.

She spent the night standing before her window, viewing the dark river but seeing nothing. Instead, she reflected on her earlier dinner with Io, trying to weigh Io's guileless declarations. Yet she was repeatedly thwarted. All objectivity seemed eclipsed by this new *thing*.

Whatever its name, it had blindsided her. And the perpetrator, she knew, was Artemis, who had, if Io was to be believed, hatched this ... what? This *liaison* years before.

Her thoughts drifted, circling like wrack afloat a river's slipstream. Or swirling like fall leaves on an updraft. Timessa could manipulate gravity and bind natural events to her will. With a mere wish she could cause storms to rake vast lands or grant fertility to the forsaken. But she appeared unable to foil love's tsunami.

The first light of day rose downriver, pinpricks of pink escaping the ocean's horizon, ricocheting over the water like bullets of light. East-facing windows glinted as if mirrors. She sensed Filly behind her and turned.

"Morning," the nymph said. She paused, then blurted, "Did you sleep with her?"

Timessa read curiosity, not jealousy. "No, but I will."

"When you do you must tell me what it's like."

"We're both so clueless, aren't we?" Together they giggled.

"Filly," she said. "Enough of this. It's hardly unusual to ..."

Filly interjected, "Have a lover?"

"Io, a lover? I'm not sure what she is. A gift, yes. Apparently. But more than that?" She tried to imagine lying with the girl, being stroked in some warm darkness. "I can't foresee."

"I can. I saw her eyes and how she looks at you."

"So, my fortune teller, what do you predict?"

"That you'll be in her arms soon enough!" She spun on her heels and walked away, pausing long enough to add, "We have more than twenty-one hundred registrants from eighteen countries!"

Timessa simply nodded. Her thoughts had shifted to the girl asleep on her bed, and whether to wake her or let time pass. She had the morning free. A single shoot was scheduled for mid-afternoon in a studio fifteen minutes away.

Filly had a full morning of meetings downtown. She appeared within minutes, dressed and holding coffee. "Io's still asleep?"

"Yes," the goddess said tiredly, "not a sound. I should check on her."

"Okay, but I have to go. There's an eight-thirty downtown, then a follow-up two hours later across the river." Filly stepped up and touched her arm. "I'm glad we talked," she said. "Lots of goddesses fall in love."

"Not I."

Filly smiled and left. Timessa remained preoccupied. Uncertain why she was so distracted, she decided to check on Io. Then she rephrased her thought: not decided to, but *needed to*. Something drew her there. She was drawn by some force. And they were alone.

The bedroom door was closed: she opened it slowly. The girl lay on her side, asleep. The blue dress was half up her thigh, her hair splayed across the pillow. Feeling vaguely like an intruder in her own bedroom, T stepped softly to the bed and sat.

Io dreamt of lions. A tawny pair, both females, was stepping through grasses, stalking something unseen. In her sleep Io watched them move, their heads turning powerfully. One suddenly leapt on the other, turning her onto her back. In the dream the two wrestled, growling and pawing each other, playfully baring their teeth.

Io smelled faintly of anise. Or maybe simply of warm girl. Sitting beside her Timessa thought, *Not anise, lavender. Or lilac.* She bent closer and smelled her hair: a faint bouquet, a trace of baby oil. Io's neck was partly exposed and Timessa brushed her mouth against the girl's skin, combing her lips lightly up to Io's ear, thinking *Mine*. The softness, the fragrance, left her heart pounding.

Still, Io slept. Timessa knew she had gotten fewer than six hours sleep and that she shouldn't be awakened. Acknowledging the thought, T placed her palm on the girl's waist, stroking her softly. *Artemis's gift.* What had Io said last night in the car? *Desire. I find it to be quite divine.*

She ran her hand up Io's ribs to her arm, then lightly down to her hips, then back to her waist. As she did so, she listened to the girl's breathing. She rested her palm lightly on Io's neck, conscious of her pulse. Timessa smiled to herself: their hearts beat in synchronization, a low forty beats a minute. The rate reflected T's tranquility, but what explained Io's repose? She found herself pleased that they shared this small attribute.

As T watched the girl's lips gently pouting as she slept, Io turned with a sigh onto her back, her dress bunching higher. Timessa had to freeze to avoid being detected. After a moment Io fell back into dreams. This time she and Timessa sat in wicker chairs on a porch. T followed the new dream as Io spun it along, watching as they held hands. Io and T talked quietly like old lovers, comfortable. Then the porch dream dissipated and Io's breathing changed.

As Timessa gently took one her hands, the girl half-opened her eyes, squinting at Timessa, "Nice to see you sitting here."

Timessa smiled, "I've woken you too soon."

There was a lush stillness between them, neither speaking. Finally, T whispered, "I waited 'til your last dream ended. Do you remember it?"

"*Oui*, I was sitting with you somewhere. There was a view of mountains far away."

They were quiet again. A minute passed and then Io reached up and took Timessa's sleeve in her hand. Timessa put her hand over Io's, and did not resist when Io tugged on her, drawing her down to within inches of her mouth. The girl whispered in the quiet, "I've always wanted to kiss a goddess."

She slipped her hand around T's neck and drew her closer. "Artemis told me that if we kissed, we'd never uncouple. Isn't that a crazy thing to say?"

Whispering as well, T replied, "Who can believe anything she says?"

Then, shocking herself, she lowered her head a final inch and took Io's mouth in the softest kiss she'd given anyone. The more experienced girl pulled on T's neck, deepening the kiss, groaning in pleasure. The morning sun had still not lit the room, and the two caressed in the soft light. To Timessa's surprise, Io pulled her down on her side and they lay touching, hip to hip.

T was aware of their bodies pressing, their breath short, their legs dazzled and converging in a startling heat of nameless hormones. Their hands drifted over each other, measuring a physicality and sensations. Time drifted. As the room slowly filled with the morning's light, the two entwined, leisurely removing pieces of clothing.

Eventually Timessa broke away, hot, lightheaded and ecstatic. Io's face, framed in the pillow that cradled her head, was flush. Timessa whispered, "Io, Io. Even saying your name is a song."

The girl said, "My goddess."

"I never dreamed of you. Never imagined being in love. Now I lie in your arms." Even then they lay side by side, Io's leg over Timessa's, her hand half-cupping the goddess's breast.

Io said, "I have been with many girls. As I confessed. Each with different needs and desires. Yet I am yours. Tell me as we play how I can please you. And I will know by your whimpering if my love satisfies you as it should."

The back wall across from the open window was now a brilliant sun-yellow, which reflected gently onto the two. Admiring the girl's perfection in the light, Timessa revisited with kisses all the soft hollows and knolls she had tasted over the hour, resampling this, that, appreciating Io's varying sounds as she played.

"You, too, must moan like this at my touch," the girl said. "Silence is not acceptable."

Timessa smiled at the girl's command, becoming more aware by the moment of the magnitude of Artemis's gift. Io was open, her every thought unsullied. She lived for one purpose: to please and adore, to wash Timessa with love and live beside her as a confidante, to give without complication or demands.

Even as Timessa had come into full power a short time before, she had sensed an emptiness, something vague and spectral. The hollowness had made no sense. How could one so powerful not be full? How could one so filled be so alone? It was unimaginable, but now she knew. However divine her molecules, they had been foraging for an accelerant that would release the sacred cocktail of love. Desire was the fuel. *Iole* was Artemis's gift.

Timessa took Io's face in her hands and kissed her again, the girl returning her passion. As they separated slowly, Io whispered, "And now we are."

"We are what?"

"We are ... one," she said with joy.

଼

They dressed, stealing occasional glances at each other. As she buttoned her blouse, the goddess said, "I would like you at my side."

"When?" the girl asked.

"Whenever, wherever I am. That often. Day and night."

Io dropped to a knee, lowering her head. T was reminded of Apollo and Poseidon; they too had yielded as readily. She recognized the action as obeisance, but would never demand such an act. And she knew that Io must be, if not her equal, her peer. If she were to be T's confidante, she could not collapse at every request. She raised Io's chin with her hand. "Stand."

The girl hesitantly stood. Timessa led her to the bed. "Sit."

Io nodded and sat. Timessa sat beside her and took her hand. "Io, you have repeatedly said you are mine."

"*Oui*, forever. However you want." Her eyes teared.

Kissing her gently, T said, "I understand. You are mine. But I am yours as well. Do you understand?"

Nodding, she said, "Go on —"

"I cannot avoid being … dominant," T said, although reluctant to use the word. "I must be frank. In so many ways, I exceed you. I do not need to describe the obvious. But because we both know — we are not arguing over this — I will, between us, always have the final word. It cannot be otherwise."

Io watched her. T saw no judgment or concern. The girl placed her hand on T's thigh, idly moving her fingers over the softness inside. Timessa went on, "That being said, except in matters you will recognize — and listen to me carefully — you must be my equal."

"Yes, Queen." A moment passed as they kissed. Then Io giggled. "Except in bed. There I may be your master." Timessa looked at her in mock surprise. "At least," Io said, "until you know fully what you want. And maybe even after that!"

Timessa leaned over, kissing her again, saying, "Perhaps in bed, Io, you will always be my sovereign. In the dark I may yield to you. You have given yourself to me, but I may surrender my senses to you. In this way, I am yours."

Io pushed her down onto the bed, saying, "Close your eyes."

Timessa moaned as Io ran her fingers inside her blouse, then lightly up her skirt, stroking her for minutes as they kissed. Finally the girl said, "Yes. I will be your mentor. And master. In love alone."

In the quiet as they smiled at each other, T said, "If we both surrender this and that, I think we'll be the best of friends."

Io's hand moved with assurance over her belly, brushing her mound and circling her breasts. She whimpered as Io's fingers played in her hair, moaning as Io bent and took her earlobe between her teeth, whispering, "Ah, now my goddess cries out in love."

T's photo shoot was in two hours. There was time to amuse themselves, to talk and to eat before they left together, arm in arm.

She had never imagined acquiescing to anyone except Artemis. Yet to this girl, this couturier, she freely surrendered, aware that in time Io might ride her into a river of stars, showing her how to drink from a cauldron of love she had been denied for millennia — and that the girl might ride her hard to places she could not imagine.

Perhaps she too, like Io, would be purified by love.

CHAPTER 49

It is important not to care too much.
—Lawrence Durrell, *The Greek Islands*

S everal days after Io's arrival in Boston, Timessa brought Io to our
Pennsylvania estate to meet me and Danaë. Timessa's her oldest
friends were here, as well. The two arrived unannounced. As T had
always done she came around to the back of the mansion where it looks
out across the fields and over Marlene Dietrich's curious old maze. I saw
her first, arm in arm with a girl who looked vaguely familiar. Both
appeared happy. Timessa's grim demeanor, so vexing during her last visit,
was gone.

I stood as they crossed the moat, which was now somewhat neglected.
Leaving my study, calling out to alert Danaë, I opened the back door.
Timessa gave me a quick hug, eager to introduce her companion. Io and
I looked at each other and I said foolishly, "I've seen you somewhere."

She said, "I think not."

Timessa interjected, "This is Jackson. You'd never guess but he was
the little boy you saw in your shop."

Io said, "Ha! And there was a little girl, as well."

At that moment Danaë appeared and said, "It was me, and I remember: you're the dress designer!"

The girl nodded. Almost singing, Timessa said, "Meet Io, the lovely Iole."

I noticed that when the hugs ended, both girls immediately linked arms again. The four of us stood quietly a moment, then Timessa said, "Yes, I know you won't believe it. I'm in love. We're in love. I wanted you to meet my girl."

Danaë lit up as if T's declaration was astonishingly good news. Io grinned as well, saying impishly, "I am hers."

Timessa smiled delightedly.

Rather than go inside, I motioned them to follow me, pointing down a path leading to a landscaped enclosure with a circle of cedar trees, a fountain, wild flowers, and two benches facing each other. "Artemis asked me to add this feature a few months ago." I said. "As quickly as I agreed, she nodded and it appeared."

Danaë laughed. "She knew exactly what she wanted. We call it the Artemis Grove."

Within a minute, we sat, Danaë and I facing the two who took a seat hip to hip, Io's arm casually around Timessa's waist. They looked at each other as if seeing some revelation. I had rarely seen such infatuation.

As Danaë took my hand, a red-headed finch flew into the grove and hovered like a fat hummingbird over Timessa's head, then softly landed on her crown. T sat with exaggerated posture until the bird hopped down lightly to her shoulder. We all watched as the finch nuzzled her neck with its head, then flew off as if it had delivered a momentous message.

Timessa said, "It, too, was smiling."

Danaë broke the spell, saying, "Tell us everything, starting at the beginning."

Time passed as the two recited details, one filling in for the other or elaborating when one hesitated. Timessa seemed determined to leave nothing out, even describing their lovemaking in enough detail to make Danaë blush and say, "Enough, enough! I'm glad the boys can't hear."

As the sun shifted, we moved from the Artemis Grove to the large room with the Phidias statue of Aphrodite which, at that moment, glowed in the warm light. Like Timessa had done on her last visit, Io circled the life-size marble, cupping its breasts and giving T knowing glances. Several nymphs brought out drinks and food, bowing to Timessa as they came and went.

As we ate Timessa said, "In less than a week I do my final shoot, a special for *Elle*. And that will be followed within days by what Filly calls an extravaganza for The Girls."

I asked if many had registered, and she nodded, saying, "Over a thousand."

Danaë looped back to the *Elle* shoot, asking what fashion house would be dressing T. She was startled when told there would be none: this would be Io's event, that Timessa had told *Elle* there would be no negotiations. If they wanted exclusives for this final bash, Io chose her clothes.

Io then explained that she had created the only dress T would wear, a sheer organza-layered piece over a bustier. She said, "Remember the dress my goddess wore when she lured Ares from his roost? It's similar, although even more alluring."

"And the bustier? *Elle* agreed?"

Io shrugged and said, "It will be worn on the outside. That's very *au courant*."

T reiterated, "All design decisions are hers. Or it's off."

The girl pulled T against her, smiling. "It's cinched with a belt just below the breasts. Artemis was my inspiration."

We talked about her backstory and how Artemis had saved her in the forest years before, appeared afterward at strategic moments, and funded the shop. None of us had been aware, but Artemis was absent at times for days. Io noted, "She was with me. I have always been promised to this one." She kissed T's bare shoulder. "Artemis says I was born for her."

"Then," I said, "she has known T's destiny far longer than she's let on."

Io simply smiled. Danaë turned to Timessa and asked, "And what will become of the Great One when the extravaganza ends and all the girls go home? In the past you've threatened to disappear, to our great dismay."

"We may live like the affluent on some private island. Or I may buy a thousand acres somewhere lush and green and hidden away from everyone but friends."

"Where you can give and get love," Danaë said. T only smiled.

To our left, from the back woods, a small group of women emerged. I stood as I recognized Artemis. Io did as well, running into the field to meet her halfway. The goddess spun her in a circle, laughing. As Artemis set her down, Timessa stepped into the grass, waiting. She, too, was taken somewhat roughly, squealing as the goddess lifted her high. Then as she set her down, Artemis knelt briefly. "Our Queen. I trust you will forgive my enthusiasm?"

T shook her head in mock disbelief and made her stand. "You are not to kneel. Goddesses do not bow to goddesses."

"Perhaps," Artemis said. "But I salute your accession. For too long you were a caterpillar, and I had to watch you so no bad crow ate you whole. Now you are wingéd and bring me joy."

I motioned for everyone to return to the Phidias room. There Artemis turned to Io and smiled. "You know I am a virgin goddess."

Io said, "And you know, like that crow you feared, I eat girls up."

Artemis laughed. "Once, you did. And now, my child, those experiences will serve you well as the Great Goddess's companion. She was once virginal, as every nymph remains."

I noticed the goddess's use of *was*.

Io smiled, "I am her companion. But I am her love mentor, as well!"

Everyone laughed, including an attendant nymph standing against a wall. Timessa blushed and half-smiled. "We've definitely worked things out."

Artemis said, "You know our reaction would be different had you chosen a man."

"I chose no one," T said. "I simply fell in love."

"With a human girl."

"With a girl," Timessa said, "you found for me."

Artemis looked at Iole. "What did I tell you, Iole, when we first met?"

"That you had never known a mortal girl as pure. I was confused. You said I reminded you of a nymph among your girls who was equally as virtuous."

"And what was her name?"

"Timessa. But I protested. I wasn't pure. Me? Hardly. I thought you crazy."

"Yes, you said that. And I replied?"

"That none of us can look into our own minds and see whether we are … what was your word?"

"Unsullied."

"*Oui*, you said my mind was the mind of one who is irreproachable."

"I said that because you encompass an innocence so pure that it is a rarity. You are like a mirror: no matter the face that appears, hideous or beautiful, the mirror is unaffected, pristine, always available for use, yet uncontaminated by the images it reflects."

"I did not know."

"And again, Iole, you protested, trying to convince me that all your affairs had tainted you."

"You said the girl, Timessa, would change into something you couldn't predict. And that I would be hers. And we would become lovers for all time. Goddess, how did you know?"

Artemis smiled. "Before Timessa absorbed the visage of the Great Goddess, she was transparent to me. I knew her every impulse, desire and thought. And she, too, was pure. All of the girls said she embodied love, more so than anyone in our tribe. I thought her unique …

"Then I found you in that dark wood, startled that your spirit perfectly mirrored hers. I felt that holding you, while you returned to consciousness from that fall, was no different than cradling my beloved nymph. The two of you were twins."

Io whispered, "You never told me. You said I had a do —, a dopp —"

"Doppelgänger."

"*Oui*, a double who would become my lover and I hers. I never doubted you. I remember trembling when you told me what you saw."

"At that time," Artemis said, "I could see Timessa as if gazing into a crystal ball. But that has changed."

She turned to Timessa, saying, "May I ask a question?"

The dynamics had changed. Before, Artemis never would have asked permission. T said, "I saw the same thing when I looked into Iole's mind. The purity was startling. I never guessed one could love so many and yet remain pristine."

Artemis sighed, "And now the two of you have joined."

Io rose from her chair, took a step and sat in Timessa's lap. She closed her eyes, resting her head over the goddess's breast. Putting her arms around the girl, Timessa said with unusual clarity, "Our love would never have happened had it not been for you, Goddess. My eternal thanks."

Io burrowed herself deeper into T's arms. It was difficult not to smile and feel pleasure at their union. Artemis lowered her head in acknowledgement.

T went on, "You have known my recent anger." She laughed. "Even Danaë has recoiled. I began to demand thysia. The poor girls. I thought thysia required the death of treasured things."

Artemis said, "And — "

"And I woke this morning before we traveled here, aware that my constant fury had vanished. This girl lay in my arms. And some ancient, aching void was gone."

Danaë stood, smiling and said, "I must have anticipated your coming as I made cookies a couple hours ago." She turned to one of the nymphs, saying, "Iphigeneia, the platter is in the kitchen on the counter. Could you, sweetie?"

Artemis shifted chairs, sitting closer to the two. Leaning forward she raised her palm, holding it out to Timessa, who returned the gesture. As they touched, I could not read their thoughts. They opened only to each other's musings. Timessa's face was expressionless.

Artemis appeared troubled and spoke thoughtfully, her attention solely on Timessa. "But you must know that what I have nurtured between the two of you is threatened."

"Oh? By whom?"

"I don't mean in the short term. Your bliss is as immortal as possible at this moment. But your love, Iole, the one we praise, is not a-mortal."

Io sat up, looking at her. She was clearly startled. With surprising anger she said, "You mean I'll die and lose my goddess."

Artemis frowned. "And she will lose you, Iole. I apologize. We speak frankly when together. At this moment you are at a zenith. Your health and beauty shine as magnificently as ours. But …"

Timessa interjected, "She will age. And then be gone."

"Yes, like all humans," said Artemis. "Like Dionysos's Ariadne. And I, for one, object. If within our power, it cannot be allowed."

To my shock Timessa's eyes filled with tears. Even when the three Fates were dying from the Thessaloniki toxin a half decade earlier, she was dry-eyed. Now in her face I read vulnerability, immense sadness, anger, and an agony of which she seemed incapable minutes before. Gripping Io, her knuckles were white.

Artemis said, "Goddess, there may be a way. A way for us to unravel death for Io. To stop its advance. If all of us can live on and on, as we do, there is a way. A way to put death to death."

The irony of her statement was lost on none of us. Less than six years ago the Fates had returned to prevent the end of death, convinced that science was redefining it as nothing more than an illness to be overcome. Other divinities had gathered to thwart their plan, Now we discussed the opposite.

Io stared at her, astonished at the discussion. She said, "*Merde*," as if her own death had never occurred to her until this moment. Then she swiveled and, taking the goddess's face in her hands, kissed Timessa tenderly.

CHAPTER 50

Sun's gold rays
rip through a thousand leaves
before striking her face,
a gentle candlelight.

A s Artemis did on occasion, she convened a small group in the
sacred grove near the house. On short notice, Athene, Apollo and
Hermes appeared. Danaë and I, Timessa and her consort, and a small
group of the senior nymphs, gathered in the late afternoon. A storm had
passed and the heat dropped. The grove was pleasant, the leaves and
grasses sparkling like jewels from the brief rain.

I was always amazed at how quickly Artemis could call these
extraordinary beings to appear. Perhaps the infrequency of the meetings
made the ones that occurred more momentous. Regardless, roughly a
dozen of us gathered in the golden light. Only one non-divinity attended:
Io.

Artemis had made our purpose clear: Iole's love completed Timessa's
transformation; her purity had largely purged T's fury. She could not be
lost.

Aside from looking slightly flushed, Timessa's appearance had returned to normal. Io's confidence, though, had vanished with Artemis's words. She appeared not to have heard the goddess's pledge to "put death to death." Or, perhaps, she simply rejected it as fantasy.

To my surprise, breaking an awkward silence, Io spoke first. "Of course I know why all of you are here. But I also accept that no human escapes death. Or aging. Overwhelmed by my love, I forgot …

"I forgot I love one who will go on, while I will not. How could it be otherwise? And know that I have no self-pity. I have never wished for more than what I am. Or what I have. My heartbreak is not for myself."

It was precisely what I would have expected from her. As she concluded, she looked helpless, as if she had only one person to turn to, and she slipped under Timessa's arm.

Apollo rose, scanning our faces. "Artemis has briefed us. In the same way that streams run dry, humans die. But in the past, gods have selected one here, one there. Almost always the one selected has been a love object, a being the infatuated god could not live without." He looked at Timessa. "As is the present case."

Athene, the most reserved of the gods, said, "Yes, Apollo. But the transformation of mortal to immortal, however infrequent, was a task left to the Fates. We would plead and petition, and if Lachesis felt benevolent, she would jigger with their DNA, and a miracle would occur. But we have lost the Fates."

"I can count on one hand the humans transfigured by her touch," Artemis said. "But however she did it, change was possible."

All of us agreed. Without chicanery Lachesis had prolonged life. Lachesis — Laine, as she had represented herself to me in the beginning — through some machination had transformed me six years before; the maneuver had taken seconds. I had felt nothing as she played. But no other mortal had been so transformed since my alteration.

Timessa exceeded her in sheer intelligence and likely exceeded the capabilities of any god that had lived, except perhaps her direct predecessor. I exclude Gaia from these considerations, as her breadth encompasses the cosmos itself, and she must be regarded as immeasurable.

Hermes, breaking his silence, interjected, "Each of us has unique powers." He turned to the group. "Did the Great One's powers, long before our birth, include making the ephemeral immortal?"

Timessa stood, still holding Io protectively. "It did not. I possess her mastery. And more. But making mortals immortal is not in my powers."

We fell silent, sensing that she held back her anger only by immense restraint. Or perhaps by Io, who was stroking her and whispering. They kissed, their preoccupation with each other obvious and, frankly, more endearing than discomfiting.

Danaë, holding my hand until this point, stood, taking her turn, enunciating clearly. "There is one of us who can make this happen."

In suspense, we waited for her to elaborate. Instead, she sat, looking down at her hands. Artemis said, "Which of us? Explain."

But she said nothing more and Artemis said, "If Iole had not been born, a god could couple with her mother. Or if the Fates had whispered their secrets before expiring, one of us might know. None of this can be. And none of us has shown we can turn human death on its head."

Danaë said quietly, "Forgive me, Goddess, but consider this: I offer a small equation. $D + L = I$. Should I go on?"

Hermes snorted. "Our scintillatingly brilliant mathematician. I once instructed Euclid and remember no such equation. We clearly waste our time —"

Danaë went on, ignoring him. "In my equation, D is death."

Artemis whispered, "That which we wish to end."

"L is Lazarus."

The goddess smiled. "I see. You refer to Jackson's gift."

"Yes," she said triumphantly. "And I is immortality. Do you understand?"

Athene said, "But the Lazarus power, his gift, raises the *dead*. Iole is alive."

"The equation," Danaë said, "is predicated on a jump. Iole jumps into an endless night. Call it self-sacrifice, self-immolation. She dies but is raised. Jackson rolls away the stone. She is the Great One's lover again, only now ageless and a-mortal."

Athene interjected, "What? You propose we kill Iole so she can live?"

Io faced us all, rapt at the turn of the discussion.

"Several of you can snap your figures and make it so," Danaë whispered.

"What if," Athene said, "Jackson's gift fails? We will be murderers."

Stepping forward Io cried, "If there is a chance that I return, let me jump!" She turned to look at Timessa.

Artemis swiveled and pointed at me. "Jackson! We are debating taking a girl's life, a rare and beautiful life, on the belief that you can … that you can bring her back. Yet, you say nothing."

Of course I followed their reasoning as they debated Io's future. And I was glad Io had spoken, however naive she might be. Her bravery was unexpected. Still, Danaë's revelation had admittedly startled me. Raise the dead? Kill a girl to bring her back as a-mortal? Even to me, it sounded absurd.

Athene had revealed the power to me, but I had never used it. It was simply spoken of, something other divinities assumed I could wield as I wished. I met Artemis's eyes and said, "All of you have heard that I can raise the dead. And that those brought back live as long as we live. And how do we know? Athene says so. But, we aware: I have never used the gift."

Io asked, "You have never actually brought someone back?"

As I nodded, Athene stood, a small white owl perched in her left hand, looking around at those gathered. "I do not excoriate Jackson for his doubts. How could he not vacillate when he has never used this tool? But whether used or not, the power — as it cannot otherwise be described — is no more a fantasy than lightning in a thunderstorm. He must, of course, wish to act —"

Then Athene turned to me. "What do I mean? Your wish to resurrect must be as strong as the desire those two have for each other. Timessa's fire burns for this girl,. You, too, Jackson, must burn with a fire as intense, except yours must be for her rebirth, if she dies. Do you understand?"

"Yes."

"And," Athene said, turning to Io, "you need not believe. Nothing is required, except that you be willing to give your life."

Io fell to her knees. "I will. I readily give myself —"

Athene lifted her hand and opened her palm. For a moment time stopped. Then the girl crumbled forward, all life draining from her eyes. Timessa gasped and screamed.

She slipped to her knees. Artemis was expressionless. A breeze swept the sacred grove.

In those same moments, something unexpected happened to me. Although I saw the divinities apparently speaking to each other in the moments after Io's death, I heard nothing. I had, for all purposes, gone deaf. I observed T and Danaë kneeling beside the body. Artemis was shaking Athene in disbelief, her mouth forming words that I could not hear.

All of this took place slowly, slowly. My limbs felt ponderous and I observed without emotion that whatever had happened to Io, serenity had the final say: her face was composed and more lovely than when she lived. She lay still, her knees half-bent, one arm turned behind her back.

I do distinctly remember Athene's owl flying into one of the cedars, its white wings a spectral blur. One of the divinities — I cannot remember who — picked up the girl and placed her on a bench. She lay on her back, her arms hanging down. Artemis lifted each arm, placing Io's hands together on her belly. The girl's hair hung through the slats of the bench, moving lightly in the breeze, rejecting the stillness required of the dead.

I remember, too, Timessa standing, then pivoting toward me, pointing, her mouth opening in what I later knew must have been another scream. Her fury was evident: that much I discerned. Yet at that moment, I simply watched them all, each immersed in a half-delayed reaction, no one certain of what to do — all of this took place as I watched with dispassion.

Then a small ringing in my ears began, no louder than a gnat circling nearby. A sound! With it I heard a half-voice, a muffled cry. The sounds increased. I was certain Danaë called my name. Athene took my arm, then with both hands she took my face. "Jackson!"

I felt myself gasp for breath and threw Athene's hands aside, stepping into a defensive posture.

Abruptly I was cognizant. Our eyes met, and she examined me.

I asked slowly, "How much time has passed —?"

"Since Iole's death? A minute." Athene pointed at the body.

I looked around. Even Danaë seemed more a wraith than real ... Timessa appeared a mere pulsing light ... Artemis stood as if a short vertical bar of colorless energy.

Yet, as I studied her, Io's figure was crystalline.

Athene whispered, "Concentrate."

I nodded. She sounded adamant and, again, pointed to the body before me.

"Yes," I said, approaching the bench where she lay. Athene walked beside me, her presence suddenly claustrophobic. "Away!" I cried. "Step back!"

She backed away. I stood alone beside Iole, or what was once Iole. As I studied her, Timessa appeared, facing me behind the bench. She said in a broken voice, "She's gone."

"No," I said. "Nothing is what it appears."

She shook her head and I wondered if in her fury she simply would destroy me. We looked at each other for seconds, and then she commanded, "Save her."

I remember nothing that followed. Whether I fell deeper into that daze or became fully absorbed by a force beyond my senses, I do not know. That evening, when most of the divinities had scattered to different parts of the estate, Danaë sat with me in the Phidias room.

I'd recovered, though exhausted.

She said, still flushed from the event, "Timessa then drove her foot into the ground and a small earthquake rippled through the grove."

"Did she?"

"I feared for your life. After all, Iole lay dead on Athene's assurance you could bring her back. You hadn't acted. Timessa's anger was evident. Yet, if she killed you, she'd destroy her only chance of saving Iole. Do you remember any of this?"

"No."

"Timessa's wrath grew. She was screaming. Yet you turned to her, and whispered, 'Say another word, and I walk.'

"She hesitated. Her rage was obvious. I couldn't help but compare this Timessa to the infatuated girl we had seen five minutes before. Isn't it funny how worlds turn upside down?"

"Death," I said.

Danaë smiled. "Death. And there before you was a body. And beside her an enraged goddess. You seemed heedless of it all. Heedless of all except Iole's form." She paused, looking at me. "Jackson, you really remember nothing?"

"Perhaps I will in time."

"You put on quite the show. After admonishing Timessa as you did, you went to Iole and ran your left hand from her forehead to her … groin. Your movement was languid, almost undirected, a gesture that might have been made by a sleepwalker. Then hesitating, your hand still soft between her legs, you retraced the passage, lingering with your fingers on her forehead, then descending again to her thighs …

"Timessa stepped forward as if to intervene, but stopped. In the meantime, like some automata, you repeated the gesture. I lost count but you switched from hand to hand, drifting from her head to her thighs, sometimes quickly but more often at a sleepy pace. I imagined you playing a slow concerto. Occasionally you would sigh, or make some indistinct sound …

"Timessa had closed Iole's eyes earlier. But after a while, you bent over her face, and with your thumbs, raised her eyelids. For seconds, inches away, you simply looked into her dark eyes. Has any living being ever stared so long into the eyes of the dead?"

Danaë shifted in her chair and leaned toward me. "After a moment, with your hand on her neck, you raised her head gently off the bench. At the same time, Iole inhaled as if she were drinking life itself. Her fingers moved and Timessa fell to her knees. And then, in response to Iole's *inhalation*, Timessa audibly exhaled …

"It may sound foolish but I found myself crying, and Artemis was in tears, as well. You released Iole's head and she turned, sitting by her own volition. As you stepped away, she rubbed her eyes, then looked at us. Still blinking she smiled and said, 'Why are you all looking?'

"No one spoke, although we were laughing. As Io stood, Timessa was suddenly at her side and slipped her arm around her shoulders. She asked Io if she remembered saying, 'I readily give myself.' The girl nodded.

"Timessa said, 'You were taken at that very moment, and then returned. What you were, you are no longer. And what we feared, we fear no longer.' It was all quite endearing."

I said, "So I succeeded?"

"Yes."

"Yet, I'm annoyed that I don't remember what I did."

Danaë smiled. "Wizards may be excused for oblivious wizardry."

Taking my hand she whispered, "Jackson, what did you see when you gazed into her eyes for so long?"

Her question triggered my first memories, admittedly fractured and partial at best. Although I could remember little else, I could answer that part with assurance. "When I raised her eyelids, I saw a distant fire. I knew that I would. Does that make sense? The fire was faint at first, then spread lazily across the horizon of her pupils …

"I knew this was the same fire Timessa had described, the one that purified all before it. For T it was devastating. But for Iole, at that moment, it heralded rebirth."

Danaë looked puzzled. "Fire?"

I continued. "Don't you see? This was Gaia's fire, that wet wildfire that infuses the womb, that dances on the edges of our consciousness. It is *life's* fire."

Danaë stood, pulling me up. "Artemis is hosting a party upstairs. I hear you know everyone. Let's show our faces. Keep your thoughts to yourself. If anyone asks you anything, just smile as if it's all so obvious. Wizards never give away their secrets."

CHAPTER 51

Discovered and cut down,
comfort or annihilation?
And the bloodied thorn
may yet be unborn.

Timessa and Io left the next morning. They had again melded utterly like some archaic alloy, a bronze lust — or love — of copper and tin, glittery and golden. And Io, no different than Lazarus, was back, her ebullience greater than ever. The two, justifiably, were more besotted than before the girl's death.

Late the previous night, after the party ended, Athene "examined" Io, purportedly to ensure she had survived the ordeal without injury, but I knew she was confirming the girl's a-morality. As they sat Athene placed her palm over the girl's heart. After a few minutes, she stood, looking down on Io. Then she turned to Timessa and said, "Yes, yours forever."

Timessa said simply, "I already know."

There was a somberness in their leaving, perhaps because none of us knew what Timessa would do or become in the coming days and weeks. Their clear joy was shadowed by our knowledge that she was making multiple shifts a week. Her outrageous success as a model was coming to an abrupt end, one of her own choosing. And The Girls's extravaganza, barely mentioned during the visit, portended another shift.

Adding to our concern, none of us could pierce her thoughts. So as she left with her couturier, at most we could wish her well. Artemis had noted that T used improvisation as readily as forethought. Given her immense intelligence, she always succeeded, gloriously, but the tribe was disquieted by what might become hubris. Timessa's instincts were softened in Io's presence, but we worried, nevertheless.

Apollo echoed Artemis, saying, "Hauteur felled Lachesis. Pray there's no repeat." But these observations were easy, obvious and nothing more. None of us could influence her; at best, we could gawk at her maneuvers.

I was thankful Athene had succeeded; I was aware that, had I failed, I would have perished. Perhaps T then would have turned against Athene, as well.

꙼

When they returned to Boston, Filly briefed Timessa on the coming event. Arrangements were untroubled. Filly said somewhat randomly, "Halcyon days while you were gone."

"Halcyon?"

"Peaceful here. I expected chaos. Sorry, none of that. Guess I'm just really good at this. And," she said, "a huge box arrived while you were gone."

She pulled a container from the hallway. It was as large as a bicycle. Io cried, "Thank god! It's the dress and all the good stuff. Sorry about the box size — I couldn't risk wrinkles."

Timessa said, "The *Elle* shoot is —"

Io said, "— three days away."

Filly found a box cutter and in minutes Io extracted the dress and accessories. The dress was wrapped in a swath of white tissue paper, and Io carefully walked the dress to their bedroom. "We'll have a formal fitting when you're ready," she smiled. "This *is* a masterpiece."

꙼

The dress was composed of multiple layers of a sheer organza to be worn over or under a bustier. Her earlier creation was her inspiration. The brilliance of this iteration was that layers of one color could be slipped off and replaced with layers of another. Or they could be combined. Or a layer could be worn as a cape. She had brought white, grey, cerulean, gold, and light pink layers. Matching silk belts could be tied beneath the breasts or at the waist. Io demonstrated how a belt could even be used as a trailing headband.

The single bustier was cut low. A black silk half-slip, included, was wrapped in separate tissue and trimmed with scalloped lace.

Io's only concern was that Timessa would object to the half-cup cut of the bustier. Everyone in the world knew she would not model lingerie. Yet upon trying it on, the goddess made a small bow to Io, saying, "Only for you."

Two telling incidents occurred within the first day they returned, both indications of Io's change. The first happened at night. In the brief time Io had been sleeping with Timessa, she went to bed around eleven, T always sitting beside her until she slept. But on the night of their return, Io couldn't drift off. Timessa suggested she join her in the living room, and try again in an hour. At about five in the morning she finally slept, waking at six refreshed.

Owls are nocturnal, as are gods and goddesses. Timessa should have anticipated that the reborn Io would mirror her own sleep.

The next morning Io shook out the *Elle* dress. During T's fitting, as Io tucked a pleat in the back of the dress, the razor she used slipped in her fingers and rolled sideways against her thumb, leaving a deep cut. Timessa gasped at the sight, but Io was used to getting cuts. Doing so came with dressmaking, and she shrugged, saying it happened all the time — she'd find a bandage. But as T held her wrist, examining the wound and the blood that flowed from the gash, the opening softened, the blood staunched and then, as they watched, began to wane.

Timessa looked into Io's eyes. "Tell me what you feel."

"Tingling."

"No pain?"

Io shook her head. The goddess said softly, "Watch."

Her wound began to close — a light pink seam at first, then in seconds, no more than a faint line. The goddess kissed the girl's thumb. "Now, finish what you were doing."

"I cut myself all the time. I'm an infamous bleeder. What just happened?"

"Keep working. I'll tell you." As Io resumed her work, Timessa explained: nymphs and gods healed instantaneously, their immune systems wildly more robust than any other living thing. "Flesh wounds, broken bones, ripped cartilage — it all regenerates in a few heartbeats."

"And you have this gift, as well?"

Timessa nodded. "What I didn't anticipate was that you would, too."

When Iole told me later about the incident, I was reminded of the afternoon Lachesis tore her leg on a fence when we were hiking. I expected to rush her to a hospital; instead, the wound healed as I watched. From Io's description of her own injury, her rebirth included similar benefits. Still, we were all surprised.

Timessa well knew the cleverness that I accrued after my remaking. In addition to the "Lazarus power," as Athene labeled it, I could shift shapes easily and move or disappear whatever I wished. Shifting was in Danaë's power as well, and we had used the ability effortlessly in Charleville. Inevitably, Timessa wondered if Io, in addition to her enhanced immunity, had become empowered with similar tricks.

Timessa tried over the next day to tease out possibilities. For instance, she asked Io, "Imagine being yourself when you were eight. Do it now!" But the girl just laughed. The goddess pointed at one of her houseplants and said, "See the pyracantha? Turn it into dust!"

Io simply giggled, saying, "What are you doing? That's not possible!"

Despite her efforts to probe her mate's potential, she discovered nothing. Perhaps the a-mortality, coupled with super-immunity, would be the extent of change. Yet T knew that, whereas her pre-death look into the girl's exquisite mind exposed the entirety of Io's thoughts, now she wasn't as certain. A thin curtain like an antique lace seemed to shield a fraction of the girl. Or perhaps Timessa imagined it.

She knew that Io was not conscious of any change. The girl's purity remained inviolate. And her ability to radiate love, a force of personality that thoroughly had seduced the goddess, was amplified after her rebirth. Consequently, the roiling fires that occasionally swept Timessa's consciousness largely disappeared, replaced with a sense of fulfillment. Her furies seemed absent.

In addition, T noticed that the girl's eyes had shifted slightly from grey to violet, what the girl called her "baby eyes." V-*iole*-t Io. Innocence or coincidence? Simply gazing into the girl's eyes made T delirious. She recognized her reaction was not a love as pure as Io's; it was simply something unfathomable.

That evening, without segue, Io said, "No one speaks of Zeus."

"What brought that up? I haven't heard his name in years."

"Why? Wasn't he above all the others?"

"At some point he disappeared. It was nothing dramatic. Perhaps he just packed a bag and left Olympus."

"He didn't die or was driven off?"

T smiled. "He was physically the most powerful of all the gods. No one came close. Not Poseidon, not even Ares. Then poof! One day he reigned, and the next he'd vanished."

"So he could still be around?"

She laughed. "Perhaps he works as a barista down the street."

Io quietly ran her fingers in half-circles below T's breasts. "And you, Queen? Zeus disappeared. Why has the Great Goddess *reappeared*?"

"You're full of questions tonight, little one."

She blushed. "Now that I'm sort of one of you."

"One of us?"

"Of course. You're stuck with me."

"Let's explore your question," T said. "The Great Goddess has filled me, and I am one with her because Gaia wished it so."

"But why?"

"I don't have a clue."

"Perhaps to spread love," the girl said, "in this troubled world?"

T laughed. "No, I have no love for 'this troubled world'."

"None? I was human, and no one has loved me as thoroughly."

"My love for you and my attachment to this world are not the same. Make no mistake: I have little compassion for anything else." As she spoke she tried to resist the rush of love she felt from the girl. "I can be more direct. However it sounds, I have no love for anyone but you."

"But aren't all gods driven to make things better?"

"Hardly. Gods are selfish, cruel. They feast on the weaknesses of others and delight in adulation. Many have been seducers, petty and vindictive. Too many of the males impregnated girls and left them to some horrible fate."

"Are you selfish and cruel?"

Timessa hesitated. "Until you arrived days ago, I increasingly demanded thysia."

She looked puzzled. "Yes, I know. But why?"

"The ancient worship is an observance, a sacrament of giving and getting. I grant favors and demand something in return."

"Like what?" she said softly.

"Some *thing* of equal value."

"Money?"

"No," Timessa said, "I had begun to demand blood."

"Blood?! Nothing else is acceptable?"

"Nothing."

"So without this bloody sacrifice, what becomes of the Great Goddess?"

"She becomes extraordinarily angry."

"I can make that go away."

"Not always. And in her hollowness," Timessa said, "fire burns throughout the world."

"Blood extinguishes that?"

"Red smothers red. Yes, the blood leaves her satiated."

"By that you mean —?" As she whispered she slipped a hand between T's legs. "This satiated …?"

Timessa, her eyes half-closed, said, "You know too much."

"To me you're obvious." Io bent and kissed until T breathed unevenly. Then Io said quietly, "I've always believed the divine were not corrupt. Not like humans. That they were examples of good. That they were exemplars of morality."

Although her eyes were clouded in her languor, Timessa whispered, "We celebrate a-morality, not morals. We distain righteousness. Can you guess why?"

Io studied her face. "No, my queen."

"Morality is an invention of men. And it constantly shifts. What is moral one century is a scandal the next. What one society celebrates, another censors. Women in one country are honored, and in another are slaves. A-morality is preferable. A-morality is more moral than morality."

"But aren't there universal principles of right and wrong?"

"Who defines 'universal'?"

"Yes, I see. It, too, is arbitrary, isn't it?" The girl paused, again studying Timessa's eyes. "Love, on the other hand," she said, "only wants the best for the beloved."

"Love can be selfish. Love often destroys the lover and the beloved."

"That's not love," Io said. "Perhaps self-obsession. Regardless, you and I will not be destroyed. And you, my queen, no longer need blood sacrifices.

"My kisses will slake your thirst, my touch will fill your emptiness. You will see."

Timessa smiled, running a finger down Io's neck. "Are you arguing with me?"

"Hardly. But in these matters, I prevail. In matters of love, your slave is your master."

The next morning as they emerged from the garage into the street beside Timessa's townhouse, their SUV idled in the sunlight, waiting in traffic to turn. A man stood across from them, oblivious, cursing in a stream of profanity both inventive and furious. He was a frequent feature in the Back Bay, wandering over several blocks through the day, swearing in a hoarse smoker's voice. As he shouted he waved his arms. City officials did nothing and residents largely had learned to ignore his foul warnings of apocalypse.

Io unbuckled her seatbelt. "Wait a moment," she said to the driver. Gripping T's arm briefly, she whispered, "I'll be right back."

The girl slipped from the vehicle, running lithely across the street and slowing as she approached the man. Ignoring her, he continued to shake his arms overhead and curse. Io snapped, "You!"

As if from a daze, he turned toward her and she reached for his shoulder. The touch lasted a second at most. At the same moment she smiled as they locked eyes. "You're through with that," she said, adding with nonchalance, "No more. Now you're suffused with love."

His eyes closed, his arms dropped and his anguish eased away. Breathing deeply, he visibly relaxed. Io said softly, "Even better, now you're free —"

He looked around as if he had never seen the street he was on, and puzzled, ran a hand through his hair.

The incident lasted less than a minute. She skipped back to the vehicle and got in. As she and Timessa watched, the man briskly walked away, his bearing spirited.

"I'd had enough of his swearing," Io said. "Weren't you tired of it, too?"

CHAPTER 52

The river's sounds,
the flow that moves sideways,
the golden turbidity and her phrase:
'Love abounds, abounds, abounds.'

The *Elle* shoot, the Last Shoot, occurred in a location Timessa had approved weeks before. The site was a half-hour drive from Cambridge, in a place somewhat similar to our Pennsylvania retreat. On a wide, gently sloping meadow of wild grasses, it featured a small cedar grove scalloped from the middle, and within it a strawberry-edged kettle pond with a stream.

On the day Timessa first saw the place, three deer walked from the grove into nearby woods, indifferent to the intruders by the road. As she strode to the pond edge, bluebirds and towhees swept over the meadow in lovely arcs.

The shoot had favorable weather, and Timessa felt extraordinarily optimistic. When Io woke her that morning, they spent a languid hour in what she called "girl-play." Io's affection always left Timessa speechless. The girl's tenderness inexplicably left her with the same fullness that followed thysia. And now that Io understood the concept of worship, she would whisper, her fingers in T's hair, "There are so many ways to sacrifice. I do them all for you."

Now they traveled in a small entourage toward the site. Someone at *Elle*, or on the photographer's staff, must have leaked the event and location. Miles away as they bumped down narrow, country roads, they noticed a nondescript van following. Her security, in a dark SUV behind Timessa's vehicle, dropped back to scan the occupants. The van's windows were blacked out.

The driver of the second SUV, now tailing the van, radioed T's driver, "Gonna pull them over. Might have to kick some butt."

Timessa heard the man driving say, "If you need backup, call."

There was silence and in five minutes the second SUV maneuvered back into the caravan. The van was missing. Io glanced at Timessa, who shrugged.

After the procession pulled off the road into the locale, vehicle doors opened and a dozen people got out, several stretching in the early morning sun. Two *Elle* editors paced peevishly, thumbing their cellphones. Assistants assembled a walk-in tent beside the grove and Io hung the pieces of T's modular frock inside on a portable rack. She commanded two stylists and a fitter. Her usual radiance had been replaced with intensity.

Wearing jeans and a grey hoodie, Timessa walked into the tent and said, "Pressure's on. Lights are up, editors are prickly, and the photog is waiting."

Io smiled brusquely, closing the tent flap, "Tell them to wait. We own what happens here, and we determine *when* it happens. Now, out of those street clothes."

Later, transformed, T stepped from the tent. Over the next two hours, with Io watching avidly, photographers captured T running through the field, slumped in a chair, balancing on a log beside the pond with her arms out, and standing legs apart, a halo breaking around her head.

The photog, a master of outdoor fashion lighting, eventually requested they move into the shadowed grove. There T was photographed with her back against old cedars or pensively strolling beside the water's edge. At her suggestion she bent beside the bank, and leaned down so that he could shoot her reflection in the green, mirrored surface of the pond.

Between shots Io functioned as T's alterations girl. During a brief argument with an *Elle* editor, T reminded her that she was an observer only; her input was unwelcome and she would be thrown off the set if she interfered. Io continued fussing with the bustier, and adjusting T's hair. The goddess caught the photographer smirking, and pointed at him, saying, "That includes you, too."

As the session approached its end, the photog said, "I have an idea, if you'll allow me to play a bit." He pointed at T and Io. "Both of you — follow me."

They did, walking together into the meadow, holding hands as if they owned the world. He turned to them, saying, "Here's what I'm envisioning: you, on your backs in the grass, head to head, feet in opposite directions. I'll take a few shots while you squint into the sky."

They nodded and sat together, giggling. Then they nodded simultaneously as if twins, and lay down, head to head, pointing away with their feet. He hovered over them, giving occasional directions, firing at rapid speed with a Hasselblad as they laughed at the silliness of it all.

It lasted mere minutes before he said, "Good. It's a take. We're done."

As they helped each other stand, Timessa saw goldfinches and orioles overhead. A warm breeze moved the vast grasses and as she watched, commanding, time slowed. Io moved at quarter-speed and assistants to the photographer seemed stuck in a golden amber. The cessation was of her own doing, and Io was her conspirator. Her Io, as she reveled in the seemingly miraculous light that fell upon them both, made it all worthwhile.

With a small sigh, she allowed time's velocity to resume, its flow to shift side to side in the dark snake-dance that felled all humans with an irrepressible speed.

Io leapt into her arms, her legs around T's waist. "Was it good?" she asked. "My dress? You were beautiful!"

"You make me beautiful," T said. "And when these photos hit *Elle*, you'll be more famous than me!"

Before the tent was collapsed, Timessa changed back to her jeans and top. In turn, Io packed up the layers of organza and the accessories she had so carefully selected. As Timessa walked to the SUV, her immense round sunglasses obscuring her eyes, one of the security team held the vehicle's door open. She thought of the van that had made such a brief foray into their caravan.

Turning to the man she said, "Was the van you stopped paparazzi?"

"Yes, ma'am."

"And?"

"We discouraged them from following."

She looked down the narrow road which faded into a summer haze of greys and browns, and climbed into her SUV.

Upon their return to the townhouse, Filly was annoyingly officious, pleading for an hour of Timessa's time. The Girls's extravaganza was scheduled in two days, and Timessa seemed more interested in Io than in the event. She couldn't, Filly emphasized, just appear. She was the grand-master and the Queen. She had to know, to approve of everything.

So the three sat down in the room with the Donatello and the implacable Queenie. Disinterested in the day's shoot and their successes in the countryside, Filly opened notebooks and passed out programs, presenting her recommendations as if in a corporate boardroom. Timessa finally raised her voice and said, "Quit pacing. Even better, sit down. This is just for fun!"

T reached for Queenie. The effigy was warm in her hand and as she stroked its belly, the flat, slit-eyed face appeared to glow. Io noticed and took her other hand, linking fingers with T, smiling quietly.

"But we have so many girls coming," Filly said. "It has to go well."

Io whispered, "It will."

Filly's eyes filled with tears. "I feel so responsible."

T said, "Relax."

Filly nodded, glancing anxiously at the two. "It's close to midnight. I know at least two of us have to sleep."

"Not me," Io said. "No more. But go to bed. We'll go through this again in the morning." She squeezed T's hand. "Right?"

The goddess said nothing. Queenie burned in her hand. For the first time since Io's arrival, she felt the primeval fire arising. As they sat talking, as Filly began to repeat herself, the fire swept into Timessa's consciousness, its flames leaping horizontally across an arced horizon. What match had set it off, she wondered, as she watched the contagion grow.

Io squeezed her hand again. "Goddess?"

T lifted Queenie up to head level, turning the statuette in her hand, studying its face. She saw an unexpected savagery, a uniquely female strength that she knew corresponded to, if not created, the fires behind her eyes. She lowered Queenie and turned to Io.

"We have wine." She smiled reassuringly. "Would you mind?"

The girl nodded. "Of course."

Filly already was retrieving a bottle, and reaching for glasses. She said, "Sorry. I've been obsessing over details. You're right: I forgot it's supposed to be fun."

She poured wine for Io and the goddess. "Thanks," Io smiled.

Filly shrugged. "I know I've been irritating. And I know the event will be spectacular." T and Io said nothing. She continued, "Well, unless you object I'm going to bed."

She turned down the hallway without waiting for comments. Io said loudly, "Thanks, Philippa." Io then turned to Timessa and said, "Goddess, I know you as if I have been at your side forever. And I know you're troubled."

T had begun twisting Queenie in her hand, clockwise, then in reverse. The marble's smoothness belied the effigy's muscular power. It had been her childhood toy and now radiated an incalculable authority. Yet that authority was hers, the dominion that had increased like a cloying vapor when she danced on Delos. That morning on the island she had not recognized the Dionysiakos for what it was, a dance that mirrored the cosmos itself.

She turned to the girl beside her. "Not troubled, Io. Reassessing. Bathing in fire. Eating fire."

"Goddess."

"I am fire and you are love. I wonder, Io, can love and fire be fused as one?"

"We have already fused. If I am love and you are fire, we have joined, have we not?"

Io could not share the burning, but could transfigure the goddess with her touch. Mischievously, she held T by the waist and said, "You are mine. And your fires are mine. And I am yours. All of this is undeniable. I'll blame Gaia," she said, "although she hides. She alone must have spun this double flower that we are."

Not waiting for T's response, Io stood and bent to kiss her goddess. As their mouths touched, T felt time stop. The braking was abrupt. Its discontinuance was not her doing. The cessation became like a river that stilled, waters that quieted while her heart, in utter contradiction, raced, aware and unable to resist Io's hands in her hair and on her neck.

CHAPTER 53

I desired my dust to be mingled with yours
Forever and forever and forever.
—— Ezra Pound

One of the many conditions T attached to the final *Elle* contract was cover approval. In the magazine's desperation to sign an exclusive, it conceded to the demand. On the evening before The Girls's extravaganza, the magazine emailed her a proof, requesting her approval within a working day.

Timessa was at her desk in the bedroom, and Io in bed, idly talking about an event from her childhood. She was wearing a simple cotton nightshirt, something she had assembled from leftover materials. When T had asked dismissively, "Aren't you too old for that?" Io had replied, "It pulls up effortlessly. Want me to show you?"

Earlier in the day, Filly had been sent ahead to coordinate the Girls event with Juliette. The extravaganza was to begin at ten the next morning, and T was being helicoptered in with Io and one of the nymphs. She had avoided copters since the incident at the farm, but now would be returning in one.

She swiveled back to the *Elle* email, asking Io to look over her shoulder, that she had a surprise. The girl came over and when T double-clicked on the image file, the cover appeared. Like children, they gasped. The front photo showed Io and T, head to head in the grass, laughing. Smeared greens and soft blues blurred the background.

T wore a pink petticoat, tied atop a yellow full slip. With the stunned look she effected, she appeared the perfect ingénue. Io's freckles descended fetchingly down her neck and disappeared below her simple dress. Her eyes shone merrily. Timessa thought, looking at the image, *My pupils are as dark as an owl's. And aren't we obviously joyous?*

The *Elle* headline, superimposed below their image, read, *T and Her Couturier. The Final Shoot.*

Io smirked, "You should reject it. It should read, *T and Io, Girl Geniuses.* I'm galled."

Timessa took Io by the waist and pulled her close, kissing between her breasts and muttering, "Around here I have the final say in *this* matter. It's an okay title. And a great shot. You'll be a sensation."

Io let her play as she wished, pleased to be taken whenever they had privacy. Here, alone, she could moan and cry as the goddess requited Io's earlier affections. As she felt T lifting her nightshirt, Io whispered, "See? Effortless, isn't it?"

They woke in each other's arms at six that morning and dressed. One of the security SUVs drove them to a VIP section at the airport. Io, the nymph and a guard followed the goddess into the copter. T shook hands with the pilot, an older woman who had flown for the military, and gave her coordinates to their destination. Running quick calculations, the pilot noted they were due to arrive around 9:45.

Weather was ideal, although thunderstorms had been predicted. T had made small adjustments to the atmospheric high, ensuring it remained stable in the vicinity of the celebration. The afternoon would now be partly cloudy and mild. As they descended toward the farm, the pilot remarked, "Quite the crowd. All girls?"

T simply smiled. At 300 feet above the ground, she saw banners being waved. One read, QUEEN, others, THE GIRLS, and still others, T = Q, and We Are One.

As the helicopter landed, a small delegation including Juliette and Filly greeted them. From their smiles she knew the morning had gone well. The helicopter would leave for a local airfield to refuel, then return at day's end to fly them back.

A day earlier T had called Juliette and cancelled the request to bring lambs and ewes; that aspect of the extravaganza was being scrapped. Filly took the extraordinary measure of checking all cameras and cellphones at entry. Each girl was assigned a numbered ziplock bag to place imaging devices. Photographs would not be allowed.

In the rear of the massive stage that faced the crowd, T sheltered with Io, preparing to appear. Io helped her change, applied light makeup and brushed her hair as a band wound up its gig. Juliette watched the two interact, then asked, "Goddess, what are your plans? No one knows."

Without hesitation T said, "No idea."

"I'd be terrified."

"Perhaps," she said, thinking of Delos, "I'll simply dance."

Juliette smiled weakly, looking at her watch. "Bought this just for today. I don't think I've ever owned a watch. You're on in one minute. I'm so excited!"

Timessa turned to Io. "Join me on the stage?"

Io nodded.

Timessa took her hand and they followed Juliette to the platform. As girls saw them on stage, applause began, rippling over the field. Juliette approached the microphone, clearly nervous. The crowd of girls quieted, the banners swaying and hands being raised until everyone was standing, arms overhead, moving in a wave.

Juliette said excitedly into the mic, "Yes, I know! Without further ado, I bring you T!"

Timessa stepped up, alone. She wore a filmy gown, golden, shimmering. It fell to her feet in soft pleats and was cinched below her breasts with a leather belt. Moments before she took the stage, Io had threaded a flower wreath of white asters into her hair. A hush fell over the crowd, and T paused, observing the girls, aware all wore identical white tees.

Filly had obviously conveyed a dress code. T smiled, whispering into the mic, "All of you are so beautiful."

From somewhere in the crowd a girl cried, "No, you!"

She smiled, continuing. "Vibrant, vivacious. I'm proud to stand before you. We are one. We *are* The Girls!" She fell silent, looking out across them all. After a moment, as if on cue they began to chant, "Queen, Queen —"

Timessa raised her hands, palms open and said, "No, I am no more than one of you. First, contrary to what you may have heard, I am well. Healthy, and in fact, more alive than I have ever been —" She paused, and again the chants rose across the field. "Queen, Queen —"

She looked at their faces, All were expectant. Years before, she had looked at Artemis identically; then, the goddess's every word was a chime, her lectures melodious. Little did they know. Each of these privileged girls, no matter the flattery each heard constantly, would face traitorous lovers, illness, the loss of children, old age, and eventually, death. She knew what they could not grasp. Or would not face. And she would not play prophet. What good could come from saying, "All of you will suffer and die"?

Instead, she continued, "Once I spoke of fire. Once I was afraid. None of you have known this. I have achieved great fame, however undeserved. But at night, alone, I used to close my eyes and see great fires sweep the world."

As she caught her breath, several girls in the front cried, "No! No!" and within seconds the entire crowd of girls was chanting "No!"

After raising her hands to quiet them again, she continued, "In a moment I will tell you more. But first, I ask you to close your eyes." She looked over the multitude of girls, all suddenly shut-eyed like sleeping birds. "Now, without opening your eyes, relax your faces … Let your jaws go slack and feel your scalps soften … Let your defenses all dissolve …"

She hummed into the microphone, the steady sound moving like a wind across the girls. "Do it," she whispered. "Do it now. Feel the tension in your lives dissolve …"

She allowed silence for a few seconds, then said, "Imagine I am beside you, touching your arm, your shoulder, touching your cheek." A shudder ran through the crowd with many of the girls gasping or crying out.

"That's my love you feel!" she said softly. "My adoration …"

Allowing another moment to pass, she said, "Now open your eyes.

Look with love at the one beside you, for she, like you, is one of The Girls. We are sisters, each of us related in our love."

One of the girls cried in a high voice, "And her blood is our blood!"

That too became a chant, echoing against the stage, resounding over the surrounding fields. "Her blood is our blood! Her blood is our blood!"

Timessa let the chant continue, then interjected, "I spoke of fire. I said it burned me, no matter my fame. You see, I have been like you. I burnt at night. My thighs burnt." Then she asked with a hushed voice, "Don't all girls have burning thighs?"

The crowd erupted in "Yes! Yes!"

Then she said as if confessing, "Well, my thighs still burn!"

Hundreds of girls hooted or cried "Mine too!" or "More than just my thighs!"

Timessa continued, "That's enough! There's more. Now quiet or I won't go on!"

Obediently, the girls became silent, their eyes on her as she laughed. To their fascination she broke into a dance that lasted seconds at most. None knew it was the Dionysiakos. None of the girls had seen it danced, or seen her dance, but all felt their hearts aflutter, a fire in their bellies at the sight.

"Fire!" she said as she again faced the microphone. "I thought I'd always burn, that to be alive meant to burn at a stake, watching without being able to stop the smoke of my life going up and away! I was just a pretty face, a fraud, someone the world had wrongly elevated!"

Cries of "No!" arose.

As they quieted she said softly, "A show of hands. How many of you believe in love?"

Without hesitation every girl reached for the sky, waving as if to get her attention. There were cries of "Me!" and "I do!" and "We all do!"

"This may shock you," she whispered, "but I did not believe. Did not believe in anything called love. It seemed a fraud. The fires that kept me up at night burned far hotter than any feelings of affection I had known. Love would never be for me. Or so I thought. I could see it in others eyes. *Love*, how glorious! But I but never felt that specialness myself."

The crowd fell silent. She paused, then said, "But then something happened. An alchemy I never believed was possible."

A girl cried, "You found love!"

Timessa smiled. "Yes! Fire and love suddenly combined." She laughed. "Fire and love? What is T saying?"

Many of the girls giggled nervously, their faces upturned as they waited. "This might happen some day to you. As it happened to me. Silly, isn't it? Fire and love? Shouldn't one destroy the other?"

A chant arose. "T! T!"

She cried, "Love can be fiery, but can fire be lovely? Of course not!" In a lilting voice, she continued, "Fire is an elemental thing, something physical. And love is ... a concept, a mere feeling. Love cannot be defined by scientists. It is something we know but can't explain. So I ask, can one combine the material world — fire — with an emotion such as *love*?"

Many of the girls cried, "No! No!"

"Yet," she whispered, "I have."

An uneasiness swept the girls. She had brought them so far. But now they wavered, unsure of where she ventured, desperate that she not destroy their own love, especially that which they felt for her. She raised an arm, sweeping it overhead in a theatrical gesture, surprising herself: it was Artemis's dramatic signal.

"Let me introduce my couturier. We appear together in a week on the cover of *Elle*. Her name is Iole —" Timessa gestured to Io. "— and she will rock the fashion world!"

Io walked slowly from the side shadows to the center stage. She slipped an arm around T's waist, and looking out across the girls, waved a greeting. T interjected, "Give it up for the lovely Iole!"

The girls applauded, hooting and whistling. Io bowed and laughed, grateful for the acceptance. T went on, "She's a genius. Perhaps someday, if you're lucky, she will design for you. She chooses whom she clothes. And who knows — perhaps she'll choose you next!"

Again, minutes of applause went by. T went on, "Now listen to me: there is more. She and I work together well. We are combined: I am fire ... and she is love. How can that be?"

There were random cries from the audience, such as, "You mean you love her work?"

"I mean," Timessa said, "that the fire I am has merged with the love she emanates. Working together, doing what we do, we are far greater than either of us alone."

A girl in the crowd shouted, "Are you in love with *her*?"

Intentionally sassy, she replied, "Yesss."

Another cried, "Tell us more!"

"Tell you more? Oh dear! So, her love struck me hard. One moment I was T, Queen, a girl who needed no one else." She smiled, whispering, "Maybe, except for all of you. Then I looked into her eyes."

A girl far in the rear yelled, "Thysia?"

"Thysia," T replied, "is worship. It is our word for that. It is our Observance. But it is not like love."

One of the elite girls in her inner circle cried, "Sacrifice?"

"Someone asks, 'sacrifice?' We sacrifice ourselves for success and adulation. It's true."

She went on, "But real love is not sacrifice. We do not annihilate ourselves for someone else. I was ignorant before I fell in love."

"Why give up modeling?" a girl shouted.

"Why not? Modeling is not like love. It is no sacred thing. Modeling falls in our lap. Why? Because we have a certain look. Clothes hang from our bones as if we were princesses. We do nothing to become these desirable girls that others envy. We can thank past generations, perhaps our great grandmother, for our high cheeks or lovely eyes. And yes, once we have been featured in *Vogue* or *W*, we burn to appear there again ...

"But modeling is no hallowed thing. It is not that fire I describe, not the sacred fire that burns for our beloved. You have heard the phrase, the flame of love. Love and fire: they are not the strange companions that they seem. That has been my revelation."

A moment passed, the reaction from the surprise confession unpredictable. Standing before them Io and T held hands, clearly joyous. Then a girl in front, grinning, started chanting, "Kiss, kiss, kiss —" and the crowd joined in.

Io blushed and T shook her head. "Kiss?" she asked dramatically. "In front of all of you?"

"Kiss, kiss, kiss —"

Io rose on her toes, kissing T's cheek, then looked with a tentative smile across the audience. Multiple girls cried, "A *real* kiss!"

T shook her head again. The chant shifted to singsong single letters: "K-I-S-S-I—"

She raised her hands to quiet them. "Most of you are too far away to see Iole's eyes. They're a lovely violet. She's French and has freckles all over her face ...." Her voice rose. "Some of you are French. You've come a long way to be here with us. Iole, say something to your compatriots—"

Io took the mic and, in a hushed voice, smiling, said, "*Salut les filles!*"

A half dozen girls, clustered together, cried, "*Salut, Iole!*"

Stepping back to the microphone, T said, "Now, girls, it is true. The *Elle* cover I mentioned was my last gig. No more. I'm done."

A girl in the front called out, "What will become of us?" Her voice was fragile, unsure.

Timessa responded, "Someone just asked 'What will become of us?' " She paused. "Have I not said since The Girls began that we are family? Do you think I might abandon my family?"

She was grateful to hear them respond, "No! No!"

"Sisters do not abandon sisters. Not only are we that, we are all like Amazons. In spirit and in strength. Almost three thousand years after they vanished, the Amazons still inspire women. They always have. Not one of you has turned to another and asked, 'What's an Amazon?' We know, don't we?

"So The Girls, like Amazons, like sisters, protect each other forevermore. The Girls go on. Best, each of you now has a thousand sisters!"

Wild applause interrupted her words. She paused, then said, "And now that I'm unemployed, I have more time to be in closer touch with each of you —"

A girl cried, "Tell us *more* about love!"

"Love. Someone wants to know more about love. Haven't I said enough?"

"No, no, no!"

"I never imagined love until Io appeared. I hope many of you will find love as grand as ours. Io and I are girls, but love knows no gender. Most of you will love men and I honor that ancient love. Without such coupling, the world will have no babies. And all of us love little ones."

As she spoke the relief in the audience was palpable. A girl in front started chanting, "Kiss, kiss, kiss," and all joined in. Timessa motioned for quiet. "No! We're being serious. "

Io, her arm still around T's waist, grinned at the audience and turning to the goddess, asked, "May I have the mic?"

Timessa half-smiled, and when she gestured that the mic was Io's, Io leaned in and said loudly, "Watch!" She quickly put her arms around T's neck and kissed her mouth. Every girl now chanted in delight, "Kiss, kiss, kiss," until Io broke away, shrugging as if she had been helpless to do anything less.

"Whoa!" Timessa whispered into the mic. "She is *so* distracting!"

To great laughter, she continued, "But before I was attacked, I was saying that Iole and I just fell in love. Before a few weeks ago, I'd never had a boyfriend. Or a girlfriend." She knew her audience listened avidly. "So I'm no example of what to do. We've never discussed it publicly, but you know the rumors. I'm accused of making babies possible —"

A girl sang out, "You mean, making us fertile!"

Timessa laughed. "Oh, most of you are fertile. Probably dangerously fertile! Most of you will find out soon enough."

Running her fingers through her loose hair, she touched her wreath, saying softly, "I should tell you, too: Iole made this garland that I wear. The flowers are asters. Do you know what asters represent?"

She opened her arms and said, "Sisters. Asters are like sisters. They stand together, wild flowers, beautiful ones like us! An hour ago as Iole pinned this garland in my hair, she said, 'Here, my darling. The wreath is a circle for our love. And the flowers are all the girls.' Wasn't that sweet?"

Io again slipped her arm around T, making no attempt to hide her adoration. As the two looked out across the throng of girls, a small cry arose which grew louder over seconds: "Queen-Io, Queen-Io, Queen-Io!"

The sound washed over them. Timessa looked back into the sea of faces and cried, "Each of you will be loved. And whomever you love, we'll applaud —"

CHAPTER 54

Once at dusk
the axe was swung, the lamb cried
and blood was blood.
Now the old dying has died.

B efore they flew back to Boston late afternoon, an event occurred
that lasted only moments, but proved monumental. Regardless of
T's promises onstage, a small group of girls feared that the day represented T's final gesture, a gratuitous goodbye — and that they would be
left adrift. In their daring — and grief — they found their way backstage
shortly after the event. When they saw Timessa in a congratulatory talk
with Juliette, Filly and others, the most vulnerable of the group, a girl of
sixteen, put her hands over her mouth and sobbed. Then, rolling her
eyes, she collapsed.

Io said, "*Elle est hystérique ...*"

The half dozen other girls fell to their knees, several attending the
stricken girl, shaking her, shouting, "Annie!"

All looked frantically from the girl to Timessa, who had not moved.
One whispered, "See, she doesn't care —!"

T recognized the fallen girl from a fashion spread in the *New York Times*. She was French like Io, petite, a redhead with luminous eyes who had been photographed hanging from ropes, upside down, sideways or grasping heavy cords with both hands, arms overhead as she wore a cape. In a brief article accompanying the spread, she was quoted as saying her greatest influence was T. In imitation, she too used a single name, Annie.

Fainting happened occasionally when The Girls met. T always discouraged it, arguing that boys never swoon. She knew of no nymph or goddess who suddenly had lost consciousness. Artemis would be appalled at such a reaction, but these were brief events. In this instance, backstage, she said quietly to Io and Juliette, "She'll come to soon enough."

Io whispered, *"Et la laisser sur le sol? Non, guérissons-la pour toujours ..."*

T responded, "Speak English."

"I said, 'Just leave her on the floor? No, let's cure her forever.'"

"Oh?"

Releasing T's hand Io rushed to the girl and knelt. With the slightest touch to Annie's cheek, Io woke the girl. Annie said, *"Est-ce que je me suis évanouie?"*

"You fainted," Io whispered. "But you're now through with such silliness forever."

As the girl's face softened, Io continued, "You're free. *Je vous ai libéré.*"

T watched with fascination. Io had done something similar when she leapt from the SUV days before to touch the man cursing about the coming of an apocalypse.

And now you're free.

Free? Timessa herself had been freed from the fires that swept her heart, although she hadn't viewed it like that. Io had not waved a wand in her case, nor had she said, "You're free."

What Timessa had experienced in Io's arms was closer to goddess seduction. Then through love they had become conjoined, T's fires consumed in Io's radiant love. The effect was to indeed free her from her own apocalypse. The raging fires that swept her consciousness had been quelled, broken like wild horses. Io had softened the anger that could flare so suddenly. The archaic fury was now ire, the wrath cooled to an ill humor.

Yes, she thought. Although anger still arose, the ancient darkness had been blunted by Io's purity.

So *this*, she thought, was Io's power as an a-mortal, to free beings from their fury. And their fears. To fill them with unconditional love.

Io walked back to Timessa. "She'll be better now."

࿔

Without her usual frenetic schedule, T began to consider leaving Boston. She could live anywhere. Io already had said, "I am yours, wherever you are." So she explored alternatives. Weeks before, she had half-joked about La Porcheria in Sicily, but anywhere with privacy would do. She knew she would be forever T, an object of fascination.

So she contacted Artemis, as well as Apollo and Hermes, noting she sought acreage and was favoring something rural in southern Europe. Within a day Artemis sent her a link to a property in France that was a thirty-minute drive northeast of Grenoble in a town called Malbourget. Artemis noted that Timessa would find parts of it familiar; the tribe had roamed it freely a half millennium earlier. Large areas were unchanged.

T pulled up the link. The estate was more than 400 acres and lay east of the Isére River. Parts of the acreage were cultivated, parts forested. A twelve-bedroom furnished stone residence built in 1720 had been modernized, and its setting in the woods would provide ample privacy.

Io smiled. "I know nothing of the region. Charleville is more than six hours north of the valley. Probably warmer there. And it's nearer Italy. But they're asking a lot of money."

Io knew nothing of T's fortune. The estate was well within her means. She said, "We should view it soon. Feel like traveling?"

At almost the same time, Hermes texted:

Several hundred acres available
on Naxos. Pleasant house and private,
difficult to access. No one would
suspect. Here's a link to listing.
Of course remember Dionysos.

She read the text to Io. Suddenly, without knowing more, T smiled. Naxos: one of the Cycladic islands. Its sharp rise was visible from Delos the morning Poseidon rose from the waters of the small embayment to greet Danaë. And as Hermes reminded T in his text, Naxos was known as Dionysos's island, a magical place where the wine god had found a sleeping Ariadne on an arc-shaped beach, marrying her in days.

There, on the island — known originally as Dionysia — they conceived children and were said to be deeply in love. But tragedy befell them. Ariadne died. A bereft Dionysos began his drunken dances in Thebes, then throughout Greece. But whiffs of the wine-god lingered on the island.

The property Hermes found bordered the sea, the θαλαττα, and looked directly north into the dun hump of Delos. It lay beside a farming community called Agia.

The next day they flew into Athens, then took a small plane to Naxos. Minutes before landing they looked down at Mykonos and Delos, strange volcanic protrusions that passed below them in a blink. The Naxos airport was a single landing strip south of the main town, which had been built millennia earlier near an old Mycenaean fortress.

They were told that the drive from the airport to Agia was at least forty-five minutes, presuming good weather. As it was dusk they would complete their travel in the morning. Although they took a room in a tourist beach hotel, neither T nor Io could sleep, so they roamed the old streets of Naxos waiting for dawn. T thought of Dionysos and his lovely wife, wondering where their house had been. She was amused that the arced road beside the town's harbor was named Ariadnis, for Ariadne's Road.

T and Io sat on a bench that overlooked yachts moored in rows under the moonlight. They held hands and said nothing for hours, content to simply watch the long shadows of the night, to hear the yachts moaning as they rocked against their anchor chains. At one point Timessa pointed to some stars, and said, "That's the Corona Borealis. Dionysos hung it there, a starry necklace for his bride."

Both knew morning would bring adventure. And both hoped the Agia property would shimmer against the sea, that the house would be habitable, and that the lands surrounding it would be unspoiled.

By nine Timessa, Io and Filly drove slowly northeast through twisting ancient roads. From Naxos to Agia was ten miles, and the green abundance on all sides spoke to the fertility of the soils. Houses were scattered and the few villages they passed — Akrotiri, Chilia Vrisi, Kampos, and Abram — hardly deserved names. A real estate agent was to meet them at ten. As they drove into Agia, Io counted fewer than a dozen buildings. Like the towns to the southwest, Agia was a town in name only.

Yet the estate was more than T imagined. A twisting gravel road off the paved highway led to two white, flat-topped residences. The largest was on a slight promontory and overlooked the Mediterranean toward Delos and Mykonos. Behind it were rows of old olive trees — hundreds, she guessed — and behind those, terraced vineyards that followed the slowly rising slope. Potable water came from a cistern attached to the main house. Dual generators provided power, as did a bank of solar panels that appeared to be an afterthought.

The agent, a deeply sunburnt man, noted the acreage was approximate; the property had not been surveyed in recent times. But the government assessed it at forty-eight hectares, around 120 acres. He asked Timessa if her husband would be viewing it at a later time, and she gave him a long look, finally saying, "No."

After a brief walk outside, he showed them the two larger buildings, both of which dated to the 19th century. One had been a main residence. The agent noted that the property was owned by an attorney in Athens who found the effort to visit too great. He sought a quick sale, but lamented that few buyers would be interested in such an isolated spot.

The interiors were simple, the plastered walls white and the furniture in a Greek country style that hadn't changed in hundreds of years. The few paintings were reproduction Madonnas. A St. Sebastian tied to a tree and punctured with arrows hung in the master bedroom. The kitchen and baths had been renovated.

Near the end of the tour, T half-joked in perfect Greek, "No helipad?" The agent almost responded. Instead, he replied, "Are you considering living here alone?"

"With these two. Perhaps others, as well."

Outside, standing beside the rental car, he sighed, saying, "I am obligated to tell you everything I know about this land."

"Of course. Legalities."

"I have been a Naxian all my life. I studied briefly in London, but returned when I was still a young man." Abruptly, he said, "Few people today know mythology, except perhaps what they have seen in movies."

Timessa smiled. "Yes, Zeus throwing lightning bolts."

"That," he said, "and Eros shooting arrows. Ares commanding

armies. Grand indeed, yet without exception, the great stories, the great gods have been maligned."

She asked him where he was leading, and he grunted. "Naxos, you may know, claims that one of the gods lived here long ago, marrying a princess from Crete."

"Really?"

"An obscure god."

"His name?"

"Dionysos."

The two girls giggled, and T thought of the mad god, now caged in Poseidon's stables below the sea. She said, "It is a familiar name. What sort of a god was he?"

"A drunk, a seducer."

"But weren't they all?"

He paused, finally saying, "The islanders have long believed that Dionysos built a house for Ariadne, his wife, on this very site."

As if an afterthought, he pointed to the right of the main house, on the seaside, and said, "There. Germans in the 1930s excavated ruins. Iron and Bronze Age pottery, a few implements. You'll see the stones if you walk a couple meters beyond the house. Not impressive, but perhaps it's true. No one really knows. But I am obligated to tell you this."

Without speaking the girls walked to the ruins, which lay in a roughly 70 x 120-foot rectangle. Massive square cut stones were scattered about. A few old trenches lined the bottom. It appeared untouched since the excavations. She turned to the agent. "Where are the artifacts they found?"

"Some museum in Berlin."

"Nothing shared with the Greeks?"

He shook his head.

She smiled. "Germans, no different than the English who ripped apart the Parthenon. All thieves." She looked at the girls. "Io, Filly — could you live in Agia?"

Io said, "With you? Forever," and Filly nodded, smiling.

As they stood beside the ruins, she gestured toward the sea and asked the agent, "Anything down there?"

"A small cove. I forgot. I apologize and encourage you to look."

They trudged down toward the shore. Rounding a laurel thicket, they suddenly faced a beach. It was shaped like a lazy crescent, a dull scimitar. T guessed it was 500 feet long. She knew instantly that ancient Greek battleships, triremes, once came ashore at this very spot. An old sailboat, its bottom rotted through, was pulled up beside the shoreline. Perhaps Dionysos himself had walked these sands.

For a moment she was tempted to take off her shoes and dance the Dionysiakos in the thin wake.

To the agent's shock, because decisions throughout Greece always were made slowly, incrementally, T said quietly, "I'll take it. The price is fine. Prepare the paperwork. I can close at any time."

EPILOGUE

She was home now,
an odd awareness, as there
had never been a home.

Danaë and I were the first to arrive on Mykonos. Charon would take us in his ancient boat to Naxos the next morning. A month had passed since T's purchase of the property, and her text invitation to selected guests promised a "resplendent" party at what she now called Theos Point.

We had had a full day beforehand, with Danaë insisting we revisit Delos. She wanted to see the cove where her father had reappeared, and sent him an invitation to surprise us there. And I was curious to view the ruins of Apollo's temple again. As we stayed at Charon's so-called AΔΠ INSTITUTE, he volunteered to ferry us over as he had before, and we made the crossing to Delos after coffee.

The ride itself was routine and we tied up as before, Charon noting he would be waiting for us when we had tired of the place. When I asked about Hermes, we were told, "He will be on Naxos tomorrow. Not here today."

We hiked south on the narrow trail toward Poseidon's cove. There, Danaë squatted in the sand, looking up at me with patience. "I know you want to move on," she said, "but I think my father will not disappoint me."

Moments later, Poseidon burst from the briny inlet, trident in hand. "My girl!" he cried and they hugged. She was joyous and I persuaded him to accompany us down the trail to the city's ruins. He had packed clothes in a knapsack and within minutes looked like any other tourist, albeit his huge frame remained intimidating. The trident has hidden beside a stone wall.

The ruins, with their cut marble, were quiet. Perhaps it was because the gods had been revived. Or that Timessa was not there to dance. Or that the crystalline sun was unrelenting. Whatever, wind swept the stones and the visit proved unenlightening. I had had no expectations, knowing we could never recreate the island as it was when we roused Dionysos and Ares that rainy day.

After a short time, the three of us rendezvoused with Charon and returned to the hotel-cum-institute. I wasn't sure what to call it. Charon certainly still housed old friends on occasion. I suspected that the institute, although duly registered with authorities, was no more than a tax write-off. Regardless, Hestia ran the little restaurant when there were guests and, on seeing us, acted as if we were old friends. I suppose in a way we were. We insisted she sit with us over wine.

At dusk the sunset brushed the sky with cerulean blues and saffron, greys and luminescent pinks. Poseidon raised his glass to the sky and said, "To the Great Goddess. I pray she prevail in all things!"

I admit years had passed since I felt such optimism. We all had a sense that elements were merging fortuitously. A certain buoyancy carried us along. It was more an undefined confidence than simply hope. As night prevailed Charon stopped at our table and said, "Weather tomorrow will be like today. I wonder if the Goddess is tweaking the skies. A few days ago we were to be swept with constant rain."

Poseidon suddenly pointed to Delos. "Look!"

As we gazed into the darkness, I saw a blinking light and knew it was the same strange phenomenon I'd observed earlier that year. It flashed twice, went dark for seconds, then flashed again. I said, "I thought Delos allowed no one on the island after dusk."

Charon stared at me solemnly. "Are you not aware?"

"Of what?"

"Why, that's old Hephaistos, signaling that he's still alive." Hephaistos was the one god who could not be revived. Before I could speak, Charon laughed and walked away.

The next morning, a bit later than the previous day, we braced ourselves inside Charon's boat, and headed due south for Naxos. In the slight headwind, the twenty miles took about 90 minutes. The boatman slid the old craft into the crescent cove below Timessa's residence. To his delight as we stood to debark, I passed him an obol, which Hestia had slipped me as we left.

As if she knew of our arrival, the Goddess stood on the shore, barefoot and in a long gown. She raised her palms in the ancient hieratic gesture, saying softly, "Greetings!" then crying into the wind, "*Aeeiii!*"

Poseidon half-bowed, as we all did, smiling at her salutation. Behind her stood Io, and walking down from the main house, Artemis, who had preceded us by a day. We clasped arms and I asked, "How many have been invited?"

"Eleven or twelve, plus some nymphs." Timessa smiled. "Hestia declined. However close, she hates these gatherings." Looking at Poseidon, she asked, "And Dionysos remains indisposed?"

"Yes, a shame he won't behave. You should hear the cursing."

"We will honor him regardless." She turned and gestured toward the house above. "Welcome to Theos Point. It was once, so long ago, the wine-god's haunts. The lovely Ariadne would stand where I do now, greeting strangers who had pulled their ships ashore. Please, follow me."

She took us up the narrow trail to the house, stopping briefly at the ruins. "Dionysos's old home, built for his beloved. Look at what remains."

Poseidon paused, saying, "I had almost forgotten. They entertained me here more than once. She was almost as beautiful as you. Alas, she was mortal, and even the wine-god himself could not save her from her fate."

Timessa cocked her head and asked, "After her death?"

"At first he drank heavily, then began down his long path of dances and seduction."

I heard music coming from behind the house and we followed the sound. Predictably, Apollo sat on a chair in the low grasses with the twins, an elaborately decorated golden lyre between his legs. Seeing us he nodded, continuing to play. I leaned over to Danaë, gesturing toward the twins, who blew coyly into pan-pipes. "I've forgotten their names. A-something."

"Aigle and Arlea."

Io disappeared into the house and Filly stepped out, looking into the sunlight, a smile flickering at the corners of her mouth. Danaë laughed, "Philippa!" and the girl ran to us.

"I'm so glad you've come!" Filly said. "Have you ever seen a place as glorious? We've been here just three weeks, but we'll never leave."

Danaë asked, "And Iole. How is she adjusting to all of this?"

Filly whispered, "It is as if she has always been one of us. I am in awe. And the Goddess is lost in her love for the girl." She grinned. "Both are radiant. It's quite infectious."

A bit past noon, we gathered at a long table to eat. Timessa, sitting between Io and Filly, said, "The wine is from our own grapes. A man has an ancient press just down the road. A bonus, indeed. And the olives are from these —" She gestured into the back toward the rows of crooked trees. "Locals say they're older than any others here."

Danaë glanced at her father. "I propose you give a toast. Remember what you said at sunset last night?"

He smiled, standing. "Of course." Raising his glass to Timessa, he said, "To the Great Goddess: may she prevail in all things!"

As we finished eating, Artemis presented T with a half dozen nymphs. She said, "All of these girls are your friends. And now they are yours to protect. They have clamored to be allowed to join you here. Guard them well. As you have proven, any one of these girls could herself become a butterfly."

Aigle muttered, "Or a caterpillar."

Timessa graciously accepted the girls, calling them over by name and hugging each. As she finished, a car eased down the long driveway, kicking up dust as it traversed the curves. It stopped in front of the house. A door slammed and in seconds a young man appeared; it was Hermes, falling to a knee when he saw Timessa.

"My apologies," he said. "I had business I could not shake." Then standing, he looked at us and loudly asked, "Am I too late to eat?"

Filly pointed toward the nymphs, saying, "Food for Hermes! He has a hunger as endless as the days he's lived."

In mid-afternoon Danaë and I sat with Io, who confided, "I am torn. On the one hand, I can't tear myself from her side. On the other — and as my goddess predicted — I have orders for dresses from around the world. Princesses, actresses, queen mothers."

Danaë said, "What a terrible misfortune. To be glamorous and in love — and in demand!"

The girl smiled. "Blame *Elle*. Even here on Naxos, I am stopped for autographs. Me, not my goddess. It's ridiculous."

Danaë nodded. "I hear the issue sold more copies than any magazine in history."

Io giggled. "I trust you have your own, framed nicely and hanging near the Aphrodite statue?"

Danaë said demurely, "Io, you should circulate. Don't spend all your time with us."

"But I have more to share! You haven't seen the second house. Part of it will accommodate the nymphs and occasional guests, as well as have an office for The Girls. But half is being converted into my studio. Last week the goddess shipped my things here from the shop Charleville. And we have the best carpenters from Athens remodeling the interior …

"Before long," Io went on, "we'll be self-sufficient."

I spread my arms. "Everywhere we look, all is enchanted."

Io looked at me with curiosity, then said in a hushed voice, "Do you mock our happiness?"

"Not at all. Perhaps I'm cynical enough to worry. Danaë and I stopped at Delos briefly yesterday, and I was all too aware that satyrs still are adrift. I half expected a few to spring from the stones."

"*Oui*, but my goddess says that those left are drunkards, old goats without leadership."

"My point," I said, "is that the world is dangerous …"

Danaë embraced her, holding her longer than necessary. "Jackson is simply saying, no matter your happiness, maintain your vigilance."

"I fear nothing," she said and stood, leaving us alone.

As we watched her stride away, Timessa appeared in a small flash and sat between us. Danaë said, "A new trick?"

T studied us with the same curious gaze as Io had, saying at last,

"What happens here is what I wish." Then in the silence, she brightened. "Don't you love my estate? I never dreamed I'd live on Naxos." She grinned triumphantly. "Now I'm a Naxian."

During a dinner at dusk, as the same blues and saffrons, greys and implausible pinks filled the horizon, a dozen of us looked out over the sea toward Delos and Mykonos. One of the twins, Aigle, sat in Apollo's lap, playing with his golden hair while Arlea pouted. Io leaned against her goddess, eyes half-closed. We had been drinking wine for hours and the world seemed Timessa's, subject to her whims and how she wished to mold it.

Reading my mind, Timessa turned to me and said, "I intend to mold nothing. Perhaps humans will become something else in time, but they are not my mission."

I understood. Advancing some temporal agenda was not our role.

Clear-eyed and radiant, Timessa rose and said to the gathering, "May all of you shine for evermore."

She took Io's arm and pulled her to her side and they nuzzled. As if their touching were a signal, the young nymphs began blowing out candles and oil lamps. Only on our table was a single candle left burning.

Theos Point fell into a soft darkness. Yet no one moved.

In the silence Aigle pointed into the northern sky. "Look!" she cried. "The Corona Borealis."

The small constellation formed an arc in the precise shape of Timessa's cove. I whispered to Danaë, "Dionysos's necklace for Ariadne must have been chosen from this very promontory."

Before she could reply, T and Io appeared from the dark. As they sat beside us, Io said, "You know, the four of us go back to the beginning."

Danaë smiled, "Of time or your love?"

"Charleville," she laughed. "My shop. When I first met the goddess."

"Yes," Danaë said. "That unforgettable morning."

Timessa reached into a small pocket of her gown. Smiling, she removed Queenie, setting her on the table, saying, "She travels with us everywhere." Then she reached again and pulled out a playing card. I noticed a black X at its top: The Wheel of Fortune, Kore's tarot.

She passed it around the table. Each of us held it a moment. The man being thrown off the wheel wore a tattered red shirt and spiraled into an abyss, his arms flailing. The naked, blindfolded woman turning the wheel looked away.

The card was returned to Timessa, who said, "It predicts that all happiness ends in ruin."

Io slipped the tarot from T's fingers. As if demonstrating a card trick, she turned the front of the card toward each of us. "See?" she asked. "Shall it be ruination or ecstasy?"

Then turning the card sideways, she angled a corner into the candle's fire. As the tarot flamed, smoke curling slyly star-ward, Io said, "Fools use these for divination. But we are the divine. And our happiness has no end."

Io took T's hand, kissed her palm and blew out the candle.

 The End ❖

GLOSSARY

&

Aigle and Arlea *Divine flute-girls who accompany Apollo.*

Aisa *One of the three Fates.*

Aphrodite *The goddess of erotic love, beauty and sensuality.*

Apollo *The god of music, arts and the bow; Artemis's brother.*

Ariadne *A mortal and the wife of Dionysos.*

Artemis *The virgin goddess of wild animals and protector of girls; Apollo's sister.*

Athene *A goddess celebrated for her cunning, wisdom and intelligence.*

Charon *A god and the boatman who ferried the dead to Hades.*

Chloé *Also known as Klotho, one of the three Fates.*

Danaë *A demi-goddess who has coupled with Jackson; daughter of Poseidon. [A demi-goddess is the female child of a divine being and a human.]*

Eos *The goddess of dawn, the herald for her brother, Helios, the sun (also, see Kore).*

Filly *Nickname for Philippa, a nymph and one of Timessa's oldest friends.*

Fates *Three sisters who controlled the life spans of mortals and* *gods alike, and consequently, were the most powerful of the Greek gods (see Aisa, Chloé and Laine).*

Gaia *The earliest goddess who, from herself, created Earth.*

Great Goddess *An ancient goddess pre-dating the Olympian gods, also known as the Great One, Inanna, Ishtar, the Triple Goddess, Cybele, Lemnos, and others.*

Hephaistos *An Olympian god and ingenious craftsman; briefly married to Aphrodite.*

Hestia *Goddess of the hearth; Poseidon's sister.*

Hermes *A divine messenger, the protector of travelers, a trickster, and guide. He escorted the dead to Hades once Charon dropped them off.*

Iole *Nicknamed Io, a dressmaker from Charleville, France, who becomes Timessa's companion.*

Jackson Night *Narrator, and a man whom Lachesis transformed into an a-mortal in* The Winnowing.

Kore *Timessa's eidolon (also, see* **Eos***).*

Lachesis *Also known as Laine, one of the three Fates.*

Laine *Also known as Lachesis, one of the three Fates.*

Orthrus *A divine dog known as the Two-Headed One for its ability to see the past and future simultaneously.*

Poseidon *God of the sea and rivers, of earthquakes and horses; Danaë's father.*

Timessa *A nymph who ran with Artemis for millennia and becomes the Great Goddess.*

ABOUT THE AUTHOR

Patrick Garner is a writer, artist and podcaster, in addition to his other pursuits. He has written stage plays and cofounded the off-Broadway Bright Lights Theatre company in Providence, Rhode Island. He was honored by the American Theater Critics Association when one of his plays was selected for a reading.

He published *A Series of Days of Change* and *Four Elements* (poetry), *Playing with Fire* and *D Is for Dingley* (biographies), as well as numerous articles and reviews in national magazines. His paintings and etchings are in museums, universities and private collections. Narrator and host of the breakout podcast, *Garner's Greek Mythology*, he lives in New England.